MURPHY'S LAW

LOOK FOR THESE EXCITING WESTERN SERIES FROM BESTSELLING AUTHORS WILLIAM W. JOHNSTONE AND J.A. JOHNSTONE

The Mountain Man

Luke Jensen: Bounty Hunter

Brannigan's Land

The Jensen Brand

Smoke Jensen: The Early Years

Preacher and MacCallister

Fort Misery

The Fighting O'Neils

Perley Gates

MacCoole and Boone

Guns of the Vigilantes

Shotgun Johnny

The Chuckwagon Trail

The Jackals

The Slash and Pecos Westerns

The Texas Moonshiners

Stoneface Finnegan Westerns

Ben Savage: Saloon Ranger

The Buck Trammel Westerns

The Death and Texas Westerns

The Hunter Buchanon Westerns

Will Tanner, Deputy U.S. Marshal

Old Cowboys Never Die

Go West, Young Man

Published by Kensington Publishing Corp.

WILLIAM W. JOHNSTONE

AND J.A. JOHNSTONE

PINNACLE BOOKS
Kensington Publishing Corp.
kensingtonbooks.com

PINNACLE BOOKS are published by

Kensington Publishing Corp.
900 Third Avenue
New York, NY 10022

PUBLISHER'S NOTE: Following the death of William W. Johnstone, the Johnstone family is working with a carefully selected writer to organize and complete Mr. Johnstone's outlines and many unfinished manuscripts to create additional novels in all of his series, like The Last Gunfighter, Mountain Man, and Eagles, among others. This novel was inspired by Mr. Johnstone's superb storytelling.

Kensington Books Hardcover Edition: March 2026
Pinnacle Books Trade Paperback Edition: May 2026

ISBN: 978-0-7860-5137-3

ISBN-13: 978-0-7860-5182-3 (ebook)

10 9 8 7 6 5 4 3 2 1

Printed in the United States of America

The authorized representative in the EU for product safety and compliance
is eucomply OU, Parnu mnt 139b-14, Apt 123
Tallinn, Berlin 11317, hello@eucompliancepartner.com.

MURPHY'S LAW

CHAPTER 1

He didn't have much to show for more than four years' service in the Confederate army. His uniform, his horse, and ten days' rations were automatic when he chose to be discharged there at Brownsville. The regiment was to be marched to Corpus Christi for discharge. But since he preferred to head straight north to reach his cabin in San Saba County, he requested his release at Brownsville. His rifle and sidearm were not army issue. He had bought them with his own money. His packhorse was "borrowed" from the cavalry horse herd, along with a packsaddle, a loan he felt was justified since he had been forced to fight a month after the war had officially ended. It was later called the Battle of Palmito Ranch and the last battle of the Civil War. From the banks of the Rio Grande River near Brownsville, a rebel force of three hundred men, under Colonel John "Rip" Ford, had defeated a Union force of five hundred men. So with that tiny victory, Sergeant Cullen Murphy gladly said farewell to his life as a soldier.

Looking back on his enlistment, he could not regret volunteering for the army when war was officially declared. It had been a matter of personal responsibility to fight to save his small ranch in West Texas. It may have been an easier choice for him than it had been for many men his age at the time. He had had no family to support, having been orphaned at the age of ten, when his mother was beaten to death by a drunken cowhand in Fort Worth. When the town marshal was summoned to the woman's room over a saloon, he found her slain body on the floor and the body of the cowhand slumped in her easy chair. There was a hole in the cowhand's temple and a larger one on the opposite side of his head. His pistol was in his hand, and there was no one else in the room. There was no sign of the boy, although the one window was wide open. The marshal easily concluded that the cowhand had beaten the woman to death in his drunken state. Realizing what he had done, he took his own life.

The years that followed his mother's death were years that would toughen the boy to the cruelties of life in the world of saloons, dance halls, and brothels. Always large for his age, he managed to find work for himself in the bawdy houses and hog ranches of the day. Then one day he met a man named John Tate, who offered him a job riding with a herd of cattle he was driving to market in Kansas. He started out riding drag with the horse remuda, breathing the dust stirred up by the cattle herd, learning to ride a horse on the way to the Kansas railheads. He worked for John Tate for four years before deciding he wanted to build his own ranch, leaning more toward raising horses than cattle. He found a property he could afford on the San Saba River in the Texas Hill Country and was just short of two years in the building of his ranch when war was declared.

Feeling it his duty to volunteer, he sold the horses he had managed to acquire to the army, then enlisted himself and the one horse he kept for active duty. Everything was in a hurry-up stage as the Confederate army rushed to train new recruits for battle. Murphy, a few years older than so many of the young men who enlisted and obviously a horseman, was put to use right away to train recruits for the cavalry. In a few months' time, he was promoted to the rank of sergeant. It was a rank he kept throughout his army career and one for which he seemed to be born. He proved to be a no-nonsense sergeant, fearless in battle and strictly by the book. In his platoon, there was "Murphy's Law," and woe unto him who challenged it.

When he was discharged, he left Brownsville and followed the Rio Grande River northwest for the first four and a half days to Laredo. He knew there was an old Indian trail that left the river from there and headed in the general direction he wanted to go. Although there were still reports of Comanche Indian parties in the area, his main concern was the scarcity of water after leaving the river. He knew there was no real source of good water until striking the Nueces River. As near as he could estimate, it would take him two and a half days to reach that river. He would hope to come across a spring or creek during that stretch of his journey. But in case he didn't, he left the Rio Grande with two canteens for his own consumption and two small kegs for his horses. Once he struck the Nueces River, he could follow it up into the Texas Hill Country, where he would cross the Llano River to finally strike the San Saba and follow that to his ranch.

When he'd left Brownsville, he had hoped to supplement his rations with some fresh game, but he was disappointed to find nothing to hunt until he left the desertlike flatlands and finally reached the Hill Country. Since it was still late in May, it was the middle of the whitetail rutting season, so when he finally reached the rugged limestone and granite hills of the Hill Country, he began to see deer signs close to the rivers. It was when he came to the Llano River that he decided to camp overnight and go deer hunting the following morning. Even as anxious as he was to complete his journey, he was more enthusiastic about some fresh meat to eat. His hunt was not in vain, for he was successful in killing a doe. So his horses got the day off while he butchered the deer and spent the rest of the day smoking the biggest portion of the meat, to be eaten later. Now that he was in country he was more familiar with, he could safely estimate that he was within about seventy miles of his cabin on the San Saba River. He had built it right where Brady Creek emptied into the river. He figured it would take two full days to reach it, due to the terrain between here and there. He crawled into his bedroll that night with a full belly of fresh roasted venison and started out the next morning for home.

Murphy arrived at the confluence of Brady Creek and the San Saba River early in the afternoon. Staring at the oak trees on the opposite bank as he approached, he watched for the first sight of his cabin, not even sure if it was still there. It seemed the grove of Texas live oaks had grown deeper since he had last been here four years ago. Then he spotted the dark form of the log cabin through the trees. It was still there, but had someone moved into it since he had left to fight in a war? This was his next question, and it was answered when he crossed the river and rode into the trees to find his cabin abandoned. The door was off its hinges and leaning against the wall beside the open doorway, the locked padlock still on the latch.

"I reckon I shouldn't have locked the door," he said. His initial thought was relief that no one was occupying the cabin at the present time, so he dismounted and continued staring at it for a long time. Then he looked beyond the cabin to a grassy clearing that held a small grave. He was relieved to see the simple cross still upright and the grave obviously undisturbed. He thought a silent prayer of thanks for that. Someone had been there, obviously, but it had been some time since, judging by the bush standing two feet high squarely in the middle of the open doorway of the cabin.

With a shrug of his shoulders, he walked over, took a good grip on the bush, and ripped it out of the ground. "Papa's home," he announced as he threw the bush over in the trees.

Inside the cabin, there was ample evidence that someone had used it, but they had not destroyed it. The front door was the only sign of destruction that he saw right away. A stone was out of place on his fireplace, and there appeared to be bullet holes in the window shutter. The bullets were evidently still in the wood, for they didn't go through to leave open holes. *Small-caliber weapon*, he thought. He checked all the corners of the cabin to make sure no critters had become tenants while it was vacant. Satisfied that it was his alone again, he decided he would fix the door that afternoon and go into town in the morning to get what supplies he needed.

He took care of his horses and freed them to go to the water. Then he put his saddle and packsaddle inside the cabin. After that, he looked in his saddlebags, found the key, and unlocked the padlock on the front door. It didn't want to work at first, so he put a little gun oil on it, and it finally cooperated. Next, he got his short spade from his packsaddle and went to the little grave beyond the cabin and started digging it up. He continued to dig in earnest toil until getting about three feet below the surface of the ground, where the point of his spade struck something solid. *Good*, he thought. *The coffin's still there.* He kept shoveling until he could take hold of one end and pull the wooden box out of the grave.

He carefully lifted the lid, so that it could be put back in place when he was through. Inside, he found all his carpentry tools, as well as his cookware and dishes. He was happy to see nails and screws, which he might need, and his axe. There was some rust but not as much as he expected. There was also an oilskin sack holding all the money he had received for the eleven horses he had sold to the army. It was all in gold Union coins, and not in worthless Confederate paper money, which had not yet been printed at the time of the sale. He was certain now that it was one of the luckiest decisions he had ever made when he buried the money, for he had no immediate prospects of earning the money he needed to get started again.

After repairing the door to his satisfaction, he cleaned the cabin as best he could without a broom or mop. Then he checked his fireplace to make sure nothing had built a nest in the chimney. When he had split enough wood for his fireplace, he changed his mind and decided to build his supper fire outside. Since it was such a nice night, he would delay cabin living for one more night. He took a look at the corral he had built, at least the half that was still there. It appeared that some of his guests had found it easier to chop up the corral rails for firewood. Taking a walk beyond the corral, he was satisfied to see the pasture hadn't been grazed out. All things considered, he realized that conditions could have been a whole lot worse. He could fix everything that needed fixing at his cabin. His major concern now was the town of Newtown, three miles north of his cabin. It was just getting a good start when the war was declared, and he hadn't heard much news from the town the whole time he'd been gone.

When he decided it was time to fix something for his supper, he built up his fire and emptied the last of the dry beans the army had given him in his ten-day rations. He had put the beans to soak in a jar of water when he left his camp that morning. Now he poured them into a kettle he'd retrieved from the grave and put it on the fire to boil while he sliced some of the uncooked meat he had wrapped in the deer hide. It was then that he heard the call from the other side of the river.

"Hello, the camp! Mind if I come across?"

Surprised, Murphy backed away from the fire and picked up his rifle. "How many are you?" he asked.

"Just me, Elmo Dillon," the answer came back. "Mean you no harm."

"In that case, you're welcome," Murphy replied. "Come on across."

Murphy stood close to the cabin and watched as a single rider entered the water on the other side of the river and rode across to come up by the fire before asking if he could step down. Murphy said he was welcome to, so Elmo dismounted.

"I caught sight of your fire back there a ways, and I was just curious to see who had took up with this cabin again. I see you're wearin' a uniform. You passin' through Newtown on your way home?" When Murphy started to answer, Elmo interrupted. "It ain't none of my business, but I felt like I oughta tell you that a lot of the boys are comin' back from the war to try to pick up the pieces they left here. That's the only reason I was wonderin' if you was just passin' through on your way home."

"Tell you the truth," Murphy said, "I plan to stay right here. I'm tired of travelin'."

"Fellow by the name of Murphy built this cabin," Elmo informed him. "I never met the man, but folks have said he was plannin' to make a nice little farm outta this place. He signed up with most of the other young men when war was declared. Don't know if he made it through the war or not."

Murphy couldn't help chuckling over what he perceived as a polite warning. He was frankly surprised that anyone would care who took over his cabin. "Well, Mr. Dillon, I can tell you that Murphy made it through the war. And if you're hungry, he's invitin' you to supper. I've got a lot of fresh deer meat that needs to be eaten before it turns. I'd appreciate it if you could help me get rid of some of it." He extended his hand. "Cullen Murphy, Mr. Dillon. Pleased to meetcha."

"Well, I'll be...," Elmo started, then shook his hand. "Ain't that something? I'd be tickled pink to help you get rid of that meat."

"Good," Murphy said. "Here's what I'm fixin' to cook over here on that deer hide. Take a look at it. It looks like it ain't goin' bad yet as far as I'm concerned. I just killed it yesterday."

Elmo led his horse away from the fire, then took a quick look at the raw meat. "It sure looks fine to me," he said. "Even if it had started to turn, it wouldn't have bothered me."

So Elmo cut a suitable branch from a tree to hold his cut of venison over the fire to roast, and Murphy emptied half of the kettle of beans onto one of the two plates that had been in the grave and handed the plate to Elmo. He apologized for not offering any coffee, but he had run out of it a couple of days before. He emptied the rest of the beans onto the second plate, and then he and Elmo held their venison over the fire. "I'm goin' into Newtown in the mornin'. I hope I can buy some coffee, if Baxter's store is still there," he said, referring to the Newtown General Store.

"Baxter's still there," Elmo told him. "A lot of the businesses that were there when you left are still there. It's just that everybody's hanging on by their fingernails. The money's damn near useless, and everybody's doing business any way they can—bartering or credit. Some folks still take Confederate paper, but it takes a knee-high stack of it to buy what used to cost a couple of dollars."

"That don't sound good a'tall," Murphy said.

"It ain't," Elmo remarked, "but we're all in the same boat together, and we're hopin' if we just hang on, we'll make it outta this mess." He paused and shook his head as if he wasn't really that confident. "The town's got other problems," he felt the need to confess. "It seems like more and more of the troublesome breed have started showin' up in Newtown. Drifters and downright outlaws have found out the town has no law."

"I can see where that could cause all kinds of problems." Murphy studied Elmo's grim face for a few moments before asking a question. "I didn't see which way you were ridin' before you called from the other side of the river. Were you ridin' to town or from town?"

"I was heading to town," Elmo answered. "I had been to my brother's farm about a mile south of here. I've got a house in town." He shrugged. "I've been visiting him and his family a lot more often since the war ended."

His remark prompted Murphy to ask if he had a business in town.

"Yes," Elmo answered. "I'm a tailor. I've got a little shop in town that was doing pretty well before the war."

"A tailor, huh? I reckon that explains why we didn't know each other when I was here before," Murphy remarked. He pulled his venison from the fire, took a bite, and tried to chew with his lips open to keep the hot meat from blistering them. "I didn't wear any tailor-made clothes," he said when he could talk again.

"Everybody thinks tailor-made shirts and pants are more expensive than store-bought, but they ain't if you compare the same quality clothes," Elmo said. "Of course, it's been mighty hard getting cheap wool durin' the war. If things get right again, I'll be glad to prove it to you."

"If you say so," Murphy said with a chuckle. "I ain't never known you to lie to me."

Elmo laughed in response. "And I'll swear I never will. At least not one you might catch me in. Welcome home from the war, Cullen. I'm glad I got the chance to meet you, and I thank you again for the venison. I expect I'd better get on my way home now. That three miles will be a lot shorter with a full belly."

"Take some more of this raw meat with you for breakfast in the mornin'," Murphy said. "It oughta be good for one more meal, and I can't eat all that's left."

"If you're sure," Elmo said. "I'll look for you in town tomorrow. I'd like to buy you that cup of coffee we were missin' tonight. We can get a good cup at Bradshaw's Saloon and Café."

"Bradshaw's?" Murphy responded. "That was just a saloon when I left here."

"That's right, it was," Elmo replied. "But with the way the economy slumped, Bradshaw had to combine his saloon business with a dining room to try to offset the money he was losing with the Confederate dollar devaluating. The Newtown Café had to close down, so Irene Floyd moved her cookstove into Bradshaw's, and they built a little eating room on the back of his saloon."

"Ain't it gonna cost a helluva lot for a couple of cups of coffee?" Murphy asked.

"No, it'll be about the same as a drink of likker used to cost, because I've got a credit arrangement with them," Elmo explained. "You see, Tyson Bradshaw still likes to have his trousers and his morning coat tailored to fit his fine figure of a man."

"I see what you mean," Murphy remarked, "but I don't know if I'll ever get used to buyin' something without real money. Can you use greenbacks?"

"Sure, if you got 'em," Elmo answered. "They're almost the same as gold. Trouble is nobody's got 'em."

"I managed to come by a few Yankee dollars, so I reckon I'll use them first thing," Murphy said as he walked with Elmo to get his horse.

"Thanks again for the venison," Elmo said when Murphy handed him the sack he had put the meat in and Elmo hung it on his saddle horn. "I'll see you in town tomorrow."

"Right," Murphy echoed, "see you in town."

First day I'm back to Newtown, and I've already made a friend, he thought as he watched Elmo ride away. *Maybe that's what I'm just naturally good at, making friends.*

Chapter 2

He was more than a little surprised when he rode into town the next morning. It had been four years since he had last seen what they had named Front Street, and it looked practically the same as it had then, only showing a lot more wear. He rode the length of the main street and saw some shops that were not there when he'd left for the war, but most of them appeared to be empty. When he spotted a small building that had a sign identifying it as ELMO DILLON, TAILOR, he pulled his horses over and tied them at the hitching rail. He went to the door and tried the knob, only to find it locked. The hour was not early by any means. He certainly expected Elmo to be open by this time of morning. He stepped away from the door and looked up and down the street. He realized then that he was the only person in sight. Finding that hard to believe, he stepped back to the door, tried the knob again, then knocked on the door.

"We ain't open yet." He heard a voice from inside. It sounded like Elmo Dillon.

"I'll catch up with you later for that cup of coffee," Murphy called back, although totally puzzled by his reception. "Sorry to bother you," he added and turned to leave.

"Cullen! Wait!" the voice exclaimed, and he heard the key

in the door lock. The door swung open, and Elmo stuck his head out and looked up and down the street. "Come in quick!"

Completely dumbfounded, Murphy stepped inside, and Elmo locked the door behind him. "I swear, I'm sorry you had to come back today. I'da told you to wait till another day, but I didn't know this was goin' on today. I was at my brother's place yesterday, so I didn't know about it."

"Know about what?" Murphy asked, but before Elmo could answer, they heard two gunshots from somewhere up the street. When Murphy's natural reaction was to go back outside, Elmo stopped him.

"Best we stay inside," Elmo told him. "You go outside, you're liable to get shot."

"By who?" Murphy responded, completely confused by Elmo's behavior.

"Rafer Polk," Elmo answered. "He's on one of his drunken binges, and there ain't nobody safe till he's had enough and leaves town."

"I don't understand," Murphy said. "Is he in a saloon this time of mornin'?"

"He's in Bradshaw's," Elmo answered. "He's been there since last night, and he won't let Bradshaw close till he's ready to leave."

When Elmo could see that Murphy didn't understand the situation at all, he went on to explain. "Rafer's just one of a gang of outright outlaws, four of 'em, that have a hideout somewhere north of town. They hit town on a regular basis now to drink and raise hell in one of the saloons. When they've had enough, they usually go back to their hideout. But last night Rafer decided he didn't wanna go back with 'em, so he won't let Bradshaw close. This ain't the first time he's done it. He threatens to shoot anybody who comes in the door, and he threatens to shoot Pete Brice—he's the bartender—if he tries to leave. Them two shots you just heard could be somebody dead or just something in the saloon he decided he didn't like. Might even be somebody passin' by out in the street. He's done that before."

"Why ain't somebody done something about it?" Murphy asked, still amazed that no one had.

"Who?" Elmo asked. "We ain't got no sheriff or town marshal. Some of us have talked about a citizens' vigilance committee, but we're afraid that gang he belongs to might take it out on the town if we tried to do anything. Besides that, Rafer by himself might be a little too much to handle. Mean as a rattlesnake and handy with a six-gun. We might lose some men tryin' to capture him."

"So you do nothing about him?"

"Just wait till he's done with his visit to town and stay off the street till he goes on back to his pals," Elmo said. "Too bad he picked Bradshaw's this time. Irene and her daughters won't be able to come to work until he's gone. But I can make you that cup of coffee I promised right here, if you still feel like having one."

"Thanks just the same, Elmo, but I've got a cravin' for some breakfast and a good cup of coffee at Bradshaw's. You're welcome to join me, if you like."

"Whaddaya gonna do?" Elmo asked.

"I'm gonna go build a fire in Irene's cookstove, so she can get started fixin' some breakfast," Murphy declared.

"Are you crazy?" Elmo blurted. "I'm serious. That man is dangerous."

"He's a bully," Murphy stated, "and I can't abide a bully. I'll leave my horses here, if that's all right with you."

He didn't wait for Elmo's response, just turned and walked back out the front door. He walked by his horses and paused long enough to draw his rifle out of his saddle scabbard, then walked up the street toward the saloon, leaving Elmo to watch him from his doorway.

As he approached the saloon, he noticed that a path had been fashioned between Bradshaw's Saloon and the barbershop next door. *Most likely so folks who only want to go to the café don't have to walk through the saloon*, he thought. Hoping the back door was not locked, he walked down the path to the back of the building. The three women standing outside the back door were startled by his sudden appearance and would have run had it not been for the fact that he was wearing a uniform.

"Sorry," Murphy said. "Didn't mean to scare you. I wasn't expectin' to find anybody back here."

"Well, if the army is finally gonna help, I wish they'da sent more than one soldier," Irene Floyd remarked. "You gave me a start, though. I thought that fool had gone out the front door and come lookin' for us."

"Sorry," he said again. "In case you ain't heard, the Confederate army's gone outta business, so there's just me. Is that door locked?"

"Yes, it is," Irene answered, "and it's gonna stay locked till that maniac goes out the front door." She held up a little chain with a key on it. "And if he doesn't get out of town any minute now, me and my girls are going home. So if you're looking for breakfast, you're gonna have to settle for dinner, if he's gone by then. If he ain't, maybe we'll see you for supper."

"I reckon I can't blame you for that," Murphy said. "But I've been outta coffee for three or four days, and I had a strong cravin' for a good breakfast, cooked by a woman's hand. So I'd consider it a real favor if you could wait a few minutes longer."

"What are you gonna do?" Irene asked.

"I'm gonna go in the kitchen and build a fire in your stove," Murphy replied. "That is, if you'll unlock the door for me." She looked hesitant to do so. "You can lock it as soon as I'm inside." She nodded, so he asked, "Have you got firewood inside somewhere, or should I take an armload off that woodpile yonder?"

"There's a stack of firewood just inside the door," she answered. "I keep it there to make sure I've got dry wood to start my fire, and there's kindling in a box beside it." She turned to exchange glances with her two daughters, who shared her opinion of the stranger. Then she turned back to Murphy and asked, "Are you crazy?"

He smiled at her and replied, "I've been accused of it from time to time. You wanna unlock that door now?"

Without another word, she stepped up to the door and unlocked it, then stood waiting while he slipped inside and closed the door behind him. He heard the key in the lock immediately after. It was quiet in the short hallway, and at the moment, he heard no noise from the front of the building, where the saloon was. He saw the stack of firewood right where Irene had said it was, and he was pleased to see part of the stack was comprised of pieces of wood that looked too big to put in a stove. Still there was no sound coming from the saloon, so he hoped Rafer Polk had finally passed out, making his job an easy one. Moving as quietly as he could, he left the hallway and walked through the small dining room. He noticed a fireplace in the far wall of the dining room, the reason for the larger pieces of firewood, he figured. About to go into the kitchen, he stopped when he suddenly heard a shot fired, followed by a warning in the slurred speech of a drunken antagonist.

"Damn," he muttered under his breath, disappointed to hear Rafer hadn't passed out, after all. He cranked a live round into his rifle and cautiously made his way into the kitchen, ready to return fire if threatened. No one was in the kitchen, so he moved up beside the door to the saloon to get a look at the situation. He saw Rafer Polk seated at a table in the middle of the room. His six-gun was on the table before him, next to a bottle of whiskey. Tyson Bradshaw was seated at another table in a front corner of the saloon, and Pete Brice, the bartender, was sitting on a stool in front of the bar. There was no one else in the room.

It didn't take any imagination to assume that Rafer was nearing the end of his endurance. It would be a simple matter to step into the open doorway and put an end to the problem with one shot from his rifle. But so far, at least on this visit to town, Rafer had not killed anyone, so Murphy didn't consider Rafer's crime one deserving of outright execution. He was guilty of drunken and disorderly conduct, destruction of property, and disturbing the peace. If there was a town marshal, he would place him under arrest and throw him in jail. So Murphy sought to take him alive, if possible.

With that decision made, he went quietly back to the stack of wood, propped his rifle against the wall, and picked up a large armload of the larger pieces of wood. He walked back through the kitchen, into the saloon, making no effort to walk quietly. Right out the kitchen door he went, holding the armload of wood in front of his chest as some hope of protection, just in case. Startled by the sudden appearance of the soldier carrying the load of wood, Rafer grabbed for his six-gun and jumped up from his chair, knocking it over in the process.

"Who the hell are you?" he demanded when Murphy walked right up in front of him.

"I want some coffee, and you're holdin' up breakfast," Murphy answered.

"Why, you dumb son of . . . ," was as far as he got as he cocked his pistol, because Murphy dropped the entire load of firewood at his feet, causing him to jump backward to avoid being hit. When he did, Murphy trapped his gun hand with his left and flattened his nose with a hard right. Rafer's knees buckled, and as he dropped to the floor, Murphy held on to the six-gun and took it out of his hand.

Bradshaw and Pete were both on their feet at the same time, so Murphy asked, "Have you got anything to tie this buzzard up with?"

Bradshaw looked at Pete, and Pete answered, "There's a

coil of rope hangin' in the pantry. I'll get it!" He left at once and was back in seconds with the rope.

Not willing to leave anything to chance, Murphy took the rope to make sure Rafer was bound securely. He tied his hands behind his back and his feet together. Then he tied hands and feet together.

"He's still out cold," Pete marveled. "What did you hit him with?"

"Just my fist," Murphy answered. "I think he was so drunk, he was ready to pass out, anyway. I just helped him along."

"What are you gonna do with him?" Bradshaw asked.

"Is there a jail in town?" Murphy asked.

"No, we don't have a jail," Bradshaw replied.

"Then I don't know what we're gonna do with him, but we'll just drag him outta the way for the time being. I've got another chore first." He started picking up the firewood. "I'll take this back. I promised the lady out back that I'd build a fire in her stove, so she can get started cookin' breakfast."

"You're joking," Bradshaw responded. "What are we going to do with Rafer Polk?"

"Oh, I ain't gonna leave you stuck with him. I'll figure out something to do with him. It's just that it's more important that I get a cup of coffee first. I hate to inconvenience Mr. Polk, but I told that lady I would build her a fire." When he had picked up all the wood, he took it back to the stack, and they followed along behind him.

"I reckon it's about time we said thank you for takin' care of this problem, Sergeant," Pete declared when it appeared that Bradshaw wasn't going to. "He had the whole town shut down, not just us. My name's Pete Brice. I'm the bartender here, and this is Tyson Bradshaw. He's the owner. We're mighty lucky you're passin' through town today. We sure appreciate your help."

"I ain't passin' through town," Murphy said as he picked

some of the kindling out of the box. "Oughta be easy gettin' a fire goin' with this lightwood. Pete, if you don't mind, grab some of that smaller firewood. I've come back to stay. I ain't a sergeant no more. I own a place three miles from here, on the river."

They followed him back to the kitchen, where he started cleaning the cold ashes out of the stove in order to arrange his kindling.

"I knew there was something familiar about you," Pete said. "You've been in here before, but it's been quite a while."

"Four years," Murphy said. "I was just gettin' started when it was time to join up and go fight that damn war. The name's Murphy, Cullen Murphy. I'm hopin' to make a go of it this time." His kindling set, he got a match from the box on a shelf beside the stove, and when the kindling developed a serious flame, he built the rest of the fire.

"I reckon we can handle it from here," Irene said as she and her two daughters came in behind them. "Unless you're fixing to do the cooking, too." She looked at Pete and asked, "Is he gone?"

"No, he's still here, but if he ever wakes up, he's gonna wish he had gone before he had a chance to make the acquaintance of Mr. Murphy."

She was obviously confused, so he explained what had taken place. As if on cue, they heard a groan from the saloon. She reacted by extending her arms, as if to protect her daughters.

"It's all right," Pete said quickly. "He's all tied up, hand and foot. He ain't gonna hurt nobody."

"What are you going to do with him?" Irene asked. She looked at Bradshaw for the answer. When he shrugged and made no response right away, she said, "You and Eliot Baxter and some of the others have been having your meetings about some kind of law and order in Newtown. Why don't you go get Baxter and decide what you should do about that piece of scum that had the whole town tied in a knot?"

"I was just going to suggest that we do that," Bradshaw claimed.

"It ain't none of my business, I reckon, since I don't live in town," Murphy suggested, "but I expect it would be a good idea to get him outta here. Put him in a smokehouse or someplace where you can put a padlock on the door while you're deciding what you're gonna do with him."

"Like that old place where we had our café," Irene suggested. "That place is still empty, and there's a smokehouse behind it, with a lock on the door. I've got the key for it at home."

"That sounds like an excellent idea," Bradshaw remarked. "Let's put him in there."

Irene turned to her eldest daughter and said, "Ginger, go back to the house and get the key to that padlock. It's in my jewelry box on the dresser."

The girl reacted at once, starting for the back door. Her mother stopped her.

"Go out the front door. If folks see you walking up the main street, maybe they'll come out of their holes and this cotton-pickin' town will come alive again. And don't dawdle, Ginger. We need to get that drunken fool outta here."

"You want me to go with you, Ginger?" Bonnie, her younger sister, asked.

Irene answered for Ginger. "No, you stay here and help me get some breakfast started for Mr. Murphy. He's our first customer today, and he needs a cup of coffee. You can roll out some dough for biscuits."

"Much obliged, ma'am," Murphy responded. "You might have another customer directly. Elmo Dillon was supposed to meet me for breakfast. I reckon we'll have to wait until I can take our prisoner to the smokehouse, and I need to take care of that horse that's been tied to the hitchin' rail all night. I expect it could use some water."

"Let me see if I can get some water heated up, enough to make a pot of coffee, so you can at least have a cup while we're waiting for Ginger to get back with that key," Irene said.

* * *

Irene's speculation about sending Ginger up the main street appeared to pay off, for when Elmo saw her, he came out to question her. When she told him what had happened, he went to the saloon to help Murphy transport the prisoner to the smokehouse. Then they went to the stable to leave Rafer Polk's horse with Paul Mathers, the owner. By the time they returned to Bradshaw's, there were suddenly people showing up on the street, like bees coming out of a honeycomb. Most of Irene's regular customers began to show up at the café now that the possibility of getting shot had been reduced, their dining expenses paid for on a credit system.

When Murphy asked the price of breakfast, Irene told him it was fifty cents in silver or twenty-five dollars in Confederate paper. "But yours won't cost you anything," she said. "I think making your breakfast is the least I can do for what you did. I also owe you for firing up my stove for me."

"That's mighty neighborly of you," Murphy said, "and I thank you. I've got some change with me, so I'll pay you for Elmo's breakfast."

"No such a thing," Elmo insisted. He said to Irene, "He fed me a big supper of venison last night and sent me home with enough fresh deer meat for breakfast this mornin'. I've already et. I thought we was just gonna have some coffee."

"We were," Murphy assured him, "but I changed my mind when I got up this morning. Decided I didn't feel like goin' to the trouble of makin' breakfast."

"So you just rode on into town, where you didn't have to go to any trouble at all," Irene remarked facetiously, causing Murphy to chuckle. "Go on into the dining room and drink your coffee, and I'll have you some breakfast in a few minutes."

Murphy did as she said, but Elmo didn't follow right away, preferring to hang back to ask Bradshaw a question. "What are we gonna do with Rafer Polk? Are we gonna call the group together and hang him, or keep him in that smokehouse for a while, then let him go?"

"Damned if I know," Bradshaw replied. "We ain't set up to take care of a prisoner for any time at all. If we hang him, I'm afraid the other three in that gang are going to ride in here and shoot the town to pieces. That might not have been the luckiest thing to happen for us when Murphy rode into town. If he hadn't, Rafer would have most likely been leaving by now." He shook his head, perplexed. "Maybe we better go talk to Eliot Baxter about this and see what he thinks."

"I agree," Elmo said. "Let's go talk to him right now, while Murphy's eating breakfast."

Bradshaw nodded his agreement, so Elmo stuck his head in the dining room door and told Murphy he had to go see the mayor. "You take your time and let these ladies take care of you. I'll be right back." He didn't wait for a reply, turning around immediately and leaving.

"He won't get no argument outta me," Murphy said. "Settin' here, gettin' waited on by three lovely ladies." He gave the three of them a wide smile and asked, "Now, which one of you is the mama?"

Irene and her daughters giggled.

"Ah, Mister Murphy," Irene said. "I think it must not have been very long since you got off the boat from Ireland. So let's fill your mouth with food to go with some of that blarney you're chewing on."

Her comment drew a chuckle from him.

Bradshaw and Elmo hustled down the street to the Newtown General Store to report the morning's encounter between Rafer Polk and Cullen Murphy. Eliot Baxter, the owner of the store and mayor of Newtown, was just opening his door, so he saw them approaching. "Looks like that maniac finally left town," he said.

"That's not quite what we're here to tell you," Bradshaw said. "Truth is, he's still in town, and the question is, what are we gonna do with him?"

"Where is he?" Baxter asked, immediately concerned.

"Locked up in the smokehouse behind Irene Floyd's old café," Bradshaw replied, then told him about the confrontation that had put the outlaw there.

"So now the town is holding him as a prisoner," Baxter stated, reacting in much the same way as they had. "How long are we gonna hold him? Has he got water or a chamber pot? We'll have to feed him if we keep him any time at all. Who's gonna do all that?"

No answers came from the two men with the blank expressions looking back at him.

"You think we oughta tell everybody to put on their masks and then hang him?"

"I don't know," Bradshaw replied. "That seems pretty drastic. He ain't killed nobody, just threatened to. Maybe we oughta keep him locked up for a day or two, then order him not to come back to town."

"How you reckon Clyde Fry and those other two outlaws Rafer runs with are gonna take his lockup in our smokehouse jail?" Elmo asked.

Baxter had no answer for him. "We'd best round everybody up today and decide what we're going to do. It might be the time we finally have to go vigilante to keep some semblance of law and order in our town. This keeps up, we ain't gonna have a town."

They talked about it for a while longer before definitely deciding to have their meeting that afternoon.

"We can keep Rafer locked in that smokehouse overnight," Baxter said. "Give him a blanket and a bucket of water and something to eat, so he can't say we treated him too badly. Then let him go."

"You really think he's gonna take his spanking and behave himself from now on?" Elmo had to ask. "Rafer and the other three will be back here raisin' more hell than they did before. We need a sheriff and a real jail if we've got any chance of growin' this town at all."

"We don't have the money to hire a sheriff or build a jail. You know that," Bradshaw said. "After seeing how this Murphy fellow took care of Rafer, I'd like to have a sheriff like him."

"I spent a lot of time talking to him last night," Elmo said. "I don't think he'd be interested in a sheriff's job. Besides, he's got a place three miles from here, and I think he's pretty much got his mind set on workin' it."

"I think I'll go back to the saloon with you," Baxter said. "I'd like to meet Murphy."

"I'm sure he's plannin' on comin' to meet you after he eats his breakfast," Elmo remarked. "He said he had to buy some supplies this mornin'."

"Even better," Baxter said. "I'll wait till he comes here. I hope he's got something to trade with."

CHAPTER 3

When Elmo and Bradshaw returned to the saloon, they found that Murphy was still seated at the table. He had finished his breakfast but was still drinking coffee so Elmo said, "If you ain't in a hurry to get goin', I'll sit down and have a cup of that coffee with you,"

"I figured you might," Murphy remarked cheerfully. "Is Mr. Baxter's store open yet?"

"Yes, it is. I told him you'd be coming his way directly," Elmo answered and pulled a chair back from the table.

When Bonnie, the younger daughter, came from the kitchen with Elmo's coffee, Murphy said, "Thank you, Miss Bonnie," and placed a quarter on the table.

"Last night I invited you for a cup of coffee," Elmo insisted, "so I surely don't expect you to pay for mine. You'd best hang on to that coin. They're gettin' scarce as hen's teeth around here."

Murphy looked at the smiling fourteen-year-old girl. "You'll take care of it, won't you, Miss Bonnie?"

She didn't say anything but nodded her head and expanded her smile as she scraped the quarter off the table. Then she turned abruptly and took it to her mother. It struck Elmo that there was quite a difference between the man he had just watched charm the girl and the one Bradshaw had described as totally destroying Rafer Polk. He couldn't help wondering if Murphy would really settle in that cabin on the San Saba or take to wandering after so long away from the farm.

Murphy sat for a little while longer while Elmo drank his coffee; then he said he had better get about the business he had come to town to do. "There's a lot of work to be done on my place to make up for four years lying fallow." He shook hands with Elmo, walked out of the dining room, and stopped at the kitchen door to thank Irene and her daughters.

"I know you said there was no charge for my breakfast," he said to Irene, "but I'd be happy to pay you for it. I know it cost you something to make it, and it sure was mighty fine eatin'."

"No, indeed, Cullen Murphy," Irene replied. "I feel I owe you much more than breakfast. I'm glad you enjoyed it. It was our pleasure, wasn't it, girls?" They both smiled in response. "Bonnie told me you paid for Elmo's coffee. You shouldn't have done that, either."

"You come back to see us, Mr. Murphy," Ginger said. "Or should I call you Sergeant Murphy?"

"Oh, I'm sure I will," he responded, just as Elmo appeared at his side. "I expect I'll get sick of my cookin' pretty quick. And you don't have to call me mister or sergeant. My name's Cullen. If you're uncomfortable callin' me Cullen, you can call me Uncle Cullen. I'm pretty sure I'm old enough to be your uncle. See you later, Elmo."

They were still chuckling after he walked out the door. "He's funny," Bonnie said. "I wish he lived here in town."

"So do I," Elmo said, thinking about Rafer Polk sitting in a dark smokehouse, getting madder by the minute. Like Bradshaw and Baxter, he wasn't sure if he welcomed Murphy or wished he hadn't showed up when he did.

Murphy collected his horses and rode up the street to the Newtown General Store. Eliot Baxter had been watching for him, and he went to the door to meet him. "Come in, Mr. Murphy. Tyson and Elmo said you would be coming to my store. Let me say that was a helluva thing you did in the saloon this morning, taking down Rafer Polk like that. It was a lesson that maniac had coming for a long time. It's also prompted a meeting of the town council this afternoon to decide what we're gonna do with him. You're welcome to come to that meeting if you're interested."

Murphy was surprised by the invitation. He hesitated a moment, then said, "I appreciate the invite, Mr. Baxter, but I expect I'd best get my business done here and get on back to my place. It sat abandoned the whole time I was in the army, and I want folks to know it's not abandoned anymore. So I don't like to leave it for too long a time until everybody knows I'm back. I'm not a citizen of Newtown, anyway, so I wouldn't have any say in whatever you folks decide what you wanna do. I'll just buy some things I need from you today and be on my way."

Baxter was disappointed, but he wasn't sure what help he could have expected, so he said, "I understand your position. Now, what can I help you with today?"

"I've got a list of things I need to get started to put my place back to where it was before I left here." He handed him the list. "I didn't write it down, but I also need some .44 cartridges. Two boxes will do right now."

Baxter looked at the list. "This is quite a good-sized list. Have you thought about how you're going to pay for it?"

"I figured cash money," Murphy said.

"Are you talking about Confederate paper?"

"No, sir," Murphy replied. "I was thinkin' about Union greenbacks. Is that all right with you?"

Baxter tried to hide his excitement. "Why, that'll be just fine. I'm just surprised when somebody comes in with Union money instead of Confederate money. It's hard to come by greenbacks these days in our part of the country."

"You're right about that," Murphy agreed. "I've had this money since before there was any Confederate money. At the start of the war, I sold some horses to the army, and they paid me with Union gold, 'cause that's the only kind of money they had."

Baxter chuckled and remarked, "It could be thought of as a sportsmanlike gesture by the Union army to pay for the expenses of a future Confederate soldier."

"I suppose," Murphy agreed. "I reckon we coulda used a helluva lot more of their generosity."

Baxter had his son, Jeff, pull all the items on Murphy's list from the shelves and gather them on the counter while he priced each one. Murphy paid him for the items and loaded them on the packhorse he had brought with him. Baxter thanked him for his business and again for freeing Bradshaw's Saloon and Café from its hostage situation. Then he and his son stood there and watched him ride out of town.

"He looks like he could handle Rafer Polk," Jeff commented. "I don't remember ever seeing him in town before."

"I guess not," his father said. "That was four years ago, when we used to call you Skeeter. I just vaguely remember him myself. That reminds me, I need to have you go and tell all the members of the town council that we're having an important meeting this afternoon at three o'clock in Bradshaw's Saloon."

Almost every member of the town council showed up for the meeting that afternoon, because by that time everyone was aware of the incident in the saloon that morning. The meeting was held in the dining room behind the saloon. Sitting up at the head of the table with Baxter were Frank Jessop, who owned the sawmill; Bert Walker, the blacksmith; and Paul Mathers, who owned the stable.

Baxter called the meeting to order. "You all know about the prisoner we're holding under citizens' arrest. Paul, Bert, and

Frank are sitting up here with me because they volunteered to take Rafer Polk a plate of food and a cup of coffee that Irene fixed for him."

"What the hell for?" Jim Anderson, the postmaster, blurted. "We ain't takin' him to raise, are we?"

"The reason we called this meeting is to decide just what we are gonna do with troublemakers like Rafer Polk. So we locked him up until we decide what our policy is going to be. In the meantime, it's just human kindness to give him something to eat, the same as if he was in jail."

"We already talked about this," Anderson said. "We ain't got the money to build a jail and pay a full-time marshal. So why don't we pull on our gunnysacks and drag him outta that smokehouse and string him up?"

"Because then we'd have ourselves three gun-slingin' outlaws come in here to shoot the town to pieces," Mathers answered him. "They think they own the town now."

"Hell, they *do* own it," Anderson shot back, "but they'll think something different if they see that piece of scum swingin' from a tree limb."

The meeting got out of hand then, with shouted arguments for one policy against the other. Baxter banged on the table until he finally calmed everyone down.

"What did Rafer say when you took him some food?" he asked Bert Walker.

"He was pretty mad," Walker replied, "especially when he found out we hadn't come to let him out. He wanted to know who the fellow was who broke his nose, and I told him he was a drifter, just like him. He said if we didn't let him outta there, it would be the sorriest day of our lives. I told him we would have a meetin' to decide if we were gonna let him go or not. He took the plate of food, though."

They argued about what to do for some time, with almost an equal split between those who wanted to hang him and those who feared the consequences if they didn't set him free. Elmo Dillon suggested that maybe they should grant Rafer his release if he gave his friends notice that any discharge of a firearm within the city limits would be a hanging offense. Although there was still an argument over the issue, enough of the members were reluctant to don gunnysacks and hang someone, so the vote was to do what Elmo had proposed. They also decided not to keep Rafer overnight. Elmo volunteered to go to the smokehouse jail with the blacksmith and Paul Mathers, who would first bring Rafer's horse from the stable. All three would be wearing sidearms. So as the meeting broke up and most of the participants spilled into the saloon part of the building, Bert and Elmo waited while Mathers went to the stable to get the horse.

"What are we gonna do if he decides to give us trouble?" Elmo asked as they walked to the smokehouse behind the vacant building.

"I don't know what he might try to do," the blacksmith replied. "I've got his six-shooter, and I emptied the cylinder. So if he even tries to shoot me with an empty gun, I'll put a bullet in his head, same as any mad dog."

"He'd have to be a fool to try anything," Paul Mathers said. "I expect he's had all of that smokehouse he wants. He'll take off and decide what he's gonna do about his arrest later. Ain't that what you think, Elmo?"

"Probably so," Elmo replied.

When they got to the smokehouse, Bert Walker had the key, so he stepped up to the door and unlocked the padlock. Before he removed the lock, he called out, "Rafer! We've come to let you outta there! You hear me? We're gonna let you outta there."

"It's about time." The voice came from the back of the dark interior.

Elmo felt Rafer was suspicious of their intent, fearing that he might be facing an attempt to execute him. And that was why he didn't rush out when Bert Walker slipped the padlock off the fastener and swung open the smokehouse door. When he finally came to the door, he stood there squinting and blinking his eyes, trying to adjust to the bright light of day. When he was able to see Mathers standing there holding his horse, he walked on out of the smokehouse. "What about my gun?"

"I got it right here," Bert Walker answered him and handed him his gun belt, which was rolled up around the weapon in his holster.

Rafer took the gun belt and immediately slapped it around his narrow hips. He buckled it and drew the Colt. "It feels light," he remarked.

"I emptied it," Bert said. "I didn't wanna take a chance on you gettin' accidentally shot if you started messin' with it. You don't need to complain. I put the bullets back in your belt."

Rafer grinned, making his face a swollen, grotesque Halloween-like mask, a result of the hard right hand that broke his nose. "I believe you," he said, still smiling, as he pointed the pistol directly at Bert and pulled the trigger.

All three in the liberating party recoiled at the sound of the hammer on an empty cylinder.

"I swear, we shoulda hanged him," Bert spat. Then to Rafer, he ordered, "Get on your horse and get the hell outta Newtown. And you can tell that pack you run with that we're not gonna put up with any more of your drunken brawls in our town. Find another place to tear down. Discharging a firearm within the city limits is now a hangin' offense."

Rafer didn't react at once; instead he just stood there grinning at Bert as if he was measuring him for a coffin. "You're the blacksmith, ain'tcha? That's quite a speech for a blacksmith." He continued to look him in the eye for a long few moments before he placed his foot in the stirrup and stepped up into the saddle. Once he had settled in the saddle, he said, "I'll try to remember everything you said, so I can tell my friends."

Then he turned the horse's head and rode off between the buildings toward the main street.

Neither Mathers nor Elmo said anything, but they both stared at Bert in amazement for a few moments before they all three hustled out to the street to see if he was riding out of town.

Elmo was the first to comment. "I swear, Bert, you put it to him pretty strong."

"I reckon it's about time somebody did," Walker replied with an air of confidence, even though he feared that he might have gone too far. He realized after the fact that he had embedded the image of himself in Rafer's mind as the bearer of the challenge.

No one else commented until they had watched Rafer ride on out the end of the street to the north road out of town. Then Walker said, "I noticed you two were pretty quiet."

"Oh, I think you carried the message to him all right. It didn't look like you needed any help from me," Mathers said.

"He knows the four of them aren't welcome in Newtown," Elmo commented. "That's for sure." He shrugged. "Well, let's go tell the rest of them that we released the prisoner and he's left town."

Most of the council were still in the saloon when the three men returned, so they told Baxter and Bradshaw about the release of the prisoner. They answered all the questions, most of which pertained to Rafer's reactions after hearing Elmo's account of Bert Walker's warning to him. There was much discussion regarding whether Walker had been too tough on the outlaw.

Baxter summed it up by saying it was something that had to be done. "And if this town is going to survive," he concluded, "we're going to have to levy a tax on every business here and hire a town marshal."

"And then he's gonna have to have a jailhouse," Frank Jessop, who owned the sawmill, commented.

"Never mind all that," Irene Floyd interrupted. "Did one of you bring my plate and my cup back from the smokehouse?"

"Why, no, Irene," Elmo answered her. "For some reason, it never crossed our minds."

She shook her head in disgust. "I reckon I can send Bonnie to get them." She went back into the kitchen. "No use to throw away good dishes, even if Rafer Polk ate off 'em," she muttered.

"Somebody's comin'," Loafer Creech called back to Clyde Fry and Johnny Shaw, who were in the process of butchering a cow beside the stream behind the cabin. The cabin was ideally located high up in the narrow valley, making it easy to see anyone approaching from the road below. They had considered themselves fortunate to have discovered the cabin beside such a strong, rapidly running stream. The old man who built it was resting in a shallow grave on the side of the valley. Clyde and Johnny paused in their butchering to wait for Creech's next call. In a couple of minutes, the call came. "It's Rafer!"

They went on with the butchering while Creech stepped down from the tiny porch to meet Rafer. "Where the hell have you been?" Creech asked when Rafer pulled his horse to a stop in front of the cabin. "What the hell happened to you?" he asked when he took a look at Rafer's face. "You look like you got kicked by a mule."

"Same as," Rafer answered. "Feller's got a punch like the kick of a mule."

"Well, I'll be . . . How many times did he hammer you?"

"One time," Rafer said. "Knocked me out cold. He caught me at a bad time, though. It was early this mornin', and I'd been drinkin' all night."

"Is he dead now?"

"No, but he will be. Like I said, he knocked me out, and I woke up sometime later, locked up in a smokehouse. And, man, I'm tellin' you I had a bad head. Still hurts like hell."

"He sure as the devil rearranged your face," Creech commented. "One of them jaspers in town? We need to go after him, or is that something you wanna do all by yourself?"

"No, that's the problem," Rafer complained. "I can't go after him. He ain't one of the town people. He was a drifter, passin' through. But I'll know him if I ever see him again, and he's a dead man if I do. I'm plannin' on takin' my satisfaction from that town for lockin' me up in that smokehouse, especially that blacksmith. He was talkin' pretty big, standin' there with three guns on me and me without mine. I'm gonna enjoy meetin' up with him again." He looked up toward the cabin. "Where's Clyde and Johnny?"

"Out back, butcherin' a young steer that followed us home this mornin'. I was settin' out here in case the previous owner might be a good tracker."

They went around to the back of the cabin, where the butchering was in the final stages. "Well, look who decided he was gonna come back to his old friends," Clyde brayed. "We thought you musta shacked up with one of them little gals in that dinin' room when you didn't even come home last night."

"I weren't ready to come back here with you three buzzards," Rafer replied. "I weren't through drinkin'."

"You gonna tell us who used your face for an anvil?" Johnny asked.

"I was wonderin' that myself," Clyde remarked. "I expect he's dead now."

"No, he ain't," Rafer answered, "and I'll tell you why. He caught me by surprise. I already told Creech what happened. Let me turn my horse out in the corral and I'll tell it again."

While Rafer related all he could remember about his confrontation with the unknown stranger, Clyde Fry was especially entertained by the stranger's reaction when Rafer said he started to shoot him. "Carryin' an armload of firewood, was he?" Clyde asked, chuckling as he formed the picture in his mind. "Then when you drew your six-gun, he dumped the firewood at your feet?"

"That's what I said," Rafer replied. "I couldn't help jumpin' to keep from gittin' hit by the firewood."

"So when you jumped, he clocked you out for a while," Clyde said.

"That's a fact," Rafer said. "I don't know for how long, but when I came to, I was tied up hand and foot."

"I swear, that's hard to believe," Johnny Shaw commented. "One punch."

"Not so hard," Rafer disagreed. "I'd been drinkin' all night. I was about ready to pass out, anyway."

"I reckon you're right," Johnny allowed. "But then they tied you up and throwed you in a smokehouse. Is that what they're usin' for a jail?"

"I don't know," Rafer replied. "It must be, 'cause they ain't got no jail. Anyway, they locked me in it, and they fed me one meal before they come to let me out."

"You say it was the blacksmith who did all the talkin' and told you about the law against shootin' a firearm in town?" Clyde asked. When Rafer said that was right, Clyde asked, "Was he wearin' a badge? Did he say he was the marshal?"

Rafer shook his head, grimacing as he did, since it still felt fragile.

"Hell," Clyde continued, "they still ain't got no marshal, and they sure as hell ain't got no jail. That's just some of them business owners tryin' to make you think they can stop us from havin' our way in their precious town."

"You think we'd be smart to move on and find another place to hole up?" Creech asked.

"What?" Clyde responded. "And leave this setup back here on this stream, with three small cattle ranches within easy ridin' distance and a saloon only a short ride away? I ain't about to ride away just because Rafer met up with a hard-nosed drifter passin' through town. We'll pay that blacksmith a little visit and see if he's as tough as he talks."

"I'm claimin' my rights to call him out for what he done to me," Rafer declared.

"I reckon you've got a right to, at that," Clyde said, "but we'll go along to back you up. We've gotta finish up the butcherin' on this cow and then start smokin' the most of it before it goes bad, so we ain't goin' into town tonight. We'll go in tomorrow night for sure."

Chapter 4

They rode into town four abreast, slow-walking their horses down the main street, as if challenging anyone who might object to their presence.

"Oh, no . . . ," Eliot Baxter muttered when he saw them pass by his store. "They're back." He was not surprised, but he had been hoping Bert Walker's message to Rafer Polk that they were not welcome in Newtown might have some effect. It appeared now that it did have some effect, but not what was intended. He assumed they were heading for Bradshaw's Saloon, so when they had passed his store, he went outside to watch them. He was surprised when they passed Bradshaw's, as well, and continued on toward the stable. But then they stopped short of the stable, and he realized they were going to the blacksmith's shop. They had come to confront Bert Walker!

What to do? He wasn't sure, but he knew he should do something. For lack of a plan, he went back inside and told Jeff to watch the store. Then he picked up his shotgun, went out the door, and headed for Bradshaw's to warn him, in case he didn't see the four outlaws.

Bert Walker was in the process of fitting a bay gelding with new shoes when he realized there was someone behind him. He dropped the bay's hoof to the ground, straightened up, and turned around to confront the four outlaws, who were still sitting on their horses. The smirks of amusement on their faces told him they had not come to employ his services.

"What's the matter, blacksmith?" Rafer asked. "You don't look glad to see me again. Oh, that's right. You told me to get outta town and don't come back. And you see, blacksmith, that hurt my feelin's when you told me that. But I'm gonna give you a chance to tell me you're sorry for telling me, and I'm gonna forgive you. And then I'm gonna tell you to get out of town and if you don't, I'm gonna put a hole right through your breastbone. But I see you're wearin' a gun yourself, so maybe we'll just decide who stays and who don't with our guns. I don't know how fast you are with that big horse pistol you're wearin', but if you was to happen to be faster than me, my friends will even the score for me. So whaddaya say, blacksmith? You ready to back up that threat you gave me?"

Bert tried to remain calm, but it was impossible for him to maintain his composure when looking up at the smirking faces, awaiting his complete collapse. "You've got no reason to call me out to fight," he said. "I was just the one the council picked to deliver the message from the whole town."

"Ahh, that's too bad, blacksmith, but I ain't got time to line up the whole town council," Rafer said, "so you're gonna have to face the music for 'em." He drew his six-gun and took dead aim at Bert's chest while Bert fumbled for his Colt Army revolver. But the sharp crack of the rifle startled Bert as well as the men still on horseback. The horses all jumped nervously as Rafer keeled over and slid from his saddle, a bullet hole in the center of his chest. Johnny Shaw pulled his pistol, thinking Bert must have shot Rafer, only to be the unlucky target of the second rifle shot.

"Hold on! Don't shoot!" Clyde shouted and held his hands in the air. Creech saw him and did the same, both of them looking desperately for the shooter.

Clyde's plea was answered by the sound of a Henry rifle cranking a new round into the chamber as Cullen Murphy stepped out from behind Bert's shop, where he had been interrupted while taking a little siesta, waiting for Bert to finish shoeing Nosy. "Just keep your hands on the saddle horn, where I can see 'em," Murphy said. "Mr. Walker, if either one of 'em makes a move toward their weapons, you shoot that one on the right and I'll take the one on the left."

"Right," Bert said, feeling the life slowly returning to his arms and legs. His weapon out now, he held it on Clyde while Murphy picked up Rafer's body and laid it belly down across his saddle. He then performed the same service for Johnny's body.

Meanwhile, Clyde was getting a little uneasy with Bert holding his gun on him. He had seen the trembling response the blacksmith showed at the beginning of the encounter, and he now worried about getting hit with a bullet due to his nervousness. So he attempted to ease the tense situation. "There's been a little misunderstandin' here, Sheriff," he said to Murphy. "Creech and me, hell, we was just ridin' along into town with them two fellers, right, Creech?"

"That's a fact," Creech confirmed.

"He said he had to go tell the blacksmith something," Clyde continued. "Shoot, we was as surprised as you were, Sheriff. We didn't come into town to cause any trouble."

"Well, that's good news to hear," Murphy said. "I expect the people of Newtown will be glad to know that. And by the way, I'm not the sheriff. I just can't abide a low-down gunslinger, that's all. I reckon you could just call it Murphy's Law. You wanna take care of the bodies and their horses, or do you want us to send for the undertaker?"

"We didn't know those two very well, but I expect we could at least take 'em back to their camp and bury 'em."

"I thought you might," Murphy said. "Too bad you two hooked up with those two. I don't know anything about the other one, but the one that caused all the trouble was a bad one. I've had a little trouble with him before. You're well rid of him. He'da give you a bad name if you rode with him very long."

"You're probably right," Clyde said, fighting to keep from biting his lip. "Sometimes things happen for the best." He looked at Bert and said, "Sorry for the trouble. Like I said, me and Creech didn't know what we was gittin' into. Come on, Creech." He grabbed the reins of Rafer's horse and rode off. Creech followed suit, taking Johnny's horse with him.

When they had gone, Bert turned to Murphy and said, "You just saved my life, and I want to thank you for steppin' in when you did. That Rafer fellow was fixin' to shoot me down, and I knew there wasn't no way I coulda pulled my pistol fast enough to stop him."

"I reckon not," Murphy said. "You'd do better to swap that old Cavalry Dragoon Revolver for the 1860 Colt Army model. It's a lot lighter and fires a .44 cartridge."

"I'd do better stayin' outta situations like this one," Bert said. "And thank you again for bringin' your horse in today." That was about all the time they had to discuss it before the crowd of spectators arrived to investigate the gunshots they had heard. One among them was Eliot Baxter, carrying his shotgun.

"Lookee yonder," Bert commented. "Here comes Baxter with his shotgun. If I coulda stalled Rafer long enough, the mayor woulda saved me."

"That's a fact," Murphy said. He couldn't help thinking about the coincidence it was that he had brought his two horses in that day for new shoes. He could have told Bert he had Nosy to thank for throwing a shoe. *Sometimes I think that horse is a lot smarter than he lets on*, he thought.

"What happened?" Baxter asked when he and the others gathered around Bert and Murphy. "We heard two shots and saw two bodies being hauled away."

"Murphy shot 'em," Bert answered right away. "I didn't

even have my gun halfway outta the holster before Rafer Polk had his out and aimed at my chest. I'da been dead if Murphy hadn't been here." He went on to tell him the whole story of Rafer's return to claim his vengeance for being locked in the smokehouse, then ordered out of town. "When Murphy shot Rafer, one of the others whipped his pistol out, but Murphy shot him before he could pull the trigger."

"Two of those four who've been raising hell in town are dead, then," Baxter said. "So we've still got the other two to deal with."

"I don't know," Bert declared. "Maybe so, maybe not. When Murphy took care of the first two, the other two started singing like a church choir. That one they call Clyde claimed they hardly knew Rafer and the other'n. Claimed they didn't have no idea they was here to kill me." He forced a nervous little chuckle when he thought about the reason for their visit. Then he grinned outright when he said, "They thought Murphy was the sheriff. He told 'em he didn't have nothin' to do with the sheriff's department, that what they ran into was Murphy's Law."

Elmo Dillon, who was part of the crowd of spectators, chuckled when he heard that. He looked at Murphy and asked, "What is Murphy's Law?"

Murphy shrugged and answered, "I don't know. It's just something that popped outta my mouth."

"Well, it's the only law we've got in town right now," Elmo declared.

"Don't count on it," Murphy quickly advised him. "I just happened to be in a position to help. I wouldn't even have been in town if my horse hadn't thrown a shoe." He looked over at Bert then and asked, "You must be pretty near done with shoein' my horse, ain'tcha?"

"I was just about finished when I was interrupted by unexpected guests," Bert answered, able to joke about the incident now. "Give me about fifteen minutes and I'll have you ready to go."

When the spectators wandered back toward the saloons, Murphy asked Bert how much he owed him. "Not a thing," Bert answered. "After what you did for me, I can't find it in my conscience to charge you a penny."

"I 'preciate it, Bert, but you can't make a livin' shoein' horses for nothing. I've got the money to pay you, in Union greenbacks." When Bert started to insist that the horseshoes were to be at no charge, Murphy stopped him. "I intend to pay you your goin' rate for shoein' two horses. Then if they turn out to be misfit and hurt my horses' hooves, I'll expect you to fix the problem. If you give 'em to me, I wouldn't have the nerve to complain about 'em, and my poor horses would have to suffer because of your work."

"My usual rate runs from a dollar to two dollars a hoof, depending on the horse," Bert said. "That's the charge in Yankee money. It's a whole lot more in Confederate money. I shoe horses because we don't have a real farrier here in Newtown, but I ain't had many complaints. How 'bout if I give you my special rate of one dollar a hoof?"

Murphy smiled. "That's fair enough, I reckon. Then if the horses make any complaints, I'll let you know. All right?"

"All right," Bert japed, "but the complaint has to come from the horse itself, so I'll know it ain't made up." He laughed at his clever remark, then added one more stipulation. "And I'll buy you a drink of likker at Bradshaw's when we finish here."

"Fair enough," Murphy said as he lightly rubbed Nosy's nose. "Is that all right with you, Nosy?" The bay gelding bobbed his head up and down, as if nodding in agreement. The horse always bobbed his head up and down when Murphy rubbed his nose.

When Bert finished the shoeing, he waited while Murphy rode the horse to the other end of the street and back to test the comfort of the shoes. He led the packhorse, as well, and saw no sign of discomfort from either horse. He was feeling the guilt of having gone so long before he had the horses reshod, but in his defense, there was no place to have it done on the long trip from Laredo to Newtown. "It's a wonder I didn't run both of 'em into the ground before I got here,," he'd confessed before Bert set to work on the new shoes.

He paid Bert eight dollars, gold, which Bert was happy to receive. So he asked Murphy to hold up a few minutes while he closed up his shop, then to accompany him to Bradshaw's for the drink he had offered to buy him. That sounded like a good idea to Murphy, so he helped Bert extinguish his fire and lock his tools up.

"I ain't causin' you to close up before you want to, am I?"

"No, I ain't got nothin' else I've gotta do this evening, and to be honest about it, I really need a drink after the way my day ended up." He shook his head slowly and confessed, "I thought I was about to die, and I'll tell you the truth, I swear I felt that first bullet go by me before I heard the rifle fire. I thought at first it had hit me, until I saw Rafer stiffen up and slide off his horse. I had my gun in my hand, but I couldn't bring it up quick enough to shoot, and the other fellow was pointin' his gun at me. I don't know what I was waitin' for. Then he doubled over and fell off his horse. I won't lie about it, Murphy. I always figured I'd be able to handle myself better than that in that kind of situation."

Murphy was sure that Bert had confessed more to him than he had intended, and that he would no doubt regret his open honesty when he thought about it later. So he decided it best to try to ease Bert's conscience as best he could. It was the kind of thing that could ruin a man's life if he let his mind labor on it.

"Don't put too much importance on your first reaction to a life-or-death situation. Every man is pretty much the same. I saw a lot of young men in their first hand-to-hand combat durin' my years in the past war. It's hard to know how you'll feel when you see the enemy coming straight at you that first time, almost close enough to shake hands. But it's a gun he's aimin' at you, and he's intendin' to take your life with it. And from what I saw, if the man wasn't killed, he became a killer, and the next time he was in that situation, he reacted like he was trained to do. So I wouldn't worry if I was you. You reacted like most men do in combat, and you survived. You'll be ready to react the next time, I guarantee it." He hesitated, then decided to add, "But get rid of that Dragoon revolver and get yourself a lighter handgun."

"I think I will," Bert said. "That big pistol of mine is hard to draw if you're in a hurry. But I notice you seem to favor a rifle, even though you wear a six-gun, too."

"That's all a matter of personal preference, I reckon. I prefer it in most situations, at least this particular rifle, because I can fire it and cock it again as fast as I can a handgun. And it's a whole lot more accurate. 'Course if I was to participate in a regular duel, I'd be better with my Colt .44, but that's why I try to avoid gettin' called out for one."

Bert laughed. "Yeah, I reckon so. But I appreciate you sharing your experience with men in their first battles. Makes me feel like I ain't that much different from everybody else."

"No, you ain't," Murphy said. "But you've faced a couple of guns and lived to tell about it, so you're one step ahead. Let's go get that drink."

Murphy tied his packhorse's reins to Nosy's saddle, so he could lead his horses as he and Bert walked down to Bradshaw's Saloon and Café. After tying the horses at the rail, they walked into the saloon, where the talk was still much about the shooting incident at the blacksmith shop.

"There they are," Elmo Dillon called out, "the gunslingers from the blacksmith shop. Pour 'em a drink of your good whiskey, Pete, and put it on my bill. They got rid of two of the town's biggest problems today."

"Pour them a drink, Pete, and it's on the house," Tyson Bradshaw declared. A little cheer went up from the customers gathered around the bar.

The cheer was loud enough to be heard across the street, a few doors down at Pratt's Saloon, just as Clyde Fry and Loafer Creech tied their horses at the hitching rail. "You sure this is a good idea comin' back here this soon?" Creech asked. "Maybe we shoulda gone on back to the hideout."

"We ain't got no reason to worry about the people of this town givin' us any trouble," Fry said. "We told that feller Murphy we didn't know nothin' about what Rafer was up to. He believed us, or he wouldn'ta let us ride off like that, free and clear. And I intend to repay him for killin' Rafer and Johnny. He cut our gang in half, and now he's holed up somewhere around here where we're gonna run into him every time we come into town."

"At least we didn't go back to Bradshaw's Saloon," Creech said. "He mighta changed his mind if he saw we didn't leave town." They had taken the road out of town but had ridden only far enough to feel it safe to dump Rafer's and Johnny's bodies in the woods for the buzzards. Then, after removing everything of value from the bodies, they had returned to Newtown at Fry's insistence.

"What's your pleasure?" Albert Smith, the bartender, asked when they sidled up to the bar.

"Whatever you're pourin'," Fry said and dropped a quarter on the bar.

Albert filled two glasses right away, relieved not to have to ask how they intended to pay. "You fellers ain't been in here before, but I've seen you in town now and again."

"That's a fact," Fry replied. "We thought it was about time we came in to give you some of our business."

"Well, we appreciate that," Albert said. "You the two fellers that was with them two that just got shot at the blacksmith's shop?"

Fry glanced at Creech before he answered, concerned that he might react the wrong way, but Creech continued to stand there, wearing a dumb expression. So Fry spoke up. "We sure are, and I wanna tell you it was mighty uncomfortable. It weren't the first time we'd come into town with those two fellers, but we didn't know about all that trouble Rafer Polk had got hisself in before. He said he had to tell the blacksmith somethin', so we weren't expectin' what he was really up to. Then, before you know it, up pops this Murphy feller, blazin' away with a Henry rifle. Well, me and Creech here backed away and let him know we didn't have nothin' to do with it. We thought he was the sheriff or somethin', but he said he weren't. We saw him once before in Bradshaw's, so we decided we'd find us another saloon to drink our whiskey at. Does he do stuff like that all the time?"

Albert shook his head. "I can't say if he does or not. Murphy don't live here. Matter of fact, he just showed up here a few days ago. Back from the war. I think he's got a piece of ground about three miles from here."

"Is that a fact?" Fry responded and glanced in Creech's direction to see if he was paying attention. "It didn't take him long to introduce himself, did it?"

"I reckon not," Albert replied and held the bottle up, ready to pour again.

"I think one more oughta do it," Fry said.

They tossed the second drink down and walked outside again. "He's got a place three miles from here," Fry said while looking up the street at Bradshaw's. "He's still in the saloon. Those are his horses tied out front. All we've gotta do is find us a place where we can keep an eye on those horses, then follow him right outta town."

"What if he don't leave town no time soon?" Creech asked. "He might stay in town to eat supper and play some cards."

"Let's hope he don't," Fry said. "We'll see how lucky we are. He's got his horses took care of. I'll bet he wants to get on back to his place while there's still a little bit of daylight left. And I wanna follow him all the way home before we jump him. I wanna see how much he's got hid around his camp. He might have a cabin and some other horses. He owes us everything he's got for killin' Rafer and Johnny."

"I reckon you're right," Creech conceded. "Let's find us a place to sit down and watch that saloon without somebody noticin' us."

"Like that empty buildin' down the street yonder," Fry said, pointing to the vacant place that had once housed Irene Floyd's Newtown Café. "There's even a bench on the front porch to set on, and we can put the horses behind the buildin'."

They rode down to the empty building and dismounted, then left the horses to stand there while they stepped up on the porch and looked back up the street to make sure they could watch Bradshaw's Saloon from there. "Perfect," Creech declared, so they led the four horses around behind the building and tied them at the back porch. "There's an outhouse back here and a smokehouse," he reported. "There's a padlock on the door. Wonder what's in there. Might not hurt to take a look inside there."

"Most likely nothin'," Fry said. "Probably put a lock on it to keep people from lookin' in it. We need to be watchin' Bradshaw's Saloon. To hell with the smokehouse."

They returned to the bench on the front porch to resume their surveillance of the main street of Newtown. They had been there for almost three quarters of an hour when Fry suddenly exclaimed, "There he is!" They both jumped up to take a better look.

"It's him, all right," Creech agreed. "He's goin' to that bay horse wearin' the saddle."

While they watched, Murphy untied the bay from the rail and climbed up into the saddle. He backed his horse away from the rail and turned, leading his packhorse. "He's comin' this way!" Fry exclaimed in surprise. They had assumed he would leave in the opposite direction, toward a camp somewhere along the higher ridges. "He'll see us settin' here on the porch!"

Creech didn't hesitate. He walked to the front door, raised his leg waist high, and jammed his boot solidly against the door, ripping the hasp off, allowing it to swing open. Creech and Fry hustled through the open door and closed it again. Once inside, they hurried to take positions on each side of the one window in front. In less than a minute, Murphy rode past the empty building, and once he continued on down the street, his two stalkers came out on the porch again to see which direction he took.

"He's takin' the path to the river road," Fry said. "He's got a place three miles down the river road."

They were in the process of untying their horses at the back of the building when they were both startled by a voice behind them.

"Clyde, Loafer."

Both men reached for their guns.

"Take it easy! It's me, Chad Tucker! Don't shoot!"

"Chad Tucker!" Fry exclaimed. "What the hell are you doin' here? You almost got yourself shot!"

"I didn't know you boys were up this way, but I heard there was a hideout back in the hills near this little town, so I've been layin' low, waitin' to catch up with you. When I saw the way the four of you come ridin' into town, I decided I'd better wait to see what you were gonna do. I reckon it's a good thing I did. Too bad about Johnny and Rafer. But if you're fixin' to leave this damn town behind, I thought I'd join up with you, if you don't mind. This damn Murphy feller ain't nobody to mess with."

"He won't be no problem after tonight," Fry remarked. "He ain't runnin' us outta town. We're goin' after him right now, so get your horse, if you're goin' with us."

"You mean you're goin' after him again?" Chad asked, surprised. "You'd best leave that rattlesnake alone. Let him be and let's find someplace where he ain't. I'm thinkin' Waco."

"Me and Creech got a score to settle with Mr. Murphy. Right, Creech?" Creech nodded. "And then we'll be right back here to have a drink."

"Well, I wish you luck, but I won't be here if you get back," Chad said. "I'll be long gone."

"Come on, Creech," Fry said as he climbed on his horse. "We don't want that rattlesnake to get too big a head start."

CHAPTER 5

This turned out to be a hell of a lot different day than I had planned, Murphy thought.

Maybe he shouldn't have let those other two losers go free, but what would he have done with them? They didn't draw their weapons, and they raised their hands right away. Besides that, he wasn't a sheriff or a town marshal. It was none of his business. He wouldn't have gotten involved at all if it wasn't for the fact that Rafer was fixing to murder the blacksmith. And he hadn't finished shoeing his horse.

Those were his thoughts when he turned Nosy down the street and left Bradshaw's Saloon. Now, as he was passing the empty building that used to be the Newtown Café, he was not dead certain, but he could have sworn he saw what looked like a man standing on one side of the front window. That caused him to rethink the situation. It was a possibility that the other two of that four-man gang might not have left town at all and were thinking about evening up the score for Rafer and the other one. So he decided to assume that he was about to have them on his tail right away, just to be safe and hope he was wrong. He figured they would not make their move on him until he was a little farther away from the town. In fact, they would probably prefer that he didn't know he was being followed until he reached his cabin. That way, they would have the bonus of taking everything he owned and not just his life.

With that thought in mind, he decided he'd prefer to ambush them before he reached his cabin. When he'd built his cabin, he had not built it primarily thinking to construct a fortress to withstand attacks by a band of armed men wishing to kill him. He had built a solid log home beside the river that would withstand the weather and the seasons, as well as a robbery attempt. It had also been built with the thought that the weary traveler was welcome if he was hungry and in need of rest. Consequently, he preferred to attack his stalkers away from his home. That way, he was the stalker. With that in mind, he kept his eye out for an ambush site that would give him the element of surprise he needed to have the advantage over both stalkers.

He asked Nosy for an easy lope in order to increase the distance between him and his pursuers. After about a mile and a half, he came to a point where the road was forced to bend around an outcropping of rock. This was made to order, he figured, so he turned his horses off the road and into the trees covering the ridge behind the outcropping. Not sure how much time he had to get into position, he dropped Nosy's reins to the ground, knowing he would stay and the packhorse wouldn't go anywhere without the bay. He pulled his rifle out of the saddle scabbard and cranked a round into the chamber. Then he climbed up to the top of the rock outcropping and found a flat place to stand facing the road and waited. The sun was lying low on the ridge behind him, throwing long shadows across the road, some fifteen feet below him. It seemed long, but it was really a short time before he heard the horses approaching. He knelt down until they were almost at the bend around the outcropping. As soon as both riders came into view, he stood up above them and demanded, "Are you lookin' for me?"

They reacted as he expected, both reaching for their handguns to fire at the unexpected figure standing above them in the setting sun. His first shot knocked Clyde Fry out of the saddle. He cranked in a new cartridge and struck Loafer Creech in the chest. Creech had time to draw his pistol but no time to aim. He squeezed the trigger as a reflex action but fired a shot into the rocky face of the outcropping as he was falling. Murphy reloaded, but there was no other response from the two who had come to kill him. He watched them for a couple of minutes to be sure; then he turned around and went back down the way he had come up. He found them still in the same positions as when he first shot them, both still alive but well on the way to cashing in. So he took the weapon from Creech's hand, cocked it, and put a bullet into his brain. Then he performed the same service for Clyde before going to retrieve his horses.

When he returned to the site of the shooting, he found the four horses that had belonged to the dead men had gone down to the edge of the river. "Good idea," he told Nosy and released him and the sorrel to join them while he stripped the bodies of anything of value. "I thought the war was over when I came back here," he said aloud as he went through the pockets of his two victims. He was surprised to find almost a hundred dollars in Union greenbacks in their pockets. "Somebody got robbed," he commented. "You boys musta been practicing your profession north of Texas."

When he was finished stripping the bodies, he walked down beside the river and took the reins of two of the outlaws' horses and led them back to the road. He tied them to a tree, and then he loaded a body on each one. In a short time, he was joined by Nosy, the bay gelding living up to his name. He untied the horses from the trees and climbed up into the saddle with their reins in hand, then rode back away from the river, toward the end of a low ridge. Once he was far enough away from the river and past the live oaks that encompassed it, he dumped the two bodies in a treeless expanse of prickly pear cactus and desert spoon. "The buzzards shouldn't have a hard time findin' you gents," he declared.

When he rode back to the river road, he continued to lead the two horses, figuring that the other three would follow, and he resumed his ride to his cabin. As he assumed, the other three horses came up from the river and followed along behind him. "Looks like I've got the start of my horse herd," he declared. "Too bad one of those losers wasn't ridin' a mare."

When he got to his cabin, he rode around behind it to the small stable he had fashioned before he had ridden off to war. His first thought when he'd returned to Newtown was to build a real barn and stable with the money he had hidden in the grave. Now, as he pulled the saddles off Nosy and the four horses he had come into possession of, he wondered if he was of sound mind for planning to raise horses. He owned a hundred and sixty acres of land, and only about half of it was good pastureland. He had planned to buy more land once he got a sizable herd of horses, and he intended to ride the perimeter of his land the next day to take a look at the land beyond his. One major disappointment for him was the development of the town. He had counted on Newtown to grow and attract more people and businesses. Instead, it appeared to have become an attraction for a lawless breed of drifters, outlaws, and deadbeats. "Well, ain't nothing I can do about that," he decided and continued to settle his "herd" of horses for the night.

After a breakfast of smoked venison and his version of pan biscuits, he filled the water trough he had built in his corral. Then he rounded up his horses and put them in the corral, now that the missing rails that had been used for firewood were replaced. He saddled Nosy and rode back from the river, following Brady Creek, which defined the north–south border of his property. There was still good pasture quite a ways back from the river, which satisfied his interests, until he saw the cows. "What the hell . . . ?" he uttered. There were three of them in the creek. He rode a little farther and saw several more grazing in his pasture. So he continued riding toward the stream that defined the east–west boundary at the back of his property, where he found a group of about fifteen cows on both sides of the stream. He pulled Nosy up close to them and dismounted. He wanted to take a close look at the brand. It appeared to be the letter *J* sitting on a rocker, easily translated as the Rocking-J. That didn't tell him who owned the cattle, but at least he knew they weren't wild strays.

"I expect you'd best step away from that cow." The warning came from a man riding out from behind a bunch of high bushes on the other side of the stream. He had a rifle resting across his forearm as his horse crossed over the stream. "Maybe you'd like to tell me what you were fixin' to do to that cow."

"Now that you're on this side of that stream, I'll be glad to tell you I was takin' a look at the brand to see whose cattle were grazin' on my property and how much I oughta charge 'em."

"If you're tryin' to be funny, you ain't doin' too good," the cowhand informed him. "I expect the best thing for you is to ride on out of these parts and find you someplace else to rustle cattle."

"Rockin'-J," Murphy declared. "Who might that be?"

"I expect you know," the cowhand replied, holding his rifle in both hands now. "Mr. Lionel Jacobson, and he don't take kindly to rustlers. So I suggest you'd best find yourself somebody else's cows to eat."

"'Preciate the suggestion, but I like it a lot better if the Rockin'-J is gonna continue to bring their cattle to me," Murphy said. "Hell, I can live on beef for as long as you wanna supply it."

The cowhand was obviously confused and not at all sure what to do about it, so Murphy thought he'd do well not to rile him further.

"I think it'd be a good idea if I was to talk to Mr. Jacobson. How can I find him?"

"If you wanna see him today, he's about half a mile up this creek at the chuck wagon," the cowhand said, relieved to have a solution to the problem. "The ranch headquarters is about half a mile farther. You need me to go with you?"

"No, that sounds easy enough to find. Just follow the creek, right?"

The cowhand said that it was, so Murphy asked his name.

"Walter," he said. "Tell Mr. Jacobson I'm roundin' up some strays down toward the river."

"I'll do that, Walter," Murphy said and climbed back up into the saddle, then rode off, following Brady Creek north. As Walter had said, he came to a chuck wagon, with a couple of saddled horses close by. He saw the cook and another fellow who looked to be a cowhand standing near the fire, talking to an older man seated on a campstool. They were all drinking coffee and paused when they couldn't identify the visitor. Murphy rode up to the wagon.

"Mr. Jacobson," he said, addressing the man on the campstool, "Walter told me I'd find you here. I'd like to talk to you. And he said to tell you he's roundin' up strays down toward the river."

That inspired a chuckle from all three, and the tall man standing beside the cook said, "He'd better be."

Jacobson laughed at that and said, "Well, step down and we'll talk. I'd offer you a cup of coffee, if you don't mind cowboy coffee."

"I'd take it and thank you kindly," Murphy said as he stepped down and dropped Nosy's reins on the ground. The cook went to the chuck wagon to get a cup, then filled it from a pot set at the edge of the fire. Murphy nodded his thanks when the cook handed it to him.

"Now, Mr. . . ." Jacobson paused to wait for a name.

"Murphy. Cullen Murphy," he responded.

"Mr. Murphy," Jacobson continued. "What do you want to talk about? If it's about employment, you'd do better talking to Mr. King here. He's my foreman."

"Mr. King," Murphy repeated and nodded, then turned back to Jacobson. "I expect it's you I need to be talkin' to. Your man Walter caught me checking the brand on some of your cows south of that stream, 'bout half a mile back that way. I really believe he was ready to shoot me until I explained that the cows were grazin' on my pasture and I just wanted to see who they belonged to." Murphy noticed an immediate interest on the part of all three and a deep frown on the forehead of Jacobson.

"Are you claiming you own that land between the stream and the river?" Jacobson asked.

"I'm not just claimin' it," Murphy answered. "I own it. Bought it six years ago and built that cabin sittin' beside Brady Creek, where it goes into the river. Then they decided to have a war, so I had to leave it until the fightin' was over. But I've still got a bill of sale, the deed, and the plat showin' my land. I'da brought it with me if I'd known I was gonna need it when I rode out to check my boundaries."

There was a swollen moment of silence that followed, the news apparently having some impact on Jacobson and King. Jacobson finally spoke. "I swear . . . So you're the one who holds the deed to that piece of land. I finally decided to add that piece of property between here and the river to my range right after I took this herd of cattle to the market this year." He paused again to think about it. "We thought it was open range but found out that somebody owned it, and I remember the name now . . . *Murphy*. But nobody could locate the owner."

"I was gone, fightin' a war for four years," Murphy remarked.

"What are you going to do with it?" Jacobson asked.

"My plan had been to raise horses when I bought it," Murphy said. "I didn't think this range was owned by anybody when I bought my property. I'd hoped that if I was successful raising my horses, I could buy up some more of this range up here. Good pastureland is kinda scarce in this part of Texas."

"That's an honest-to-God fact, Mr. Murphy. I guess things don't always go the way we plan them, do they?" Jacobson asked. "As far as my cattle are concerned, I'll tell my men to keep them off your land south of that creek. Like I said, we knew we were grazing private land, but we couldn't find any trace of the owner."

"Why, that's mighty neighborly of you, Mr. Jacobson. I appreciate it. But the fact of the matter is, I'm a little slow gettin' my herd started. And lately, with all the trouble they're havin' in town, I ain't sure I ever will. So don't worry about your cows grazin' on my land. I don't see how it could hurt, as long as you don't graze it out."

Jacobson got up off the stool then to shake Murphy's hand. "Mr. Murphy, you are a true gentleman, and I'm glad to make your acquaintance. We won't destroy the pasture. I give you my word."

Jim King grinned then when it struck him where he had heard the name. "Mr. Murphy," he declared. "Are you the Murphy everybody in town's talkin' about?"

"I don't know that I am," Murphy replied.

"The Murphy who knocked one of those four drifters out and locked him up in a smokehouse?" Murphy just shrugged, so King went on. "And the Murphy that killed that outlaw and his partner when they tried to kill the blacksmith?"

"I reckon you don't always have a choice when you have to fix something that ain't right," Murphy answered.

Jacobson looked at King, then back at Murphy, thinking this surely could not be the man his foreman was talking about. "If you are that man, then I salute you. I wish there were more like you in Newtown. Eliot Baxter and Tyson Bradshaw are going to have to build a jail and hire a sheriff. If they don't, they're going to see more people leaving, and we need that town."

"Yes, sir," Murphy said, "that's the way it looks to me, but I reckon they just ain't got the money." He downed the last of his coffee and returned the cup to the cook. "Thank you for the coffee. Pleased to meet you, Mr. Jacobson, Mr. King. I'd best be gettin' back to my place." He stepped up into the saddle and wheeled Nosy around. "Don't worry about the cattle. I'd appreciate it if you told your cowhands that somebody lives in the cabin, though."

On his way back to his cabin, he met Walter herding a bunch of cows back north of the boundary stream. They nodded to each other in passing. As he approached his cabin, he looked at the corral and decided to use the rest of the day to cut trees down for it. He wondered if he should ride into town one day that week and let Bradshaw and some of the other saloon owners know they didn't have to worry about Fry and Creech showing up again. He needed to take those extra four saddles in to see if he could sell them for whatever he could get for them to add to his treasury. Then it occurred to him that he hadn't even searched their saddlebags yet. He decided he would do that as soon as he got home.

When he got back to the cabin, he turned the horses out of the corral and took the saddle off the bay gelding. The horse went immediately to join the other horses at the creek, and Murphy went to the shed he used for a barn to go through the four saddlebags. What he found was too good to be true. In each of the four saddlebags, he found a sack of Union money. The four outlaws had robbed a bank or a train, judging by the canvas sacks the money was in. When he finished counting all four bags, he added the money to the cash he had already saved up and exclaimed, "Hell, I can buy a *herd* of horses!"

His declaration caused him to stop and give it some serious thought. His ambitious plans for what he was going to do were suddenly illogical. He would need to hire help to maintain a herd the size he intended, but that was not the restriction he had only recently discovered. He was going to need a greater range than the hundred and sixty acres that he owned. He had planned to move into the open range north of his land as he needed it. But now it was no longer open range. It was the Rocking-J Cattle Ranch.

He thought about that for a long moment, then suddenly declared, "Shoot! I don't wanna raise horses for a livin', anyway. And the Lord is sure sendin' me enough messages lately to discourage me. The first time I had the notion, He let a war get started. If I keep tryin' to raise horses, He's liable to have an earthquake or something, so I'd better find something else to do."

He spent the rest of the day working on his barn, with the intention of taking a ride into town the next day to see if he could get rid of the four saddles and the four extra horses. With his latest decision, he no longer needed to increase the size of the corral.

Chapter 6

He decided to take all six of the horses into town the next morning, with all four of the outlaws' horses saddled. He had in mind the possibility of selling or trading the four for whatever he could get for them. He figured his best bet for what the horses were carrying would be Eliot Baxter's Newtown General Store. As for the horses themselves, he would talk to Paul Mathers to see if he was interested in taking them at some ridiculous price. His first stop when he reached town, however, was the blacksmith shop.

Bert Walker saw him coming up the street and walked out to meet him. "Mornin', Murphy. Where you headin' with that parade?"

"Mornin'," Murphy returned. "The other night I had occasion to acquire some extra horses and hardware. I'm hopin' to sell or trade 'em, but I wanted to drop one item off with you before I get rid of the rest."

Bert stared in wonder at the four horses carrying empty saddles, thinking they could have come from only one source. "Those other two drifters?" he asked.

"That's right," Murphy answered. "They followed me home that night, after our little party here at your place. I don't expect to get much for any of it, but I thought you might want to take a look at that pistol hangin' on the saddle horn of that gray horse. It's a Colt 1860 Army model. Takes a .44 caliber bullet, and it's a good deal lighter than that hogleg you've been packin'. It's the same kind I carry, and I've been pretty satisfied with it."

Bert was immediately interested, and he walked back to the horse and lifted the revolver out of the holster to test the feel of it. "Which one of 'em was carryin' this?"

"I don't know," Murphy confessed. "I don't even know who was ridin' which horse, and I'm sure I got the guns mixed up after I took 'em off the bodies."

"I sure like the feel of it," Bert said.

"Good," Murphy replied. "It's yours."

"How much do you want for it?" Bert asked. "Or maybe we can trade for blacksmith services on your horses."

"It ain't for sale," Murphy said. "It's yours, if you want it, the pistol, the holster, and the belt. And make sure your belt is full. If it ain't, take some cartridges out of one of the other belts."

"Really?" Bert asked. "You're gonna give me the gun for nothin'? After you went through all the trouble to come by it? You ain't even told me what happened when the last two of those killers followed you home. It don't take much imagination to figure out who came out on top, though, so I'm damn glad to see you this mornin'. But you saved my life. I oughta be givin' you presents."

"Don't consider it a present," Murphy told him. "I just wanted to make sure my blacksmith wore a gun he could get outta the holster a little quicker. I reckon I don't have to tell you that things are just going to continue to get worse in this town when more and more no-good drifters and outlaws find out there ain't no law in Newtown. And if you find yourself in a situation like the one you were in the other day, I want you to be able to get your weapon out a little quicker than you did then."

"I guess I should take some practice time with my new gun," Bert said.

"Wouldn't hurt," Murphy agreed.

Bert couldn't resist asking, "Are you fast with a six-gun?"

"Well, that's hard to answer," Murphy replied. "Not especially, I'd say. Depends on the circumstances. Ever since I wasn't much more than a boy, I have spent most of my time avoidin' face-offs and shoot-outs. They don't make much sense. I always prefer to fight with my rifle, instead of a six-gun, anyway, if fightin' is the only choice. I've done a lot of killin', but most of it was done when I was in the army, and we were supposed to do as much killin' as we could. It still didn't make much sense, though. After a while, you get to the point where you just can't abide useless mischief and killin'." He paused then when he realized he was exposing his innermost thoughts, and that was always a good time to end any conversation. "But I'd best get over to Baxter's store and see if I can get rid of some of this stuff."

Bert thanked him again for the revolver, then asked, "Are you gonna sell the horses, too?"

Murphy told him that he had thought he would.

"How much are you askin' for that gray?"

"I'm hopin' to get forty dollars apiece for 'em," Murphy said, "and that includes the bridle and saddle. You lookin' for a horse?"

"That old sorrel of mine is getting pretty old. I think he's been wantin' to retire for some time now. Would you be interested in a trade for forty dollars' credit?"

"I would," Murphy said. "Look him over good."

They both checked the gray over thoroughly and decided the horse was about five years old and a real deal at forty dollars.

He left the blacksmith a happy man, and he was satisfied, as well, grateful in fact for getting anything for the horse. He would use that credit. His dealings with Eliot Baxter were a sight different, however. Baxter was not at all interested in the horses, but he did want to take advantage of the opportunity to buy guns, ammunition, bridles, saddles, saddlebags, and bedrolls at dirt-cheap prices. He was sure he could sell them all in his store. Like the blacksmith, Baxter was interested to know the source of the merchandise Murphy was trading with him, but seemed overly relieved to hear the last of the four outlaws were dead. "It's good news this morning to know our town is peaceful again." He wrote a figure down in his ledger for the credit he was extending Murphy for the items he traded, showed it to Murphy, and said, "Business as usual."

"Mr. Mayor," Murphy said, "you do understand that there's gonna be more trouble ridin' in here, don't you? The word's bound to be spreadin' that there ain't no law in Newtown. We need a jail and a sheriff to enforce the law, or we're gonna be a ghost town before you know it."

Baxter released a sigh of frustration. "I hear what you're saying, Murphy, and I totally agree with you that we need a sheriff and a jail. But the fact of the matter is we don't have the money to pay for them at this point. Getting a sheriff or building a jail isn't like a business that just decides to set up shop in this town, with the prospect of selling a product. The town has to pay for the law, and we don't have the money."

Murphy left the store, feeling his own frustration after talking to the mayor. It didn't help when a couple of men on horseback decided to have a race from one end of the main street to the other. Their galloping horses caused several early shoppers to run for the boardwalks to escape being run over. This apparently caused the loser of the race to complain that it wasn't a fair race, because he had had to swerve around them. So they decided to race again, back to the other end of the street. The disgruntled rider decided this time to fire his six-shooter in the air to warn everyone to get out of his way. It would prove to be a bad decision on his part, for Murphy was already annoyed by the race they had just run, which had sent women and children scattering as they ran for their lives.

Now, when the one rider started firing his gun in the air, Murphy pulled an axe handle out of a barrel of them that Baxter had set outside his front door. He walked calmly out into the middle of the street, stopped, and turned to face the charging horses. Both riders yelled at him to get out of the way. The one firing his gun emptied it into the air, but it had no effect on the man standing in the middle of the road, so the two riders veered to go on either side of him. Murphy turned toward the one firing his gun. Timing it perfectly with that of the passing horse, Murphy's swing of his axe handle caught the rider in the chest, taking him off his horse to land on his back, the wind knocked out of his lungs. Still holding his six-shooter in his hand, he aimed it at Murphy and pulled the trigger, only to find he had emptied it already. With his chest feeling about to cave in, he couldn't put up much resistance as Murphy grabbed his boot and dragged him out of the street to his horses, which were tied in front of the store.

Keeping one eye on his prisoner's partner, Murphy took the rope from his saddle and quickly tied the gasping man's hands together behind his back and left him sitting there while he watched his partner make up his mind. After a few more moments of hesitation, his partner walked his horse back to the store, where Murphy waited, his six-gun in hand.

"Who the hell are you?" the rider asked.

"I'm the law here," Murphy answered. "And we don't allow any horse races inside the town limits. And your partner here is lookin' at some time in jail for dischargin' a firearm inside the town limits." He looked down at the young man on the ground. "And attempted murder is a hangin' offense."

Still straining to regain his voice, the man claimed, "I was just funnin' when I aimed at you. I knew my gun was empty. I never meant no harm a'tall. I was shootin' up in the air, just so folks wouldn't get in the way and get hurt."

"Honest, Sheriff," the man on the horse declared, "we didn't know nothin' about them rules here in town." After getting a close look at the formidable image that Murphy projected, he had decided it best to play humble. "Nobody ever said anything when we was in town before."

"He's right, Sheriff," the one on the ground said, able to talk a little easier now. "We was at the saloon, and we was just gettin' ready to head back to the ranch. We didn't know anything about those rules."

Murphy pretended to be considering their pleas. They reminded him of the young men who had served under him when he was in the army. "I'm thinkin' you've both earned a little time in jail, but since you say you didn't know the difference, and you said you were leavin' town, I'm gonna let you go this time. And think about how much better it would be if the folks in town would be happy to see you come in, instead of dreadin' it."

"Yes, sir," the young man with his hands tied remarked, "that sure makes a lot of sense. We 'preciate you lettin' us off with a warnin'. Don't we, Harry?"

"We sure do," Harry agreed at once. "I'll go fetch your horse."

Murphy helped his prisoner up on his feet and untied his hands while Harry rode down the street and got his horse. Once they were both mounted, Murphy stood there and watched them ride out of town while he wound his rope back into a coil.

"Murphy's Law." He heard the simple statement behind him and turned to find Elmo Dillon approaching him. "Did you really tell those two fellows you were the sheriff?"

"No," Murphy answered, "I told them I was the law. They decided to call me Sheriff."

Elmo smiled. "But you didn't bother to correct their mistake, did you?"

"I saw no need to, and I think they might have felt like they had to protest if they thought I didn't have any real authority to arrest them. I could have told them I was makin' a citizen's arrest, but I think that would have caused them to put up a fight. And I didn't want it to come to that."

"You knocked that one fellow off his horse," Elmo said.

"I had to get his attention," Murphy replied. "How long were you hidin' back there?"

"Long enough to see the whole thing," Elmo answered, still grinning.

"You coulda helped," Murphy said.

"Didn't look to me like you needed any help."

"Seems like that's the attitude of the whole damn town," Murphy said. "Tell me this, is there anybody in town who does carpentry work?" He was ready to change the subject.

"Sure," Elmo replied. "Frank Jessop's brother, Robert. He built my shop. You know Frank, don't you? Owns the sawmill. You gonna build something onto your cabin?"

"Nope, I reckon I could do that myself. I built the cabin and the barn. I've got something else in mind, and I need a real carpenter for that."

That answer was not going to satisfy Elmo's natural curiosity at all. "Whaddaya gonna build? Are you talking about something here in town? What's the big secret?"

"I'm thinking about buildin' a tailor shop," Murphy japed, "one with a bar and some sportin' women."

"Doggone it, Cullen, you can tell me what you're thinking about doing. I ain't gonna tell anybody, if you're wanting to keep it a surprise for some reason."

"I don't want to tell you or anybody else what I want to do until I find out if I can do it with the money I've got saved up. If I can't, then everybody would know how dumb I am, and I don't want anybody to know that, includin' you."

Elmo shook his head, frustrated. He considered himself Murphy's first friend when he came back from the war.

Murphy read it in his expression, so he said, "When I find out whether I can do it or not, you'll be the first person I tell about it. Right now, I've gotta take these horses to the stable to see if Paul Mathers is interested in buyin' the three totin' saddles."

"What you selling 'em for?" Elmo asked. "I thought you were planning to raise horses."

"I changed my mind," Murphy said.

"You gonna go to farming?" Elmo asked as a joke.

"I might," Murphy said as he stepped up into the saddle. "It's one of the things I'm considerin'."

"That'll be the day," Elmo remarked, trying to picture Murphy behind a plow. "You going back to your cabin right away?" he asked as Murphy prepared to ride.

"No, I've got a couple of things to do before I go home," Murphy answered.

"Stop by Bradshaw's at dinnertime and I'll buy your meal," Elmo offered.

Murphy told him that he would be happy to. Bradshaw's was one of the stops he had planned for the day, anyway, so he figured he might as well let Elmo spring for some grub.

Murphy rode up the street, passed the blacksmith's forge again, and pulled Nosy up before the stable. Seeing no sign of Paul Mathers at the barn or the corral, he tied the horses beside the corral and walked into the stable, where he found Mathers cleaning out one of the stalls.

"Howdy, Cullen. What can I do for you?" he asked.

"Howdy, Paul," Murphy replied. "I'm gonna be in town for most of the day, and I've got some horses with me that I'd like to leave in your corral till I'm ready to leave."

"How many horses are you talking about?" Mathers asked.

"Well, I've got my bay and my sorrel packhorse, but I've also got three other horses. The thing is, my bay and my sorrel could use a portion of grain. It's been a while since I've had any to feed 'em, and I generally like to feed 'em grain or oats every once in a while. So I'd like to pay you for that." He paused, as if stopping to think, before he continued. "I've got no idea if the other three were accustomed to bein' fed grain or not. I just came by them yesterday. Probably wouldn't hurt to give them a portion, too."

"Just five horses, right?" Mathers asked. Murphy nodded, so Mathers said, "Sure, I'll take care of 'em for you." He propped his pitchfork against the side of the stall and walked out to the front of the stable with Murphy. "What are you fixin' to do with the three extra horses?"

"I'm thinkin' about sellin' 'em," Murphy answered. "There were four of 'em, but I sold one to Bert Walker for forty dollars."

This sparked some interest from Mathers, so he took a closer look at the three horses. "I recognize that buckskin. Those horses have been in my stable before." It struck him then. "That gang of four drifters, Rafer Polk and his partners . . . But how'd you come by 'em? I know you done in Rafer and one other one. What happened to the other two?"

"They followed me home last night," Murphy said. "They had all four horses with 'em."

"Damn . . . ," Mathers drawled. "Don't reckon there's any chance they'll be coming to look for 'em, is there?"

"I don't expect so," Murphy said.

Mathers nodded thoughtfully. "So you're gonna try to sell 'em, huh?"

Murphy nodded then. "Might as well. I've got no use for 'em."

"You know, from time to time, I buy some horses, but forty dollars is a might steep for me. At forty dollars, it doesn't leave me much room for profit."

"I can understand that," Murphy said. "That horse I sold Bert included the bridle and a fancy saddle. I'm just looking for thirty dollars apiece for these three."

"Well, that is some better, but it's still a little too much for me to make a profit." He shrugged his shoulders, as if truly disappointed. "I'll give you seventy-five dollars for the three of 'em."

"Are you talking about seventy-five dollars in Confederate paper or seventy-five dollars in Union greenbacks?" Murphy asked. "'Cause that makes a helluva difference."

"Genuine Yankee greenbacks," Mathers responded. "And I'd appreciate it if you didn't tell anybody about it."

"I understand," Murphy said. "Real paper money is hard to come by these days." He paused to think about it, then continued. "I'll make you a counteroffer. How about thirty dollars apiece for ninety dollars in trade and you can hang on to your Yankee greenbacks?"

Mathers smiled in appreciation for Murphy's obvious consideration. "I'll counter that offer with my final offer, the three horses for one hundred dollars in trade."

"You bought yourself some horses," Murphy said, and they shook on it.

He took his saddlebags and rifle with him. He left the stable and walked back down the street until he came to the vacant building where he had spotted Clyde Fry and Loafer

Creech watching him before they followed him home. There was still a padlock on the door, but the hasp had been pried loose. Irene Floyd, owner of the building, was either unaware of the loose hasp or didn't care. He pushed the door open and went inside. The building was of simple construction, having been built for a café. The front door opened into a single large room, which had been the dining room. Behind it was a short hallway with the kitchen and pump room on one side and two small rooms on the other. Murphy presumed the two small rooms had been the living quarters for Irene and her daughters.

He spent some time trying to visualize how the building could be adapted to fit his purposes with the addition of some new walls and the boarding up of some windows. He looked the structure of the building over thoroughly and decided it was in good condition. It would serve his purposes. With the money he had accumulated recently, added to what he had buried when he went off to war, he could afford to build a new place. But that would take longer plus the inconvenience of not being in the center of town, as this building was. So the question now was whether or not he could strike a reasonable purchasing price with Irene Floyd. It was now close to the time when the café would open its doors, so he expected to get an answer to the question shortly.

He walked into Bradshaw's Saloon a few minutes before the door to the café opened, so he went over to the bar to talk to Pete while he waited.

"Mr. Murphy," Pete greeted him.

"Mr. Brice," Murphy responded.

"What's your poison?" Pete asked.

"Is that corn whiskey you're pourin'?" Murphy asked, and Pete said that it was. "Give me a shot of that. I'm just waitin' for the dinin' room to open up." He didn't know if the whiskey was watered down or not, but one shot wouldn't start much of a fire in his empty belly.

"Word's goin' around that the last two of that wild bunch have passed away," Pete remarked. "You hear anything about that?"

"Yeah, I heard," Murphy answered. "Kinda sad, ain't it? They were good boys, every one of 'em. Just got off on the wrong start, I reckon."

"Story's goin' around that they run afoul of Murphy's Law."

"Is that so?" Murphy responded. *Elmo Dillon*, he thought to himself. *He's worse than a gossipy old woman.* "I expect what they ran afoul of was the law of right and wrong accordin' to what the honest folks of this town believe in."

The door between the saloon and the café opened at that point, and Bonnie Floyd turned the CLOSED sign around. Murphy downed his whiskey and dropped a coin on the bar. "See you later, Pete."

"Good afternoon, Uncle Cullen," Bonnie said with a giggle when he walked inside the dining room. "Are you gonna drink coffee with your meal?"

"Always," Murphy answered. "As long as you've got food to serve, I'll have coffee with it. And if you run out of food, I'll just have coffee."

"I'll take that as a yes," Bonnie said and giggled again as she went to the kitchen to tell her mother and sister that Murphy was in the dining room.

"I called him Uncle Cullen," Bonnie told Ginger.

"You didn't," Ginger insisted, in disbelief.

"He said we could call him that if we didn't want to call him Cullen," Bonnie reminded her.

"I know he told you that," their mother said. "But you mind you don't show him any disrespect. He's a customer, and we need every customer we can get." Her concern went a little deeper than that, but she preferred not to share that with the two girls. The fact of the matter was that no matter how friendly and polite Cullen Murphy seemed, he was evidently a brutal killer when triggered.

In spite of their mother's warning, both girls managed to show Murphy plenty of attention while he ate his dinner. When he had finished, he asked Ginger if she would tell her mother that he would like to talk to her, if she could spare a couple of minutes. When Irene heard of his request, she took her apron off and went into the dining room, prepared to hear his complaint.

"Good afternoon, Mr. Murphy. Was there something wrong with your food?"

"I declare, when are you folks gonna stop callin' me mister? My name's Cullen. Is it all right if I call you Irene?"

"Of course it is," she responded. "Was there something wrong with your meal?"

"No, ma'am. The food was excellent. Your cookin' always is. I wanted to talk to you about something else."

The girls, she thought. "Was there something wrong with the service?" she asked, wondering if he thought he was eating at a fancy New Orleans restaurant.

"No, ma'am, your girls are top-notch. I wanted to ask you if you still own that vacant buildin' where your café used to be."

"Yes, I still own it and the lot it's settin' on. Why?"

"I was just wonderin' what you plan to do with it," Murphy said.

Caught off guard for a second when she realized he wasn't complaining about anything, she hesitated before replying. "Well, nothing, really. I can't afford to do anything with it, if you're talking about moving my café back there. Eliot Baxter has been talking to me about possibly selling it to him. It cost my late husband twelve hundred dollars to build that place."

"How much did Baxter offer for it?" Murphy asked.

"He said he'd pay me the twelve hundred dollars we spent

to build it, but he'd do it in three years, at four hundred a year."

"Do you think that's a good deal for you?" Murphy asked.

"No, not especially. That was the cost five years ago, and that's why I haven't ever sold it to him."

"I think you're right," Murphy told her. "Would you consider sellin' it to me? I'll offer you two thousand dollars for the property, genuine official Union greenbacks, the whole sum upon closing. Whaddaya say?"

She was speechless for a moment, not sure she had heard him properly, so she repeated his offer to confirm it. "Two thousand Yankee dollars, all in one payment?"

"That's right," he said. "Whaddaya say?"

"I say, 'Yes, I'll take it!'" she exclaimed. "Hell, yes! When do you want to do it?"

"While I'm here in town this afternoon, if you can get your deed and any other papers you have for the property. Can you do that?"

"I sure can," she replied at once. "What are you going to use the building for?" she had finally thought to ask.

"I'm gonna make some changes on it, fix it up for a shop of some kind," he answered. "I'm still in the plannin' stage, but I knew I needed a building in the middle of town whatever I decided on. I've got a thing or two to do before I leave town today, so what time do you want to sell your buildin' to me?"

"We have to keep the dining room open until one thirty, and it'll take us about half an hour to clean up after that. But just to be safe, can we meet at two thirty at my house?"

"Yes, ma'am, that'll be fine," Murphy said.

She gave him directions to her little house on a side street a short distance off Front Street. He paid her for his dinner, picked up his rifle and his saddlebags, and left the café on his way to the stable to get Nosy and his packhorse. Mathers was eating his dinner out of a metal pail he had just heated up on the stove. He offered Murphy a cup of coffee and a piece of corn bread, but Murphy said, "Thanks just the same, but I just came from Bradshaw's Café. Don't interrupt your meal. I just came to pick up my two horses, and I'll be outta your way."

The bay gelding came to the corral gate as soon as he saw Murphy walking toward it. The sorrel followed the bay, and Murphy led them both out. He threw his saddle on Nosy and rode half a mile down the river to Frank Jessop's sawmill.

Chapter 7

Frank Jessop was standing outside the little shack that served as his office, talking to another man, when Murphy rode up to his sawmill. He had seen Frank before at Bradshaw's, but he had not become very well acquainted with him. The two men stopped talking to watch him approach. When he pulled Nosy to a stop and dismounted, Jessop greeted him.

"Mr. Murphy, what can I do for you?"

"Mr. Jessop," Murphy returned, "I'd like to talk about doin' a little business with you, but I don't wanna interrupt."

"You're not interrupting," Frank said at once. "I was just talkin' to my brother, Robert. Don't know if you've ever met him or not." Both Robert and Murphy shook their heads, so Frank introduced them. "Robert, this is Cullen Murphy."

Murphy stepped forward and extended his hand. "Glad to meet you, Robert. Matter of fact, I came here hopin' to meet you and your brother. Elmo Dillon said you built his shop. I'm fixin' to do some work on a vacant buildin' in town and fix it up for my needs. I'm gonna need some more lumber as well as some carpentry work."

"What buildin' is it?" Frank asked.

"The old Newtown Café buildin'," Murphy answered.

"Irene's old place?" Frank asked. "You thinkin' about puttin' another eating place in that building?"

"No, it'll be a different kind of business, and I'm gonna need some heavier wood on some of the walls. I'm thinkin' about four-by-sixes maybe," Murphy said.

"So you'd need the walls took out and replaced with heavy walls," Robert said.

"No, I'm thinkin' about leaving the walls and just nailin' the four-by-sixes to them. They still looked to be in pretty solid condition. There'd be some walls that might come out. I'd just have to draw up a little plan, and you could get a better idea of what it would take."

"Damn," Frank said. "What kinda business you thinking about starting? A bank or a jewelry store?"

"Something like that," Murphy said. "I'd like to keep it a secret until I'm ready to open. That would be part of the deal. All right?"

Frank shrugged, amused. "Sure, we can keep our mouths shut. Can't we, Robert?"

"You bet," Robert answered and grinned at Murphy. "As long as we get invitations to the grand opening."

Murphy grinned back at him. "I can promise you that."

"I'm pretty sure we can provide the lumber for you," Frank said. "Robert can take a look at the job with you and figure what we'll need. Then I can give you a price for materials and labor. So let me ask you now, what kind of payment plan are you thinkin' about?"

"Cash deal, Union-guaranteed greenbacks," Murphy answered.

"When do you want to get started?" Frank asked.

"I'm goin' to meet with Irene Floyd at two thirty to pick up the deed to the property." He paused to pull his watch out to look at it. "That's about thirty minutes from now. I don't expect that to take very long," he said to Robert. "You wanna meet me at the old café about three thirty? And we can get a pretty good idea what we're gonna need."

"That sounds good to me," Frank said, looking at his brother when he did and receiving an enthusiastic nodding of his head in return.

"I'll meet you at the old café at three thirty," Robert confirmed.

"Right," Murphy replied and stepped back up into the saddle. He wheeled Nosy and rode back toward town.

The two Jessop brothers stood watching him depart. "Doggone, that sure is a surprise source of business," Robert said. "It couldn't come at a better time."

"Yeah," Frank agreed, "and payin' for the job with real money. I hope he has a realistic idea what things cost these days. He's been off fighting in a war for the past four years. He might not know how prices have gone up."

"I wonder why he doesn't want anybody to know what kind of business he's planning to open," Robert remarked. "You reckon it's something illegal?"

"I don't care if it is," his brother replied. "They ain't likely to send us to prison for building it." He forced a chuckle and added, "I just hope he's easier on us than he was with Rafer Polk and his pals."

At promptly two thirty, Murphy pulled up in Irene Floyd's front yard and dismounted. He stepped up on the front porch and was about to knock when the door opened and he was greeted by a smiling Ginger Floyd. "Come in, Cullen," she said. "Mama's in the kitchen, making a pot of coffee. She said you'd probably want a cup."

He smiled and said, "I wouldn't turn one down. I must be earnin' a reputation in town."

"You sure are," she said. *But it's not for drinking coffee*, she thought. "Come on in the parlor, and Mama will be right in." She led him into the small living room and pointed to a large chair beside a low coffee table. Then she went into the kitchen to get her mother.

He had just sat down when Irene came into the room, carrying a folder of documents, and she waved him back down when he got to his feet. Bonnie followed along behind her with a cup of coffee. She placed it on the table beside him and said, "Hope you enjoy your coffee, Uncle Cullen."

"Bonnie!" Irene scolded. "Mind your manners. Please excuse my daughter's lack of courtesy, Cullen."

He chuckled and replied, "I've been called a lot worse things than *uncle*. Besides, I think I like havin' a niece."

"You're a patient man, Cullen," she declared.

"Now that's something I've never been accused of before," he responded with another chuckle.

"Well, here's the deed and a little plat thing that shows the outline of the property," she said as she handed him the documents. "I signed it down there at the bottom of the last page, where it says I'm selling it and dated it. I guess that's all you need. If it's not, I'll be glad to tell anyone that you bought it."

"That oughta be good enough. I reckon I'd best pay you since you've already signed it over to me. Do you still want the money?" he joked.

"I should have gotten the money before I signed it, I guess. But I'm still holding the keys to the front door and the smokehouse," she countered.

"Well, you got me there," he laughed. "I need that key to the smokehouse. Here's your money." He handed her an envelope with the money in it.

She took it and thanked him.

"You'd best count it to make sure it's all there. It's a big stack of bills."

"Oh, I trust you," she assured him.

"No, really, count it," he insisted. "I wanna make sure I didn't accidentally short you."

"All right," she said and sat down at the table. "You can help me. Here, you take half the stack and we'll count it again."

"Irene," he scolded, "you haven't known me long enough to know if I'm a sticky-fingered money shark or not. If you want help countin' it, let Ginger or Bonnie do it."

Ginger, who had come in from the kitchen at that moment, said, "Here, Mama. Bonnie and I'll count it." She took the stack and gave Bonnie approximately half, and they began counting the money. When they finished, they came up with the correct amount.

"You're an honest man," Irene said. "I knew it wasn't necessary to count it."

"It never hurts to make sure," he said.

"You still haven't told us what you're going to do with that old building," Ginger said.

"I'm afraid you might try to talk me out of it, so we'll just wait to see what I decide on. Right now, I'm thinking about Murphy's Café, to try to give you a little competition. I'm gonna have to find me a place to buy some cookbooks and recipes, though."

"Fiddle!" Ginger uttered. "You know what you're going to do with that place. You just don't want anybody to know yet."

Irene handed him the keys. "Here you go, Cullen. Good luck with whatever you're going to put there. I'm just glad it's too small to be another saloon."

"Maybe I'm just tryin' to give myself a reason to live in town, instead of in my little cabin up the river," he said. "Maybe I can help you folks save this town." He got up and headed for the door. "Looks like I might still be in town at suppertime. I've got one more stop to make."

"Well, come on back to Bradshaw's," Irene said, "and we'll give you supper on the house tonight."

He got back on his horse and rode back to his newly purchased investment in Newtown. "This is your new home, Nosy. You and the sorrel might as well get used to it." After he tied the two horses at the back of the building, he went inside to make sure there weren't any drunken homeless people taking temporary residence there. The first time he looked through the building he had found some evidence of past visits, and he wanted to put a stop to that right away. He was thinking about the danger of a fire getting started by a drunk when he heard someone come in the door up front. He hurried back to find it was Robert Jessop.

"Looks like the first job needin' some attention is to fix the lock back on the door," Murphy said. "I woulda done it myself if I had any of my tools with me."

"Ain't no worry about that," Robert replied. "I've always got a hammer and some nails in my saddlebags. So I'll fix that for you today at no charge. That oughta do temporarily, and we can do a more permanent job on it later. You might be thinking about taking this door out and putting in a double door."

"No, a single door will work just fine," Murphy replied. "But I do want a good lock on it." When Robert shrugged in reaction, Murphy explained. "This front room is gonna be an office, and it doesn't have to be as big as this room, so we'll be addin' a wall across here."

He went on to go through the building, showing Robert where he wanted to change the current walls and where he wanted to have the extra-thick walls. Robert had a pencil and a pad he was taking notes on, and when they had gone over the entire building, he had a pretty good idea of the finished floor plan. So he had to ask, "What are you building? A jail or a jewelry store?"

"One or the other," Murphy answered, still choosing to be evasive. "But that's why part of our deal is that you and your brother can't tell anybody what we're buildin' till it's finished. I expect I'll have to get the same commitment from Bert Walker, 'cause we're gonna need quite a bit of hardware from him before it's done."

"I'll get together with my brother, and we'll work you up a price for all these changes, but I gotta warn you, it might be higher than you were figuring on," Robert warned.

"Maybe so," Murphy said. "You just come up with a number and I'll see if I can make it." He didn't really have a clue, and they didn't have the blacksmith's price for the items he would have to furnish. But he felt that it could surely not take the entire sum of money he had managed to collect. And he couldn't think of a better use for the money that Clyde Fry and his gang had robbed from either a bank or a train than to build a jail with it.

"Like you insist, I ain't gonna tell a soul what you're fixin' to make outta this old café. But I gotta ask you outright, are you building a jail?"

"Saw it right off, did you?" Murphy asked, no longer evading the question.

"But why?" Robert asked, finding it hard to believe.

"The town ain't got one, has it?" Murphy asked.

Robert shook his head.

"The town needs one, doesn't it?" Murphy asked.

Robert nodded his head.

"There you go, then," Murphy continued. "Anybody with the brains of a chicken can see that this town is goin' down unless there's some semblance of law and order. The drifters and the outlaws are well aware there's no law and order here. I know you folks on the town council have been talking about some vigilante justice, but that ain't a permanent solution to the problem. Sooner or later, the US marshal would be down here to put a stop to that. And it ain't likely to attract new people to come to Newtown to live if they hear there's a lot of hangin's by masked vigilantes."

"Are you wantin' to become the sheriff?" Robert asked.

"Hell, no," Murphy responded.

"You'd make a good one," Robert insisted, "and you're the only one who's ever made an arrest and locked somebody up, even if it was in the smokehouse."

"That was just something anybody is apt to do with somebody that don't know how to act like a human being and respect the rights of others," Murphy said. "I can't abide a man that bullies other people."

"I have to say that most of us feel the same way you do," Robert confessed. "But there wasn't much we could do about it till there were enough new businesses here to pay for a sheriff and a jail."

"And there ain't ever gonna be enough new businesses until the town's got law and order. When we get this jail built, maybe that'll be a kick in the butt for the town council to put a man in it."

"I can't wait to get it built," Robert said.

"Here, take one of these keys." Murphy handed him one of the keys to the padlock on the front door. "Irene had two keys to the door. You might as well keep one of 'em, so you can go in if there's something you want to take a look at again."

He took the key and said, "I'll sit down with Frank, and we'll go over the materials and labor figures and get you a price in the morning. Is that all right? You gonna stay in town tonight?"

"No, but I'll be back tomorrow," Murphy said, "and I'll ride out to the sawmill, and we'll see if we can get this thing started." He looked at his watch. "I've managed to stay today until it's time Irene will be open for supper, so I reckon I'll let her feed me before I go back to the cabin."

They locked the building, and Murphy headed for Bradshaw's Saloon. Instead of tying his horses in front of the saloon, he took the path beside it that led to the back entrance to Irene's café. One saddled horse was tied there. He dropped

Nosy's reins on the ground beside a small window to the dining room. A quick look in the window told him was no one sitting at the small table beside it. *Good*, he thought, *I'll take that table, and I can keep an eye on my horses*. He climbed down from the saddle and paused a moment to decide. "It might take me too long to get back out here," he said and pulled his rifle out of the scabbard and his saddlebags off the horse. He didn't know why he had even considered leaving the saddlebags, with every dollar he had acquired, out behind the building while he ate.

When he went inside, he walked past the dining room door and went to the kitchen. He stuck his head inside, but there was no one in the kitchen. Figuring all three women were in the dining room, he parked his rifle and his saddlebags in an out-of-the-way corner of the kitchen, then headed for the dining room. Just as he opened the door, he heard what sounded like a threat of some kind delivered by a female voice. When he stepped inside, he heard Irene repeat the threat she had just made to a snarling brute of a man who had Ginger's wrist locked in one of his hands.

"Let her go, Kirby, and get yourself out of here, or I'll dump this pot of coffee over your head!" Irene demanded.

"You do that, you old witch, and I'll break her arm off and beat you to death with it," the brute threatened, still seated at the table. "This little tease comes sashayin' by me like she was in heat and darin' me to do somethin' about it. It's time she learned to put up or shut up. So go back to the kitchen and mind your own business."

Irene took a step back when she saw Murphy approaching the table, an instant look of relief in her eyes. Puzzled by it, Kirby turned to see him. He released Ginger and got to his feet, dropping his hand on the handle of his six-gun.

"Who the hell are you?"

"I'm your guide," Murphy said. "I've come to see you get

safely out the door before you get in more trouble than you can handle. You ready to go?"

"Ha!" Kirby responded, as if delighted. "Am I ready to go?" He smirked and walked around the table to stand almost face-to-face with Murphy. "What if I say I ain't ready to go? Then what?"

"Then I'll have to escort you outta here, and believe me, it'll go a whole lot easier on you if you just go ahead and leave without my help. Whaddaya say? Wanna take the easy way out?"

"Mister, this is all the warnin' I'm gonna give you. If you ain't turned tail and walkin' out that door you just came in by the time I count to three, I'm gonna put a .45 bullet right through your breastbone. Now do you understand that?"

"Yes, I think I do," Murphy answered. "You're too damn dumb to go the easy way."

Kirby grinned in response and lifted his hand up from the handle of his pistol to let it hover over it. Then he began his count. "One . . . two . . . ," and drew his six-gun.

Anticipating that Kirby would draw before he said three, Murphy grabbed his wrist as the gun came out of the holster, and with all the strength he could muster, he forced the man's arm to keep going up until the six-gun's barrel was jammed up under his chin. With one hand holding the weapon up under Kirby's chin and the other holding the back of his neck, so he couldn't pull away from it, Murphy taunted, "Go ahead. Pull the trigger! You're so anxious to kill somebody. Might as well make it somebody the world would be better off without. Pull the trigger."

He kept straining to free himself from Murphy's grasp until Murphy suddenly let go of everything except the six-gun and Kirby landed on his back without his gun. Murphy stuck the gun in his belt and waited for Kirby's next move, hoping he had had enough and would now go peacefully. But he knew better, so he watched him carefully as he took an extra-long time getting to his feet. Once he was up, he suddenly charged like a bull. Murphy braced himself as if ready to meet the charge. At the last instant, however, Murphy stepped aside, then planted a haymaker on the side of the charging man's face as he lunged by. It served to stun him to the point where he couldn't stop before crashing headfirst into the wall. Murphy grabbed one of his boots and dragged him out of the building. While Kirby was still unconscious, Murphy tied his hands and feet. Then he lifted him up and laid him across his packhorse and led the sorrel down the street to the smokehouse.

"What the hell?" a groggy Kirby asked, just beginning to regain consciousness.

"You broke a few laws of this town and earned yourself a little lockup time to sober up," Murphy told him. "We usually leave you tied up overnight, but I'm gonna go easy on you and untie you. You'd do well to try to sleep some of that likker off that made you act like an ass." He unlocked the smokehouse and opened the door.

Kirby remained where Murphy stood him up in the doorway, looking into the dark interior, his hands and feet still tied together. "You can't put me in there. That looks like a smokehouse."

"It does kinda resemble one, don't it?" Murphy said.

"I ain't goin' in there," Kirby insisted. "That ain't no jail."

"You'll get used to it, and I'll let you out in the mornin'. Gimme your hands." Kirby held them out to him, and Murphy untied them. Then he spun him around and placed his foot on the seat of Kirby's trousers and sent him sprawling into the dark interior. "You can untie your feet. Sleep tight." He closed the door and put the lock in place but didn't close it. He planned to be back in the morning, but in case he wasn't, someone else could let Kirby out.

Too bad the jail ain't finished, he thought as he headed back to the dining room.

The three Floyd women were all waiting for him to return, but he made a quick stop in the kitchen first to make sure his saddlebags had not been disturbed. When he found that they had not, he went to the dining room.

Ginger was the first to speak. "I was so glad to see you, Cullen!" she gushed. "He said he was going to have his way with me!"

"Well, we can't have that, can we?" Murphy said.

"What did you do with him?" Irene asked.

"I put him in jail," Murphy said. "We'll see if he's learned to respect the nice ladies of our town in the mornin'."

"You put him in the smokehouse, didn't you?" Irene asked.

"I prefer to call it solitary confinement," Murphy said. "It ain't gonna hurt him. I plan to be back in town in the mornin' to let him out. But just in case Eliot Baxter finds out he's locked up and he's worried about it, like he was with Rafer Polk, the lock ain't closed. So he could let him out if I don't get back early enough." He paused to grin at her. "Of course, Ginger might wanna let him out," he japed.

"That's not funny, Cullen," Ginger responded. "Look at the bruises that animal put on my wrists."

"I wasn't gonna let him drag you out of here," Bonnie said. "I was gonna get the shotgun out of the pantry if he tried."

"There you go," Murphy commented. "You didn't need me a'tall. I coulda been eatin' my supper."

Irene placed her hand on Murphy's arm and said, "Thank you, Cullen. Sit down and I'll get your supper."

"Does this happen very often?" he asked, no longer joking.

"Every once in a while," Irene replied. "That's the reason I brought my late husband's shotgun from the house. I thought I was gonna have to use it this evening."

He was tempted to tell her about his plans for building a jailhouse and his hopes that it might help to persuade the town council to go ahead and hire a sheriff. But he thought it better to see the project completed before he told them what he had in mind. There was no need to get anyone's hopes up, in case he wasn't successful.

"What about his horse tied out back?" she asked. "What are we gonna do about that?"

"I'll take care of it," Murphy told her.

Chapter 8

He got up the next morning at sunup, made some coffee and cooked some bacon, mopped up the grease with some hardtack, and figured that would see him through till dinnertime. There had been no evidence of anyone having visited his cabin the day before, but it was of some concern for him, knowing he was going to be spending most of his time in town now. It didn't make a lot of sense to ride three miles every day to get to town, then three miles back at night when he could just as well stay at his new property. He couldn't help but wonder if his idea for building a jail was a ridiculous one. But he loaded his packhorse up with his tools and weapons and everything else he thought he might need and headed into town.

When he got to town, he went straight to his "jail" and unloaded his packhorse. It struck him then that his prisoner was mostly suffering for water. So he used the quart bottle of water beside the pump to prime it and filled the bottle again. He emptied the cartridges out of Kirby's gun and dropped them in his pocket. Then he stuck the gun back in his belt and walked back to the smokehouse. He found the padlock just as he had left it, so he opened it and removed it from the hasp. Then he swung the door open, and Kirby fell halfway outside, evidently having been sitting there with his back against the door. He struggled up to a sitting position again, looking dazed and confused.

"Here," Murphy said and held the bottle of water out to him. He took it without a word and immediately gulped half of it down, most of which came right back up. "Take it slow," Murphy said. "A swallow or two at a time." He emptied the bottle then and handed it back to Murphy.

"What are you gonna do with me now?" a much more subdued Kirby asked.

"I'm gonna give you your gun and let you go, if you're through acting like a horse's hind end," Murphy told him.

Kirby slowly rose to his feet, and Murphy handed him his gun. Murphy watched him carefully. When he returned the gun to his holster, Murphy reached into his pocket and took the cartridges out. "These belong to you, six cartridges. Take my advice and just load five of 'em back in, so you can rest the hammer on an empty chamber. Might keep you from shootin' yourself in the leg sometime." Kirby took the cartridges and put them in his pocket.

"Can I go now?" Kirby asked.

"Yeah, you can go. Your horse is at the stables at the end of Front Street. Mr. Mathers has already been paid for takin' care of him."

Murphy watched him as he walked away, unhurriedly, as if expecting to suddenly be ordered to stop. When he reached the street with no sound of a rifle being cocked, he broke into a trot toward the stable. *Oversized, tough-talking gunslinger with the brain of a ten-year-old*, Murphy thought. He locked the smokehouse again, climbed on Nosy, and rode out to the sawmill.

He found both brothers waiting for him, and they waved him over to the little office shack, where they had talked before. Inside, the brothers sat down at a large desk and invited him to sit down in the empty chair on the other side of the desk.

"You've got a helluva project planned to convert that café into a jail," Frank commented in greeting him. "Whatever put the idea in your mind?"

"Like I told your brother, the town sure as hell needs one," Murphy answered. "You got a price figured up?"

"We do," Frank replied, "but I ain't sure you're gonna like it." Before he showed him the figure, he tried to prepare him for it. "You're beefing up every wall in that place, and we don't even know how much it's gonna cost for all the iron bars and slats the blacksmith's got to make."

"I understand," Murphy said. "What did you come up with?"

Frank appeared hesitant to say the figure out loud. He pushed the pad with the number on it across the desk; then both he and Robert leaned back to give him room to explode. Murphy looked at the number, and it was big, but not as big as he had anticipated. He slid the pad back toward Frank and said, "All right. Will a thousand dollars be enough to get you started?"

Both brothers exhaled the breath they had been holding. "Yes, sir, Mr. Murphy," Frank replied grandly. "We'll start right away."

"Good," Murphy said. "I want to talk to Bert Walker to let him know we need to keep this project a secret, just like I did with you. Then when you're ready, you can get together with him to show him what he'll have to make up for you." He got up from the desk they had gathered around. "I'll be right back with the first thousand," he said and went out to his horse.

"You can give me that five dollars you bet me now," Robert said to his brother. "I told you he knew what he was doin'."

"They must pay sergeants damn good in the army these days," Frank japed. "I swear, I'd think he musta robbed the bank, if we had one." They both had a quick chuckle before he walked back in. Then they watched as he counted out one thousand dollars.

"All right, we've got this thing started now," Murphy said. "I'm goin' to talk to Bert right now to make sure he can do the work we need."

They both thanked him for the opportunity and sealed the deal with a handshake.

The blacksmith was as skeptical as the Jessop brothers had been when Murphy told him what he had in mind for the old Newtown Café building. Like Frank and Robert, he had to be convinced that Murphy wasn't out of his mind. When he learned that the Jessop brothers were already on board with the project and would be working with him, he became enthusiastic about what Murphy was trying to do for the town.

It was dinnertime by the time he left the blacksmith's forge, so he left his horses with Paul Mathers and walked down to Bradshaw's Saloon and Café. He stopped for only a minute to say howdy to Pete at the bar before going on into the café. Ginger and Bonnie both rushed to meet him when he walked in the door.

"What's goin' on?" he asked.

"You let Kirby Case out of the smokehouse!" Ginger declared.

"Case?" he asked. "Was that his last name?" He shrugged. "I said I would. Why?"

"He came in here this morning," Ginger said.

At once alarmed, Murphy exclaimed, "Damn! I never counted on that. What did he do? Are you all right?"

"Yes," she said. "He came in and wanted to see Mama. When she came out of the kitchen, he told her he just wanted to stop by to say he was sorry for the way he treated us last night. He said his mother taught him better than that and he was drunk, but that was no excuse."

"Well, I'll be . . . ," Murphy started. He found it hard to believe, based on Kirby's attitude the night before.

"He told Mama it was pitch black in that place you put him in, and he couldn't see if anyone else was in there or not. But after he was in there for a while, he decided he was alone, and he tried to go to sleep. When he finally did, he said his mama and his sister came to him in a dream and asked him if he would treat them the same way, then told him to go apologize. Mama made him sit down in the kitchen and eat some breakfast before he went back to see if he still had a job at the Lucky Six Ranch."

Murphy was dumbfounded, scarcely able to believe what she had said. Maybe he should make sure to keep that smokehouse just like it was. Maybe it had some special effect on lawbreakers. Then he reminded himself that it hadn't done much to help Rafer Polk's attitude.

Irene walked out of the kitchen when she realized he had come in. "Ginger tell you about Kirby Case?" she asked.

"Yes, but I'm havin' a hard time believin' it," Murphy answered.

"He was pretty convincing," Irene said. "Wasn't he, Ginger?"

Ginger said he was, and Bonnie agreed.

Murphy was still unwilling to believe the smokehouse was a miracle cell. "I don't know," he commented, "but I was already thinking about putting a big cross on the roof of it." He pointed his finger at Bonnie and said, "Then you could call me Reverend Murphy instead of Uncle Cullen."

"That would most likely cause lightning to strike your little smokehouse," Ginger told him. "When are you gonna tell us what you're really gonna do with that old café, anyway?"

"As soon as I decide for sure," Murphy answered. "I'm thinkin' about two or three different things this town needs. One of 'em for sure is a fortune teller. When I was in the army, I was stationed down in Brownsville, on the Rio Grande. There was a fortune teller right across the river in Mexico, and she made a lot of money."

"You're just talking nonsense," Ginger said. "You know nobody in Newtown would go to see a fortune teller."

"They would if the fortune teller was always right with her predictions, like that woman in Mexico was," Murphy claimed.

"Nonsense," Ginger insisted. "How do you know she was always right?"

"I talked to a lotta soldiers who told me they gave her money, and she predicted they were gonna be really happy, and they always were."

"You dog!" Ginger blurted and punched him on the shoulder. "Maybe you ought to build a jailhouse to put disrespectful people like you in."

He responded with a big chuckle, hoping she had not noticed his surprised reaction to her suggestion. He looked at Irene, who was grinning at him and shaking her head, so he said, "I apologize for disrespectin' your daughters. Can I still buy something to eat?"

"I suppose so, if you'll promise to behave yourself in my business establishment from now on," Irene said. "Set yourself down and Bonnie will get your coffee."

He sat down at a table close to the kitchen door to eat his dinner, and the two girls offered suggestions for a new business to occupy the old café building as they went back and forth to the kitchen. He had to admit that some of them made a lot more sense than a privately owned jailhouse. But he knew that if he got stuck running it until the town hired a sheriff, he was pretty sure he could handle the job temporarily. He was absolutely certain that he didn't want the job as his permanent vocation, however.

While he was still eating, Bert Walker came into the dining room and walked back to join him.

"If I'd known you were gonna eat here, I'd have waited till you were ready to go," Murphy said.

"I fixed my dinner at the shop, like I usually do," Bert said.

"Right after you left, Robert Jessop came by and said he was gonna meet you over at the old café this afternoon and go over some things he wanted to be sure of. He said it'd be a good idea for me to be there, too."

He was interrupted then by Ginger, who asked if he was there for dinner.

"No, Ginger, I've already et, but I'd enjoy a cup of coffee, if you don't mind." She left to get it, so he returned his focus to Murphy. "Anyway, I thought I'd check with you to make sure it's all right with you."

"Of course it's all right," Murphy said. "Matter of fact, I shoulda told you to meet with us. It'd be a good idea if we were all thinkin' the same way about what we're gonna end up with. You and Robert are gonna be workin' together on this job. As soon as you see what we'll need to have you make, you can give me the cost, and hopefully, I can afford it." Ginger returned with Bert's coffee at that point, so Murphy asked, "You sure you don't want something to eat with that? A piece of pie or something?"

Ginger paused to hear his answer. "Apple," she said when he hesitated.

"You talked me right into it," Bert said.

Ginger looked at Murphy then and waited.

"All right," he said. "I'll try a slice of pie, too."

"You won't be sorry," she said. "And this is the last of the dried apples, too. I don't know when Mr. Baxter will get some more."

When the apple pie and coffee were finished, Murphy settled the bill with Ginger, and he and Bert went to the old café, where they found Robert Jessop already marking the walls he planned to work on first.

"I drew up a little plan of what it'll look like after we make the changes you said you wanted," Robert said. "Take a look at it and see what you think."

They all three hovered over the floor plan, and Robert pointed out the office and the cell room and the fact that the rooms would be a little smaller than the present rooms because of the added four-inch thickness in the walls. "They gonna have to fire a cannon to get through those walls. You kept the hallway back to the kitchen and the pump room, but it ain't gonna be as wide as it is now, because of the thickness of the walls. You said you didn't need but one room for your livin' quarters, so we're using the other one for cells. You're gonna have four cells." Then he showed Bert where they needed iron-barred windows and doors inserted into the heavy cell walls.

"You ain't gonna have iron bars floor to ceilin' in your cell room?" Bert asked.

"No," Murphy answered. "It would take too long and cost too much. I'd have to have them shipped from an ironworks up north. That's why we're goin' with the thick wood walls and the barred windows."

They decided on the size of the windows and the design that would permit someone to see through them and talk through them but would provide no opening large enough to pass a revolver through. Bert said he would do his figuring on his cost and give Murphy his price in the morning. "It's a good thing I just got a load of charcoal," Bert said, " 'cause it looks like I'm gonna need some hot fire in my forge." There were also hinges, locks, and other articles that would have to come from Waco to be figured in.

When they agreed that everything had been covered, Bert and Murphy decided to meet for breakfast in the morning to go over Bert's cost estimate. Robert said he would start the work in the morning. "I'll let myself in with the key you gave me," he said.

"No need," Murphy told him. "I'm gonna sleep here tonight."

So when they parted, Murphy walked up to Mathers's stable

to let Paul know he would leave the horses overnight. Then he got his bedroll off his saddle and took it back to his building.

By the next morning news of Cullen Murphy's mystery construction project had spread all around Newtown. There was obviously a major change in the works for the inside of the former café, but questioning Robert Jessop, who was doing most of the work, left the curious citizens no closer to an answer. Even Eliot Baxter, the mayor, was told that Murphy was just intent upon making a strong building suitable for housing any number of businesses and was hoping to attract some merchant's interest. Baxter was soon convinced that Murphy's intent was to rent the building. Then as soon as he did, he would fix up another vacant building to rent to another merchant. Considering the problem the town was currently laboring under, the lack of law enforcement, Baxter felt obligated to advise Murphy he was wasting his money. Murphy thanked him for his advice but said he was already committed to the project, so he would see it through.

As the days turned into weeks, with the building still under remodeling construction, it became the subject of a lot of guessing games. This was especially so when near the completion of the work, Murphy draped a canvas over the signboard Robert had nailed over the front entrance. Finally, the day arrived when the construction was completed. Murphy met with Frank, Robert, and Bert and settled up with them financially. Since he had money left over, he was tempted to name the building the Clyde Fry Memorial Building in honor of the outlaws who had stolen the money to build it. But the sign was already painted with the name he had chosen. He thanked the three of them for keeping the purpose for the building to themselves, and they all hoped it would encourage the town council to hire a marshal.

When Murphy started to pull the canvas off the sign, Bert stopped him. "Don't take it off now," he urged. "Wait and take it off tonight, after the town's closed up, and let's see how long it takes for somebody to notice it in the morning."

The Jessop brothers thought it was a good idea, as well, so Murphy said he'd wait and uncover the sign later that night. They parted, feeling as if they were playing a joke on the whole town.

Since it was suppertime at Irene Floyd's dining room, Murphy went up to Bradshaw's Saloon and took the path along the side to the café's back entrance. "The Reverend Murphy is here," Bonnie called out when Murphy walked in. Murphy made the sign of the cross in response to her announcement.

"You two better watch out," Ginger warned. "Keep it up and you're liable to get struck by lightning." She followed him to a table. "When are you gonna be done with your building?"

"Funny you asked," he replied. "We wrapped it up today. Drove the last nail and it's ready for occupancy."

"What kinda business are you gonna put in it? Are you ready to let us in on the big secret?" Ginger asked.

"I ain't sure," Murphy responded. "I'm gonna decide tomorrow for sure."

"Well, what businesses are you thinking about?" Bonnie urged. "Maybe we can help you decide."

"That's just crazy," Ginger remarked. "Just because you decide what kind of business you want doesn't mean that business will come to town and buy your building."

"Well, like I said, I'll decide tomorrow, and we'll see what happens," Murphy said. "I'm just hopin' I'll get a cup of coffee before then."

"I'll get it, Reverend," Bonnie volunteered and went to fetch the pot. Irene followed her back into the dining room.

"Bonnie said you've finished your store," Irene said and placed a plate of food down for him. "What's the big secret?"

"It's no secret," Murphy insisted. "I just wanted to be sure before I told anybody. I'll decide for sure tonight and open it up in the mornin', if anybody wants to see how we fixed the inside."

"You sure are making a big thing out of it for no reason at all," Irene declared.

"I reckon," he said and turned his attention to the sliced ham and potatoes. While he was eating, he thought about his grand opening. He knew a lot of people would accept his invitation to come inside and see everything that had been done. Too bad he didn't have blankets for the bunks, chamber pots, and water buckets for the four cells yet. He decided he could catch Eliot Baxter before he closed his store and pick up one of each item, so he would have at least one cell furnished.

With that thought in mind, he didn't linger over his supper. He made it to the store just at closing time. Eliot was happy to accommodate him and sold him the items he requested, plus one small pillow, which Murphy thought to add to his order. He took his purchases back to the jail and placed them in the first cell. Satisfied that it looked like a real jailhouse, he decided to go back to Bradshaw's and celebrate its completion with a drink of whiskey.

When Pete asked him to name his poison, he said, "Pour me a drink of that good rye whiskey. I'm celebratin' the completion of my building."

"Well, congratulations," Pete said and reached behind him to pull a bottle of rye whiskey off the shelf.

When he turned back around, the bottle of whiskey exploded. Murphy didn't know what had actually happened until he saw the foolish grin on the face of the young cowhand sitting at a table alone, holding a six-gun up while he cocked it again. Murphy didn't wait to see what the drunk's next target was. He reached the table before the cowhand could bring his six-gun down to aim at another target, grabbed the edge of the table, and turned it over on the startled shooter, but not before he buried a .44 round into the tabletop. The men at the tables on either side of the shooter's cleared out of the way in a panic.

Murphy shoved the table aside in time to grab the young man's wrist before he could aim the gun. He jerked him up to meet a right-hand flush on his nose, which turned his lights out long enough for Pete to throw Murphy a short rope. "That's what's left of that rope you used on Rafer Polk," Pete exclaimed.

Murphy took the six-gun out of the drunk's hand and stuck it in his belt. Then he turned him over and tied his hands together behind his back. He looked at the spectators standing around and asked if anyone knew who the man was. No one claimed to know anything about him other than he had consumed a lot of whiskey, he had said his name was Billy Daniels, and he had said he could outshoot anybody in the saloon.

"He's ridin' a paint horse," one man volunteered. "I seen him when he rode up."

"He needs to sleep that drunk off. Put him in that cooler you've got in your backyard," Pete said, referring to the smokehouse.

"Good idea," Murphy said. He picked him up to lay across his shoulder, then walked out the front door to drop him across the saddle on the paint horse at the rail. By the time he led the horse down to his building, he had decided to make him the first prisoner to be put in the town jail. "I can't think of a greater honor than to be known as the first prisoner in the Newtown jail," he announced to himself.

He pulled Billy off the horse and hefted him up on his shoulder again. Although Billy was beginning to make slurring attempts to talk, he was still not making sense. Murphy unlocked the office door and carried Billy to the first cell in the cell room and dumped him on one of the bunks. He started snoring immediately. Murphy put the blanket where Billy could see it and made the "thunder mug" handy. He put water in the bucket and untied Billy's hands. He had ordered a badge and some handcuffs, which he hoped would arrive on the stagecoach within a couple of days. The handcuffs would make arrests a little bit easier.

His original plan had been to sleep in that first cell that night himself, but he decided to spread his bedroll on the floor of the sheriff's quarters to avoid another confrontation with Billy in the middle of the night. He thought he should have emptied the prisoner's pockets to see if he had enough money to pay for the bottle of rye whiskey he had destroyed, but he hadn't thought about it at the time.

He thought about the paint horse then. It was too late to take the horse to the stable, so he took the saddle off and threw it on the back porch. He tied the horse's reins to the corner of the porch where there was a little patch of grass. Then he filled an old washtub that was lying in the yard with water from the pump. "That's about the best I can do for you," he told the horse, scratched the gelding's ears and face for a few minutes, then picked up Billy's saddlebags and went inside for the night.

A little while later, he remembered to come back outside and remove the canvas from the sign on the front of the building.

Chapter 9

"I don't believe it!" Ginger Floyd fairly screamed.

"What?" Irene responded, normally having little interest in the sights between her house and her place of business behind Bradshaw's Saloon. She was accustomed to the bland awakening of Newtown so early in the morning.

"Son of a . . . ," Bonnie blurted before she caught herself.

"You watch your mouth, young lady!" Irene scolded. "Where do you learn to talk like that?"

"Mama, look!" Ginger exclaimed. "Look at Cullen's building!" And she pointed.

"Well, kiss my . . . ," Irene started to say. "I don't believe it!" She stopped in her tracks to peer at the sign over the door. SAN SABA COUNTY JAIL. She turned to look at Ginger to see if she was reading it correctly.

"He did it," Ginger told her. "He built a jailhouse!"

"I knew from the beginning that he was a little bit crazy," her mother remarked. "But now I think he's downright insane. What are Eliot Baxter and Tyson Bradshaw gonna do when they see this? I know Baxter will explode."

"I'm sure he will," Ginger replied, finding the development exciting. "Let's hurry up and get to the café. I don't wanna miss any of the fireworks. I sure hope Cullen is coming in for breakfast this morning."

At that particular moment, Murphy was checking on the welfare of the first official prisoner of the San Saba County Jail. He unlocked the door to the cell room and went to the first cell, the only one that was locked. Looking through the small window in the top of the door, he saw Billy Daniels sitting on his bunk, evidently contemplating how he came to be in jail when he woke up that morning.

When he saw Murphy peering at him through the small heavy-wire window in the cell door, he asked, "Where the hell am I?"

"You're in jail," Murphy informed him.

"Where in jail?" Billy asked, confused.

"Newtown," Murphy answered.

"There ain't no jail in Newtown," Billy informed him.

"And yet you're sittin' in one," Murphy declared. "Ain't that rich? I reckon things happen a little too fast for slow brains in this modern world. You want a cup of coffee and maybe a rag to try to clean some of that dried blood off your face?"

Billy reached up to feel his face and winced when he put his hand on his nose. "Yeah," he said then. "Bring me a wet rag and a cup of coffee."

"Bring that bucket over here and set it in front of the door," Murphy told him. "Then go back and sit down on your bunk again and I'll get you some fresh water and a cup of coffee."

Billy got up from the bunk, picked up the water bucket and brought it over to the door, and waited for Murphy to unlock the door.

"Go back and sit down on the bunk," Murphy said.

"Oh, I forgot that part," Billy said and turned around to go back to the bunk. "And bring some sugar for that coffee."

Murphy waited until he sat down again before he unlocked the cell door and pulled the bucket out of the cell. "We don't serve coffee for women and children here. Nothin' but black jailhouse coffee. You still want it?"

"Yeah, I want it," Billy answered while he studied the man standing in the doorway. "I remember you," he stated then. "You're the big SOB that punched me in the nose. You're lucky you caught me when I was drunk."

"Yeah, I reckon I was lucky," Murphy said as he locked the cell door. "If I was a little bit luckier, you might not have showed up in Newtown."

"So, hell, why don't you just let me go? I'm ready to leave town now. I was drunk when you arrested me, but I ain't drunk no more. Ain't no harm done."

"Well, now," Murphy said, "I can see why you'd think that, but there's more to it than that. You broke a few laws last night—dischargin' a firearm in the city limits, destruction of private property, disorderly conduct, and endangerment of human lives. Any one of them calls for jail time. Add 'em all up and you earned yourself a nice little stay in jail. You might as well make yourself comfortable."

He went back to the pump and drew some fresh water in the bucket and poured a cup of coffee. He had sugar, but he didn't want to bother with it, so he took the cup and the bucket back to the cell, along with an old towel he had brought from his cabin on the river. After he set the bucket and the cup of coffee inside the cell door and locked it, Billy got up from the bunk and came to get them.

"You can dip one end of that towel in the bucket and use it to wash your face and dry it with the other end," Murphy instructed.

"I expect I coulda figured that out," Billy remarked.

"Maybe." Murphy shrugged. "But you didn't know better than to start firing a gun in a crowded saloon last night, so I thought I'd better not take a chance. By the way, when I checked your pockets last night, I found a little cash money in one of 'em. So next time you count it, you'll find it two dollars short. That two dollars is to pay for a new bottle of rye whiskey you shot out of the bartender's hand. Well, that about does it for right now. I'm goin' to go get some breakfast, and I'll bring your breakfast back with me." He went out of the cell room and locked the door after him.

Due to the heavy wooden walls, Billy couldn't hear a sound from the office, so he didn't know if there was anyone else in there or not. This was not Billy Daniels's first time in jail, but there was something totally different about this jail. This one was built more like a dungeon, with its thick walls and tiny windows. And there was no one else in the jail, just this one man who wore no badge and made no claim to be a lawman. He suddenly had a feeling that he might be in this jail forever. When he let his mind run with it, he realized that he had been unconscious when he'd been taken out of that saloon. He had no memory of how he had got to this medieval cell room. He might not even be in Newtown.

He went to the one window in the wall and stood up on his tiptoes to look out. His view was of a short section of a street, but he could not see enough to tell if it was Front Street in Newtown or not. *I've got to get out of here!*

"Morning, Cullen," Ginger Floyd greeted him. She, her mother, and her sister were all standing in the middle of the dining room, facing the door, all with knowing smiles on their faces.

"Mornin'," he returned casually, knowing without doubt that they had seen the sign over the jail. "Am I too early for breakfast?"

Unable to maintain the pretense of innocence, Irene was the first to cave in. "The San Saba County Jail," she blurted. "You've got to be out of your mind."

"I don't know why you'd say that," he said. "We sure as the devil need one. I just opened for business yesterday, and already I've got a customer. And that reminds me, I'm gonna need to take a plate of food with me when I go back to the jail."

"You've already got a prisoner in a cell?" Bert Walker asked when he heard the comment as he walked in the door.

"Mornin', Bert. That's right. Locked up the first customer last night. You mighta heard a couple of shots in Bradshaw's. It was after ten o'clock," Murphy said. "If he's still there when I go back, we'll know you and the Jessops did a good job."

With a wide grin on his face, Bert declared, "Eliot Baxter will have a hissy fit when he sees that sign. You better be ready for his visit."

"I know that's true," Murphy said. "I'm goin' back as soon as I eat some breakfast and wait to see how long it'll take before he notices it."

"Or somebody tells him," Irene said. "I better get your breakfast for you. You're gonna need a good one."

"I'll have some breakfast, too, Irene," Bert said. "Cullen might need some protection. I'll go back to the jail with you," he told Murphy.

" 'Preciate it, Bert," Murphy said.

Bert sat down at the table with him, and the girls ran to fetch the coffee. "Have you really got somebody in a cell right now?"

"That's right," Murphy said. "A young fellow named Billy Daniels." He went on to tell Bert the situation he had walked into the night before that led to Billy's arrest. "Just a young gun too likkered up to have good sense, and he coulda killed Pete Brice. It was a helluva shot, though, unless he was aimin' at Pete, instead of the bottle of whiskey. I'm plannin' to take him back some breakfast, and then I'm gonna let him go. From what Pete told me, the young fellow wasn't out to fight anybody. He just wanted to have a good time, and the likker got the best of him."

First one person, then another, noticed the new sign over the old café building, and by the time Murphy and Bert finished breakfast, the word had passed through most of the town. Bert went back to the jail with Murphy, and they walked through a group of townspeople who had come to see if the rumor was true. One of the spectators was Elmo Dillon, who was trying to hide the fact that he was extremely disappointed to have been left out of the project.

"You shoulda named it Murphy's Law," Elmo said. "You might be in for some trouble calling it the county jail."

"Do you know if there's another jail in this county?" Bert asked him, and Elmo said there wasn't. "Then this jail is the county jail until the state politicians decide to build one somewhere else."

"I appreciate what you're sayin', Elmo," Murphy told him. "I know you and maybe most everybody else in town think we just built a sign to nail up over an old building. So what I'd like to do is to invite you and Eliot Baxter and Tyson Bradshaw and anybody else to come and inspect the project. Then you'll at least see it's built to be a jail. It's all finished now and ready for your inspection. Now, I'm lettin' my prisoner's breakfast get cold, standin' out here in the street. So I'd best take it inside now."

They went inside the office, and Elmo followed them. "You need a desk and some more furniture in here," he said as he looked around the barren room.

"Yeah, I reckon," Murphy said. "I've got some stuff comin' in sometime in the next couple of weeks. We'll just have to make do till it gets here."

"I've got an old desk in the back room of my shop," Elmo offered. "You're welcome to use it till you get a better one."

"Thanks, Elmo. I 'preciate it. Robert Jessop's makin' me a table and a couple of benches." He took a ring of keys off a hook in the wall and unlocked the door to the cell room. When he opened the door, he found Billy Daniels standing at the door to his cell, having heard them come into the building.

"Here's some breakfast for you, Billy. Go back and sit down on your bunk and I'll put it inside the door." Billy didn't respond immediately, seeming to be puzzled by the two men who had come to gawk at him. "Or if you don't want it, I'll throw it in the slop bucket in the kitchen," Murphy said.

"No, no, I'm goin'!" Billy exclaimed and retreated to his bunk.

Murphy unlocked the cell and set the plate inside. "Bring your cup and the water bucket with you," he said and drew his Colt in precaution until Billy did as he was told. Then he retrieved the cup and the water bucket and locked the cell again.

"I swear," Elmo declared, "this place really is a jail. It looks like a blamed fort."

"I'm glad you appreciate that," Murphy said. "Maybe you can help Eliot Baxter and the rest of your town council decide it's time to do something about your lawless problem before it's too late."

Elmo followed him back to the kitchen, where he put a few sticks of firewood on the dying fire in the small iron stove and poured some fresh water into the coffeepot. Then he put the water bucket aside. "These grounds oughta be good for another cup," he said. "I don't want him to think the coffee's so good he won't wanna leave."

They went back into the cell room, and while Murphy gave Billy the coffee and water bucket, Bert pointed out some features of the jail to Elmo. He stressed the thickness of the cell walls, as well as the small windows and the iron grillwork, which let in air and light but little else. By the time they returned to the office, Elmo was convinced that it was a solidly built jail, but he had to ask Murphy, "Why the hell did you build a jail?"

"Because the town didn't have one and the town needs one," he answered. "It's been one of the reasons you folks ain't hired a lawman."

"This had to cost you one helluva lot of money to build this place," Elmo declared. "Is it because you want the job of town marshal?"

"Hell, no," Murphy insisted. "I built it hoping you folks would do something about your problem and I'd sell the jail to the town."

Elmo sighed and exhaled. "You spent a fortune on this place, and you know the town council ain't got the money to spend on a jail. How much would you have to ask for it?"

"Well, I figured I'd make a special price for the city of Newtown," Murphy answered.

"How much?" Elmo insisted.

"One dollar," Murphy answered.

"How much?" Elmo repeated, thinking he had not heard him correctly.

"One dollar," Murphy repeated. "But there's a stipulation. The town has to commit to hiring a town marshal or sheriff and pay the jailhouse expenses, like breakfast for Billy Daniels and such."

"Damn!" Elmo swore. "You're serious. I had no idea you were that wealthy."

"I ain't anymore," Murphy remarked, "now that I've built this jailhouse."

"I've got to go talk to Eliot and Tyson and get them in here to look at this building. They need to know what an opportunity we've got to keep this town civilized and growing. You gonna be here at the jail for a while?"

Murphy said that he would be, as far as he knew. He had to release his prisoner.

Elmo hurried out the door. "I'll be back!"

Murphy gave Billy a little more time to eat his breakfast, using the time to get Billy's horse ready to ride. He found the paint gelding grazing at the short grass beside the corner of the back porch, looking none the worse for wear after his night behind the jail. Murphy got the saddle off the porch and put it on the horse, then led it around to the front of the jail and tied it to the short stoop. He opened the door to the cell room, went inside and unlocked Billy's cell.

"Come on out, Billy," he said and turned around and went into the office.

Billy quickly grabbed his hat and followed behind him, almost colliding with him when he suddenly stopped and turned to face him. He was holding Billy's gun belt and six-gun, which he held out to him. Billy hesitated to take them at first, not sure he was not being baited for some kind of trick. So he slowly reached out to take the belt, surprised when Murphy released it. He strapped the belt on, then shifted it until it rested comfortably just the way he liked it. Then he drew the weapon and held it up before him.

"You're mighty damn trustin', Sheriff."

"Not really," Murphy said. "I took the cartridges out of it."

"I knew it felt light," Billy claimed.

"Right," Murphy replied. "Your horse is tied out front. I'm lettin' you go this time because I don't think you meant any harm to the bartender. But if you're plannin' to come back to Newtown and get that drunk again, I'll put you in that smokehouse out back and throw away the key."

"Fair enough, Sheriff. I'll keep that in mind, and I'd appreciate it if you told that bartender that I was aimin' at the bottle and not him."

Murphy walked out to the front stoop with him and stood there while he climbed up on the paint. He backed the horse away from the stoop, then paused to ask, "I heard them fellows callin' you Cullen. Is that your first or last name?"

"My name's Murphy," he said. "Cullen Murphy."

"Yessir, I'll remember that name," Billy said and wheeled the paint toward the street.

* * *

He spent the rest of the morning working on some short tables he had been making out of some pieces of scrap boards. He planned to put them in the cells for prisoners to place their plates on when they were eating. He wasn't the carpenter Robert Jessop was, so he had to work on the tables a little longer to get the wobble out of them. He was placing one of the little tables in the fourth cell when he heard someone come into the office, so he went back to see who it was.

"Murphy," Eliot Baxter acknowledged when Murphy came into the office. "Like everyone else in Newtown, I was curious to see what you had in mind when you started rebuilding this old café. But I've got to admit, I never would have guessed you were building a jail." He glanced at Bradshaw, who was standing beside him. "Did you, Tyson?"

"No," Bradshaw agreed, "that would have been my last guess. Any municipal building, like a library or a jailhouse, would have been voted on by the town council, with a plan for how the money would be raised to pay for it. A jail is hardly a private business—"

Elmo interrupted then. "Before you form any set opinions on the unusual approach to solving our lawlessness problems, take a look at the rest of the building."

"Yes, I'd like to see the actual cells," Bradshaw said. Then looking at Murphy directly, he asked, "Is it true what Elmo said, that you'd sell it to the town for one dollar?"

"That's a fact," Murphy answered, "but like I told Elmo, that's with the guarantee that it will be used for a jail and not resold to somebody lookin' for a place to start a business."

"I see," Bradshaw said. "Come on, Eliot. Let's take a look at the rest of it."

Elmo led the way into the cell room, and Murphy decided to remain in the office and let them inspect it. He figured they'd be more thorough in their inspection without his presence.

They took quite a long time in the cells before taking a look at the back of the building, with the kitchen and living quarters for a lawman. When they came back to the office to talk to Murphy, Baxter was quick to report, "There's no doubt about it. It's as solid as any jail I've ever seen."

"I'd have to agree with you, Eliot," Bradshaw said. "Of course, I may not have seen the inside of as many jails as you have." He paused to wait for the chuckles, then said, "But that's a helluva deal for the merchants and the people of Newtown. We need to call for a council meeting and draw up some agreement on how much to tax each business. We knew the day was gonna have to come, if the town is gonna survive."

"I've already been working on some numbers that the members might have to come up with to sponsor a town marshal," Baxter said. "But it was always the amount of taxes we'd have to come up with to cover a jail building and the land to build it on that made it too expensive for us."

"Let's call for a meeting tonight and work out the taxes it would take," Bradshaw suggested. "The whole deal, not just a salary, but the cost of prisoners' meals and the upkeep of the jail." He turned his attention to Murphy again. "If we decide to take your offer and buy this jail from you, can we count on you to stay here in the jail until we find a permanent man for the job of marshal?"

"Are you talking about being an acting marshal or just takin' care of the buildin'?" Murphy asked. "'Cause I ain't got any experience as a lawman."

"You musta been born with some in you," Bradshaw said, "judgin' by the way you took care of Clyde Fry and his gang. Not to mention the fellow who damn near killed my bartender last night. Elmo said you locked him up here in your jail to let him sleep off his drunk, and you even brought him his breakfast this morning." He grinned at Baxter, then back at Murphy. "If that ain't' exactly like what a marshal does, I don't know what is."

"Wait a minute," Murphy responded as he looked at the same smiling countenance beaming at him from all three faces. "I just can't abide folks that take advantage of other folks and do what they please. That's the only reason I did what I did."

Bradshaw's grin expanded. "That sounds like the definition of a perfect lawman to me. What do you think, Eliot?"

"I think I'd have to agree with you," Baxter answered. "What do you think, Elmo?"

"There ain't no doubt about it," Elmo answered, "and there ain't no question in my mind that there ain't no more honest a man than Cullen Murphy. All this rebuilding of this old café took a helluva lot of money, and I'm sure I know where he got the money to pay for it. He took down all four of that Fry gang and got their horses and everything else they had. They were spending money like it grew on trees. I think he got all that money they stole somewhere. But being an honest man, he used it for a good purpose, to buy a jail for this town when we couldn't afford one."

Murphy found himself in a quandary. He hadn't counted on Elmo or anybody else thinking about where he had got the money to buy the café from Irene, plus pay for all the work he had done on the building. For a man who had just spent four years in the army, then received his separation pay in worthless Confederate money, he should have known he would have to come by his real money dishonestly.

"I reckon I ain't got much to say for myself," he finally confessed. "When the last two of those four outlaws came after me that night, I was just worrying about protectin' myself. I didn't know they had all that money. They must have held up a bank or a Wells Fargo shipment or something. I didn't know where they stole it from, so I didn't know who to return it to. And I didn't wanna just turn it over to the government and let them waste it on who knows what. So I decided to put it to some use that would help a lot of folks who needed the help. I used every bit of it on this jailhouse. Thanks to those four outlaws, I paid for everything with stolen money and didn't get into the money I had before I went to join the fight."

Baxter and Bradshaw were both amazed by his apparent confession.

"Well, Cullen Murphy," Baxter said, "let me say the city of Newtown thanks you for your unselfish gift of the money you came by honestly. Now we're gonna get these merchants together and finish what you started."

"Amen," Bradshaw added.

Chapter 10

When the three members of the town council finally left the new jailhouse, it was close to dinnertime, so he locked the front door and made his way up the street toward Bradshaw's Saloon. He walked into the barroom and went to the bar. When Pete saw him coming, he reached behind him for the rye whiskey, poured a drink, and set it down.

"Howdy, Cullen. Have a drink."

"I reckon one wouldn't hurt before dinner," Murphy said. "What's the occasion?"

"I ain't really sure," Pete replied. "When the boss came in a few minutes ago, he said when you come in, to pour you a drink of the good rye, on the house."

"Is that a fact?" Murphy responded. "Well, thank you kindly."

"Whatcha got there?" Pete asked.

Murphy held up the plate he was holding. "My prisoner's breakfast dishes from the dinin' room. I got something for you, too." He pulled out a couple of dollars he had folded up and put in his pocket. "I just stopped in on my way to dinner to give you this two dollars." When Pete was obviously surprised, Murphy said, "That's from Billy Daniels for that bottle of rye whiskey."

"Well, I'll be . . . ," Pete started. "I didn't expect to get paid for that bottle. Is he still locked up?"

"No, I let him out this mornin' after breakfast. He said to tell you he hit what he was aimin' at and he hopes there ain't no hard feelings."

"I reckon not," Pete said. "He was just showin' off, but if it ever happens again, I'm gonna shoot back with my shotgun."

Murphy laughed and replied, "Don't do that, because then I might have to put both of you in jail."

"You gonna take over the job of sheriff?" He seemed quite excited about it, at least as excited as Murphy had ever seen Pete before. "Every time that subject comes up between the boss and Eliot Baxter, one of 'em says you'd be the best man for the job."

"Is that a fact?" Murphy responded. "Well, I ain't interested in takin' on that job, and I told 'em so."

Pete shrugged. "So you ain't gonna be the sheriff, huh?"

"Well, not the permanent one," Murphy said. "I just agreed to be the acting sheriff or marshal, whichever they decide, until they find a man for the job. I've got a good piece of ground and a cabin on it three miles up the river. That's where I wanna get something started."

"I don't see how you're going to do much of a job as marshal or sheriff, whatever they call you, if we need to ride three miles to get you," Pete commented.

"Well, I reckon not," Murphy replied. "I'll be stayin' here in town, in the back of the jail, while I'm the actin' sheriff. If you need the sheriff late at night and the office is closed, come around to the back door. I'll be sleepin' in the back room."

"I'll keep that in mind," Pete said.

"Thanks for the drink," Murphy said. "I'll go get something to eat now." He walked back to the door to the café, thinking he should go tell the bartenders in the other saloons to go around to the back of the jail if they needed him after hours.

"Afternoon, Marshal Murphy," Bonnie greeted him when

he walked into the dining room. "Are you going to need to take any food back to the jail with you after you eat?"

"No, I let my prisoner go after he had breakfast. I brought your plate and fork back." He handed them to her. "And I ain't the marshal. I'm the temporary help till they hire one."

She turned the plate over, looking at one side, then the other. "You washed it," she said, surprised.

"I gave it a lick or two," he said. "I didn't wanna get anything on your dainty hands."

"Well, ain't you the thoughtful one?" she teased. "When are you gonna show me the inside of that fancy jail?"

"When you do something bad enough to get arrested," he said. "Most likely won't be too long to wait."

"Well, I beg your pardon," she responded, pretending to be offended. "Go sit yourself down and I'll get you some coffee."

She headed for the kitchen, passing Ginger, who was coming out. Bonnie held up the plate and fork. "He brought the plate back," she said. "He washed it."

"I told you he would," Ginger said and continued on to greet him. "Howdy, Cullen. Today's meat loaf with mashed potatoes day. How's that suit the new sheriff?"

"It suits me just fine," he answered, "but I don't know how it suits the new sheriff. He ain't been hired yet. I've done my part for this town. I built you a jail. Now the town's part is to find a good man to take the job as sheriff and pay him a livin' wage."

"Looks like you'd consider taking the job," Irene said, having heard Murphy's response to Ginger as she entered the dining room. "I know Tyson Bradshaw really wants you to."

"Yes, ma'am," Murphy said. "But I don't know anything about being a sheriff. I just know that I can't abide some men's lack of respect for another man's life and possessions. And when I cross paths with men like that, it galls me something awful. So I try to avoid crossin' their paths, if I can. If I was a sheriff, it would be my job to go huntin' for them." He shrugged. "Besides, I've got a nice little cabin about three miles from here that's callin' for my attention."

"Well, I reckon you've got to do what your mind and your heart tell you to do. It ain't every man that's cut out to be a lawman. But you'da made a helluva lawman. Here, I filled a plate for you. Sit down and enjoy it."

Meat loaf was one of Irene's best dishes, and enjoy it he did, leaving a clean plate for the girls to wash. He was enjoying another cup of coffee when Otis Crutcher hurried in the door and asked Ginger if Murphy was there. She turned and pointed to Murphy near the kitchen door, and Otis hurried to his table.

"Are you Murphy?" Otis asked frantically.

Murphy said that he was.

"You've gotta come with me!" Otis blurted. "Jake Pike has got Maggie Tatum prisoner, and he's threatened to kill anybody who tries to help her!"

"Who told you to come get me?" Murphy asked.

"Albert Smith," Otis replied. "The bartender."

"Has he got the woman in Pratt's Saloon or somewhere else?"

"He's in the saloon!"

"All right," Murphy said and got up out of his chair, reached into his pocket, and left the money for his dinner on the table. Then he picked up his rifle and went out the back entrance of the dining room.

Otis hustled along behind him as he headed down the street at a trot. When he got to Pratt's Saloon, he stopped at the batwing doors to catch his breath and look inside before walking in. He saw the problem at once. A man, who he assumed was Jake Pike was sitting against the back wall, his chair tilted back and resting on the two back legs. One of his arms was stretched out next to an almost empty whiskey bottle on the table, his hand resting lightly on a Colt .44 lying on the table. In his other hand, he held one end of a short piece of rope, the other end of which was tied tightly around the neck of a sobbing woman. Even from as far away as he was, Murphy could see that the woman's face was swollen and bleeding from several blows. His initial impulse was to cock his rifle and put a .44 slug into Pike's chest. But he checked his natural tendencies when he remembered he was acting as a law officer. So he turned to Otis, who was standing behind him, and asked, "Who is the woman?"

"Maggie Tatum," Otis responded, wondering why Murphy didn't act at once. "She works here at the saloon. She's a good woman. She don't deserve that kind of treatment."

Murphy nodded his head. "How 'bout the man? Who's he?"

"Jake Pike, a sorry deadbeat drifter," Otis said. "He hung around here a couple of years ago, but he's been gone ever since then. He just showed up here again today."

Murphy nodded again, then pushed on through the batwing doors and walked straight across the room to confront the man at the table who was holding the woman close beside him on the floor.

"What the hell do you want?" Pike asked, and his fingers closed around the handle of the Colt on the table.

"Is that your dog, Mr. Pike?" Murphy asked.

"My dog?" Pike responded, confused. Then the question amused him, and he gave the rope a little jerk. "Yeah, that's right, the little cur *is* my dog. What's it to you?"

"Just thought you oughta know it's against the law in Newtown to bring a pet on a leash inside a public establishment. So I'm gonna have to ask you to take that rope off your dog and let her run outside."

Pike wasn't sure he was hearing what he thought he was hearing. "If you wanna walk outta here, you'd best get outta my face. What I do with this woman ain't none of your business, and I'm sick of lookin' at you."

"So now you're callin' her a woman," Murphy said. "I thought you said she was a dog."

"When she acts like a dog, then I treat her like one," Pike said. "Who the hell are you, anyway?"

"I'm the man who treats you like you treat women," Murphy replied.

"Why, you thickheaded coyote! I've had all of your crap I'm gonna take!" He suddenly grasped the Colt, but as he started to bring it up to aim, Murphy kicked one of the two legs supporting the chair, causing it to deposit Pike on the floor with his six-shooter aimed at the sky. The one shot he got off went straight into the ceiling. Before he could recover, the butt of Murphy's rifle made solid contact with the side of his face, cracking a cheekbone and leaving him unable to resist as Murphy took the gun out of his hand and stuck it in his belt.

"You all right, miss?" Murphy asked Maggie as he loosened the knot and took the rope off her neck.

"Yes, sir, I am now. Thank the Lord for you coming to save me. I just wanna get away from here right now." She stared at Jake Pike, who was lying there unconscious, afraid he might suddenly wake up.

"I think that's a good idea. Have you got someplace to go to get a little doctorin' on your bruises?"

She glanced at Otis, who was standing by with a worried look on his face. She nodded her head, and he nodded in return.

"Good," Murphy said. And when Maggie took another worried look at Jake Pike, Murphy said, "Don't worry about him. He's going to jail." Then he picked up the rope, put the noose over Pike's head, and tightened it around his neck.

Otis and Maggie went outside, and he helped her up onto the wagon seat and drove his team of mules out the north road, headed for his cabin back down the river. Murphy pulled an unresponsive Pike up from the floor, hefted him on his shoulder, and walked out of Pratt's Saloon, his rifle in one hand.

One of the spectators asked Albert Smith, the bartender, if he was the sheriff.

"Not as far as I've heard," Albert answered. "That's just Murphy's Law."

When he walked outside, Murphy looked at the half dozen horses tied at the hitching rail and decided he wouldn't take the time to find out which one belonged to Pike. The jail was practically across the street, only a few doors down. He figured it best to just keep walking and get rid of Pike before he became fully conscious, then come back for the horse. When he reached his jail, he thought to himself, *Two days and the jail has already had two customers. I hope to hell this ain't typical.* When he started toward the office door, he thought of how pathetic Maggie Tatum had looked with a rope around her neck. With that picture in his mind, he abruptly turned and took Pike to the smokehouse instead.

"I think a night in the cooler is what you need," he told Pike, referring to the smokehouse by his pet name for it.

Pike mumbled incoherently in response but was too groggy to put up any resistance. Murphy wasn't sure what to do with him. There was no judge to decide his prisoner's punishment, so he figured it was up to him to decide how long to keep Pike in jail. It was still early afternoon, but he decided to leave him in the smokehouse until the next morning before he worried about feeding him. So he went into the jail to get the water bucket from the first cell, rinsed it, and refilled it. Then he went back to the smokehouse and set the bucket just inside the door. He figured it wouldn't be too long before Pike's brain cleared enough for him to realize he was locked up somewhere, and there would be enough daylight around the edges of the door to enable him to see the water bucket.

Feeling no compassion for his prisoner beyond not letting him die of thirst, he went back to Pratt's Saloon to get Pike's horse. He went inside and addressed the customers, who were still talking about the arrest. "Who's got a horse tied out front?" he asked. Five men raised their hands. "Better come claim 'em, 'cause I'm fixin' to take one of 'em with me."

There was no delay on the part of the five men, so Murphy was left with a dun gelding. Back to the jailhouse then, he tied the horse and searched Pike's saddlebags and found an extra handgun, which he confiscated along with his rifle.

When he was struck with a feeling of compassion, it had nothing to do with Jake Pike. He went to the stable to give his horses some attention. They had been spending too much time in the stable lately, so he wanted them to know he hadn't forgotten them. He had to take Pike's horse to the stable, anyway, so he rode the dun gelding to the end of the street.

"I heard you made another arrest this mornin'," Paul Mathers greeted him when he pulled up by the corral.

"That's a fact," Murphy answered. "This is his horse. Belongs to a fellow named Jake Pike. He was treatin' a woman like a dog and threatenin' to shoot anybody that tried to help her."

"Jake Pike. I remember him. A while back, maybe a year or two ago, he used to hang around Pratt's Saloon. I think he was seeing one of the gals that worked there."

"Maggie Tatum," Murphy reminded him.

"Right," Mathers remembered. "It was Maggie Tatum. But Maggie got religion or something, and she quit the upstairs business. All she does now is help Mack Pratt sell whiskey."

"Well, I reckon that didn't set too well with Jake Pike," Murphy said. "From the looks of her face, it looked like he had beat her up pretty good."

"So he's a guest of the new jail, eh?" Mathers replied.

"Not yet," Murphy said. "My jailhouse is too good for the likes of Jake Pike, so I threw him in the smokehouse. I can't abide a man who'll beat up a woman." He pulled the saddle off Pike's horse and turned him out in the corral with the others. Mathers said he would take the saddle and bridle in the barn, so Murphy remained at the corral to give Nosy and the sorrel some attention.

When he started to leave, Mathers said, "Listen, Cullen,

you've already got a big credit on the books, but there ain't gonna be no charge to take care of your horses." When Murphy looked surprised to hear that, Mathers said, "That's for as long as you're doin' the job of sheriff. There's a lot of us in town that appreciate what you're doing. I'll take good care of your horses."

"I swear," Murphy responded, "that's mighty generous of you, Paul. I can't tell you how much I appreciate that."

He walked back to the jail, thinking he'd try to do a decent job for the town.

He had been back at the jail for only an hour or so when Bert Walker pulled up to the front door in a wagon.

"What you haulin' there, Bert?" he asked the blacksmith.

"This here is the official desk for the Newtown sheriff or marshal," Bert declared. "We ain't decided if you'll be the sheriff or marshal yet. But we thought you needed to have some decent furniture in your office, like a desk better than that old one Elmo offered you."

"Is that a fact?" Murphy responded. "Where did you get a desk?"

"It was in the back of Eliot Baxter's storeroom," Bert said. "He said he used it when he first built his store, but a couple of the legs got broke off, so he got a new one. He had me make a couple of legs for it and put some handles on the drawers, and it's as good as new."

"Well, I'll be doggone . . . ," Murphy uttered. "I thought I was pretty lucky to have that old one."

Bert chuckled and remarked, "I think this desk will make it look a lot more official when somebody comes in lookin' for the sheriff. And before you start makin' a bench to sit on, hold off till you see the desk chair Tyson Bradshaw said he never uses. He said I could pick that up for you tomorrow."

When Murphy smiled and slowly shook his head, Bert was quick to comment. "I know what you're thinkin', Cullen. We're trying to fix things up for you so you'll feel more like taking the job permanently. But, believe me, it's also because we're really appreciative of what you've done for this town. Mack Pratt said it best when he told me how you walked into his place and put a stop to a situation that's become typical in our town. The lawless breed finds out there's no law in Newtown, so they know they can do what they please. Like Mack said, that brazen outlaw Jake Pike settin' at a table in his saloon with Maggie Tatum beside him on the floor with a rope around her neck. And him hopin' somebody will try to do something about it. But nobody, not one man, would make a move to help her."

"Yeah, I reckon that pretty much describes the whole picture, although I think there are some men in town that would have tried to help. I figure you're one of those men. There must be more. I sure as hell can't guarantee you folks that I ain't gonna get shot down. You need more than one lawman who's willin' to try to maintain law and order. What the town needs is a sheriff and a deputy or two that ain't afraid to stand up for law and order. Then this town will grow and be too big for the lawless crowd."

"Damn, Cullen," Bert exclaimed, obviously impressed, "you just made quite a speech. Maybe you oughta make it again at the town council meeting."

"I was tryin' to impress you enough to make you volunteer to be my deputy," Murphy said.

"Me?" Bert responded. "Hell, I've got a business to run. If I was a deputy, the town wouldn't have a blacksmith."

"Hell," Murphy insisted, "you wouldn't have to shut down your forge. You'd just be available if some extra help was needed. I mean, now that you don't carry that hogleg pistol anymore, you've got a handgun you can handle. A little practice and we might make a genuine fast gun outta you."

"Now you're talkin' crazy," Bert said. "I can't see myself in that role."

"Maybe not, but I'd like to think I could count on you if I needed some help," Murphy said.

"I can give you that guarantee right now," Bert declared. "I still don't know how much help I would be, but I'm willin' to answer the call if it comes."

"I think I already knew that, but right now, what I really need is for you to help me get that desk inside the office."

So the two big men muscled the desk through the door to the office and moved it twice more before a final spot was decided upon. "That's a mighty fine piece of furniture," Murphy joked after it was in its final resting place. "It's a good thing it's officially property of the town of Newtown, or I might be tempted to try to sell it."

It occurred to Bert then to ask a question. He nodded toward the door to the cell room. "Jake Pike ain't makin' no noise a'tall in there, is he?"

"He ain't in there," Murphy answered.

"You let him go?"

"No, I threw him in the cooler," Murphy replied.

Bert was confused for a moment before he understood. "You put him in the smokehouse?"

"That's right. I figured he could use a day and a night in there. I wanna see if it has the same effect on him that it had on Billy Daniels," he japed. "If it does, then we'll make it a standard practice for everybody we arrest."

Being a practical man, Bert chuckled in response to Murphy's remark, but he saw fit to comment, as well. "You know, sooner or later, somebody's gonna have to clean that smokehouse out, and that ain't gonna be a job I'll volunteer for."

When Murphy walked into the dining room at Bradshaw's for supper, Ginger Floyd greeted him with a question. "Are you going to want a plate to take with you?"

"No, ma'am," Murphy replied.

"We heard you arrested that man who caused the trouble in Pratt's Saloon. Aren't you supposed to feed him?"

"I'll start feedin' him in the mornin' for breakfast," Murphy said. "I don't think he wants anything tonight, anyway. His jaw is kinda swollen up. It might hurt him to chew. Maybe you can fix him up something in the mornin' that ain't hard to chew."

Without thinking, she asked, "What happened to his jaw?"

"When he was gettin' up out of his chair, he bumped into my rifle butt. Nothing serious."

"Is that poor woman he was holding all right?" Ginger asked.

"I think so. She was pretty bruised up. He'd been rough on her, but that fellow—Otis, I think his name was—who came to get me took her off somewhere to take care of her."

He walked back and sat down at his usual table when Ginger went into the kitchen to get his coffee. When she came back with the coffee, she was followed by Bonnie carrying a plate of food, and she questioned him on the arrest, as well. When he had answered the younger sister's questions, he attacked the meat loaf for the second time that day. He was not halfway finished when he was joined by another investigator, this one unusual.

"Howdy, Cullen. Mind if I sit down?" Tyson Bradshaw asked. "I heard about the arrest at Pratt's. Damn good work. Glad you're doing the job of a marshal. How long do you figure on keeping that Pike fellow in jail?"

"I hadn't thought about it, to be honest. Like I said, I don't know much about being a marshal. A few days, I suppose, for what he did to that woman."

Bradshaw stroked his chin thoughtfully. "Here's the thing, Cullen. Some of the members of the council who are working on the town marshal project are trying to keep our costs down until we can implement the new tax system to pay the marshal and the jail expenses. So it would help if we could cut expenses where we can until we get an agreement from all the merchants. And it would help if you just ordered men like that Pike fellow out of town, instead of a long jail sentence. I mean, for something like just roughing up a saloon girl, maybe a long time behind bars isn't required." He could see by Murphy's expression that he was not in agreement. So he quickly continued. "Unless you think some jail time is called for, then we wouldn't object."

"I'll let him go tomorrow after breakfast," Murphy stated flatly.

"Fine. It's strictly at your discretion. I'll leave you to eat in peace, and thanks again."

Chapter 11

Murphy was still a little disgruntled about Bradshaw's visit at supper the night before, especially when he had insinuated that Pike's attack on the saloon girl was nothing important. Orphaned at ten, he grew up in a world of prostitutes and dance-hall girls, but he didn't know them as such. To him, they were people, some bad, some with hearts of gold. Because of bad luck, however, they found themselves traveling a rougher road of life. He pictured the bruised and bleeding face of Maggie Tatum, and he hoped Pike's face was going to be at least equally disfigured when he took him out of the smokehouse this morning.

When Pike heard the lock on the smokehouse door being opened, he immediately cried out, "Let me outta here!" His voice was hoarse and strained from apparent exertion. "Open this hellhole!"

Murphy took the padlock off and swung the door open. Pike rushed out to run blindly into Murphy's fist, landing him flat on his back. Murphy reached down to grab a handful of shirt and picked Pike up, stood him on his feet, and held him there until he managed to stand on his own. Pike wobbled for a minute, in extreme pain from the punch in his already swollen face.

"Good morning," Murphy said. "I hope you had a restful night. I'm gonna put you in a jail cell while I go to get you some breakfast, unless you prefer to wait back in there for your breakfast."

"No, damn it. Take me to jail!" Pike exclaimed. "It stinks in there, like somebody died in there."

"Somebody did," Murphy lied. "I thought we got most of him outta there. We coulda missed some of him, though."

He marched Pike to the front of the building and into the office, then took him to the cell room and locked him in the one cell ready for prisoners. Seeing the bunk, Pike went immediately to it and flopped down on his back.

"When I get back, I'll make you some coffee to drink with your breakfast," Murphy said. He locked the office up then and went to the dining room.

"Morning, Marshal Murphy," Bonnie greeted him when he walked into Irene's café. "Bert Walker's waiting for you."

He said good morning and sat down at the table with the blacksmith, who was already eating. "Get tired of your own cookin' again?"

"Yeah," Bert answered. "I thought I'd give my belly a break and have one of Irene's breakfasts. I hoped I'd catch you here. Tyson Bradshaw told me to be sure and pick up that office chair and take it to the jail today."

Murphy had to chuckle. "He did, did he? Well, I ain't surprised."

"Why's that?" Bert asked.

Murphy told him about the visit he had with Bradshaw when he was eating supper the night before. "He's afraid I'm gonna keep prisoners in jail too long and cost the town money. I told him I'd let Jake Pike go right after I feed him some breakfast."

"He's afraid you're gonna quit, and there ain't nobody to

take your place," Bert said. "And I'm afraid he's gonna put the pressure on me to take the job."

"That' s why I gotta make sure you're ready to take it," Murphy said, with a second chuckle.

"I'll volunteer to be your deputy, and they won't have to pay me anything, if you'll promise me you'll stay here."

"I don't like to make promises," Murphy said. "But I'm plannin' to stay here till you folks get some solid law enforcement. I've already got too attached to the town not to try to help somehow." He paused when Ginger set his plate down and Bonnie filled his and Bert's cups.

"Are you going to take some breakfast back for your prisoner?" Ginger asked. "Or are you going to make him skip another meal?"

"See what I mean?" Murphy said to Bert. "As sassy as those two little gals are, I'd still miss 'em." To Ginger, he said, "Yes, Miss Floyd, I'll take a plate back for my guest."

"I'll bring that chair by after you get back, all right?" Bert asked.

"Sure," Murphy answered. "I'm gonna make Pike some coffee. Then while he's eatin', I'll go to the stable and get his horse, so he can jump right on it and get outta town."

Bert finished eating shortly after, so he decided to go back to his shop and get the chair. "I'll meet you at the jail," he said. "I wanna put a little oil on those springs under the seat."

"Right," Murphy said. "I don't want no squeaky chair," he japed as Bert walked away.

"What's wrong with your chair?" Bonnie asked after overhearing Murphy's last remark to Bert when she brought Jake Pike's plate to the table.

"Not a thing," Murphy told her. "And tell your mama there's not a thing wrong with the breakfast, either. I'll see you for dinner." He picked up the extra plate and walked out the door.

As he walked across the street, he looked up toward the stable and saw Bert walking down the street with an armchair upside down, the seat on his head and the arms resting on his shoulders. He met him at the front door of the jail and helped him get the chair into the office. Then he sat down in the chair after they'd moved it around behind the desk.

"That thing's so comfortable, it might be hard to get me out of it," he said. "Might take a bank robbery to get me outta this chair. Good thing we ain't got a bank." He got up out of the chair and said, "You try it, Bert." Bert sat down in the chair, and Murphy said, "That's what I thought. It didn't throw you, did it?" Bert jumped up out of the chair immediately.

"You mind if I take a look at your prisoner?" Bert asked. "I wanna make sure those hinges I made are workin' like they're supposed to."

"Why, of course not, Deputy," Murphy replied. "Make yourself at home." He opened the door to the cell room and held it for him. "Be a good idea for you to see how we have to pass anything in or out of the cell."

Pike was still lying on his back in the bunk, and when they came into the cell room, he started to sit up.

"You just stay right there on that bunk, if you want this breakfast," Murphy ordered. Pike lay back on the bunk. Murphy unlocked the cell door and set the plate inside on the floor. Then he closed the door and locked it. Pike came at once to pick up the plate.

"What the hell are you lookin' at?" Pike said to Bert, who was staring at his swollen jaw and cheek.

"Now, you mind your manners, Jake," Murphy warned him. "I was thinkin' about turnin' you loose after you had some breakfast, since you ain't caused any trouble since I arrested you. Maybe you ain't ready to get outta jail, after all. I ain't sure I wanna make you some coffee, either."

"I ain't gonna cause you no problems," Jake said at once. "I just didn't like the way he was lookin' at me."

"He's a deputy sheriff, Jake. He's paid to keep an eye on you." He winked at Bert, who was not enjoying the ruse any more than Jake was. "Here's the deal, Jake. I'm willin' to release you from this jail on the condition that you get on your horse and ride out of Newtown and don't let me see your face here again. If I do, I'll shoot you on sight and ask questions later. Do you understand?"

"Yeah, I understand. I can't wait to leave this town," Pike declared.

"Good," Murphy said. "I'll go make you some coffee. Bert, you want some more coffee?"

"No, thanks just the same. I need to get to work. I've gotta make two rims for that wagon I delivered your desk in."

Murphy walked to the cell room door with him, and when he started to close the door, Bert asked, "What's gonna keep him from goin' to Pratt's after Maggie again?"

"She ain't at Pratt's," Murphy said.

"Did Otis Crutcher take her home to his farm?"

Murphy nodded and closed the door quickly, afraid that Pike might have overheard him. Bert left then, and Murphy went to the kitchen to stir up the fire in the little stove and get some coffee working. After he took Pike's coffee to his cell, he locked the office and went up to the stable to get his horse.

"You already lettin' him go?" Mathers asked when Murphy arrived at the stable.

"Yep," Murphy replied, "after a special request from your town council to save that seventy-five cents a day to feed him."

Mathers claimed he didn't remember having that discussion at the last council meeting.

"I think Baxter and Bradshaw are tryin' to work out a tax on you merchants that you can afford and employ a sheriff at the same time."

He led Jake Pike's horse back to the jail and tied it at the hitching rail Robert Jessop had erected in front of the building. He went inside to find his prisoner still working on his breakfast, painfully trying to chew a strip of bacon on the plate. "Ain't you through eatin' your breakfast yet?" Murphy asked when he walked in the cell room. "I thought you were in a hurry to get outta here."

"I am, dammit," he blurted, "but I can hardly chew anythin', thanks to you."

"I know you're blamin' me for your jaw, but you need to remember it was what you got for beatin' up a helpless woman. If you've got half a brain, maybe you'll figure out that it's painful beatin' up a woman."

"It weren't nobody's business but mine and hers," Pike declared. "She ain't nothin' but a tramp, and nobody else shoulda stuck their nose in it. I warned 'em that it weren't none of their business, and that little worm that sneaked outta there and ran to fetch you, I'da put a bullet in his head if I'da caught him."

Murphy felt his temper rising. He cautioned himself against rising to the bait. "I swear, I think I'll take your horse back to the stable and throw your sorry butt back in the cooler."

"Hold on!" Pike blurted. "You want me outta here! So just as soon as I get on my horse, I'm gone! I'll be outta here, and you won't never see me again! I'm through eatin'. I'm ready to go."

"All right," Murphy said. "Get outta here before I decide beatin' up a woman is a hangin' offense." He unlocked the cell and opened the door.

Pike plopped his hat on his head and hurried out. "How 'bout my gun belt and my gun?" he asked as he walked out the front door.

"They're hangin' on your saddle horn," Murphy said and followed him out the door. He watched him as he first untied his horse, then took his gun belt off the saddle horn and strapped it on his hips. He paused for a few moments until it felt comfortable while he met Murphy's gaze.

"Go ahead and pull it, if you think this is your lucky day," Murphy said.

Pike hesitated for a few more moments before a smile broke out across his swollen face. "It's empty, ain't it?"

Murphy smiled back at him. "There's one way to find out."

"I think I'd better cut my losses and get outta town," Pike said and climbed up into the saddle. "It's been nice knowin' you, Marshal." He wheeled his horse away from the rail and galloped up the street.

Murphy went back inside to get Pike's plate and cup. He took them to the kitchen, dumped the uneaten food into the slop bucket, and dropped the dirty plate and cup into the bucket of water to soak before he washed them and returned them to the café dining room.

Jake Pike rode out the north road toward the stark hills of limestone and granite with their sparse covering of vegetation. About half a mile north of town, he turned the dun onto an old Indian trail leading in a more westerly direction before crossing a rapidly running stream. Instead of continuing on the trail and crossing the stream, he followed the stream west for a mile or so before it led him up a narrow valley formed by two steep hills. He could now see the cabin farther up the stream.

As a precaution, he pulled his Colt and aimed it up in the air and pulled the trigger to hear the hammer fall on an empty cylinder. He cocked it and fired again with the same result, only then remembering he had not reloaded the weapon when it was returned to him. He smirked when he pictured the smug face of the man called Murphy. If he had gambled on whether or not Murphy had emptied the gun, he would have given Murphy an excuse to shoot him. He loaded the Colt and fired one shot up in the air. In a short while, it was answered by a single shot, so he rode on up to the cabin.

It had been two years since he had left the cabin. Wanted in Kansas for robbery and murder, he and his two partners had fled to the out-of-the-way Texas Hill Country. They had expected to join Clyde Fry and his gang when they got there. He had told Clyde how to find the cabin, but there was no sign of Clyde or the men riding with him. So he didn't know for sure whether Clyde had ever found the cabin or not. There were plenty of signs that someone had used it recently, however. He was glad to find it in pretty good condition. Hank Dougherty and Ron Blake were tickled to find the cabin was in as good a location as he had promised, close by a healthy stream and convenient to fresh beef. Best of all, close to an isolated town with no law enforcement. He paused in his thinking to note, *I'll have to tell Hank and Ron there's been a change in that part of it*.

Maybe it was a good idea for him to ride into Newtown alone this first time, so he could see if there were any big changes since he had left. There had not been much growth in his two-year absence. One of the reasons he had not encouraged Ron or Hank to go into town with him on that first occasion was Maggie Tatum, a young prostitute in Pratt's Saloon. He had spent a lot of time with her when he was in Newtown, and when he left two years ago, he'd told her he didn't want her to be with anybody else. He started getting angry again when he thought about the reception he had gotten from her when he showed up after two years. Expecting a hero's welcome, he had gotten a cold shoulder instead. When he'd said he would pay her, she'd claimed she didn't do that anymore. She'd said she would be glad to have a drink with him, but that was as far as she would go.

"She damn sure found out that I'm the one who'll decide how far she'll go," he said as he approached the cabin.

"Jake?" Hank Dougherty called out as he holstered his six-gun. "What in the world did you run into? Ron! It's Jake. Come look."

"What is it?" Ron Blake asked when he came out of the cabin. "Great day in the mornin'! What happened? You fall off your horse?"

"It was a sight worse than that," Jake replied. "I got kissed by the butt of a Henry rifle and blindsided by a fist that was more like the kick of a mule. I spent the night locked up in what looked like a smokehouse outside the jailhouse."

"Oh," Hank said, "as long as you was havin' a good time."

"You never came back last night, so we figured you musta found that little gal you was lookin' for," Ron said. "We figured you musta shacked up with her, so we was fixin' to go into town to look for you."

"Do I look like I've been shacked up with a woman all night?" Jake demanded. "You ain't listenin' to what I said."

"I take it you didn't find the little gal. What was her name?" Hank replied.

"Maggie Tatum," Jake said. "I found her, but she got religion or something."

"Why, that little tramp," Hank remarked. "I expect you taught her some religion, then."

"I sure as hell did," Jake replied. He told them the whole story then since it appeared they were now interested enough to let him tell it. When he got to the part where the town marshal came into the picture, they realized something was going to have to be done to make things right.

"I reckon we'll have to go visit that little town and straighten that marshal out," Ron declared.

"I don't think that's a good idea," Jake said. "I was ordered out of town, and he told me he would shoot me on sight if I showed up there again. You and Hank can go into town. He don't know anything about you two. I got something to take care of outside of town, and I'd like to take care of that first before I settle things with Cullen Murphy. I came back here to get Maggie Tatum, and I plan to have her. And she ain't in town. I heard Murphy's deputy ask him if a feller named Otis Crutcher took her to his farm. Murphy pulled the deputy out the door real quick, but I made out like I didn't hear him. I wanna find her and bring her here. Then I wanna take care of Murphy."

Hank and Ron looked at each other and nodded. "Whatever way you want it done, Jake. This is your show," Hank said and looked at Ron again and smiled. "I reckon you can bring her out here and we'll help you watch her."

"You sure you're up to goin' after that woman?" Ron asked. "You don't look like you're ready to go."

"I'm all right now," Jake said. "It's just my face that hurts. But I wouldn't care if both my legs was crippled. I'd go after her after she stuck her nose up like I was dirt."

"This feller, Otis what's-his-name, how you gonna find his farm?" Hank asked.

"I know where it might be," Jake said. "There ain't that much land that's any good for small farms around here. There's a road leadin' north outta town that forks off to follow the river, and there's a bunch of small farms along it. I'm headin' that way this afternoon and just taking a look-see. Maybe I'll ask somebody where Otis Crutcher's farm is. Somebody oughta know where he lives."

"You sure you don't want me and Ron to go look for that gal with you?" Hank asked.

"Nah, he's right," Ron answered for him. "He's got a better chance of slippin' up on her by hisself. Me and you oughta go on into town to see what's there and pick up a couple of bottles of likker. We been out for two days, and if I don't get a drink of likker pretty soon, I'm afraid I'll get religion like Jake's gal did. No offense, Jake."

Jake ignored him. He was already deep in thought about what he was going to do when he found Maggie Tatum. So he went to the small corral behind the cabin and led one of the three packhorses out and put a packsaddle on it. When he found her, he planned to put Maggie on the horse. When he was ready to ride, Ron and Hank saddled up to go with him. They followed the stream back down the narrow valley until they reached the old Indian trail. Then they followed that trail back to the road out of Newtown, where they split up. Jake followed the road to the fork that led to the small farms, and his two partners rode to Newtown.

Chapter 12

It had been two years since Jake Pike had left Newtown, and he had spent very little time in the part of the county where some folks had settled along the river to farm. But the fork off the main road was obvious when he came to it, so he followed it until he came to a house built close to the river, with a large field of cotton behind it. There were a couple of small children playing in the yard, a boy and a girl. When he was almost even with the house, a woman came out of it and called to the children. When she turned and saw him approaching, she stopped and waited, staring at the stranger.

"Howdy, ma'am," he said as politely as he could, knowing she was transfixed by the condition of his face. "I was wonderin' if I could ask you something."

She didn't reply but continued to stare at him.

"I'll ask you to excuse my appearance. I came headfirst off a wild horse I was tryin' to saddle break."

She relaxed then. "My goodness' sakes, it looks like it really must have hurt," she said, sympathizing.

"Yessum, it surely did, but it didn't do no permanent damage. I raise horses, and somebody told me that a feller name of Otis Crutcher was lookin' to buy some horses and he had a farm up this way."

She looked genuinely astonished. "Otis wanting to buy some horses?" she questioned. "Otis has a farm on this road, but I'd be surprised if he's looking to buy some horses." She smiled then and added, "But I don't know what Otis is planning to do."

"Maybe you're right," Jake said, "but as long as I rode all the way out here, I reckon I oughta find out. You say his place is on this road?"

"That's right. Two houses farther," she said, "about a quarter of a mile."

"Thank you, ma'am," Pike said and continued on along the road, passing cultivated fields along the river.

He passed the next house on the road, which was similar to the first house, but he didn't see anyone out around the house. He rode a little farther, until he saw the next house up ahead, sitting in a small clump of trees. It appeared to be a smaller house than the two he had already passed, not much more than a good-sized cabin. His first thought was that Otis most likely had no family. That was enough to raise his anger even more. *I'd best be careful*, he told himself and turned off the road to ride under cover of the trees beside it.

He tried to look the place over as best he could while he approached the cabin, riding parallel to the road. There was no sign of anyone outside the cabin, but while he was watching, a man walked out the back door and started for the barn, where a mule was standing, hitched to a wagon. Pike felt the muscles in his forearms tighten as he considered his competition. A skinny sodbuster, he observed, not half the man he was. He started to pull his rifle from his saddle sling, then thought better of it. It would be better to make sure Maggie was there before he fired a shot. So he decided to wait and see what Otis was going to do before he decided to act. While he waited and watched, Otis climbed up into the wagon seat and drove away from the barn to follow a well-beaten path beside a cornfield. Pike continued to watch until the wagon was well out of sight.

Inside the cabin, Maggie Tatum was also watching Otis. Standing in the back door, she watched him until he disappeared before she went back and cleaned up the dishes from his dinner. A grateful smile still lingered on her lips as she considered the shy, thoughtful young man who had caused her rescue and volunteered to take care of her with no demands in return. She knew that she would do anything for him to repay him for giving her a new life.

"Maggie, I come to get you."

The sound of the voice shattered her reverie like a bullet through a windowpane. Thinking it an illusion, she turned to see him standing in the front door, not ghostlike but real, his face grotesque in its swollen detail. She felt the strength drain from her knees as if she might faint, but she forced herself to run to the kitchen for the butcher knife she had left on the table.

Spotting the knife, as well, he raced her to it and arrived a split second before her. He grabbed her arm and stopped her. Then he picked up the butcher knife and held it up in front of her face. "Is this what you was runnin' for? Was you fixin' to use it on me? I oughta just jam it in your belly and walk clean around you. And I would, but you owe me something. And I always collect the debts people owe me. Maybe we'll wait for your friend to come back, so I can pay him for his part in this. I'll fire a couple of shots in the air and see if he comes to save you."

Her mind was still not functioning properly from the sudden shock of seeing him again, but she recovered enough to surrender. "Leave him alone. I'll go with you if you do. He's not the one that put you in jail. He just gave me a place to rest up from the beating you gave me. So let him be."

"I'm thinkin' I might give him a little something to teach him to mind his own business before I go," Pike said.

"If you do, I won't go with you," she said. "So you'll have to kill both of us."

He hesitated a moment to consider that option. It would serve to teach both of them that he was not someone to mess with. His passion for her had become an obsession, however, and he was determined to have her. "All right," he finally decided. "Get your things and let's go."

"I don't have any things," she said. "Everything here belongs to his late wife."

"Good. Let's go." He flipped the butcher knife in the air and caught it by the blade. Then he threw it across the room to stick in the kitchen wall, grabbed her wrist, and went back out the front door, pulling her along behind him.

Hank Dougherty and Ron Blake rode the length of Front Street, then stopped halfway back when they pulled up before Bradshaw's Saloon, where they tied their horses. "Not a bad little town," Hank remarked as they stood outside the saloon and looked up and down the street. "I thought Jake mighta still been a little drunk when he told us about spendin' the night here last night."

"Whaddaya mean?" Ron replied.

"Didn't you notice?" Hank asked. "When we rode by the jail just now, there was what looked like a smokehouse behind it."

"Is that a fact?" Ron responded. "I swear, I never noticed." He looked up at the sign over the door then and read it. "Bradshaw's Saloon. That don't sound like the name of the saloon he said he got arrested in."

"Nah, it don't," Hank agreed, "but it looks like it's the busiest one, so let's go get a drink."

They walked into the saloon with the carefree attitude of

two outlaws in a new town where nobody knew them, in a state where they were not wanted for anything, with money that was worth the value printed on it. They were met at the bar with a friendly smile.

"Welcome to Bradshaw's, gents. Whaddaya have?" Pete Brice asked.

"How 'bout a shot of rye whiskey," Hank replied.

Pete glanced at Ron then, and Ron nodded, so Pete put two glasses on the bar and poured two shots. They both tossed their drinks down and motioned for seconds.

"That ain't half bad," Ron said while he watched Pete fill his glass.

"You boys ain't been in before, have you?" Pete asked.

"No, we ain't," Hank said. "We just rode into town, and I'm glad to find a good drink of likker in your saloon. We've rode all the way down here from Kansas, and I'm tellin' you the truth, every drink of likker we've had tasted more like the Red River than rye whiskey."

His comment was good for a chuckle out of Pete. "Well, welcome to Newtown," he said. "My name's Pete. You've already picked the best saloon in town, so you might as well know the best place to eat is right through that door right there." He pointed to the door to the café. "It's operated by Irene Floyd, and there's a door to it in the back of the building, if you don't wanna go through the saloon."

"Come to think of it," Ron remarked, "I didn't notice any eatin' places when we rode up and down the street. I didn't see a hotel, either. Jake didn't say nothin' about eatin' places in town."

"Who?" Pete asked.

"Jake Smith," Hank quickly answered and poked Ron with his elbow, "a feller up in Kansas that told us about Newtown."

"Right, ol' Jake Smith," Ron said. "He was right sorry he couldn't come down here with us."

"I reckon we'd best take us a bottle of this over and sit down at a table," Hank said, and when Pete reached in a cabinet behind the bar to get it, he added under his breath, "Before you tell him everything you know."

When Pete came back up with a new bottle of rye whiskey, Hank asked how much, and Pete answered, "Two bucks." Then he prepared to explain that the Confederate money was of no value. He was surprised and pleased when Hank peeled two Union dollar bills off a roll and placed them on the counter. "Good," Pete said. "I see you've got Union bills."

"That's the only kind we ever earned," Hank said. "We also owe you for a couple of shots apiece."

"Fifty cents," Pete said.

Ron slapped two quarters on the bar, and they took the bottle and their glasses to a table. They were sitting there deciding whether or not to wait right where they were and then go in and try out the café when a large, rather rugged-looking man walked into the saloon.

"Evening, Cullen," they heard Pete greet the man. Both men seated at the table thought the name familiar, but neither one could remember why. "You're a little early for supper," Pete said.

"Yeah, I know," Murphy replied. "Elmo said he wanted to meet me here before supper to buy me a drink."

"Well, that don't exactly sound like Elmo," Pete said with a chuckle. "He must need something."

"Most likely," Murphy agreed. He didn't bother to discuss it with Pete, but he suspected both Baxter and Bradshaw had been approaching him with hints about spending less of the town's money when he made arrests. So now they probably had some other complaint and had enlisted Elmo to present it to him.

As if on cue, the next body to come through the batwing doors was Elmo Dillon. He walked straight to the bar. "Pete,

Marshal Murphy," he greeted them enthusiastically. They returned his greeting.

The two strangers at the table exchanged quick looks of discovery. "That's Murphy," Hank whispered. "No wonder Jake's face looks like he fell off a high building."

"He looks like a handful, all right," Ron whispered back, "but I don't reckon he's bulletproof. He'd be easy to take right now, wouldn't he?" He released his index finger from the glass he was holding and pointed it straight at Murphy like a pistol barrel. "Bam, bam," he whispered.

"You don't wanna rob Jake of the pleasure," Hank mumbled.

"Give us a bottle, Pete, and a couple of glasses and we'll sit down at a table," Elmo said.

Pete got them a bottle and put it on Elmo's account. Then he said, "Say howdy to Hank and Ron there. This is the first time they've been to Newtown. This is Cullen Murphy and Elmo Dillon." The four men exchanged greetings.

"What brings you fellows to the little town of Newtown?" Elmo asked.

"We're in the cattle-buyin' business up in Abilene, Kansas," Hank answered. "We've got reports about the cattle country around this part of Texas."

"That's right," Ron said. "So we thought we'd ride down this way and take a look for ourselves."

"I'm afraid you're gonna be disappointed you took the trip down here," Murphy remarked. "This hill country ain't much for big cattle operations. Lionel Jacobson's Rocking-J Ranch is the only sizable cattle ranch along the San Saba River. Most of the others are just small ranches that will combine their herds with Jacobson's when he drives his cattle to market."

"Is that a fact?" Hank replied. "You seem to be right up to date on the cattle situation in this part of Texas . . . Mr. *Murphy*, was it?"

Murphy nodded.

"Too bad we had to ride all the way down here, Ron. If we'da known, we coulda just wrote Mr. Murphy a letter."

"We hope you find it better to your liking after you've spent a little time around Newtown," Elmo said. "There's a lot of folks startin' up ranches in San Saba County. The cattle business is bound to get bigger, too."

He took Murphy by the arm and led him to a table across the room. "I swear, Cullen, I thought you knew we're trying to lure business, not scare it away."

"If those two drifters are cattle buyers, I'm a lady's garter inspector." He frowned. "What's on your mind, Elmo?" Murphy asked after they sat down.

"Everybody is really pleased with the new jailhouse," Elmo started, "and the way you handled those two arrests—"

"But . . . ," Murphy interrupted.

"No *but*," Elmo insisted. "They know you're doin' a helluva job as marshal, and that's what we've decided to call you, town marshal. Is that all right with you?"

"Yeah, sure. I don't care what you call me. Whatever suits you best. Was that all that's botherin' Baxter and Bradshaw?"

"Yeah," Elmo said. "They just wanted to make sure you were okay with it." He hesitated. "There was one more little thing they were worried about."

"I thought there might be," Murphy remarked.

"Nothing earthshaking," Elmo insisted. "The sign, San Saba County Jail, might cause some problems with the county and the state of Texas, since Newtown isn't the county seat. They were thinking it might be better to just call it the Newtown Jail."

Murphy smiled. "Hell, I don't care what you call it, as long as it's still a jail. The town bought it under the condition that it would be used for a jail. Frankly, there ain't no other town in the county. So I thought if you named it the county jail, it might influence them to make Newtown the county seat."

"Well, see, that's where you're wrong. There is another town in the county. It ain't much more than a little settlement, and they named it San Saba. It's about twenty miles east of here, and about ten years ago, they made it the county seat."

They sat there a little longer while Murphy thought about that. When Bonnie opened the café door to hang the OPEN sign, Murphy asked Elmo if he was going to eat supper.

"Not right away," Elmo said. "I've got to take care of something first."

"Well, I'm gonna see what Irene's cooked this evenin'," Murphy said, "and maybe I'll see you later." *After you report to Baxter and Bradshaw that I'm not going to raise hell if you want to change the name of the jail*, he thought.

He got up and followed the two strangers into the dining room, while Elmo went out the front door.

Murphy enjoyed a peaceful supper before taking an evening walk up and down Front Street, since that was what he supposed a town marshal would do. Finding nothing to concern himself with, he returned to his office at the jail to sit behind his new desk in the comfort of his armchair. To amuse himself, he looked through a stack of wanted notices that Jim Anderson, the postmaster, had accumulated and was now happy to get rid of. He was accustomed to hitting the hay about this time, but since he had taken on the chore of town marshal, he now made it a point to stay up later to see that the town closed for the night. The night was still fairly young when he heard the frantic knocking on his office door.

He went to the door and opened it to find Otis Crutcher in an obvious state of distress, standing on the stoop. "He took Maggie!" Otis cried as soon as the door was opened. "She's gone! He come and took her!"

Murphy stepped back and held the door open for him. "Tell me what happened. Are you sure somebody took her?" He was not sure she hadn't just decided to return to Pratt's Saloon on her own.

"It was him, Pike," Otis insisted. "Couldn'ta been nobody else! Maggie cooked me a big dinner, and we sat around the table and talked a long time. We was plannin' to get married, so she wouldn't have to live in no saloon. When I took the mules and wagon down to the lower field to work, he came in the house and took her. When I came back for supper, she was gone, and there was my butcher knife stuck in the wall."

"Have you got any idea where he mighta took her?" Murphy asked. "He might have a camp somewhere near your place?"

"No," Otis said. "There ain't no place on that road where anybody's camped. I ain't got no idea where he coulda took her. I don't know how he knew where my place is."

"He must have asked enough folks where your farm was until he found somebody who knew," Murphy said. "Pike had hung around Newtown for a pretty good while before he left two years ago. Were there any farmers on that road two years ago?"

"Sure there were," Otis answered. "I was there two years ago."

"Most likely that's how he found you," Murphy said. "He musta asked somebody on that road, and they told him which place was yours. It's already gettin' dark, so we'd have to wait till tomorrow to even try to track him. He found you. Now we've got to find him. You were here two years ago, when he was hangin' around town, right?"

"Yes, but I didn't know him," Otis said. "That was before my wife got sick and died. I didn't spend much time in town."

"Did you ever hear of a place where drifters, outlaws, or army deserters had a hideout?" Murphy asked. He was looking for any possibilities now, with no clue whatsoever to go on.

"There was always talk about some outlaw hideout back up in the mountains northwest of town, but I never talked to anybody who'd ever been there or knew where it was supposed to be." He shook his head in despair, aware of the hopelessness of the situation. "I'm sorry. I should have been there at the house with her, instead of workin' in the field. I didn't know what to do, so I came to find you. I don't know why I thought you could do anything."

"I'll be honest with you," Murphy said. "I probably can't. But I'll try, and I don't want to waste any more time. You go on back home. There ain't anything you can do to help me, but I'll let you know, good or bad."

With no time to lose, he strapped on his Colt .44 and picked up his rifle while he walked Otis out the door. He locked the office and said again, "I'll let you know." Then he left the forlorn little man and hurried up the street to Bradshaw's Saloon but stopped short of going in the door. Standing just outside, peering over the batwings, he scanned the room until he saw what he was looking for. Then he left at a trot to go to the stable to get his horse. Up to that point, luck was with him, for Mathers was just in the process of closing the stable.

"Cullen," Mathers said when he saw him rush in, "what's wrong?"

"Nothin', Paul. I need my horse, and I'm in a hurry, that's all." He ran to the stall where his saddle was kept, grabbed it and his bridle, and ran to the corral. Mathers was close behind, anxious to hear an explanation for the panic. Nosy came to meet him, and Murphy slipped his bridle on him and saddled him.

"Cullen, what the hell?" Mathers blurted impatiently.

"Long story," Murphy responded as he climbed aboard the eager bay. "I just ain't got the time to talk now. I'll tell you the whole story when I get back."

After leaving the stable, he made another quick stop at the blacksmith's forge, where he found Bert eating his supper. Murphy didn't bother to dismount. "I've gotta leave town for a little while. I ain't sure how long. But I'm dependin' on you to keep your eye on things till I get back, *Deputy*," he announced, emphasizing the final word. Then he galloped away, leaving Bert in the same state of shock as he had left Mathers.

He knew he was following a hunch that had a very slim chance of being accurate, but he had nothing else to gamble on. He was gambling on that hunch and nothing more, and he had to move fast to make sure he wasn't too late. So he went straight back to Bradshaw's Saloon, hoping they had not already left. He pulled up in front of the saloon and left Nosy at the hitching rail. He intended to stand just outside the door and scan the barroom to make sure the two "cattle buyers" were still enjoying themselves inside. He was startled, however, when the two strangers came out the door just as he approached it.

"Mr. Murphy," Hank exclaimed, surprised, as well. "Or is it Marshal Murphy?"

"Just plain Murphy will do," Murphy responded. "You boys fixin' to take a look at some of the other saloons in town?"

" 'Fraid not," Hank said. "We've had a long day, so we're gonna call it a night. We thought you'd already gone to bed."

"Nope," Murphy replied. "I'll go in and have a couple more drinks before I call it a night. I still have to make a midnight walk on the street to make sure everything's tidy."

"Well, have a good night," Ron said. "Maybe we'll see you tomorrow sometime."

"Right, the same to you," Murphy said and went on inside the saloon.

As soon as he was inside, he hurried to the front window and watched to see what the two strangers did. *Another couple of minutes and I would have missed them*, he thought. As he watched, they climbed on their horses and rode off toward the stable and the north road out of town. He was operating on a slim gamble that they might know of a popular hideout back up in the hills that a few other outlaws knew about. And he was putting all his chips on the possibility that Pike was at the same place. He had not revealed his intentions to anyone else, because they were based on nothing more than a wild guess, and he preferred not to have anyone tell him so.

When he felt sure they wouldn't see him come right back out the door, he slipped outside and climbed on his horse, then followed the two strangers out the north road. In the rapidly growing darkness, the two men he trailed soon turned into little more than two clumps in the road ahead that were just a shade darker than the night around them. He held Nosy to a walking pace that kept the two riders at that distance, reining the bay gelding back whenever the dark clumps became slightly darker. He felt confident that the odds were greatly in his favor that the two men would not spot him if they happened to look back. Had he known that the two men he followed had zero concern about being followed to the hideout, he might have trailed them even closer.

CHAPTER 13

"I can't wait to see this beauty queen ol' Pike has worked his-self all up in a lather about," Hank Dougherty commented to Ron Blake.

"You reckon that crazy fool is gonna find that gal?" Ron wondered aloud.

"He ain't got no idea where that gal took off to, but I ain't countin' him out. I'll tell you what I'm really wonderin', though, is whether he's plannin' to share his pleasures with his friends."

"Hell, why wouldn't he?" Ron replied. "She's a tramp, ain't she?"

"Maybe so, but Jake ain't got good sense when it comes to that gal, and she told him she ain't that no more, so he couldn't have his way with her. I reckon that's what set him off in that saloon. I expect that's why he's so determined to find her, so he can show her he'll damn sure have his way with her. And I'm afraid when he's done with her, he'll kill her, and never mind what me and you might need."

"Well, I expect that's when we'll have to remind him that we're partners," Ron said, "and we're entitled to . . ." He stopped in midsentence when it struck him.

Behind them on the dark road, Murphy suddenly realized they had stopped, for he was gradually catching up. The two dark clumps were not moving—waiting for him to catch up perhaps—so he guided Nosy off the side of the road and prepared to defend himself. Still the dark shapes remained in the same spot, no longer moving. An ambush, maybe? Then they suddenly disappeared. There were no more dark shapes, only the total darkness of the night. That could mean they had left the road and were now doubling back to ambush him.

Retreat like a wise man, or charge ahead like a fool? he wondered. "This whole thing is a fool's mission, so I might as well take my chances," he muttered to himself. He pulled his rifle as he dismounted and walked, leading his horse toward the spot where the dark clumps had disappeared.

Straining to see through the darkness, he continued to advance until he came to a break in the bushes beside the road. He felt certain that he was close to the spot where the two riders had disappeared, and it suddenly struck him. He walked through the break in the bushes and discovered a trail leading away from the road. That was why they had suddenly stopped. They had wanted to be sure this was the trail they were looking for. He almost laughed to think what a mystery he had created over it. *But now I've got to catch up with them again*, he thought.

He found out immediately that it was much more difficult to keep the two riders in sight on the small Indian trail. It led into the tall, rugged hills of granite and limestone, with many exposed rocks and boulders that made for perfect ambush sites. When he was going through a long grove of live oak trees, the trail became so narrow and winding that he was forced to slow down to make sure he did not suddenly catch up to them. In the middle of the grove of oaks, he came upon a strong stream flowing down a narrow valley formed between two tall granite hills.

He had been riding the Indian trail for quite some time

by then with no sight of the two men he followed, so he dismounted and let Nosy drink from the stream while he tried to examine the trail. He took a knee so he could determine if there were fresh hoofprints on the trail. The recent appearance of a full moon helped a little to assure him that the two horses he was following had not turned off before reaching that point. He felt the hoofprints with his hand to make sure they were fresh. With no choice but to continue, he started to get back in the saddle, then hesitated when he discovered an even smaller trail beside the stream, one leading up toward the top of the valley. Something told him this was the trail to the hideout. To confirm this, he crossed over the stream, stepping from rock to rock. As he suspected, there were no fresh hoofprints on the other side of the stream. The hideout was somewhere up this stream. The question was, how far? So he climbed back into the saddle to find out.

He climbed another fifty feet before he got a glimpse of the cabin beside the stream. He could see the glow of a fire burning behind the cabin, so he rode up a little closer before stopping. "This is about as far as you need to go, boy," he said and got down from the saddle. It was time to find out if Jake Pike and Maggie Tatum were here or if he had just wasted the whole night seeing that two drifters got home safely. If it was the latter, he gave serious thought about not returning to Newtown. It didn't take long before he had the answer to his question.

Remaining on the side of the stream opposite that of the cabin, he worked his way up to a position above the backyard of the cabin, where the fire was burning. There was no sight of anyone in the yard, but he could hear the voices of men talking in the small barn across the yard. Ron and Hank had just arrived, so it made sense that they were taking care of their horses. He saw no sign of Jake Pike or the woman, which was a bitter disappointment, but he remained where he was, thinking he was going to have to get a look inside the cabin before he admitted his failure. The horses taken care of, the two men he had trailed to this hideout came out of the barn, followed by Jake Pike. Murphy felt his muscles tense. He was here! But where was the woman? Had the animal killed her?

The three men were all talking at once as they walked back toward the fire. From his position on the other side of the stream, he couldn't understand what they were talking about. But evidently, it was amusing, for they were laughing as a result. The woman, Maggie Tatum, where was she? She had to be there, unless Pike had killed her. Murphy could feel the anger welling up inside him. Then they walked past the fire, over to the back porch of the cabin, and Pike untied a rope from the corner post. Then he put the rope over his shoulder and walked away from the porch, dragging the woman out from under it, the rope tied around her neck.

Thinking she was dead, Murphy gripped his rifle so hard his knuckles were white. But she struggled to her feet when Pike cursed at her and threatened her with his pistol.

"I swear," Hank said, "you sure got a special way with women, but you ain't left much for your partners, have you?"

"Since when have you two coyotes got so particular?" Pike asked. "But I reckon I done got all the good out of 'er. I'm done with her. Be my guest."

Hank and Ron each grabbed an arm and stood Maggie up on her feet. "Don't look so skeered, darlin'," Hank said. "You might enjoy a ride with me after puttin' up with Pike."

"Who said you was first?" Ron said. "She don't look like she can go two times. We're gonna flip a coin."

He was stunned then when he heard the slug impact Hank's chest and the sound of the rifle at almost the same time. "What the hell?" He gasped when Hank released Maggie and stumbled a couple of steps before collapsing. In the next second, he felt the impact on his own chest and his knees suddenly felt weak and he sank to the ground.

Pike was terrified, not sure which way to run. He drew his six-gun and looked right and left, then decided to run for the cabin. He made it to the back steps before Murphy's third shot struck him in the back and he fell face forward on the porch.

Murphy came out from behind the bushes where he had hidden. Seeing both Hank and Ron struggling to pull their weapons, he pulled his six-gun and methodically finished them off with a shot to the back of the head for each one of them.

Then he walked over to the porch steps where Pike was lying facedown. When Murphy turned him over, Pike was holding a pocket pistol, and it was aimed at him.

Murphy grabbed his hand and jammed the pistol up under Pike's chin and squeezed the trigger.

Only then did he go to Maggie. He lifted her up from the ground as if she were a small child. "You're gonna be all right now. It's all over, and nobody else is gonna hurt you. All right?"

She nodded her head rapidly.

"Otis is waiting to take care of you," he continued. "But I think we better rest you up some before we go back home. I'll see what I can find inside to fix you a little something to eat. Then while you're restin', I'll clean up this mess here."

With tears streaming down her battered face, she tried to speak but could not seem to form the words she wanted to say.

"Just rest now." He tried to reassure her. "Ain't nobody gonna hurt you now," he repeated. "I'll take you inside, and you can lie down and rest while I see if I can find something for you to eat."

He stepped over Pike's body and started to go into the cabin. She immediately clutched his neck and started to whimper. He saw at once that she did not want to go back inside that cabin, and he could only imagine what she must have suffered in there.

"I shoulda thought of that," he said. "You don't have to go back in there. I'll fix up a place for you to lie down out on the front porch. All right?"

She nodded and relaxed in his arms, so he went back down the steps and walked around the cabin to the front porch. "I'm gonna set you down right here while I go inside and see what I can find to make you comfortable. I'll be right back," he said. Then he saw the threat of panic in her eyes. "All right?"

She nodded, having yet to speak a word since he had appeared. He lowered her gently to the porch floor to sit with her back against the cabin wall. He went inside the cabin then.

He understood her reluctance to revisit the inside of the cabin, for there was ample evidence of the torture she must have endured. There were four bunks in the front room, three of them obviously in use, the other one with a straw mattress rolled up. Murphy glanced in disgust at the one that must have been Pike's. *It's a miracle that poor girl's still alive*, he thought.

Aware now that she didn't want to come into contact with anything Pike or his two friends had touched, he took a blanket from the bed farthest from Pike's and folded it neatly. Then he lifted the rolled-up mattress off the fourth bunk and took them both out to the porch. "We're in luck," he announced. "I got the mattress off the extra bunk in there, and I found a blanket on a shelf, so you're all set." He unrolled the mattress and laid it down. Then he picked her up again and placed her on it. Since she was not very tall, the mattress was plenty long enough to position her down from one end of it, so he could fold that end under to form a makeshift pillow.

Once she seemed comfortable with that, he spread the blanket over her and said, "You just rest up now. Let yourself go to sleep if you can. There ain't nobody anywhere around here but you and me, and I ain't gonna be sleepin'. I'm gonna walk about thirty yards down the stream to get my horse and bring him up here. And that's the only time I'll be gone . . . maybe five minutes. The rest of the time, I'll be right here, gettin' rid of those three men, just like they never existed. Okay?"

She smiled faintly for the first time since he'd found her, nodded her head, and soundlessly formed the words *Thank you.*

He smiled and nodded back, then went back down the stream to get his horse. When he got back to the cabin, he checked to make sure Maggie was all right, and she seemed to be sleeping. He figured she was probably so exhausted she couldn't help passing out. So that was good: he could take care of the bodies and the horses while she slept. *I just hope to hell they weren't expecting any more of their friends tonight*, he thought.

He went into the cabin to get the one lantern burning, and while he was there, he checked the supply of food in a couple of open packs. There was bacon and flour, salt and sugar, coffee, and some dried peaches. *That'll do us just fine*, he thought, since he was planning to fix only one meal before they went back to town.

He took the lantern and then went out to the barn and the corral to look through their packs and saddlebags. Finding nothing of value, he emptied one of the large canvas bags and went back outside to search the bodies for anything useful. He put guns and cartridge belts into the bag, along with a considerable sum of money. *That's gonna help my expenses, boys, since Newtown don't seem to be making much progress in paying me*, he thought.

Once he had searched them, he went about the business of taking care of the three bodies. He had no intention of digging a grave for such obvious mistakes of their birth mothers. But he wanted to take them out of Maggie's sight, as well as to a place where the buzzards could easily dine upon them. Farther down the hill, away from the stream, seemed a good place to stage the feast. So he loaded the bodies on the backs of two of the horses in the corral and led them down the narrow valley until he found an easy place to go over the low ridge that formed one side of the valley. He decided there wasn't going to be any better place, so he went over the ridge and dumped them.

When he led the two horses back up to the cabin, he put them back in the corral, then went to check on Maggie. She was evidently totally unconscious, her breathing steady and rhythmic. He decided she was going to sleep all night, and that was a good thing. He wished her sweet dreams, far away from the nightmare she knew when awake.

He thought maybe it would be a good idea if he got a little sleep, as well. It had been a long day and part of a night. He took his pocket watch out of his pocket and walked over to the lantern to see what time it was. "Damn," he mumbled in surprise. It was already four thirty. It was getting along toward getting-up time. He had no idea it had taken the whole night to get everything done. Maybe he had neglected to wind his watch, and it had stopped at four thirty that afternoon. He held it up to his ear and heard the steady ticking of the timepiece. How long would the girl sleep? He wanted to be awake and ready to fix something for her to eat when she woke up. Even though she was sleeping soundly, and had been for a long time now, she might wake up any minute. And when she did, he wanted to make some coffee for her and cook something for her to put in her stomach, then take her home.

He decided to see if he could catch an hour or two before she woke up, so he put a little more wood on the fire in the backyard to keep it going all night. There was a little iron stove in the kitchen, and he planned to do the cooking on it, so he carried some small wood into the cabin. He took the coffeepot to the stream and rinsed it out, then filled it with water for coffee in the morning. As a precaution, he carried his rifle out to the porch, along with the blanket from the bunk that had belonged to either Ron or Hank. He wrapped the blanket around his shoulders and sat down on the other side of the door from Maggie, with his back against the wall.

He didn't know how long he had slept, but when he woke up, he was at once alarmed, for a tiny ray of light was shining right in his eyes. He blinked a few times, trying to get rid of it, before he realized it was sunshine. It was morning! And he had slept right through sunrise. He looked toward the other side of the doorway, and the straw mattress was empty. Maggie was gone! He jumped up, pulling the blanket from his shoulders, and charged into the cabin. She was not there! He ran through the cabin and out the back door, and she was nowhere to be found, so he ran to the little barn, but she was not there, either.

She must have awakened after he dozed off, and, in the state she'd been in, seen him guarding her and decided to escape. Either that, he thought, or some more of Jake Pike's friends had come in and stolen her right out from under his nose. He discarded that notion because had that been the case, he would still be sitting on the porch, with his throat cut. So he was back to the theory that she had awakened and, in her panic, had run for her life. He started to go back to the front porch, thinking maybe he'd see her tracks and get an idea which way she had fled.

"Were you going to cook on the stove?"

The sound of a woman's voice stopped him in his tracks. Shocked speechless for a moment, he turned to see Maggie coming from behind the barn and realized where she had been. Hoping she had not guessed what he had feared, he replied, "Yes, that was what I planned to do. I was lookin' to see if there was an old bucket in that barn, so I could use it to get a fire going in the stove."

"I can do the cooking," Maggie said, "if you get a fire started in that stove."

"Are you sure you feel like it?" Murphy asked. "You've been through a helluva lot. I didn't figure you'd come back this strong."

"I'm sure," she said. "I know that I am safe with you. You have saved my life twice, and I don't know how I can repay you for that. When I woke up this morning and saw you sitting on the porch, I knew I was all right."

"Even though I was asleep?" he couldn't resist asking.

"I knew everything was all right, or you wouldn't have been asleep," she said. "I know you must have been up most of the night, until it was safe for you to sleep. So I tried to get up without waking you. Thank you for coming to get me again," she said humbly.

"You're welcome," he said. "Now, I wanna fix you something to eat and take you wherever you wanna go." He had heard Otis Crutcher's version of their relationship, and he wanted to hear hers to see if it was the same.

"I wanna go back to Otis's farm," she said without hesitation. "Otis and I want to start a new life together."

"Good," he said. "That's what Otis told me, so that's where I'll take you. Let's get some breakfast started. I'll get that fire going in the stove."

"All right," she responded. "That old bucket you were looking for is settin' behind the barn."

"Right. I knew I saw it around the barn somewhere," he lied. "I'll get it."

He walked around the barn and saw a beat-up old bucket sitting by the back corner, not far from a damp spot on the ground. He picked it up and banged it against the side of the barn until a cake of dirt fell out to reveal a jagged hole in the bottom. He put enough of the dirt back in it to cover the hole and took the bucket over to the fire in the yard. The fire had died down to a small stack of burning sticks and branches, which he carefully transferred to the bucket, along with some glowing hot embers. These he took hurriedly into the cabin before the bucket got too hot to handle and dumped it into the stove. He then arranged some of the fresh firewood over the burning remains of the outside fire. In a few short minutes, the new firewood was blazing and the little stove was ready to cook on.

"I'll smash some of these beans and get us some coffee started," he volunteered. "I cleaned the pot out last night and filled it with fresh water. If you're sure you feel like cookin', I got some of the stuff out of their packs that they were eatin'. I didn't find but a few things worth messin' with. You might see more possibilities."

She took over the cooking with a positive spirit, which was hard for Murphy to believe, considering her bruised and battered physical appearance. She had come so close to the moment of her death that she had accepted it. Now to have been spared from a horrible execution, she felt she had been sent an angel in disguise, and she wanted to show her appreciation by brightening Otis Crutcher's lonely life. And as anxious as she was to leave this outlaw hideout, she thought it was best to eat before starting back to Otis's farm. So she cooked their breakfast and freed Murphy to prepare the horses for the trip back to town.

When they were ready to leave, Murphy was tempted to burn the place down but decided to let it stand on the possibility that an honest family might find it. Then he picked a gentle horse for Maggie and led her and the extra horses down the narrow valley.

"Well, I'll be . . . Look comin' yonder!" Bert Walker exclaimed to Paul Mathers as they stood talking beside Mathers's corral.

Mathers turned to look where Bert pointed. "I swear, speak of the devil and up he pops. I told you he'd be back."

"He sure had me worried," Bert said. "I'm sure glad to see him. I didn't know what to tell Baxter or Bradshaw." They watched the two riders and the string of horses as they approached from the north road. "Who is that behind him? It looks like a woman." Then Bert recognized her. "That's that little gal that works at Pratt's Saloon. Boy, I can't wait to hear this story."

"What in the world would he be doin' with Maggie Tatum?" Mathers asked. "It was because of something between her and that Pike feller that caused Murphy to throw him in that smokehouse."

They stepped away from the corral rails to meet them. "Cullen," Mathers acknowledged when he pulled his horse to a stop.

"Mornin', Paul, Bert," Murphy returned. "I've got a few extra horses I'd like to leave with you. Those last four behind her horse. I need to take Maggie out to Otis Crutcher's farm right away, so I'll come back later and we'll settle up, if that's all right with you."

"Sure, Cullen, whatever you say," Mathers replied. "I'll take care of 'em. Where'd you pick 'em up?"

"I don't know exactly. Somewhere back up in the hills northwest of here," Murphy answered honestly. "I'll tell you the story when I get back." He really didn't want to talk about Maggie's horrible experience when she was right there to hear it.

"You coming right back?" Bert asked.

"Yep, I'll be right back, by dinnertime, I reckon," Murphy answered. "I have to ride out to Otis Crutcher's farm and back. Did you have any problems?"

"No, not a one," Bert replied. "It was an unusually quiet night."

"Well, there you go," Murphy responded. "It's kinda obvious that I must be the problem here. Maybe I oughta go on back to my cabin on the river."

"Don't even think about it," Bert said.

"I 'preciate you takin' care of things while I was gone," Murphy told him. "I'll buy your dinner when I get back if you meet me at Irene's."

I can afford it, he thought, thinking about the money he had found when he'd searched the outlaws' bodies. So far, he had no firm commitment from the town council regarding his compensation as the town marshal, but as long as he kept showing a profit, he wasn't worried about a salary. He supposed he could try to find out where the money came from that he'd found in the saddlebags of men like Jake Pike and Clyde Fry, but he wasn't sure he was that good a detective. If he was religiously honest, he supposed he could turn any monies he found over to the town council, but he knew he was not that righteous.

"Right," Bert called after him as he wheeled Nosy and rode away. "I'll meet you at Irene's." He turned to Mathers then and said, "I wonder what he has to go to Otis Crutcher's place for."

"To take Maggie Tatum there, I expect," Mathers answered. "That's where I heard she was staying now." He paused, then said, "She sure as hell looked in pretty rough shape."

"You don't suppose he . . . ?" He couldn't bring himself to finish the question. "But where did he get the extra horses?"

"Ain't no tellin'," Mathers replied. "He seems to come by 'em naturally. I quit askin'."

Murphy knew how to find the road Otis's farm was on, but he needed Maggie to tell him which house was his. When they got there, Maggie didn't wait for Murphy to help her down.

She jumped from the saddle and ran into the house. Murphy waited and held her horse. In a few seconds, she came back outside and announced, "He isn't here. I'll bet he's down at that lower field he's been clearing."

"Hop back on your horse," he said. "Let's go find him."

He pulled Nosy up close enough to her to reach down and take her elbow to help her up in the saddle. Then he followed her as she rode down the lane beside the cornfield. They rode down past the cleared field to the end, where the scrub and bushes began. Otis was working with an axe when he heard the horses coming down the lane. When he saw who was riding the first horse, he dropped his axe and ran to meet her, waving his arms wildly.

Murphy reined Nosy back to a walk and let Maggie go along ahead of him. "I believe they're glad to see each other," he said to Nosy as Maggie came off the horse into Otis's arms. Her momentum took both of them to the ground, and they rolled over and over, laughing like two kids. Their reaction upon seeing each other caused Murphy to laugh, as well. He turned the big bay gelding around and started back up the lane.

"Cullen, wait!" Maggie yelled.

He hesitated, then stopped.

When they caught up to him, she said, "You can't just ride off like that. We both wanna tell you how much we appreciate what you've done for us."

"You already did," Murphy told her, "and I'm just as glad I was able to bring you home."

"I need to thank you," Otis said. "I don't know if I can ever repay you for what you've done. If I'd lost Maggie, I weren't even gonna try to stay alive anymore. You gave my life back to me. How can I ever pay you back for this?"

"Easy," Murphy said. "Just treat her right and take care of her. You do that and it would square things with me. All right?"

"Yes, sir," Otis exclaimed, "you can count on that."

"I'd best be gettin' back to town now," Murphy said. "I told Bert Walker I'd meet him for dinner." He turned his horse again and started toward the road.

"Wait!" Maggie called after him again. "You forgot the horse!"

"That's your horse," Murphy called back. "It's a wedding present." He nudged Nosy with his heels, and the big bay broke into a lope.

Chapter 14

It was just a little past noon when Murphy pulled his horse up behind Bradshaw's Saloon and went in the back entrance to Irene's café. Bert was already there and had been ever since Bonnie had turned the sign around to OPEN. He raised his hand to signal Murphy, and when Murphy walked over to the table and sat down, he asked, "Did Maggie stay there?"

"Yep," Murphy answered. "That's where she's been stayin', and now she's back home with Otis."

Their conversation was interrupted at that point when Ginger came out of the kitchen with Murphy's coffee. "You didn't show up for breakfast this morning," she announced. "Did you have trouble getting out of bed, or have you found someplace you like better?"

"I reckon I just wasn't hungry this mornin'," he said, "so I just made myself some coffee and let it go at that."

Bonnie arrived at the table then with his dinner.

"Thank you, Bonnie," he greeted her. "Ginger was just telling me how much you ladies missed me this mornin'."

"She did, did she?" Bonnie replied. "I didn't know you weren't here."

He shook his head and asked, "Who taught you to lie with a straight face like that?"

She laughed and went back to the kitchen. Murphy looked back at Bert, who was staring at him with a mischievous grin on his face. It struck him then. Surely Bert couldn't be thinking such a ridiculous thought; however, his next question confirmed it.

"Listen, Cullen, just tell me it ain't none of my business and I won't mention it again, but I gotta ask the question. Where did you and Maggie go last night?"

Murphy just stared at him for a long second, hardly able to believe Bert could ask such a question. Then he admitted to himself that Bert's conclusions were his fault for all the secrecy he had insisted upon because he had not wanted to share the fact that he was committing himself totally on a hunch. Now that Maggie was safe, almost strictly because of shear dumb luck, he could tell him about the events of his night away from the town. The mayor and Bradshaw might be very upset with his tendency to go on a wild-goose chase, but they could not deny the fact that a young woman's life was saved and three outlaws were eliminated.

"All right, Bert, here's the whole story. Jake Pike went out to Otis Crutcher's farm yesterday and abducted Maggie Tatum. Otis rode into town to tell me. And this is where the story gets hard to believe, unless you believe in dumb luck." He went on to tell Bert the whole story and his reasons for not telling anyone he was going to follow two strangers who had just ridden into town that day. After he finished, he confessed that he had no clue as to where Pike had taken Maggie. His hunch was the only possibility he had, and it was sheer luck that it was a correct one.

"Man, that was a helluva hunch," Bert declared. "One in a million chance of being the right one." He shook his head slowly back and forth while he thought about the dumb assumption he had made. "I hope you didn't think I thought . . ." He hesitated to say it. "I mean with Maggie being a saloon girl, she most likely wouldn't mind showin' her appreciation if you was to . . . but you being . . . And you had to shoot all three of them?"

"I had no choice," Murphy answered. "They were in the process of harming her. It was the only chance I had to stop it." That might have been true, or he might have had an opportunity to arrest them. The fact of the matter was he had given no thought toward arresting the three men. To him, it was no different from if he had chanced upon three rabid wolves attacking a woman. The solution to save the woman was to put the wolves down and rid the world of three beasts who might go on to attack other helpless victims.

"So those two cattle buyers turned out to be friends of Jake Pike," Bert said. "How 'bout that? How 'bout that?" he repeated, his thoughts actually captured by the bold action the man had taken to hunt the perpetrators down and execute them, judge, jury, and executioner. *Murphy's Law*, he thought but did not say it. Bert knew enough about the law to know that if he was the town marshal, his jurisdiction would be the city limits of Newtown, and he would have no authority to make arrests outside the city limits. He would have to be appointed to the office of county sheriff before he could arrest anyone outside the town limits. So actually, Murphy had committed a crime, if you looked at it the way a judge would.

Lost in his thoughts, Bert happened to glance directly at him and realized Murphy was studying him with a question on his face. "What?" Bert responded.

"I thought I lost you there for a minute," Murphy said. "Where'd you wander off to?"

"Oh," Bert replied, "I don't know. I was just trying to remember if I locked the gate when I left the forge to come down here."

"You been havin' trouble with somebody comin' in your shop when you ain't there?" Murphy asked.

"No, not at all," Bert quickly answered, wishing he'd thought of something else to say. "It's just that when some of the folks come to town, they turn their young'uns loose to wander all over the place. And I'd hate for some of 'em to mess around my forge when I'm not there."

"I wouldn't worry about it today," Murphy said. "I didn't notice any kids runnin' around today, so far." He wondered what was really on Bert's mind. A few minutes later he found out.

"You know what, Cullen? It might not be a good idea to tell Baxter or Bradshaw about trackin' those three outlaws down and killin' 'em. I mean, it being outside the town limits, where a town marshal wouldn't have any jurisdiction. They might be a little worried about you shootin' three men down instead of arrestin' 'em, and without any witnesses."

Murphy shrugged, unconcerned. "Maggie Tatum was a witness. I expect she could tell 'em why it had to be done that way. Besides, I ain't worried about their opinion, anyway."

"Yeah?" Bert exclaimed. "Well, I am!"

"You are?" Murphy responded, surprised. "Why are you worried?"

"'Cause if they decide they shouldn't hire you as the marshal, I'm afraid they're gonna want me to take the job. And I ain't ready to!"

Murphy cast an impatient glance at him. "Why in the world do you say that? You're a strong young man. You ain't cross-eyed, and you've got good hearin'. You're wearin' a decent sidearm now since you started carryin' that 1860 Colt Army model." He paused then, and his glance changed to one of suspicion. "How many times have you fired that gun?"

"Oh, I've fired it a couple of times already," Bert assured him.

"A couple of times?" Murphy responded. "A couple of times?" he repeated. Then he shook his head as if exasperated, and his mind suddenly went back to his days in the army training new recruits. "You've got to get to know that gun like it's your sweetheart," he preached. "You need to know what it can do and what it can't do and if you can depend on it if you get in a tight spot. How you gonna know that if you don't spend some time with it?"

"I've been meanin' to do some practicin' with it," Bert replied in his defense, "but I just seem to be pretty busy at the shop. You oughta know that, with all them hinges and iron straps for your jailhouse."

Murphy couldn't stifle a chuckle. "Yeah, I reckon you have been, at that," he allowed. "I'll tell you what. Why don't we ride down the river a ways tomorrow and do a little target practice? And we'll see if you and that Colt are a good marriage."

"Why don't we do it this afternoon?" Bert responded. "You got anything goin' on?"

Murphy hesitated while he thought about it. "No, I reckon not," he answered.

"Other than doing the job of town marshal and protecting the citizens of Newtown," Bonnie said, having overheard his response. "What are we supposed to do if somebody comes in and robs us while you're out in the woods, practicing?"

Murphy smiled at her. "Same thing you did before I came back from the war," he said. "Call your mama and she'll come running with her shotgun." Bonnie didn't find his comment amusing, so he said, "Fact of the matter is, I've agreed to a temporary job as marshal, but the council has yet to offer me the job. I think they prefer Bert, so it's important to make sure he's familiar with his new weapon."

She pretended to be unimpressed, so he continued to tease her. "Anyway, the town council isn't payin' for my meals here, so I don't have to protect the dinin' room."

"Is that so?" she replied, then looked at Bert. "Just as a suggestion, Mr. Walker. You should be very careful when you eat here not to get your plate mixed up with Reverend Murphy's.

There's no telling what might have fallen accidentally into his food."

"You heard that, Bert," Murphy said, pretending alarm. "If anything happens to me, you know who to arrest and send to prison."

Bert shook his head. "I don't know, Cullen. She might put up a fight."

Bert went by his forge to make sure no one was seeking blacksmith services, and when there was no one, he saddled his horse and went back down Front Street to the jail. Murphy locked the jail and got on his horse. Nosy was still saddled, since Murphy had planned to take him to the stable after he ate dinner. The big bay had traveled more than a few miles since the night just passed, but he had been watered and rested ever since Murphy got back in town. But in order not to push the horse too far, they rode only a little over a mile from town.

They picked a heavily wooded stretch along the riverbank in which to conduct their target practice. Murphy pointed out targets of different sizes and distances away. He started with the targets which were farther away from them, at what he considered the longest shot to expect any accuracy from a pistol. Bert performed very well at the longer range—after a few shots to determine his Colt's tendency to shoot low or high, right or left—when he had the time to take dead aim and used his left hand to steady his gun hand. Then Murphy had him shoot at different trees to his right and left, but he hurried his shots, still trying to take dead aim when there was less time to do it. Next, Murphy pointed out targets at close range, similar to the distance across a saloon floor and even closer. Bert's tendency was still to hold the weapon with both hands, and he could not keep up with the time when Murphy called out targets quickly, shifting quickly from one direction to another.

So Murphy tried to plant the notion in Bert's mind that he

didn't have to consciously think about aiming the gun in a close-up situation. Instead, Murphy instructed him to mentally throw his shots with one hand, as if he was merely pointing at the target with his trigger finger. In a short time, Bert was spinning right and left, nailing targets as quickly as Murphy called them out. By the time they were finished, Bert already had a sense of the feel a real gunslinger felt, that his sidearm was not just an object you picked up to shoot something with. When you drew it, it became an extension of your arm. Murphy was well satisfied with Bert's natural motion after the brief practice session. *Now, if he can remember to pull the trigger, he might be ready to take over the job of marshal*, he thought.

When they returned to town, Murphy took his horse to the stable, while Bert went back to his shop, where he found a stranger waiting to have his horses shod.

"I thought you were out of business, thought I was gonna have to go hunt you down, and I was hopin' I wouldn't find you in a saloon. You do shoe horses, right?"

"Yes, sir," Bert replied, "I shoe horses. I hope you haven't had to wait too long. I ain't usually away from my shop very long, but you caught me when I had to go somewhere with the town marshal."

He stepped down from his horse and looped the reins around a fence post. He took a casual look at the stranger and immediately knew he wasn't a cowhand. Dressed in black from his boots to the modified derby hat on his head, he wore a black hand-tooled gun belt with a fast-draw holster, secured to his leg with a rawhide string. He rode a black horse and led a gray packhorse.

It wouldn't be too hard to guess what this fellow's favorite color is, Bert thought. "This your first visit to Newtown?" he asked.

"Yeah, that's right, first time in your little town. I heard it was startin' to collect a few more people, so I thought I'd ride out here and take a look for myself. You said you were gone somewhere with the town marshal. I didn't think Newtown had a marshal, so I wondered about that when I rode by the jail on my way up the street."

"Fact of the matter is we don't officially have a town marshal yet, but the town council is workin' on it. Right now, it's a question of how much we can levy taxes on the businesses to pay a marshal's salary. So in the meantime, we have a good man to fill in until we hire one."

"Is his name Murphy?" the stranger asked.

"Yes, it is," Bert replied, surprised. "How'd you know that?"

The stranger smiled. "Just a guess," he said. "Word travels pretty fast about things like that. I heard he killed Rafer Polk. Is that a fact?"

"That's a fact," Bert said. "Rafer didn't give Murphy much choice in the matter. He kept causin' trouble. He even came here to my place to shoot me. This is where Murphy finally killed Rafer Polk."

"What was he gonna shoot you for?" the stranger asked, truly curious.

"I don't know," Bert said, not particularly interested in recreating that scene for the stranger's amusement. "Probably because I've helped some in controlling criminal activity in the town. But Murphy's the man who gets the job done."

"And he's not on the payroll?" the stranger asked.

"Not yet, anyway," Bert answered. "He said from the beginnin' that he didn't want the job as marshal, but there ain't nobody as qualified as he is." He paused then before leading the black horse over near his forge to take a look at its hooves. "Excuse my manners. Welcome to Newtown. My name's Bert Walker, Mr. . . ." He waited for his reply.

"Liam Black," the stranger said, pronouncing the name very distinctly, as if he wanted Bert to remember it.

There was no response from Bert other than a "Pleased to meetcha."

So Black shrugged and said he was going to visit one of the saloons for a drink of whiskey while he waited for Bert to shoe his horses. He asked Bert for a recommendation, and Bert naturally suggested Bradshaw's Saloon and pointed out the fact that it was also the best place for a good meal.

"There ain't no other restaurant-type places in town, and there ain't no hotel. But if you're stayin' over and wanna sleep in a bed, there is a roomin' house on that side street beside the post office. Pearl Johnson owns it, and it's decent."

Black thanked him for the information and walked back down the street toward Bradshaw's Saloon. As he looked the town over, he thought that maybe Chad Tucker's report about Cullen Murphy was basically true. Tucker was a small-time outlaw, and Black believed him when he said he had missed being a victim of Murphy's because he had had better sense than to accompany Clyde Fry and Loafer Creech in their plan to bushwhack him.

It pleased Black to notice that the people he passed on the street all took second looks at him as he walked past them. It was not simply because he was a stranger. He knew it was more than that. It was because of the way he looked and dressed and moved like a well-oiled killing machine. When he got to Bradshaw's Saloon, he reached down and eased his Colt Army revolver up and down to make sure it was riding free and easy as he looked over the batwing doors. He thought it best to take a look at the barroom he was walking into to make sure there were no surprises. *Peaceful enough*, he decided and pushed on through the doors.

Pete Brice saw him when he stepped into the room. Unlike Bert's innocent appraisal of the stranger, Pete's first thought was, *Here comes a stick of dynamite just looking for somebody to light his fuse.* "Howdy," he said. "Welcome to Bradshaw's. What's your poison?"

"I'm partial to a drink of rye whiskey, if you've got some that hasn't been watered down too much," Black answered.

"The whiskey we serve at the bar comes right outta the bottle it arrived in," Pete told him. "We don't cut our whiskey here at Bradshaw's. If you still don't want to risk it, I'll open a new bottle for you and pour you a drink outta that one."

Black smiled at him and replied, "That won't be necessary. You seem like an honest man. I'll take your word for it."

Pete reached behind him, picked up a half-full bottle of rye, and poured a drink. Then he slid it over toward the stranger and waited. Black picked up the glass and passed it under his nose a couple of times, then tossed it down. He set the glass back on the bar and said, "You're a man of your word, Mr. . . ." He paused.

"Pete Brice," he answered. "Everything's been cut back and watered down so much ever since the war, but Mr. Bradshaw says we oughta draw the line when it comes to a man's drink of likker."

"Well said," Black replied. "Pour me another one and I'll drink to Mr. Bradshaw." He turned to look around the barroom again while Pete poured his second drink.

"What brings you to our little town, Mr. . . . ?" He paused, but the stranger didn't reply at once, so he continued. "You just passin' through on your way to somewhere else?"

Black turned back to face him, picked up the glass, and held it up as if in a toast. "To Mr. Bradshaw," he said and tossed the whiskey down. "My name's Liam Black, and I heard about this little town of yours. I'm always interested to check on any word of a new town in a part of the state where there wasn't a town of any size before. Right now, I'm killin' a little time while your blacksmith is fixing my horses up with some new shoes."

"What line of business are you in, Mr. Black?" Pete asked.

"I'm a facilitator," Black said, drawing a blank stare from Pete.

"You're a what?" Pete asked, thinking that was a name for a gunslinger he had never heard of before.

"A facilitator," Black repeated. "I'm not surprised that it's an occupation you're not familiar with. It's a term more often used in the large cities up north. Maybe you'd be more familiar with an organizer or business consultant. It's not someone you'd often see in towns the size of Newtown."

Genuinely interested in where Black could possibly be going with that line of talk, Pete continued to question him. "I've gotta be honest with you, Mr. Black. I don't see how you could do much philer . . . fill-her . . ." He tried to remember the word but couldn't.

"Facilitator," Black repeated. "I'm a facilitator."

"Right," Pete said. "I don't see how you can *facilitate* anything with the stores and shops here in Newtown. We got hit hard by that damn war, and everybody's just tryin' to hang on till better times get here."

"You misunderstood me," Black said. "I won't try to sell anybody anything in Newtown. I work with big investors in New Orleans. My job in Newtown is to see what kind of businesses the town needs and tell the big investors if Newtown is a good bet to invest in. So I just thought I'd stop over for a couple of days to get a feel of the town."

"Oh," Pete responded, still not sure if Black was on the level or out to fleece some of the merchants in town. "You know ain't nobody got anything but Confederate paper to buy anything with, right?"

Black smiled. "Right," he said. "I'm not sellin' anything."

"It's a good thing you ain't," Pete concluded, " 'cause you'd go broke, like most of the rest of the town."

He decided his first impression of Black was more apt to be accurate. He was a gunslinger, and the only reason he'd come to Newtown was Murphy. Pete knew it was inevitable that word would get out about the outlaws who had come to their final end at the hands of Cullen Murphy. Tales of Murphy's Law had to have traveled through the outlaw population. And since it was inevitable, Pete had hoped it would cause outlaws and gunmen to stay away, instead of being drawn to Newtown in hopes of making a name for themselves.

If I had the guts to do it, I'd pull my shotgun out from under the bar and blow Liam Black to hell, he thought. He was glad when a couple of the saloon' s regulars came in and he had an excuse to move down to the other end of the bar to wait on them.

"Who's the slick gent at the other end of the bar?" Robert Jessop asked.

"He says his name is Liam Black," Pete said. "Bert Walker's shoeing his horses, and I expect he'll most likely leave 'em with you, Paul, since he says he's gonna hang around town for a couple of days."

"Did he say what for?" Paul Mathers asked.

"I'd have to let him tell you," Pete said. "He claims he's lookin' the town over to see what kind of businesses would do best here."

"Horse manure," Robert remarked. "He's a damn fast-draw gunslinger. He might as well be wearin' a sign sayin' 'Test me, sucker, if you feel like dyin'.' Look at the way he's wearin' that six-gun."

"He must be lost," Mathers remarked, "showin' up in Newtown." He gave Black a quick appraisal. "Unless you wanna try him out, Robert," he japed.

"He ain't lost," Pete declared. "Newtown ain't on the way to anywhere. Newtown is where he was headed. Think about how many gunmen have been killed in our little town this summer. He's come lookin' for the man who killed 'em."

"Murphy?" Mathers questioned. "Murphy ain't no gunslinger. He was acting more like a sheriff. He didn't participate in any fast-draw shoot-out with any of the men he killed. He ain't got no reputation as a fast gun."

"Maybe not," Pete insisted, "but the man who took Murphy down would sure as hell have one."

Neither Mathers nor Jessop replied to his comment as the possibility of it struck home with both of them. They were left to discuss it between them when Black signaled to Pete for another drink of whiskey and Pete moved back up the bar to accommodate him.

"I think that'll be enough whiskey before supper," Black told Pete as he reached for the money to pay for his drinks. "I'll go see how the blacksmith is coming along with my horses now, but I plan on comin' back here for supper. I see the door at the back of the saloon with the CLOSED sign. I take it that's the way to the dinin' room."

"Yes, sir," Pete replied, "that's the door to the café. One of the girls will flip the sign over to OPEN at five o'clock."

"I might have time to take my horses to the stable before they open the café. I noticed the stable is just past the blacksmith's shop."

"That's right," Pete said. "If you wanna talk to the owner of the stable, that's him down at the other end of the bar. Paul Mathers's his name. He's the one wearin' the flat-crowned hat."

"Good," Black remarked. "I'll go speak to him." He put the money for his whiskey on the bar and walked down to the other end.

"Mr. Mathers? My name is Liam Black. Pete said you own the stable up past the blacksmith's shop." Mathers nodded and said that he did, so Black continued. "I've got a couple of horses gettin' new shoes right now, and I'd like to have you take care of them for as long as I'm in town. I'm not sure how many days I'll be here. Two or three, I imagine. But I want to make sure my horses are well taken care of."

"Yes, sir, Mr. Black. I'm headin' back to the stable right after I have a little drink of likker," Mathers said. "I'll be glad to take care of your horses for you."

They watched him all the way until he disappeared between the two swinging doors of the saloon before Robert saw fit to comment. "Yessir, I think ol' Pete is right. If that man ain't a quick-draw gunslinger, he oughta be arrested for impersonatin' one. You know, I've heard tales of gunmen who make a name for themselves based on how fast they are in a duel with another idiot. But I ain't ever seen one. Have you?"

"No," Mathers answered, "unless we just saw one. What did he say his name was? Liam Black? We oughta go to the post office and see if Jim Anderson's got a wanted notice for anybody by that name."

"That's a good idea," Robert said. "Let's go."

They paid Pete and hurried out the door. Looking up the street, they could still see Black on his way to the blacksmith. They crossed the street and hustled down to the post office.

Jim Anderson was equally as interested to hear about the stranger in town as Mathers and Robert had been. "I don't keep all those wanted posters that come in anymore," Anderson told them. "Since Murphy built the jailhouse and marshal's office, I took all the old ones I had and gave them to Murphy. I figured he oughta be the one interested in 'em, not me."

They started to head out the door, but he stopped them when something occurred to him. "You know, if he was a real fast-draw gunman, he wouldn't necessarily be on a wanted poster unless the other fellow didn't know he was in a duel."

"Damn, that's right," Robert said. "If they go to face each other with the intent of settlin' an argument with their guns, it's a duel. And the winner of a duel ain't prosecuted by the law. Let's go see if Murphy's at the jail. We can go through those posters, anyway, just to see if there's one with Liam Black on it."

"You go ahead," Mathers said. "I think I'd best get back to the stable, just in case Bert's through with his horses and he takes them there. I told Black I'd be there to take care of his horses. If he's as deadly as he looks, I don't want to give him any reason to call me out."

"Wise thinkin'," Robert japed. "But don't take any guff from him."

CHAPTER 15

Murphy was in the process of cleaning his Henry rifle when Robert Jessop came into the marshal's office at the jail. "Robert," he greeted him. "What's up? You come back to admire your carpentry work again? Or are you finally here to admit you overcharged me and you brought some of my money back to me?"

"Neither one, Cullen. I thought I'd best let you know you may have some trouble in town, if you ain't already aware of it."

This captured Murphy's attention, so he laid his rifle down on his desk and waited to hear what was on Robert's mind.

"You ever hear of a man named Liam Black?"

Murphy shook his head.

"Well, a fellow who calls himself Liam Black rode into town this afternoon. He left his horses with Bert to get shoes, and then he came to Bradshaw's, where me and Paul Mathers were havin' a drink." He went on to relate their and Pete Brice's conversation with the stranger. "The thing of it is the man looks like a professional fast gun, dressed in black from head to toe and wearing his handgun in a quick-draw holster. He told Pete he was gonna stay in town for a few days, because he was wantin' to see if the town could handle some more businesses."

"Sounds pretty mysterious, all right," Murphy said. "But what do you want me to do about it? Did he threaten anybody or do any damage?"

"No, see, that's the thing that make us suspicious about this jasper," Robert insisted. "He's calm and polite to a fault."

"I can see where that would make you suspicious," Murphy said facetiously. "This might be that time when we have to call out the citizens' gunnysack gang and hang the sucker."

"You make light of it, but you ain't seen this fellow. Mathers and I both thought it was important to let you know about this stranger."

"You're right," Murphy said, "and I apologize. But I can't go out and arrest a stranger for being calm and polite to a fault. Accordin' to Baxter, they want the man to commit the crime before I arrest him for it. But I appreciate you tippin' me off about the stranger."

"Is it all right if I look through your wanted posters just to see if you've got anything on somebody named Liam Black?"

"Yeah, sure," Murphy said. He pulled a bottom drawer open, where he had been piling the posters. "Help yourself."

Robert took the whole stack out and pulled a stool, the only other piece of furniture in the office besides Murphy's desk and chair, up to the other side of the desk. He began leafing through the wanted papers while Murphy continued to clean his rifle.

Murphy finished cleaning his rifle and placed it back on the rack he had made for it on the wall right behind his chair. He glanced over at Robert, who was almost to the bottom of the posters, and it occurred to him that this was one of the reasons he had no real desire to be the town marshal.

"No luck, huh?" he asked when Robert got to the bottom sheet of paper. "You could still be right about the man," he told him. "He might be lightnin' fast with a six-gun, but if he played by the rules, he never committed murder if the other man was trying to kill him. And thanks for warning me. I'll keep a sharp eye."

It was approaching suppertime when Robert left the jail to go back to the sawmill, where his brother Frank's wife, Edith, would be cooking supper. Murphy locked up the jail and walked up the street to Bradshaw's Saloon, where he would indulge his desire for one drink of whiskey before he went into the dining room for supper.

"Have you seen Liam Black yet?" Pete asked him when he walked up to the bar.

"No, but Robert Jessop told me all about him," Murphy replied.

"What did you think?" Pete asked.

"About what?" Murphy asked in return.

Pete gave him a look of exasperation. "About what the hell a fast gun is lookin' for in Newtown."

"How do you know he's a fast gun?"

"By lookin' at him," Pete insisted, getting more and more frustrated by the second. "Have you seen him?"

Murphy said again that he had not.

So Pete said, "Well, that explains it. You'll see what I'm talkin' about. You just be damn careful around him."

"I will," Murphy said. "Can I have my drink now?"

"I reckon," Pete replied. "One ought not hurt you. You goin' in to eat supper now?"

Murphy said that he was.

"Good," Pete said. "It'd be a good idea to stay sober."

"Pete, I appreciate the fact that you're concerned about my welfare tonight, but I think it's gone far enough. You're cookin' up something in your mind based on the clothes a stranger is wearing. Make no mistake about one thing. I don't answer challenges to participate in duels. Only a damn fool does that. And I won't arrest anybody for what he's wearing, unless he ain't wearin' enough to cover his privates. So why don't we just welcome this stranger to our town until he does something that proves he doesn't deserve it?"

"I know you're right, Cullen," Pete replied patiently. "That's the attitude we all oughta have with strangers. But it don't pay for a man in your boots to be careless when a walkin' signboard rides into town."

"I'll try to stay out of his way," Murphy promised, tossed his drink of whiskey down, and went directly to the door of the dining room. When he opened the door, he was surprised to find Ginger Floyd standing just inside it. Without a word, she placed her hand on his chest and pushed him back out the door before closing it again behind her.

"Ginger!" he exclaimed, immediately alarmed. "What's wrong?"

"Thank goodness you didn't come in the back door today," she said, almost breathless. "I was afraid I wouldn't head you off."

"What is it, Ginger? What's goin' on?" He started to push by her, but she held on to his arm.

"Liam Black!" Ginger pronounced solemnly. "He's in the dining room, waiting for you!"

"What's he done?" Murphy asked. "Has he hurt anyone?"

"Not so far," she answered. "Right now, he's just sitting there eating supper."

"Why do you think he's waitin' for me?" Murphy asked. "Did he say he was waitin' for me?"

"Not to me he didn't, but Elmo Dillon said Paul Mathers told him that the stranger had come to town to have what he called a shoot-out with you. Elmo said that's what gunslingers call a duel. So the best thing for you is to go back to the jail and I'll send your supper over there."

"Ginger, I appreciate your concern for my life, but I don't want to eat my supper at the jail. Don't worry about your din-in' room. There ain't gonna be any shoot-out in the dinin' room, or anywhere else in town. So don't worry your head about it. You just carry on like you would any other night." He paused to think if there was anything else. "Did he ask about me or mention my name at all?"

"No," she answered. "I didn't hear him mention your name. He seemed to want us to know his name was Liam Black. Other than that, he just asked what we were serving for supper. He talked very politely, just like he was friendly as could be. But his eyes shifted with every sound, like he was watching every corner of the room."

He listened to her description of the stranger. It was the same as Robert Jessop's description but emphasized the man's manner more than his dress. He put more stock in her report, so he decided it might not be a bad idea to take a cautious approach upon meeting this dark stranger.

"Thank you again for warning me, Ginger. Let's go in now, and just do what you always do when I come in. I'll handle it so that nothing happens in the dining room. You tell Bonnie and your mama not to worry about it. If there's any trouble, we'll take it outside." He reached past her and opened the door, then went in first in case Liam Black was excited to the point where he might open fire at first sight.

It was easy to spot Liam Black simply by his all-black attire, accented by his coal-black hair and pencil-thin mustache. He paused his meal when Murphy walked into the room, and watched him until he sat down at a table near the kitchen door, Elmo Dillon having frantically signaled him to join him.

"Did you see him?" Elmo asked.

"Yeah," Murphy replied. "It'd be kinda hard not to. Wouldn't it?"

"Whaddaya gonna do?" Elmo asked.

"I'm gonna eat supper," Murphy replied. "What did you think I came in here for?"

"You know what I mean," Elmo insisted. "That gunslinger

came to town for one purpose only. And that was to add the name of Cullen Murphy to his list of kills."

"Did he tell you that?" Murphy asked, and Elmo said that of course he had not. So Murphy told him that he had no reason to ask the stranger anything as long as he made no trouble in Newtown.

Bonnie brought him his coffee, and Ginger brought his supper, served with grave expressions of concern from both sisters. Elmo had already finished eating, but he remained at the table while Murphy ate. Murphy also noticed that Liam Black finished his supper at almost the same time as Elmo had. And, like Elmo, Black remained at his table, even though Ginger had removed his dirty dishes and he had declined her offer of more coffee. It soon became obvious that Black was watching him and waiting for him to finish eating.

We might as well get this over with, he thought and told Elmo it might be best if he left the table now.

Elmo didn't question the suggestion. He got up and went to the kitchen to tell Ginger to remove Murphy's dirty dishes. Ginger went at once to the table.

"Leave the coffee cup," Murphy said. "I'm gonna want another cup." She gave him a worried nod and left the cup.

Evidently, this was a signal to Black that it was time to act, for he rose slowly to his feet, left some money in the middle of his table, then walked deliberately toward Murphy's table. Facing him directly, he stopped a few feet short of the table. Murphy felt sure Black was not fool enough to draw on him without warning while he was still sitting at the table. For it was obvious that Black's motivation was a reputation as a fast gun. There was a possibility that he was wrong, however, so that was the reason he had slipped his Colt .44 out of his holster and laid it in his lap, under the table.

"Are you Cullen Murphy, the acting town marshal?" Black asked.

"I am," Murphy replied.

"I wonder if I might have a few moments of your time?" Black asked politely. "I didn't want to bother you while you had your supper. I hope you didn't think I was staring at you."

Totally astonished for a couple of moments, Murphy recovered quickly and said, "Sure. What can I do for you?"

"Mind if I sit down?" Black asked.

"Have a seat," Murphy said. "I'm gonna have one more cup of coffee. You want a cup?" He didn't know whether to laugh or worry. This might be the most polite invitation to a gunfight he would ever get.

"No, thank you very much, but I'm afraid I might not be able to go to sleep tonight if I drink another cup of coffee. My name's Liam Black, and I always think it's a good idea to check in with the sheriff or marshal in any town I haven't been in before. For some reason, the law in some little western towns gets suspicious when I show up and hang around town for a few days. You see, I'm like a scout, if you will, who goes ahead of the column. But in my case, I'm here to see if it would be profitable to build a bank in Newtown. And I don't want the folks here to think I'm up to anything suspicious."

"I take it that's happened to you before," Murphy said. "Is that the case?"

"Yes, indeed it has, more than once."

"Have you got any idea why?" Murphy couldn't help but ask.

"Oh, yes, it's my outfit. It makes me look like an outlaw or something. But I kinda like to wear the clothes of the rugged West. My partner picked these clothes out for me. He said he wanted me to look like I belonged in the West."

"Where are you and your partner located?" Murphy asked.

Liam answered, "New Orleans."

"You rode all the way out here from New Orleans?"

"Oh, no, I came to Waco by train and stagecoach," Liam said. "But I rode all the way from Waco."

"Whose idea was it to wear that gun and fast-draw holster?" Murphy asked.

"That was my partner's idea, too," Liam said. "He said it might give me a little protection if I was wearing the gun. But don't worry. It's all right. It's not loaded."

"How well do you know your partner?" Murphy asked. "He might be tryin' to get you killed. My advice to you is to take that gun off before somebody expects you to use it. Your partner's right. You look like a real gunslinger, and the worst thing to have in a gunfight is an unloaded gun."

"I guess I should confess that I was enjoying the masquerade as a real western gunfighter. I even played the part with Mr. Walker, the blacksmith. But I ran into a real outlaw in a Waco saloon, and he thought I was a gunslinger. His name was Chad Tucker, and he told me about you and two outlaws who were going to kill you. I guess I just got carried away with my costume and my gun. I realize now that I could have been killed. I just thought those were exaggerated tales about all the gunfighters in the untamed West."

"They probably are exaggerated, but there are some desperate men roaming these hills and ranges, especially since the end of the war. And they'll shoot a man down to take what little bit he has. It's best not to tempt them." Ginger came to the table then with the coffeepot. "You sure you don't want another cup, Mr. Black?" Murphy asked, causing Ginger to react with a look of genuine astonishment.

"Oh, maybe I'll risk one more," Liam conceded. "I really enjoyed the supper, by the way," he said to Ginger.

She just stood there amazed until Murphy said, "He'll need another cup, Ginger."

"Of course," she replied and went to get a clean cup.

"I hope you'll find that Newtown is a perfect place to build a bank," Murphy said to Liam. "This town is goin' to grow sure as sin, and there's no bank here right now."

Ginger returned with another cup of coffee for Liam, and Murphy made it a point to sit there with him while they both finished their coffee. Murphy told him about the different people and businesses in the town and answered Liam's questions. Elmo came out of the kitchen before they got up from the table, and Murphy introduced them.

"Elmo's the town tailor," Murphy said. "He could probably make you an authentic western outfit that wouldn't tempt people to take a shot at you while you're here. But in the meantime, get rid of the gun, or load it if you don't. I need to take my after-supper walk around town now. If you want me to, I'll show you where Pearl Johnson's roomin' house is."

"I would appreciate that, Marshal," Liam said, and they walked out of the dining room to go back through the saloon.

As soon as they walked through the door, the noisy saloon went almost deadly quiet. Murphy knew at once that Pete had spread the word that a gunfighter had gone into the dining room to wait for him. At first sight of Black, the crowd drew away to give them a clear path out the door. It was kind of amusing to Murphy, so he didn't say anything. He just kept walking toward the door, with Liam beside him. Everything remained quiet until they had almost reached the door, where they were suddenly confronted by a wild-looking man plunging through the batwing doors, holding two six-guns aimed at them.

"Who the hell are you?" he demanded of Liam as he looked him up and down. "You think you're fast with that fancy rig? Well, buster, you're gonna get your chance to find out what fast is. My name's Ed Trask, and I know you've heard of me. So I'm gonna give you your chance to run or die. I rode over sixty miles to see if Cullen Murphy has got the guts to stand and face me. After that, if you've got the guts, I'll give you the chance to stand up and face the man who shot Cullen Murphy down." He dropped both guns back in their holsters and looked at Murphy. "Draw when you feel lucky, Marshal."

"You're making a mistake!" Liam blurted. "I'm not a gunfighter! This gun is not even loaded. Look, I'll show you!"

He reached down to draw the pistol, and Trask reacted immediately, reaching for one of his six-guns, but his weapon was only halfway out when a bullet from Murphy's .44 struck him in the chest. He squeezed the trigger, putting a bullet in the floor beside Liam's foot. Knowing he was dead, he tried to pull his other six-gun, so Murphy stopped him with a shot in his forehead. He dropped to the floor. Liam staggered backward until coming to a chair and sitting down in it.

Murphy exclaimed, "Are you all right? Were you hit?"

"I don't think so," Liam answered, "but I thought I was for a moment. I was just going to show him the gun was empty." "My goodness," he blurted, as he sagged in the chair, "you saved my life!"

"Your empty gun mighta saved my life," Murphy said. "That man was not lying. He was mighty damn fast." He didn't explain what he meant by his first statement, but he had had no way of knowing how fast Trask really was. So he had reacted the same as Trask and reached for his .44 when he saw Liam make the mistake of reaching for his. Luckily, his bullet had found Trask's chest before Trask had his weapon aimed high enough to kill Liam. He wasn't really sure if he would have been faster than Trask in a direct face-off with him. They might have shot each other.

"I told him my gun was empty," Liam repeated, shaking his head at how close he had come to being shot. "I told him I would show him."

"I know you did, Liam," Murphy said, "but you shoulda unbuckled your belt and took it off, leaving the gun in the holster instead of pullin' it out of the holster."

"I see that now," Liam replied. "I certainly do. As a matter of fact, I'm taking it off right now, in case there might be another maniac roaming the streets of this wild town."

"That's a good idea," Murphy told him. "But I hope this experience won't tarnish your opinion of Newtown as a good place to build a new bank. This business wouldn't have happened any differently if it had been in any other little town in these parts. You just sit there for a couple of minutes while I drag Mr. Trask outside. Then I'll get Doc Ennis to come pick up the body. And on the way, I can show you where the roomin' house is."

Liam nodded his head and remained seated there while Murphy picked up the body by its boots and dragged the late gunfighter out the door. When he got outside, he pulled Ed Trask's corpse away from the door so as not to hinder passage in and out of the saloon.

"You gonna need me?"

Murphy turned around to see William Ennis, whom everyone called Doc, coming toward him. Ennis owned the drugstore and the funeral parlor, in addition to acting as the town doctor.

"I heard the shots. I reckon I shoulda brought my cart. How many is there?"

"Just this one," Murphy replied. "If you want to, we can just throw him on his horse, and you won't have to go back for your cart. I'll take his horse to the stable later." He turned then to look at the horses at the hitching rail. There were only three, and of the three, not one of them looked as if it was worn out. This, plus the fact that none of the three had a packhorse's reins tied to the saddle. He checked each horse carefully and decided one of them, a buckskin, had been ridden recently, while the other two had not. That encouraged him to pick it. With a hand from Ennis, he laid Trask across the buckskin's saddle.

"Hold on a minute, Dr. Ennis," he said just to be sure and

stepped back inside the saloon door. "Anybody in here ridin' a buckskin?" When there was no response, he told Ennis to take the horse.

Then he went back inside to see if Liam had recovered from his scare. "You ready to go, Liam? Come on."

Liam got to his feet and walked out of the saloon.

Standing next to Pete, Elmo remarked, "If that ain't the damnest thing I've ever seen."

Pete chuckled and responded. "It's just Murphy's Law," he said. "Don't matter how it starts out, it always ends up the same."

CHAPTER 16

"I heard him say it," Tyson Bradshaw declared. "Walked right in my front door and pulled his two guns out and said he rode sixty miles to come face-to-face with Cullen Murphy. Said his name was Trash, or something like that, and said he wanted to face the fancy-pants fellow pretending to be a gunslinger after he put Murphy in the ground."

He pointed his finger at Eliot Baxter and said, "It's starting to happen, just like we talked about. I'm afraid it's going to continue to get worse. This kind of news just spreads like wild-fire, and every empty-headed gunslinger in the state of Texas is gonna start showing up to try to be the man who takes Murphy down. And one of these times it's gonna be the right man to take Murphy down. And then where will we be?"

"Done, that's where we'll be," Eliot Baxter answered him. "We've talked about this before and what it might lead to. And I agree with you, Tyson, it surely looks like word is spreading about Murphy."

"But we can't deny the good that Murphy has done since he got back from the war," Elmo Dillon insisted. "We were losing businesses because of the influx of petty outlaws like Rafer Polk, Clyde Fry, and the like. That scum is gone, thanks en-tirely to Cullen Murphy. We couldn't even afford to build a jail and Murphy built one for us and it didn't cost us a dime. He's even made a first-rate deputy outta Bert Walker."

"He gave you the deed to that jailhouse," Jim Anderson saw fit to point out to Eliot Baxter. "Said it belongs to the town now. He can't take that back."

"Hell, he ain't gonna try to void that dollar sale," Elmo remarked. "The only thing he said was that it had to be used for a jail. He wouldn't try to take it back. The fact of the matter is Newtown is safer with Cullen Murphy as the town marshal."

"That's like saying the henhouse is safer if you keep a coyote in it," Anderson quipped.

"Another thing that worries me about Murphy is he's apt to go after anybody," Mack Pratt said. "I'm talkin' about that little gal that was working in my place, Maggie Tatum, and that damn Jake Pike carried her off. Now, I ain't sayin' it was wrong that Murphy took way off to hell and gone from Newtown to rescue a simple saloon gal. But what if some trouble happened and he weren't here where he'd been paid to be? I expect he took care of Jake Pike and the other two strangers, who never showed up in town again."

"You're right, Mack," Baxter remarked. "That is something we talked about before. There is a question in the minds of some of us, and that is, will Cullen Murphy get too big for us to handle?"

"I don't know about that," Bradshaw commented, "but I agree with Jim. He's bound to attract would-be fast-gun outlaws."

"Like coyotes to the henhouse," Jim Anderson repeated.

"But I think we can thank him for one more thing," Bradshaw continued. "I think Bert Walker can take over the job of town marshal now, and that would eliminate most of our worries right there."

"And we wouldn't have to pay Bert as much as I'm sure

Murphy's gonna want," Baxter pointed out. "He can still count on some blacksmith work to help him out."

"Maybe that's true," Elmo commented, "but what if Bert starts to get more business at his shop? We might find him spending more time at his forge than he does at the jail."

"And we need a blacksmith," Frank Jessop felt the need to point out. It was the only comment he had made in the meeting, having had a reluctance to support Murphy's firing because of the money Murphy had paid him in the construction of the jail.

"That's true," Baxter said, "but we have to do what's best for the town right now, before it gets out of hand. I don't know if Bert's the man for our permanent marshal, but I think he can handle the job for the present, at least until we are ready to hire a more qualified lawman." He paused before going on, then added, "One without a reputation." He paused again. "Anybody got a better idea than asking Murphy to leave?"

No one responded, so Baxter said, "We've got enough of us here to vote on it, so all in favor of firing Murphy, raise your hand."

Everybody raised a hand but Elmo Dillon and Paul Mathers.

"Looks like most of us think it's time for Murphy to leave," Baxter said, directing his comments toward Elmo and Mathers. "That doesn't mean the rest of us don't appreciate what Cullen has done for Newtown. We'll always be grateful that he stepped in when he did. But it's our duty to make the hard decisions when it comes to what's best for the future of Newtown."

"I understand why you feel the way you do, all of you," Elmo replied. "And you may be right. I just believe that Newtown is better with Cullen Murphy in the marshal's office than it is without him."

Most of them shifted their gaze toward Mathers then. He shrugged and responded simply, "What he said."

"I know this was a hard decision to make, but it was past time to make it," Baxter said. "It's not going to be a very pleasant job to notify Cullen of the council's decision. Since I'm the mayor and the one who called for this meeting, however, I'll take the responsibility for it and give Cullen his notice."

"You're right, Eliot," Elmo remarked. "It will be an unpleasant job to inform Murphy that he's been fired. But I'll volunteer to give him the news if you want me to. I feel like I was the first one of us to befriend him when he came back here, and I think I can tell him what a hard decision it was for us to make."

Baxter made no effort to hide his immediate sign of relief. "It might be better received coming from you rather than me," he said. "If you're sure you want to do it, I appreciate it."

"I'll tell him today," Elmo said. He looked at the clock on the wall. "Is that thing right?" He pulled out his watch to check. "Pretty close," he announced. "Irene's gonna run us out of here any minute so she can set up the tables for dinner. I'll most likely catch Cullen here and give him the good news."

"Take my advice and don't wear your sidearm," Jim Anderson quipped. His remark was met with several groans as they all got up to leave.

"One other thing," Baxter said, having almost forgotten. "I've got to inform Bert Walker that we've decided to offer him the job of town marshal." He paused to scratch his beard. "Tyson, why don't you come with me to do that?" he said to Bradshaw.

"All right," Bradshaw responded. "What are we gonna do if he doesn't want to take the job?"

"Then one of us is going to have to start wearing a sidearm," Baxter japed. Then he said, "That's the reason I want you to come with me. I'm sure you can talk him into it."

Overhearing their exchange, Elmo shook his head in disbelief. In his opinion, Bert Walker was a good man and might one day make a good marshal. But right now, he was better suited for the deputy's job. He was big and husky and was still a young man. But Elmo was not convinced that Bert would give up his blacksmith business to accommodate the marshal's job. He shook his head again, thinking he might write on his calendar that this day was the beginning of the end for Newtown, Texas.

Murphy was locking the front door at the jail when he heard a wagon pull up behind him. He turned to find Otis Crutcher and Maggie Tatum sitting in the wagon seat. "Well, good mornin', folks," he greeted them, then remembered he was on his way to dinner. "Or good afternoon. I reckon it's near 'bout noon, ain't it? What are you two doin' in town?" "It ain't Sunday, is it?" he asked, because they both looked as if they were dressed to go to church.

"No, sir," Otis answered. "It ain't Sunday, but I reckon it's about the same as. Ain't it, Maggie?"

"I reckon so," Maggie replied and giggled.

"We ain't up to nothin' much. Are we, Maggie?" She giggled again.

Murphy had his mind very much on dinner, so he asked, "What can I do for you?"

"Nothin'," Otis said. "We just decided we wanted you to be the first person to say howdy to Mr. and Mrs. Otis Crutcher." His grin covered his face. "We stood up before the preacher, and he married us and give us a piece of paper to prove it. Cost me a dollar, but it was worth it. Weren't it, sweet pea?" She grinned in response.

"You're the only soul we wanted to tell for sure. Ain't that right, Maggie Crutcher?" She giggled at the use of her married name and nodded vigorously. "We're gonna name our first young'un Cullen, even if it's a girl. 'Cause there wouldn't be no Maggie Crutcher if it weren't for you."

Murphy was truly touched. "Well, that would surely be an

honor for me," he said, while trying to think of something more dramatic to say but coming up with nothing. "I would consider it a real honor for me if you would let me pay for the ceremony." He dug into his pocket for his folding money. "Here's a dollar for the preacher and ten dollars for a weddin' present. Buy Maggie something nice with it."

Otis and Maggie were both speechless for a few moments while they stared at the real money.

"Cullen," Otis gasped, "them's Union greenbacks!"

"What kinda friend would I be if I gave you Confederate dollars?" Murphy said. "Now, you promise me you'll take care of your wife."

"I'll swear that before God," Otis said, and Maggie gave his arm a little squeeze. He looked at her and said, "We done took up enough of this man's time. Let's go to Baxter's store and see if there's anything you might need."

Murphy stood there for a few moments as Otis drove his wagon down the street toward the Newtown General Store. "The best eleven dollars I ever spent," he announced aloud.

Then he started up the street toward Bradshaw's Saloon.

"Good afternoon, Marshal Murphy," Ginger greeted him when he walked into the dining room. "Elmo Dillon is sitting at your usual table, waiting for you."

"Good afternoon, Miss Floyd," he returned, no longer trying to convince her and her sister to call him Cullen. He wondered what Elmo had on his mind, so he didn't bother japing with Ginger over the name game she, and especially Bonnie, liked to play. He walked on back to the table and was surprised when Elmo stood up to greet him and extended his hand.

He shook his hand and said, "Howdy, Elmo. What's goin' on? They send you to tell me I'm fired? Either that or there ain't no money to pay a marshal, so I'm gonna have to work for free?" He paid no attention to the startled expression that popped out on Elmo's face, and sat down at the table. When Elmo didn't sit back down at once, Murphy asked, "Is something wrong, Elmo?"

"No," Elmo replied immediately. Then he said, "Well, yes, there is something wrong, something terribly wrong, and I got the job of telling you about it." He sat back down then and waited until Ginger put their coffee on the table and returned to the kitchen.

"What's the matter? Did Baxter and Bradshaw find out I left the town without a marshal all night when I went to get Maggie Tatum?" Since he had just seen Otis and Maggie before he came to the dining room, that was the first thing he thought of. "They might be interested to know that Maggie and Otis got married this mornin', so something good came from it." When Elmo still hesitated, Murphy asked, "What is it, Elmo?"

"What you said at first," Elmo answered. And when Murphy didn't understand, he said, "I've come to tell you we're firing you from the marshal's job. We think it's best if we don't have a marshal with a reputation. That was the council's vote, and I say 'we' voted that way. But I want you to know, and anyone at that meeting will tell you, that I stood up and said that I thought Newtown was better with you than without you."

Ginger came back from the kitchen then with two plates of food and placed them on the table. She noticed the sudden silence between the two men, so she said, "Sorry to interrupt. I'll check on your coffee later."

When the silence remained after she left, Murphy said, "That meat loaf looks good enough to eat. Don't let it get cold!" He broke off a bite with his fork and shoved it in his mouth. "I'm gonna miss eatin' at Irene's table, I'll be honest with you."

"Cullen, I can't tell you how hard it is for me to bring you this decision the council came up with. Baxter put it to a vote,

I'll give him that, but he knew they would all go along with whatever he thought best. Almost everybody at the meeting voted to let you go. Only two voted against letting you go, myself and Paul Mathers. I'm sure Paul would like for you to know that, same as I do. After all you've done for this town, I can imagine how all this must make you feel. But all those who voted to fire you didn't vote that way because they didn't like you. They voted that way because Baxter and Bradshaw told them it was the only way to save the town."

"Don't fret yourself over this thing, Elmo," Murphy said, seeking to console him. "They might be right, and I hope they are. I won't hold any grudges. There ain't a man on that council that I have any dislike for. A few of 'em I ain't had enough contact with to like or dislike 'em. I got no problem with their decision. It's your town. You ought to run it the way you think best. Hell, I never wanted to be your marshal in the first place. I told you that, but nobody would listen to me. Now maybe I can take a few of those horses Mathers is takin' care of for me and rethink that idea of startin' a little herd of my own. I talked to Lionel Jacobson at the Rocking-J Ranch, and he said he'd most likely do business with me, if I got up a good herd."

He changed the subject then. "What about Bert? Is that who the new marshal is gonna be?"

Elmo said that he was and that Baxter and Bradshaw were meeting with him after dinner to offer him the job.

"So he doesn't know I'll be leavin' yet," Murphy remarked.

"I expect he'll be finding out any minute now," Elmo said. "He usually makes his own meals, so they'll most likely be up at his shop right now." He gave Murphy a sympathetic smile and said, "I expect Bert will be more disappointed to hear about his new job offer than you seem to be over your firing."

"I'm telling you the truth, Elmo," Murphy said, trying to reassure him. "I ain't upset with anybody over my short stretch as the town marshal. Maybe it's because I was in the army for four years, and I got used to sudden changes in the marchin' orders for the day. Wasn't ever any use to complain about 'em, but we always did. After a while, you quit complainin', because it never did any good. You just did what the general said. So we'll just do what General Baxter says and see what happens."

"Ain't that the truth?" Elmo responded and sighed. "But doggone it, don't lose touch with us."

"Oh, I ain't goin' anywhere," Murphy assured him. "I'll be just three miles away, and I expect I'll be in town from time to time to buy supplies or one of Irene's dinners. So whaddaya say we enjoy the rest of this one, and I'll get back to the jail to get my little mess out of there?"

"I don't reckon there's any big hurry about that," Elmo said.

"Maybe not," Murphy replied, "but there ain't no reason to delay it, either. We're already into the middle of summer, and I've still got work to do on my place, if I'm ever gonna make a workin' ranch out of it."

Their conversation was interrupted then when Bonnie arrived at the table with the coffeepot.

"You two look like you're having a real serious talk about something," the precocious girl commented. "I don't know if I should give you some more coffee or not."

Murphy gave her a smile and answered, "When you run into a situation like that, it's always the safest bet to pour more coffee. Ain't that what you say, Elmo?"

"Yeah, I reckon," Elmo managed but with little show of enthusiasm.

His demeanor was enough to convince Murphy that of the two of them, Elmo seemed the most upset over his firing. So he asked Bonnie if they had baked a pie or a cake for dessert.

"We sure did," Bonnie replied. "We've got apple pie, and it's a good one, because I rolled out the dough for the crust."

"Then I'll have a slice of pie to go with this coffee," Murphy said. "How 'bout you, Elmo? You save a little room for a slice of pie?"

"What the hell," Elmo responded. "I might as well, although this don't seem like a day to be celebrating."

Bonnie went back into the kitchen to get the pie. When she got a couple of dessert plates off the shelf, she remarked to Ginger, "Something's going on between Cullen and Elmo."

"Whaddaya mean?" Ginger asked.

"I don't know," Bonnie answered. "They're just acting like something's happened, and Elmo acts like he's not comfortable with it, but Cullen is his same old carefree self." She shrugged and added, "But they both ordered a slice of pie, and that's unusual for both of them."

"Hmm," Ginger responded. "That *is* unusual." She walked over to the kitchen door to look at the two men sitting once again in what appeared to be serious conversation. "They are acting a little odd today," she said to Bonnie when she went back to the pie safe. "I'll take the pie with you."

Overhearing, Irene asked, "What are you girls up to? If they're having some serious talk about something, don't you two go interrupting them."

"We're just gonna take them some pie, Mama. We're not gonna interrupt them," Ginger said. They picked up the plates and hurried out the door with them before their mother said more.

"All right, you two," Ginger asked, "what's the occasion? I don't remember either one of you ever having dessert unless it's a big occasion. So what's the occasion?"

Elmo looked at Murphy, and Murphy shrugged indifferently, so he said, "Cullen isn't the town marshal anymore."

Ginger and Bonnie exchanged puzzled expressions. Then, expecting Elmo to reveal Murphy's new title, Ginger asked, "What is he, then?"

"Unemployed," Murphy couldn't resist answering with a chuckle.

It was enough to leave the two sisters speechless for several long seconds before Ginger asked, "You're not the town marshal anymore?"

"That's right," Murphy answered her. "So that means the next time I come in here to eat, you have to ask me how I expect to pay you. And you'll be seein' a lot more of Bert Walker here in your dinin' room."

Suspecting Murphy of joking with them, they both looked at Elmo for confirmation.

He answered with a helpless shrug. "I'm afraid so," he said, not waiting for the question.

"Why?" Ginger could not help but ask. "After all Cullen has done for this town . . . Most of the people here even call it 'Murphy's Law.'"

"I'm afraid that's the problem," Elmo tried to explain. "Cullen's made a name for himself that's getting around, and the town council thinks it's important to stop it before it gets any worse. We've already had someone in town for no other reason than to face Murphy in a shoot-out."

"Well, I don't think that's fair," Bonnie declared.

Murphy was touched to think the two girls cared one way or the other, but he was quick to speak on behalf of the town. "Don't think ill of the town council," he told them. "They're just doin' what they think they have to do to keep your town from attractin' notorious gunslingers who want to carve another notch on their gun handles. And they figure there are only two ways to prevent that. One is to fire me. The other is if somebody shoots me. And I have to admit I'm pretty partial to the first option. I'm sorry things turned out this way, but I can understand how they did." He paused and shook his head before continuing. "And, hell, we even had one fellow from back East pretendin' to be a gunfighter."

They finished their apple pie, and Irene and her daughters said a tearful goodbye, which totally surprised Murphy, and he promised that when he was in town, he would never fail to visit them. Outside the dining room, Elmo thanked Murphy for his understanding of the problem and the gracious way he had explained it to Irene and her daughters. They parted then, Elmo headed back to report to Baxter about his meeting with Murphy, and Murphy to the stable to talk to Mathers about his horses.

CHAPTER 17

Paul Mathers stood in the open door of his barn, watching Murphy approaching. He couldn't tell from his walk whether he was angry or not. It was the same determined stride that he was accustomed to seeing when Murphy was on foot. Still, he was relieved when Murphy was close enough to speak and he heard his friendly greeting.

"Howdy, Paul," he said. "I reckon I need to talk to you about my horses."

"Elmo tell you?" Mathers asked.

"Yep, he told me," Murphy answered.

"Did you talk to Bert yet?"

"No, I haven't talked to Bert," Murphy replied. "Did he take the job?"

"Yeah, he took it," Paul said. "But Bradshaw said he weren't sure he wanted it dumped in his lap. He said he was fine workin' with you as your deputy, but he ain't sure he's ready to take on the full responsibility of the town marshal."

"You folks give him all the help and support you can," Murphy said. "Bert's a fine young man, and if he can survive the initial stages of enforcing the law here, he'll be a good marshal. He's just got to grow into the job. I hope he has the time to do it. And there's no reason to think he won't. Nobody comes to

Newtown on purpose. You end up here by accident when you're tryin' to go somewhere else. There's very little pastureland, so it ain't good for cattle, and there's no farmland to attract settlers, unless you've got some land on one of the rivers. It's tough to raise anything on these high hills of granite and limestone, unless you know where a market is for prickly pear cactus or desert spoon."

"I reckon I can't argue with all that," Mathers said. "But we still get these drifters and gunslingers showin' up here. How do they know to come here?"

"I think the main reason the town attracts 'em is that outlaw hideout I followed those two friends of Jake Pike's to. Back up a strong stream that came down a narrow valley, that place was more than a rough cabin. Somebody built that for a home to raise a family. Back behind the cabin there was a barn and a corral. Beyond the corral there was even a small pasture. I doubt I'da found it if I hadn't been following those two outlaws.

"Those outlaws I had trouble with were all holed up in that hideout. They weren't passin' through town on their way somewhere else. Think about it. Every damn one of the gunmen I've dealt with since I came to Newtown had money. They weren't broke. They were hidin' out from robberies somewhere else, and the law was after them. So my concern is, how many other outlaws know about this hideout? If we're lucky, maybe there's not a great number of them that know there's a nice cabin not too far from a small town where there's no law, at least as far as they know."

He paused to bite his lip. "I shoulda burned that place to the ground before I left it." He looked at Mathers as if he needed to explain why he didn't. "That little girl, that Maggie, was damn near dead by the time I found her, and all I thought about was gettin' her someplace where she wasn't afraid."

"Maybe you're right," Mathers said, "but that fellow you

just shot at Bradshaw's Saloon claimed he rode sixty miles just to stand up to you."

"Yeah, I was thinkin' about that," Murphy admitted. "I ain't convinced that fellow wasn't half-crazy. His horse didn't look like it had been rode hard a'tall, and he didn't have a packhorse. Seems like he woulda had one if he rode sixty miles to get here."

"Yeah, it does, don't it?" Mathers allowed. "Maybe Bradshaw hired him to call you out," he japed. "He mighta been one of those drunks that hang out in front of the saloon, and Bradshaw promised him a bottle of whiskey to do the job."

Murphy laughed, but he remembered how fast the shooter was and the fact that he had wondered if he would have beaten him if he had faced him first instead of Liam Black. It caused him to consider riding back up to that camp in the hills to see if he might find a horse in the corral and a packsaddle in the barn. Another thought occurred to him. He didn't know Doc Ennis that well, but he wondered if the undertaker would admit it if he had found a substantial sum of money on the shooter's body. *That was careless*, he thought. Ordinarily, he would have searched the body of a man he had killed, and paid the undertaker his fee.

Reminding himself why he was there, Murphy said, "I need to talk to you about my horses. Since I'm not the marshal anymore, I'll be movin' 'em outta your way and drivin' 'em out to my place on the river. I was wonderin' if I could just take my packhorse and leave the other four for a couple more days and then take 'em off your hands."

"No problem a'tall," Mathers quickly responded. "You've still got a lot of credit left on my books for those horses you sold me. Don't worry. I'll take good care of 'em."

"I know you will, Paul, and I appreciate it. I need to tell you that Elmo told me it was just him and you that voted against firin' me. I appreciate that, too." He paused to think about it but couldn't resist saying, "And I always thought you were smarter than Elmo, but you fooled me."

They both enjoyed a chuckle.

Then Murphy said, "Well, I'd best go find Bert now and see how he's taking his promotion. I expect he's lookin' for the keys to the jailhouse." He could see Bert's blacksmith shop from the stable, but there was no sign of Bert. So he figured he was more than likely waiting for him to show up at the jail.

Mathers helped him cut Nosy and his usual packhorse out of the herd of horses in the corral and put the packsaddle on the sorrel while Murphy saddled the bay. "I expect I'll be back in a day or two for the other horses," he told Mathers.

"No hurry," Mathers told him as he rode away. "Take all the time you need."

He rode down Front Street to the jail, where he found Bert Walker sitting on the jailhouse steps, waiting for him. "Sorry, Bert," Murphy said. "I meant to give you the key I got back from Robert. You been waitin' long?"

"No, fifteen minutes, maybe. Baxter and Bradshaw were talkin' to me for quite a while. You know, you don't have to move out of here right away."

"I 'preciate that, but there's no need for me to hang around." He unlocked the door and handed the key to Bert. "Here ya go, Marshal Walker. That other key is in the desk drawer. I'll just pick up my possibles, and I'll be out of your way pretty quick."

He stepped into the office and took his rifle out of the rack behind the desk and picked up a couple of the extra handguns he had accumulated. Then he busied himself going through the desk drawers, picking out any items he thought he might have use for at some point. As he did, he purposely avoided the eyes watching him intensely, afraid Bert might become emotional and say something he might regret later on.

He quickly finished collecting his personal things from the

marshal's desk and went back through the cell room to the living quarters behind it with Bert following close after him. "You know, you're gonna have to hire you somebody to do all the cleanup and housekeepin' chores. The town has to pay for it. You make sure that's part of your deal. They know they can't expect the marshal to do household chores. You've got more important things to take care of."

"They said they would hire somebody to do all that," Bert said.

"I'm just takin' stuff I brought from my cabin," Murphy went on. "Nothing that the town furnished." He rolled up his bedroll to put behind his saddle; then he stuffed his extra clothes in a sack, which he would put on the packhorse, along with his coffeepot and a couple of cups. He looked around the room and decided he had everything he wanted. "That's pretty much it. The rest belongs to the town," he said. "You oughta be in good shape to take over the job. You ain't got but one fast-draw gunslinger in town now," he said, referring to Liam Black in an attempt to lighten the mood. "And you don't have to worry about him, because his gun ain't loaded."

"I don't even have one that I know about," Bert said. "He left town this mornin', headed back to Waco."

"Is that a fact? He said he was gonna hang around town two or three days to see if Newtown was ready for a New Orleans bank. You can tell Baxter that you've already got rid of a notorious gunslinger your first official day on the job."

"Cullen," Bert started, and Murphy was afraid this was the talk he had been trying to avoid all along. "I didn't have nothin' to do with this."

"Hell, I know that," Murphy responded. "But it just might be the right time for it. You've got the tools for it, and they could be right about me havin' a reputation. And I don't want to do anything to hurt this town. I'm just glad they've got somebody like you that's ready to take the job."

"I'm not sure I'm ready. That's what's worryin' me. I know I'm strong. I can lift my anvil and move it anywhere I want. And I know I can handle a horse that don't want to be shod. I'll stand up against any man in a fistfight. But when Rafer Polk walked into my shop and told me he was gonna give me a chance to try to kill him, and if I did, the three men with him would kill me, I froze up so bad I could hardly breathe. I'll admit that to you because I think you already know I ain't got any confidence in myself."

"You're right about one thing," Murphy responded. "I think I know you, and what I know ain't what you just described. During the war, I had the opportunity to see hundreds of raw recruits thrown into battle with not near enough training for it. Their first time facing the enemy toe-to-toe was pretty much what you faced when four gunmen with no prior warnin' walked into your shop. There woulda been something wrong with you if you hadn'ta been scared. You were facing a cocky gunslick wearin' a fast-draw holster and a weapon twice as handy as that hogleg you were wearin'.

"But that's all changed now. You've got a weapon you can handle as fast as anybody now, and I've seen you shoot with it. You just don't know it yet. It's always best to avoid having to shoot someone, but you're already fast enough to hold your own against the so-called gunfighters, a title they picked for themselves. Having said that, let me advise you to avoid all the fast-draw confrontations you can, because there is somebody out there who is faster than you are. So why take the chance?"

"I don't know, Cullen. I appreciate what you're trying to tell me, but I'm still not a hundred percent sure I'm the man for the job." He didn't admit it to him, but the image of Murphy's explosive reaction to Rafer Polk's threat to kill him in his shop that day was not one he could see in himself.

"It'll come to you when the time comes that you need it," Murphy said. "I can see it in you. You've just got to learn to trust your natural instincts. It'll come quicker when I'm out of your way. I'm confident that you'll do a good job."

He extended his hand, and Bert shook it. Murphy took one quick look around before they walked out of the living quarters and went through the office to go out the front door. "I'll see you on the occasional trips I take to town," Murphy said. "And I'll be damn sure to behave myself, since I know who the marshal is," he joked as he tied the sack on his packhorse. Then he climbed up into the saddle, rode out into the street, and turned Nosy's head toward the river road.

Had he known that evil was descending upon the unsuspecting town of Newtown via the north road to town at the same time he was leaving on the south road, he would have turned around at once. This evil was in the form of Clay Barnett and the five outlaws who had followed him on a robbing and killing march from Missouri, through Arkansas and Oklahoma, to Texas. Since their reputation now followed them, they had one destination in mind. It was a town by the name of Newtown, which until recently neither Barnett nor any of his gang had ever heard of. And that was the reason it was their destination. An outlaw who used to ride with Barnett had told him about the existence of Newtown, a little development that had sprung up like a weed where no other life existed. Clyde Fry had told him how to find a hideout close to town, but Barnett wanted to look the town over before going to the hideout.

They slow-walked their horses down the main street of the town, surprised to find that it was not the stagnant little settlement they expected. When they came to a building that had a sign identifying it as the jail, Barnett pulled his horse to a halt. "Fry told me there was no law in Newtown," he said to Emmett Rice, who was riding right beside him. "They've damn sure got a jail. We need to see just how much law they've got. We'll ride the rest of the street. I wanna see what else they've got. Then we'll ride back to that saloon called Bradshaw's. It looks like the busiest one. Maybe because of that sign that said 'Café.' We might as well get something to eat."

As Barnett had ordered, they rode the length of the street, then turned around and rode back to Bradshaw's, where they tied their saddle horses, with their packhorses tied to the saddles. When they walked into the saloon, Barnett paused to look it over as if he was considering taking it over. His men, accustomed to his actions, stood patiently, waiting for the signal to proceed. Finally, he pointed to one side of the room and said, "Push three of those tables over there together, and I'll get some whiskey." They went at once to follow his orders while he walked over to the bar, from where Pete, the bartender, was already eyeing them.

"Bring me an unopened bottle of rye whiskey and six glasses over there," Barnett said and pointed to the tables. He turned around and walked across the room without waiting for Pete's response.

Not prone to argue with six strangers who looked like they thrived on trouble, Pete delivered the bottle and the six glasses. "Afternoon, gents," he said cheerfully. "That'll be two dollars for the bottle."

"We'll test it first to see if it's worth two dollars," Barnett said, and he handed the bottle to Luther Boyd to open. Luther, accustomed to the heavy jobs because of his size, took the bottle and broke the seal as he pulled the cork. Then he poured whiskey in Barnett's glass, and Barnett tossed it back.

When he slammed the empty glass back on the table, he said, "Drink up, boys. It's the real thing." To Pete, he said, "We're gonna be spending a lot of money before we leave here, so you just keep an accurate bill, and I'll pay you all of it in one lump when we're done." His comment caused some chuckles among his five men, for it was a joke of theirs that the lump he referred to was usually a lump on the head.

Pete knew he had big trouble coming. "We usually do business on a 'pay as you're served' basis. Maybe you'd best talk to Mr. Bradshaw, the owner, if you wanna deal on a credit basis."

"I'd be happy to talk to Mr. Bradshaw," Barnett said. "Just tell him to drop by."

"Hey," one of the men asked, "where are the women? Ain't there no women workin' here?"

"No," Pete answered him, "no women. If that's what you're lookin' for, you'll find them down the street at Pratt's Saloon."

"Damn, Clay. Maybe we picked the wrong saloon," one of the other men said. Back to Pete then, he pointed to the stairs. "What's upstairs?"

"That's where the owner lives," Pete answered.

"The whole upstairs?" Lefty Birchfield asked.

"Well, not all of it," Pete answered reluctantly. "There's some rooms up there to rent, but there ain't no saloon girls at Bradshaw's."

Hoping that would end the questions, Pete turned to go back to the bar. But he was stopped by another question, this one by Barnett. "The sign outside says 'Café.' Where's the café?"

"It's through that door yonder," Pete said and pointed to it. He didn't want to tell them, but he was afraid not to. They were a dangerous-looking crew, and he hated to aim them toward Irene and the girls.

The six strangers sat there until they had emptied the bottle of whiskey; then Barnett said he was ready to eat. So, much to Pete's regret, they left their tables and headed for the entrance to the café. When they filed past the bar, Barnett read the expression on Pete's face and said, "Don't worry about your two dollars. You'll get what you've got comin' when we leave here."

It didn't sound like a promise of payment in cash to Pete. When the last of the six filed through the café door, Pete immediately took most of the cash out of his register and hid it under the counter. Then he went over to a cord hanging down beside a stack of shelves from a small hole in the ceiling. He pulled the cord three times rapidly. In a couple of minutes, Tyson Bradshaw appeared at the top of the stairs, and Pete waved him over.

"What is it, Pete?" Bradshaw asked when he got to the bar. Pete told him about the dangerous-looking group of obvious outlaws and said that he was suspicious of their intentions. He advised him to take any large sums of money out of his safe upstairs, just in case.

"Where are they now?" Bradshaw asked.

"They went to Irene's to eat dinner," Pete replied.

"Damn," Bradshaw swore, "and we fired Murphy this morning. Do you know if he's still in town?"

"I think he's already gone," Pete answered. "Maybe I'm just overreacting. So far, they're just into us for two dollars."

"I'll go back upstairs and empty my safe, just in case," Bradshaw said.

In the dining room Ginger and Bonnie were both surprised by the sudden entrance of the six heavily armed men.

"Lookee here, Lefty!" Squint Bates whooped. "This is where they keep the women!"

"Hot damn!" Lefty blurted. "I know what I want for dessert!" The others started whooping it up, as well, entertained by Squint and Lefty's antics, encouraging their misbehavior, until Ginger put her foot down.

"If you want us to serve your dinner, you're going to have to behave yourselves and act like you're civilized," she declared.

A couple of customers wolfed down the last of their dinner and went out the back door. One other customer, Eliot Baxter's son, Jeff, was seated at a small table for two, eating alone. As much disturbed as the two who had just hurried their meal and left, he was not one to be forced out by rude behavior.

"All right," Clay Barnett said, "stop the foolishness so the girls can bring out the food. I'm hungry." It was enough to calm his men down, since they were hungry, too.

"Damn, boss. This is pretty good eatin'," Luther Boyd said

after they'd been served and he'd dug into his dinner. "I could get used to this." He got a couple of "Me too" comments from around the table. So he said, "It's gonna be hard to go back to our own cookin' when we go to that hideout."

Their behavior slid from raucous to just noisy, and Bonnie deemed it safe enough to fill the coffee cups again. Almost all the way around the table, she was fine, until reaching over to fill Squint's cup, which he had pushed to the center of the table in order to make her have to reach way over to get the cup. When she reached for it, he grabbed her around her waist and pulled her down on his lap. She screamed and struggled to escape, much to Squint's delight.

It was too much for Jeff Baxter to allow. He came out of his chair and charged across the room. Squint saw him coming, dumped Bonnie on the floor, and drew his six-shooter, but Jeff was too fast for him, and they both spilled over on the floor, struggling for possession of the one gun between them. Probably five or six years older than Jeff and twice as big, Squint finally managed to get a knee up between Jeff's legs and jerk the revolver free. Jeff nevertheless charged him again, but he was stopped in his rush by a bullet in his chest.

Hearing the gunshot in the kitchen, Irene grabbed her shotgun and sent Ginger out the back door to get Bert Walker. When Irene rushed into the dining room to see Bonnie on the floor and Squint standing over Jeff's body, his six-gun now aimed at her, she raised the shotgun to shoot.

"Now, hold it right there!" Clay Barnett shouted. "You pull that trigger and you're gonna start a killin' like you ain't ever seen before. It's six crack shots against you. That boy layin' yonder took it on hisself to attack my man. Your daughter ain't been hurt, not one bit. We're sorry for the disturbance, but my man has a right to defend himself."

"Mama, I'm all right," Bonnie said. "It's poor Jeff I feel so bad about. He came to save me when that man grabbed me."

"Squint wouldn't hurt a hair on her head," Barnett insisted. "I think that young feller mighta been sweet on the girl. It's just a mistake he made."

Bonnie got up from the floor and took her mother's arm and led her back into the kitchen.

Barnett looked at Squint and said, "Put your damn gun away, Squint. What was you gonna do? Shoot the cook? Drag him out the back door."

Squint replaced the spent cartridge and holstered his gun. Then he grabbed Jeff by his ankles and dragged him out the back door. He had dropped Jeff's boots and was turning to go back in when Bert Walker came running down the path beside the saloon, heading to the dining room, with Ginger right behind him.

"You!" Bert commanded. "Stop right there!"

Squint ignored him and went back inside.

"That was one of them!" Ginger shouted.

So Bert ran after him. Inside, he saw Irene and Bonnie standing just inside the kitchen as Squint ran into the dining room. When they saw Bert, they rushed to meet him.

"He shot Jeff Baxter," Bonnie exclaimed, "and Jeff didn't even have a gun!"

"You're sure of that?" Bert asked.

"Yes, they got in a fight when that man grabbed me and pulled me down on his lap, but that man had a gun and Jeff didn't, so then he shot Jeff."

"The three of you stay in the kitchen," Bert told them. Then he went into the dining room, where he was met with the smug faces of six confident gunmen and promptly made the mistake of allowing Clay Barnett to take charge of the investigation.

"Are you the law in this town?" Barnett asked before Bert had a chance to speak.

"I am," Bert answered him. "I'm Town Marshal Walker, and I'm here to arrest that man for assault and murder."

"Let's not jump to conclusions, Marshal," Barnett said. "Who said he attacked anybody?"

"I've got a witness that said she was attacked by him and that the man he killed was murdered when he came to her defense," Bert charged.

"Well, I've got five witnesses who saw that man attack Mr. Bates after that young woman sat down in his lap. Mr. Bates has a right to defend himself, and that's what he did. If you wanna arrest somebody, arrest that girl for causin' that feller to get shot."

Realizing he was being made a fool of, Bert decided enough was enough. "I'm tired of playin' word games with you." He turned directly to face Squint and said, "I'm placin' you under arrest. Is Bates your name? What's your first name?"

Squint didn't answer him right away. He just looked at him and grinned, and the more his grin widened, the more his eyes seemed to close, until he was just squinting at him. "Why don't you guess?" he finally said.

Bert found himself in a situation where he wasn't sure what he should do. The man refused to be arrested. "I'll have to ask you to hand over that gun. Draw it out of the holster with your left hand and hold it with your thumb and one finger."

Still, Squint stood there, not moving, the wide smile set in place.

After a long minute with no response, Bert blurted, "Am I gonna have to shoot you to take you to jail?"

"That's what you're gonna have to do," Squint answered smugly. "'Cause I ain't goin' to no damn jail standin' up."

Feeling like a stray calf who suddenly found itself confronted by a pack of hungry wolves, Bert wondered what Murphy would do in such a situation. He knew a big mistake was not having his gun already drawn when he first entered the room. Murphy had told him never to give the perpetrator an even chance. Too late to rectify the situation, he started to reach for his Colt. Seeing his move, Squint automatically reached for his six-gun. The result was a near draw, but Bert proved to be a split second faster, sending a shot into Squint's chest while Squint's shot went into the floor.

Hit almost as hard by the sensation of having been faster than his adversary than he would have been had he lost the competition, Bert stood there in a mild state of shock for a brief moment before he holstered his weapon. "That was an unnecessary shooting," he managed to say.

In a greater state of shock, Clay Barnett was speechless for a moment, as were the other four members of his gang, for they all had assumed Squint would be the winner in a duel with the young marshal. But none were as shocked as Squint Bates as he stared down at the front of his shirt and the blood oozing out of the hole left by the bullet. He sat down heavily in the chair behind him and continued to stare as his life trickled away.

Furious now to have lost one of his men, Barnett drew his own weapon and held it on the startled marshal, thinking to retaliate. Then he had a better idea. "Grab him, Luther!" he ordered, and the big man wrapped his arms around Bert, pinning his arms to his sides. "Get him!" Barnett bellowed, and Bad Eye and Lefty pulled Bert's legs out from under him as Luther took the helpless marshal to the floor. "Hold him there," Barnett commanded. "Emmett, go out and get some rope to tie this coyote up with. Bring plenty of it. We're gonna try this lawman!"

Remembering Irene and her shotgun then, he went to the kitchen, where he found her and her daughters huddled together after hearing the gunfire. "You three, he ordered, "come in here." When he saw Irene glance at her shotgun, propped against the wall, he warned her. "By the time you get to that shotgun, both your daughters will be dead, and I'll shoot you before you can pick it up. Now, we're gonna have a trial, and I want you to witness it. Get movin'."

He herded mother and daughters into the dining room and directed them to sit down at one of the tables. Shocked to see Bert Walker held down by three of the men, they were even more devastated when Emmett came back in with two coils of rope from off the horses. They watched in horror as Bert was then tied hand and foot, then left on the floor.

Satisfied to that point, Barnett said, "Lefty, you and Luther go back to the saloon and run anybody still hangin' around outta there and lock the doors. Then bring that bartender and the owner in here."

Already downstairs in the saloon, having heard the shooting, Tyson Bradshaw was frantically asking customers what it was about. Pete yelled from behind the bar that gunshots had come from the dining room, but he had no idea the cause. Luther and Lefty came in at that point with guns drawn.

"All right, everybody out!" Lefty ordered. "Saloon's closed."

"You and you," Luther ordered, pointing at Bradshaw and Pete, "you're goin' to the dinin' room for the trial." He grinned foolishly when they were confused by the mention of a trial.

When everyone was out of the saloon and Bradshaw and Pete had been taken back to the dining room, Clay Barnett took over again. "All right, ladies and gentlemen, come to order. The court is in session for the trial of this murderin' lawman." He paused. "What was his name?"

"Walker," Emmett Rice responded. "He said his name was Marshal Walker."

"Right," Barnett said. "Anyway, Judge Clay Barnett presiding." This caused a couple of chuckles to come from Lefty and Bad Eye. "Order in the court!" Barnett responded. "After witnessin' the brutal slayin' of Squint Bates, I find Marshal Walker guilty of murder. And the penalty for killin' any one of my men is to be hanged by the neck until dead."

"You animal!" Irene could not keep from protesting. "You can't hang the town marshal!"

"That's where you're wrong, old woman," Barnett responded. "We're the law in this town now, and you damn sure better remember it. This saloon is going to be our headquarters until we're ready to move on. I can't tell you how long that'll be. Just depends on how we like it here. We'll take rooms upstairs, and we'll permit you to stay open for business. That goes for the saloon and the dinin' room, too. Old lady, your life and your daughters' lives depend on how good the cookin' is. And my men won't soil your sweet little girls as long as I approve of the cookin'."

Barnett went on. "Bradshaw, I ain't gonna be bothered by payin' you for every drink of likker I or my men take. You just keep a book on what we spend, and I'll settle up when we decide to go. But if I ain't satisfied with the service we get, I'll burn this place to the ground. Is that understood?"

"What about that hideout, Clay?" Bad Eye asked. "Ain't we gonna go lookin' for it?"

"What for?" Barnett responded. "We own the whole damn town. We've got everything we need right here and nobody to stop us from takin' it, 'cause we're the law. And you heard my verdict, so let's get on with the hanging."

When Bad Eye asked where, Barnett said, "Right out in front of this saloon, and anybody that cuts him down will be shot on sight."

Chapter 18

Cullen Murphy searched his mind, wondering why he had no feelings of guilt or disappointment upon having been fired from a job that he thought he had been handling as well as his employer could expect. Instead, he had a feeling of freedom from a chore he hadn't wanted in the first place. His brief career as town marshal for Newtown had given him the opportunity to meet many more of the town folk than he would have. And most of them he liked.

Now he was ready to see if he could make anything out of his little ranch. He thought of Otis Crutcher's farm north of town, on the river road, but he couldn't raise any crops on his land, even though he had all the water he would need. His cornfield would be filled with Rocking-J cattle twenty-four hours a day. He would have to fence in his entire acreage, and he was not prepared to do that. He figured the only way he could continue to get along with the Rocking-J was if he went back to his original plan to raise horses.

His only source was going to be wild horses, and he needed to capture some mares among the first of them. He was well aware of how difficult it was going to be for one man to drive a herd of wild horses. But he had no partners, so he was going to have to find out if he could do it at all. When he had talked to

Lionel Jacobson, the owner of the Rocking-J, Jacobson had said there were reports of wild horses near the Pecos River. That was a long drive for one man, maybe impossible. He supposed he would just have to wait and see. He figured he had only two options: try it and succeed, or try it and fail. These were the thoughts that filled his mind during the three-mile trip from Newtown. They were promptly forgotten when he arrived at the confluence of Brady Creek and the San Saba River and the smoky remains of his cabin.

He rode Nosy into the water and crossed over to the other side. No words came to him as the big bay gelding climbed up the bank and came to a halt before the blackened remains of his labor. Before dismounting, he looked beyond the cabin to see a similar picture of his barn. The sturdy cabin had survived the four years he had been away in the war, broken into more than once but never abused. This was not accidental. This was a deliberate act of destruction. He stepped down from the saddle to take a close look around and discovered a lot of hoofprints around the cabin and the barn. He was struck by the fact that they were all from unshod hooves.

Indians? Commanche maybe! If so, they were a long way from home. The tracks were not fresh, but no more than a day or two old. Under the limbs of a tree by the creek, he found the remains of a cow. *So they stopped here to butcher their cow and eat it before they burned everything down and went on their way. I suppose I ought to feel lucky that I wasn't here at the time,* he thought, *but I don't feel lucky.*

There was plenty of daylight left, so while the horses were drinking at the creek, he took a more extensive look around. He found the tracks of at least four horses coming from the Rocking-J range down Brady Creek but none going back that way. So he scouted the San Saba riverbanks and found their tracks following the river to the southwest. Since it wasn't close to dark yet, he decided to follow their tracks to see if they had left the area or might circle back to kill more cattle. He didn't follow the tracks very far before he was disappointed to find they circled back to the north again. Another mile led him to the remains of a camp beside a small stream. They had evidently camped there for the night. He was warned not to come any closer by a pack of snarling coyotes that was cleaning up the meat and scraps the Indians had left. With no desire for direct contact with the coyotes, he circled around them until he struck the Indians' trail away from the camp. He figured he was getting close to that creek where he had first met Lionel Jacobson when he saw the smoke against the late afternoon sky. Surprised, for he would not have expected them to stop this soon after leaving the camp where they had spent the night. It was time to become cautious.

Up until then, the trail left by the four ponies had been easy to follow, due to the barren terrain it led through: rocky and hilly, almost desertlike. That advantage turned against him now. For just as easily as he could trail them, they could easily see him coming if they were watching their back trail at all. They probably weren't, he figured, but why risk it? So he left the trail and rode off at an angle to a narrow valley between two steep rock-faced hills that stood north of the column of smoke. Riding up the narrow valley between the two hills, he stopped when he was opposite the smoke, pulled his rifle, and dismounted.

He dropped Nosy's reins on the ground so he wouldn't move; then he climbed up through the rocks to the top of the hill. Trying to work his way around a limestone outcropping so he could see the fire, he stopped suddenly when he heard a scream of pain. With his rifle ready to fire, he crawled around the limestone protrusion to discover two Indians holding a white man close to the flames of a fire while a third Indian held a burning limb against his bare back. Murphy saw at once the game they were playing. The man's chest was being held so close to the fire that when the Indian with the burning limb pressed it against the man's bare back, he couldn't help but flinch, causing him to stick his chest in the flames.

Murphy didn't delay. His first shot struck the Indian holding the flaming limb in his back. He ejected the empty cartridge and put his second shot in the chest of one of the two holding the tortured man. The third Indian dropped the victim by the fire and ran for his horse, falling dead from a shot in the middle of his back when he was halfway there. Murphy quickly cranked another round into the Henry and scanned the width of the little valley to make sure there were not four Indians.

Then he hurried back down to his horses and rode around the hill, where he jumped off Nosy and ran to make sure the white man was not actually in the fire. He was not, but he had been dropped close enough for his trousers to begin scorching. Murphy pulled him away from the fire and said, "I'll be right back." He ran over to the first Indian he shot, the one who had held the flaming limb. He was crawling on his belly toward a rifle propped against a rock a few feet away but was stopped forever when Murphy put a round into the back of his head. The other two had not moved, but they received the same treatment.

He went back then to see how badly the victim of their torture was hurt. The man, a cowhand, looked up at Murphy as if seeing an archangel appearing from Heaven. Murphy blinked to be sure before he asked, "Walter, is that you?"

Walter responded with a weak nod of his head, fighting to keep from screaming again from the pain of his burned skin.

"Are you hurt anywhere besides your chest and back?" Murphy asked.

"No," Walter managed. "They said that was comin' after I was cooked over the fire."

There was no water close by, so Murphy got his canteen and

a couple of rags from several he carried in his saddlebags in case of gunshots. He soaked the rags with water and held them against Walter's burned skin. "Maybe this with help with the pain. I ain't sure, but I can't think of anything else to try."

He looked around him and saw the horses standing idly by. Three with Indian saddles and one packhorse were now joined by Walter's horse. "Do you think you can stay on your horse?" Murphy asked. "I need to get you back to the ranch house. There oughta be somebody there who can take care of your burns. Right?"

"Yes," Walter gasped, as if it pained him to speak. "Corky or Miss Atha. I can ride if you'll help me get my boots on and help me on my horse. I'll damn sure stay on him till I get back to the ranch."

Murphy remembered that Corky was the chuck-wagon cook; he assumed that Miss Atha was possibly the housekeeper at the ranch house.

"You just sit there a minute. I'll get your boots. Did they take 'em off you?"

"Yeah, they said they was gonna cook my feet, then put 'em back on me and watch me dance a war dance." He paused to catch his breath. "I'm kinda glad you come along."

Murphy could see that the cowhand wasn't hurt as badly as he had first suspected, but he was in a great deal of pain. It was really fortunate that he had decided to track the Indians, for it sounded to him that they had planned to gradually torture Walter to death. He found Walter's boots and put them back on his feet. Then he led Walter's horse over beside him and dropped the reins. Walter's gun belt and sidearm were hanging on the saddle horn. His shirt was lying across the saddle. Murphy took that and stuffed it in his saddlebag. When Walter said he was ready, he reached up with his arms, and Murphy took hold of his wrists and pulled him to his feet.

"How ya feel?" Murphy asked. "You gonna make it?" He just then noticed the lump on the back of his head.

Walter stood there for a minute, holding on to Murphy's forearms tightly. "I'll make it," he finally said, "if you'll give me a little boost up." He let go of Murphy's arms and grabbed the saddle horn. Murphy lifted his foot for him and placed it in the stirrup, and when Walter said he was ready, Murphy boosted him up to settle in the saddle. When he said he was ready to ride, Murphy left him while he got his horses after deciding to let the four extra horses make their own choice. He stripped them of their saddles and reins; then he collected the Indians' weapons and put them on his packhorse.

"How far is it to the ranch house?" he asked, once he was astride Nosy again and had sidled up to Walter's horse.

"About a mile and a half," Walter said, sitting in the saddle, shirtless, with two large wet rags wrapped around his bare torso and his hat hanging on the saddle horn with his pistol. The large knot on the back of his head and a bad bruise over his eye made it uncomfortable to wear the hat. "I can lead the way," he declared nonetheless.

Leading his horse out of the stable, Jim King, the foreman at the Rocking-J Ranch, stopped suddenly when he caught sight of the two riders approaching the barnyard. "What in the world . . . ?" he uttered. "Corky! Look yonder! Ain't that Walter?"

Corky looked in the direction Jim pointed and saw what looked like Walter on his horse, with no shirt or hat on and something wrapped around his bare chest. "It's Walter, all right. Looks like he's picked up somebody and some stray horses." They stood there and waited for them, and when they were a little closer, Corky asked, "Ain't that that Murphy feller that owns the cabin down by the river?"

"It sure is," Jim said. He tied his horse's reins on a corral rail and walked forward to meet them. "Murphy," he acknowledged, but he turned to Walter for an explanation. "What happened to you? What's that wrapped around your chest?"

"I ran up on those damn hostiles that have been slaughterin' our cattle," Walter said. "It was on the other side of Brady Creek. The only problem was them devils musta saw me, because they ambushed me, and when they found out there weren't nobody with me, they decided to amuse theirselves with my long, slow death. But they didn't count on Murphy strikin' their trail." He went on to tell them about the torture games they had dreamed up to make him squirm and how they had planned to kill him a little bit at a time. "I could feel the skin on my chest and my back scorchin' and puckerin' up in big blisters. I started prayin' for them to go ahead and kill me. Then I heard *crack, crack, crack*, and I dropped to the ground—"

"He's hurtin' a lot more than he's lettin' on," Murphy finally interrupted. "We need to get him someplace where you can do something for those burns he's got on his chest and his back. He got knocked in the head pretty good, too. I don't know what you can do about that, but I know he's in a lot of pain from those burns. I didn't know what to do for 'em, so I wrapped some wet rags around him. I hope it was the right thing to do."

"I don't see how it could make it any worse," Corky said. "I don't know much about treatin' burns myself. All I know is that you have to keep 'em real clean, so they don't get infected. I'll go get Miss Atha to take a look at him and see what she thinks. Take him on into the bunkhouse. There's empty bunks on that far end."

Murphy and Jim led the two saddled horses to the bunkhouse and got Walter down off his horse, into the bunkhouse, and onto a bunk.

"You'll have to lay on your side, Walter," Murphy told him. He looked at Jim and said, "Maybe there's some extra blankets or something to pack on both sides of him to keep him from rollin' over on his back."

"Right," Jim King said and went to a little room at the front of the bunkhouse. When he returned, he had four blankets, and he and Murphy rolled them up and wedged them on both sides of Walter.

He looked up at them with eyes beginning to show the pain he was suffering. " 'Preciate it," he said. "Murphy, I ain't thanked you near enough yet for savin' my life. I don't know how in the world you happened to be there, but I'd be chopped up in pieces and throwed on a fire right now if you hadn'ta been."

"I'm just sorry I didn't get there sooner," Murphy said. "Maybe I coulda saved you a lot of the pain you're sufferin'."

Murphy and Jim stood back away from the bunk when Corky came back with Miss Atha. She promptly took charge of the patient, and they gave her the room she needed as she carefully removed the wet rags.

It occurred to Jim to ask Murphy, "What were you doin' out on that part of our range?" Were you on your way to somewhere?"

"No, I was followin' the tracks of those three Indians. They burned my cabin and my barn down to the ground a day or two ago," Murphy answered. "I just got back from Newtown this afternoon."

"So Walter ain't the only one they were out to burn up," Jim said. "I swear, Murphy, that's rough news. Are you gonna build another cabin? I mean, you're livin' in town now. You have to be if you're the town marshal. Maybe it would be better for you if you didn't have a cabin and a barn out here to worry about."

"And go ahead and sell my hundred and sixty acres to the Rocking-J, right?" Murphy concluded for him, since the deal was obvious to both parties

Jim laughed sheepishly. "Well, that is one natural option, ain't it?"

"I suppose," Murphy answered, "except for one thing."

"And what's that?"

"I ain't gonna be livin' in town, 'cause I ain't gonna be the town marshal."

"You quit?" Jim couldn't believe it.

"I got fired," Murphy declared.

Jim found that even harder to believe. "Fired? For what?"

They were interrupted at that point by Atha Barnes. "Can I get your attention for a minute?" she exclaimed. "I need you to help me move Walter up to the house. I need to put him in the back bedroom, because I'm going to have to see him often to change the vinegar poultices."

They jumped at her command and came up to the bunk, where they stopped to decide the best way to transport him to the house that would cause him the least pain. She made the decision for them.

"The two of you take hold of each other's arms and make a chair for him. That way Walter can sit upright, and you can carry him into the house."

They looked at each other and nodded.

"I was gonna suggest that," Jim claimed.

"Right," Murphy responded. And they created the chair, and Miss Atha helped Walter off the bunk, then held him steady while he sat down in the "chair."

When it proved to be the answer, they transported him across the barnyard toward the ranch house and resumed the conversation that had just been interrupted.

"What did you mean when you said you got fired?" Jim asked.

"I meant just what I said. I was fired," Murphy insisted.

"From everything I've heard, I thought you were doin' a great job."

"I thought I was," Murphy replied.

"Was money the problem? Did they think they were paying you too much for the job?"

"I don't think that was the problem," Murphy said. "So far, they haven't paid me anything. You go first."

"Whaddaya mean?" Jim asked.

"We gotta go up the kitchen steps," Murphy replied. "I'll try to keep him as level as I can. If we try to go in like we're walkin' here, we can't get through the kitchen door. So you go first."

Jim swung around and started up the kitchen steps first, lowering his arms as much as he could without stumbling. Murphy followed him, lifting his side of the chair as much as he could to make it level. They made it through the door with no accidents.

"You're not really gonna build another cabin and barn on that piece of land, are you?"

"Why not?" Murphy said. "I've gotta live somewhere, and I own that spot."

"What's gonna keep somebody else from burnin' down the next cabin you build there? Then whaddaya gonna do?" Jim asked as Atha led them down the hallway.

"Same thing I did this time," Murphy said. "Track 'em down and put 'em in the ground."

Atha opened the door to the bedroom and held it for them. They carried Walter in and sat him down on the bed.

"I'll take it from here, boys," Miss Atha told them. "Murphy, what is your given name?"

"Cullen, ma'am," he replied.

"Well, Cullen, I appreciate what you've done for Walter. And from the constant jabbering between you and Jim, I would speculate that you haven't had any chance to eat supper. If that's the case, you're welcome to go into the kitchen and help yourself to a cup of coffee from that pot that's sitting on the stove. I expect Walter might be hungry also. So as soon as I can make him comfortable, I'll be in the kitchen to see if I can't come up with something to fill your bellies. Jim, you're welcome to join us."

"Why, thank you, ma'am," Murphy responded. "I am hungry. I figured I was gonna have to backtrack the way we rode in here to see if I could find some of that beef I know those Indians hid somewhere."

They were joined at that point by Lionel Jacobson, who had been enjoying his after-supper brandy in his study in the front part of the house. "Well, Marshal Murphy!" he exclaimed, surprised to see him in his house. He looked back and forth at Atha and Jim, waiting for a quick explanation for the lawman being in his house. "Are you here on official business?"

"Ah, no, sir," Murphy responded and stepped out of the doorway so Jacobson could see Walter sitting on the bed. "I was just returnin' someone who belongs to you."

Jacobson paused when he saw Walter, his face still half covered with dried blood, shirtless, with rags wrapped around his bare torso. "What the hell? Was he in town? What did he . . . ?"

"Walter wasn't in town," Jim King said, quick to keep him from forming the wrong impression. "He got ambushed by three Comanche. The ones who have been killin' our cattle. Murphy brought him home."

"Oh. Then I reckon we owe Marshal Murphy our thanks," Jacobson replied, but it was obvious that he was still confused by Murphy's presence this far out of town, and on his range at that.

"I'm not the town marshal anymore, Mr. Jacobson. The town council decided I was attracting gunslingers to Newtown. That's why I happened to be out here this afternoon. It was just lucky I was at the right place at the right time." He paused, then said, "At almost the right time. I woulda liked to have been there a little sooner."

Jim stepped in again, in case Jacobson was still wondering what Murphy had been doing on Rocking-J range. He explained the circumstances that had brought Murphy far up Brady Creek and onto their range.

"Well, that is a piece of bad news," Jacobson said then. "Burned your whole place down to the ground, did they? You can find an empty bunk in my bunkhouse if you need a place to stay while you're rebuildin' it. Right, Jim?"

"Yes, sir," Jim answered. "We might talk him into sellin' that piece of land to the Rocking-J, and then he wouldn't have to worry about his cabin gettin' burnt down."

Jacobson chuckled. "There's some wisdom in that line of thinking, Murphy."

"Yes, sir," Murphy chuckled with him. "I'm beginning to consider it myself." When he saw Jacobson's eyebrows rise in response, he quickly added, "Right now, I'm only sure of one thing. And that's to accept Miss Atha's offer of a cup of coffee."

"I'll join you in the kitchen," Jacobson said, realizing he should be showing more concern for his injured cowhand. He went on into the room in time to help Miss Atha position a bedside table next to the bed so she could treat Walter's burns. "Those blisters look painful as hell," he said to Walter. "Miss Atha will take care of you, though. I'm just glad Murphy came along when he did."

"Yes, sir, me too," Walter replied while clenching his teeth as Atha applied a poultice to one of the large blisters on his back. "I wish he'd come about half an hour before he did, though."

"You hang in there," Jacobson said. "You'll be back in the saddle in no time. I'll check on you later. I'll get out of Dr. Atha's way now." He turned to leave.

Atha fixed her bored expression upon him and said, "There's leftover biscuits in the warmer oven. It's gonna take me a little bit before I'm done with this. There are two kinds of jam on the shelf in the pantry. Maybe that'll keep Murphy from starving."

Jacobson found Jim and Murphy sitting at the kitchen table, drinking coffee, while Murphy was telling Jim exactly where he had come upon Walter's ambush. Jim repeated the information to him, along with his intention to take some of the men and scout that area of their range.

"We've been missin' some cattle in the last couple of weeks," he said. "I'm wonderin' if we might find the remains of a helluva lot more cows than we suspected. And we need to find out how many more of those damn Indians are rustling our cattle. Murphy's volunteered to stay over and go with me and a couple of the men in the mornin' to scout that section from his place and northwest of there."

"That's mighty neighborly of you, Murphy," Jacobson said. "I think that's a damn good idea. We need to know just how many Indians we've been feeding. And since you've agreed to go along, I'll get the biscuits Miss Atha said to feed you for supper. Look in the pantry, Jim. She said there are two kinds of jam to put on 'em."

Murphy grinned as he watched Jacobson take the biscuits off the pan and put them on a plate. Then he opened a drawer and got a spoon for the jam Jim had brought from the pantry. He decided he liked Lionel Jacobson. He reminded him of another rancher, named John Tate, who had hired him as a rough-edged boy to help drive a herd of cattle to a Kansas railroad. Totally inexperienced, at least as a horseman, he was a hard-riding cowhand by the time they had driven the herd to market. He worked for John Tate for four years before he left to find his own little ranch.

And how'd that work out for you? he had to ask himself, sitting in Lionel Jacobson's kitchen, his own cabin a pile of burned-up boards. He was halfway inclined to tell Jacobson to make him an offer to buy his land and hire him on as a cowhand. *But not tonight*, he decided.

By the time Miss Atha had her patient settled down for the night and joined them in the kitchen, the biscuits and the coffee were a memory. She looked at them with her hands on her hips for a couple of moments before addressing Murphy. "Did you get enough to hold you till breakfast? Or did these two coyotes wolf 'em all down?"

"I think I got enough to take the edge off," Murphy answered.

"Because if you didn't, my stove is still hot enough to fry up some bacon," she insisted.

"No, ma'am. Thank you very much, ma'am, but I think I got enough. That's awful kind of you. How's Walter? You think he's gonna have problems with those blisters on his chest and back?"

"I don't know," she answered honestly. "That poor boy was getting cooked just like a ham over a fire. I guess you could say he is lucky that the burns are just in spots, especially on his back, where he said that brute was pressing that stick against his skin. We'll just have to wait and see how he heals." She shook her head slowly. "If he heals."

Her prognosis put a damper on the conversation, so Jim said, "Maybe you can tell better if he gets some sleep tonight." He stood up and plopped his hat on his head. "We'd best go take care of those horses, and you can pick out a bunk for the night," he said to Murphy. Then he told Jacobson that he was going to take Matt Stokes and Curly Granger with him and Murphy in the morning. "We'll eat breakfast before we go."

Chapter 19

It had been a long time since Murphy had slept in a bunkhouse with a working crew of cowhands. When morning came, he was satisfied with the sleep he had gotten. He was surprised to have found it to be a relatively quiet bunkhouse. He was not aware of the fact that all the Rocking-J cowhands were well aware of who Cullen Murphy was. About half of them had been witnesses to some of his arrests. One of the men picked to ride with him that morning had been in Bradshaw's Saloon when Murphy and Liam Black were challenged by Ed Trask. So there was a certain amount of respect for the man whose intolerance of wrongdoing was responsible for the creation of the popular term *Murphy's Law*.

After a reasonably good breakfast at Corky's cookshack, the four-man scouting party left the Rocking-J to follow Murphy and Walter's trail from the lower quarter of the Rocking-J range. Murphy led them back over the trail for approximately a mile and a half. After about a mile, however, it became unnecessary to rely on his memory, for there was already a flock of buzzards circling the spot of the massacre. The four riders pulled up short of the grisly scene of the raucous, squawking buzzards as they perched on the three bodies and tore away strips of their rotting flesh.

"Well, nobody came to pick them up or bury them. That might mean there's nobody else in on this cattle rustlin' and there was just the three of them," Jim said. "I'm surprised you didn't dig a grave for these poor devils," Jim joked.

"I thought about it," Murphy replied, "but Walter was kinda in a hurry to get back to the ranch. And I figured those buzzards mighta been gettin' tired of all the beef they've been feedin' on."

"Those three Indians must have followed the San Saba up this way to strike our range," Jim speculated. "There ain't no tellin' how many of our cows they slaughtered before they went a little farther and found your cabin."

"That sure as hell turned out to be their unlucky day, didn't it?" Curly Granger declared when he recalled the picture of Murphy's encounter with Ed Trask in Bradshaw's Saloon.

"I'm just wonderin' how many more are back along that river," Jim said, "and why nobody else showed up lookin' for the three you killed. Those three mighta been supplying the food for a village."

"I don't think they were," Murphy said, "because they're eating the cows where they killed them. At least that's what they did when they burned my cabin down. I think they mighta been there a couple of days before they left. When I started trackin' 'em and found one place they camped, it was the same story. They cooked the meat right there. Then they ran up on Walter. I ain't no expert on Indians, but it looks to me like those three were all alone . . . renegades or something. I don't know. Why don't we follow this river back a few miles and see if that's the way they came in here?"

"Might as well," Jim King said. "I don't have any better idea."

So they headed in a more southernly direction and rode until coming to the San Saba River a short distance upstream from the remains of Murphy's cabin. This was the place where Murphy had left the river the day before, when he'd followed the Indians' trail. They followed what appeared to be a definite game trail close to the banks of the river for barely a quarter of a mile before Matt Stokes pointed to a few buzzards circling in the sky a short distance ahead.

They continued on until coming to a wide stream, and whatever the buzzards were circling appeared to be up that stream, so they followed the stream, thinking that the carrion might be a single cow's remains. To their surprise, however, they came upon the remains of a camp that looked to have been used for more than a few days. Anxious now to see what the buzzards might be circling, they continued along the stream until coming to a fork made when a smaller stream joined the one they were following. In a small clearing between the forks, they found the mostly skeletal remains of about a dozen cattle, with some scraps of flesh or enough skin to attract the attention of the few buzzards overhead.

It was easy to assume this was a more permanent camp of the three dead Indians. They had obviously been there for quite some time, living off Rocking-J cattle they had led back to their camp. It was also reasonable to assume the three were alone in their cattle rustling, for whatever reason. Consequently, Jim King decided it useless to scout further. He was convinced their Indian trouble was over, so they took a direct line back to the ranch headquarters to report their findings to Lionel Jacobson. Murphy went back with them to get his packhorse and his belongings.

They made it back to the Rocking-J in time to eat the noon meal at the cookshack, so Murphy took advantage of that before he departed, preferring it to the bacon he would cook for himself back at what was left of his cabin.

Lionel Jacobson came back to the cookshack with Jim to

thank Murphy for ridding him of his Indian problem. "I just wish you had come a little sooner," he told him. "Jim said it looked like bones of over a dozen cows in that clearing."

"Yes, sir, I expect there musta been," Murphy replied, "and it smelled like there was still some for the buzzards to clean up."

"If you don't mind me asking, what are your plans now?" Jacobson asked. "Jim tells me you're dead set on building another cabin."

"I don't see as how I've got any other option," Murphy replied. "I'm gonna need a place to live, no matter what I do for a livin'."

"You ever work with cattle?"

"Yes, sir, for about four years, back when I was a younger man, not much more than a boy actually. That was back before the war. I rode for a man named John Tate, on the Triple-T, west of Fort Worth."

"If you're not sure you're ready to start building that cabin, I'm sure I can use you to work with Jim at the Rocking-J until you are ready to go on your own again. And if you change your mind about raising horses, I'll buy that hundred and sixty acres of yours for the same price you paid for it."

Murphy didn't respond right away, pausing to consider it. He told himself he wouldn't have even considered it before his little homestead was destroyed. Now he wondered if he really wanted to try to build a horse herd. "That's a lot to think about," he finally said. "I can understand how my property would extend your range all the way to the river. Let me think about it for a day or two, and I'll let you know what I'm gonna do. Is that all right?"

"Certainly," Jacobson replied. "Take all the time you need. You're welcome to bunk here at the Rocking-J while you're thinking about it."

"I 'preciate the offer," Murphy said, "but I think I'll go on back to my place and camp there while I give it some thought."

"The offer's open, if you change your mind," Jacobson said.

"Thank you, sir." He started to leave but paused to ask, "How's Walter after a night's sleep, if he did go to sleep?"

"He didn't get much sleep, I'm afraid," Jacobson said. "Atha told me he said he passed out sometime close to sunup but woke up not long after when he rolled over on his back."

"I expect before he heals up, he's gonna wish I'd shot him, too," Murphy said.

He left the Rocking-J right after the noon meal in order to have plenty of daylight left to try to put a camp together, one that would be more than just an overnight camp. It was going to take some time to build another cabin and barn like the ones he lost. One of the first chores to confront him was the necessity to drag the remains of the cow the Indians had slaughtered in his backyard to the other side of the creek, beyond the tree line. He wanted them to be out in the open so the sun and the buzzards could work on them, and hopefully downwind.

Once the cow was out of the way, he took the saddles off his horses and started an inventory of what was left to make a temporary shelter. There was not much to work with. The fire had burned long enough to destroy even the foundation logs. "I'm afraid you're in for a lot of work," he said to Nosy when the big bay gelding nudged him in the back as he stood staring at the burnt timbers. He remembered the gray gelding named Trouble that had the hauling chore when he built his cabin. Trouble was a good horse. Murphy took him with him when they both joined the army. Trouble got halfway through the war before a sniper's bullet took him out from under Murphy. He tried two or three other horses before he found Nosy, and they'd had a tight working relationship ever since.

Luckily, there had been no sign of rain for the past couple of days, so he decided not to worry about trying to rig up something to keep him dry that night. He would just spread his bedroll on a flat piece of ground and use his saddle as a pillow. He would look through his packs to decide what he would cook for his supper. He knew he had plenty of bacon, but he wasn't sure what he had to cook with it. "I should have stopped at Baxter's store before I left town yesterday," he said to Nosy. "Maybe we'll catch a deer sneakin' around that creek in the mornin'," he speculated, "or one of Jacobson's cows." He laughed at the thought. "Hell, they owe me at least one cow for shootin' those three Comanches."

He looked over at his cabin and the only thing left standing was the stone fireplace and chimney. At least they didn't steal the iron grill over the fireplace, so he could still place his frying pan and his coffeepot over the fire and cook his supper. As darkness settled in over the San Saba River where Brady Creek joined it, he sat by the fireplace and thought about the first time he saw the little clearing. It struck him then that it was the most peaceful spot he had ever happened upon. It still had a peaceful feeling even now, as the night deepened and hid the charred remains of his cabin. He fell asleep under a starry sky, thinking about his plans for the new cabin.

He started early in the morning to clear the rest of the burned timbers away from the fireplace. He intended to build the new cabin around it. Once that was done, he would saw down the trees that would form his new foundation as well as the walls for the cabin. He worked continuously, but it seemed his progress was slow. He was sharpening the edge on his chisel when he had a visitor.

It was late afternoon when he spotted the lone rider approaching on the trail beside the river, often referred to as the River Road. He paused in his work to watch the rider. Something about him looked familiar, even that far away. A little closer and he identified him. It was Elmo Dillon. *Probably on his way to visit his brother's farm again*, Murphy thought. He put his hatchet and his chisel down and walked outside the walls of the partially built cabin to meet him when he came across the river.

"Howdy, Elmo," he called out cheerfully. "What brings you out of town this evenin'? You goin' to visit your brother?"

"Howdy, Cullen," Elmo returned. "No, I've come to see you." When his horse came up out of the water, he saw what Murphy was working on. "What happened? You have a fire?"

"I sure did," Murphy replied. "Three Indians burnt the cabin down while I was still in Newtown."

"That sure is sorry news," Elmo said. "How do you know it was three Indians?"

"I was lucky enough to track 'em down."

"So I reckon they haven't started any more fires," Elmo said.

"No, but I hope they're tending one big one right now. What did you come to see me about?"

"Some more sorry news," Elmo said. "I hate to come beggin' after we kicked you outta the marshal's job. But I rode out here to ask you to come back to Newtown. Things have gone to hell since you left. An outlaw by the name of Clay Barnett hit town right after you left. He's got a gang of five men, and they've managed to take over the whole town. They've taken up permanent residence in Bradshaw's Saloon, including Irene Floyd's café. They're using Irene's as their own personal dining room, and none of her old customers go there anymore. They're afraid they'll get shot down like Jeff Baxter if they refuse to dance while Barnett's hoodlums shoot around their feet with their six-guns."

"They shot Eliot Baxter's son?" Murphy gasped, finding it hard to believe. "Why?"

"Jeff went into the café to eat dinner, and one of 'em, a foul-mouthed scoundrel they called Squint, laid his hands on Bonnie Floyd and wouldn't let her go. Jeff went to help her, and he and that Squint fellow got into it. Squint pulled a gun, and Jeff didn't even have one. So they fought over it, but Squint pulled free and shot Jeff in the chest. Ginger Floyd slipped out the back and ran to get Bert. Bert was on his way, anyway, because he heard the shot. He told Squint he was under arrest for murder, and Squint refused to be arrested and pulled his gun on Bert. But Bert was faster than he was and shot him down."

Murphy nodded thoughtfully. "I told him he was fast enough with that Colt, and I reckon that proved it to him."

"It ain't gonna give him much satisfaction," Elmo said. "Bert's dead."

"What?" Murphy blurted. "How? I thought you said he was faster than the other fellow!"

"He was," Elmo said. "But Barnett ordered his men to grab Bert. He said the penalty for shooting one of his men was death by hanging. A couple of his men are big animals, and they tied Bert up and carried him out on Front Street and hung him on a rope from the second-floor porch railing. Barnett said anybody cutting Bert down would be shot on sight. He's still hanging there, right in front of the saloon, for everybody to look at. The whole town is scared to death. Eliot Baxter is sick with grief. I rode out of town this afternoon, when I was pretty sure Barnett and his animals weren't outside to see me."

Murphy was stunned. He couldn't imagine the town could have been taken over like that. There had been previous gangs that preyed on the unprotected little town, miles from any real law authority. But to have a gang of cutthroats come into town like an invading force was beyond imagination. He was hit hard by the news of Bert Walker's death, and he felt totally responsible for it. Before he worked with Bert and built up his confidence in handling his sidearm, Bert would not have had courage enough to face up to a gunslinger like this Squint character.

"So Baxter and Bradshaw sent you to get me?" he asked.

"No, they didn't send me," Elmo replied. "Bradshaw is like a prisoner in his saloon, so he couldn't come talk to me, anyway, and Baxter's been in a bad way ever since they shot Jeff. So I decided to come to tell you myself, because I didn't know what else to do. The situation might just be too much for one man to handle. Bert killed one of them, but there are five more, and they are all killers."

He paused, wringing his hands nervously. "I didn't know what else to do but come looking for you. Cullen, I know this ain't your problem, and I can't blame you a bit if you tell me to go to hell after the way we cut you loose without no warning at all. And for no other reason except you were too good for the job. If you decide you'll come back to Newtown, I'll help all I can, although I don't know how much good I can do you. I've got a shotgun I know how to use."

"Of course I'll go back with you," Murphy said. "I have some good friends in Newtown." He had made that decision when Elmo told him that the outlaws had lynched Bert Walker for the town to gawk at. The thought of it had lit a fuse to his inner fury, and he would do whatever it took to punish the men who would mistreat a fine young man in that fashion. "Let me bury my tools and pack up my horses. Who's got the keys to the jailhouse?"

"I don't know," Elmo answered. "I expect Bert mighta had them in his pocket. At least the key to the office door."

"I'll find out about that when we get to town, because that's where I plan to stay. If his killers searched him when they hung him, maybe Clay Barnett has the key." He wrapped his hatchet and chisel, along with his handsaw and axe in a piece of canvas and quickly dug a little trench with his shovel. Then he laid the bundle in the trench and covered it up with dirt. He looked at Elmo, who was watching him intensely. "That's just in case I make it back here." He started to load his things on his pack-horse but stopped when he had a second thought. "You say that gang is holed up in Bradshaw's Saloon?"

Elmo said that was a fact.

"Then I think I wanna catch 'em early in the mornin', before breakfast. You can stay here tonight if you don't wanna ride back to town. I've got enough grub to make some supper, and I can fix up a bed for you, if you don't mind sleepin' on the ground."

"I'll stay here and go back with you in the morning," Elmo decided immediately.

They covered the three miles to Newtown in about half an hour's time. Since it was still early morning, there were only one or two people on the street. Murphy pulled up to a sudden stop when he saw Bert Walker's body hanging from the second-floor porch railing. It sickened him to see the young blacksmith turned marshal, his hands tied behind his back, his boots tied together.

Murphy spoke for the first time since they had left his cabin. "Elmo, I don't know what's gonna happen from this point on. But it might be a good idea to let me handle this alone from here." He was being honest in his evaluation of his plan of attack, because, in truth, he had none. He would take it step-by-step and react to whatever he encountered. It was going to be difficult enough to take care of himself, so he preferred not to have Elmo to worry about, as well.

Elmo understood his meaning. "All right. I'll get out of your way. Is there anything I can do to help you?"

"Do you know any of the other names besides Barnett and Squint?" Murphy asked.

"I know a couple of the names. Barnett called one of them

Bad Eye. He wears a patch over one eye. And he called a big brute of a man Luther. I don't know the others' names." He apologized for not knowing them all. "What are you going to do?"

"Well, the first thing I'm gonna do is cut Bert down from that rope and take him to Doc Ennis, so he can prepare him for a decent burial. Then I think it'll be Clay Barnett's move. While he's thinkin' about it, I'll take my horses to the stable. If Mr. Barnett hasn't contacted me by then, I'll most likely go lookin' for him."

Elmo said he would be at his shop, if Murphy needed him. Then he remained there, sitting on his horse, while Murphy moved toward the body hanging on the rope.

Nosy hesitated for a moment when Murphy guided the big horse up beside the motionless body, but Murphy urged him forward until he was beside it. Then Murphy drew his skinning knife from his belt and stood up in the stirrups. With one hand gripping the hangman's knot, he reached above it and cut the rope, then helped ease the body down to the ground with the one hand on the rope. He dismounted and took a look all around him to make sure there were no guns pointing at him from any direction. He saw no threat, only two spectators who had witnessed the defiant action, both of whom seemed to be shocked motionless. Knowing he was most vulnerable at this point, he wasted no time picking Bert's body up from the street. Finding the body still rigid from rigor mortis, he raised it up like a log and tilted it on his shoulder until he could transfer it over to lay across his saddle. It appeared that Bert's body might be starting to limber up again, as it bent a little when he placed it on the saddle. Murphy found that this helped balance the body enough so that he could lead his horse slowly without tipping the body to either side.

It was not a long walk to the drugstore and the funeral barn behind it, but it was a definite feeling of relief to get the body out of sight before one of the unwanted visitors saw him. He tied Nosy's reins to Doc Ennis's barn door and went to the back door of the drugstore and knocked. No one answered right away, so he knocked again, this time louder. In about two minutes, the door opened.

"Cullen Murphy!" Ennis exclaimed. "Boy, am I glad to see you! We've got a helluva mess on our hands."

"Yeah, I know," Murphy said. "Elmo Dillon told me. I've got Bert Walker's body out back. You need to prepare him for burial."

"Did you take him down?" He didn't wait for his answer. "They said anybody would be shot if they tried to take him down."

"Yeah, well, they ain't makin' the rules no more," Murphy replied. "Bert Walker gave his life for this town, and we owe him a decent burial. Nobody needs to know where the body is, if that's what worries you."

"You're right about that," Ennis said. "We owe Bert at least that much. Let's get him inside." He walked back into the room to put his shoes on and slip into a bathrobe while Murphy waited inside the barn door. Then they walked out the back door to find Bert standing there, leaning against Murphy's horse. The sight gave both of them a start.

Ennis recovered before Murphy and said, "They ain't usually that anxious to get here." Evidently, Murphy's horse had moved enough to cause the body to slide off the saddle and land on its feet to lean against the horse. Not sure if Murphy would appreciate his second thought, Ennis didn't voice it. But it occurred to him that if the horse had shifted the other way, Bert might have been standing on his head when they came out.

Murphy took hold of Bert's boots and picked the body up

so Ennis could take his shoulders as they slid off the saddle. They carried the body inside and put it down on a table. "You're right," Ennis said. "Rigor mortis is starting to work its way back. He'll be getting limber pretty quick now." He pulled Bert's shirt open to bare his abdomen. "Yes, he's already got that green tint to his skin, and he's starting to smell already. Looks like I better get to work right now."

With no reason to linger over Bert's putrefying body, Murphy walked out of the barn, and Ennis followed him. "What are you going to do now?" Ennis asked him. "I know you've come back to set things right again." He hesitated, then had to swear. "Damn, we made a helluva mistake when we voted to let you go. Nobody could blame you if you just told us to sink or swim. Why did you come back?"

"You folks have got the makings for a good town," Murphy said. "It just ain't right for a gang of outlaws to ride in here and destroy everything honest folks are workin' to build. And I just can't abide a man who makes his livin' by takin' another man's livin' with his gun."

"You know there's five of 'em, don't you?" Ennis asked.

Murphy said he did.

"And I'll swear, they're the roughest-looking bunch that's ever hit this town. And they ain't gonna leave until they've bled every one of us dry."

"They've kinda made Bradshaw's their headquarters, is that right?" Murphy asked.

"That's right," Ennis answered. "And I feel sorry for poor Tyson. They've run all his business off, and it's especially bad for Irene and her daughters. They're trapped in that saloon with him." He paused to let that sink in with Murphy. "Where are you heading when you leave here?"

"I've gotta take my horses to the stable, and then I'm gonna go tell Clay Barnett that somebody cut Bert Walker's body down. So I expect I'd better get goin'."

"Doggone it, Murphy," Ennis couldn't help exclaiming, "you be careful. You're the only weapon we've got."

"I will be," Murphy replied. "But whatever happens, you've got one more weapon that's bigger than me. You've just hesitated to use it. And I know you've talked about it. But I reckon you just ain't been pushed to that point yet."

"You're talking about a vigilante committee, aren't you?"

"That's right," Murphy answered, "and if I don't do what I came to do, that's your next step, and I advise you to take it." He stepped up into the saddle then and rode back to the street, heading to the stable.

Ennis stood there and watched him ride away to what he perceived to be a voluntary suicide mission. He was confident that Murphy might take out one or maybe two of Barnett's gang of murderers, leaving three or possibly four to take their vengeance on the town. Vigilante action was brave talk when there was no immediate threat, but an entirely different thing when going up against three or four cold-blooded killers. True, there had been a lot of discussion about organizing a vengeance committee when the town council met in the saloon. But when individuals were talking privately, no one wanted to participate in a vigilante arrest and hanging. Too often they uttered, "I didn't bring my family out here to fight outlaws." That made it necessary to depend on men like Cullen Murphy, men who had no family, no home, and no business. Murphy might disappear just as mysteriously as he had appeared a short time ago.

Holding his shotgun with both hands, Paul Mathers watched the street from his hayloft, his eyes on the rider and packhorse turning off Front Street and coming up the path to his stable. "I hope to hell that ain't some more friends of Clay Barnett's," he muttered aloud, "especially this early in the mornin'." He was already taking care of a dozen of their horses, and so far, there had been no payment of any kind.

"Cullen Murphy!" he blurted when the rider came close enough to identify. He hurried to the ladder and almost fell off the hayloft headfirst when he tried to grab the ladder while still holding his shotgun. Forced to slow down and be careful, he still made it down in time to greet Murphy when he rode up.

"Cullen Murphy!" he called out. "I swear, I believe I'm happier to see you than I would be to see another feller I won't mention for fear I'd get struck by lightning."

"Howdy, Paul," Murphy returned the greeting. "I'm happy to see you, too. But I wish it was under better circumstances."

"So you know what's goin' on here, right?"

"Yep, Elmo Dillon rode out to my place last night with the news about Bert Walker."

"I reckon Elmo told you all about the situation we've got for ourselves here in town," Mathers said. "Did you see poor Bert's body hangin' in front of Bradshaw's Saloon?"

"Yes, I did," Murphy replied. "I took it down and carried it over to Doc Ennis's place. He's gonna get Bert ready for a decent burial."

"You know what that damn outlaw said was gonna happen to anybody who cut Bert down?"

"Yeah, I heard," Murphy replied. "I need to leave my horses with you. You wouldn't happen to know where the key to the jailhouse is, would you?"

"No, I ain't got no idea," Mathers answered. "I wasn't there when Barnett's men jumped Bert. Robert Jessop was, and he told me they searched Bert, took everything out of his pockets. If they got his jail key, they didn't say nothin' about it. And as far as I know, there ain't been anybody in the jailhouse night or day."

"Maybe it'll turn up somewhere," Murphy said. "If it doesn't, I might break into it, because that's where I'm plannin' to stay while I'm in town."

Mathers looked at him as if he was born the day before. "Did Elmo or Doc tell you how many outlaws we're talking about?"

"He said five," Murphy responded. "Have there been any more show up since this mornin'?"

"Ain't five enough for you?" Mathers blurted.

"It's less than half a dozen," Murphy replied. "I've got Bert Walker to thank for that." He started pulling his saddle off Nosy. "Same stall I used to be in?"

"No, I'll clear out another one for you," Mathers said. "Clay Barnett and his friends are using those three stalls down at that end of the stable. They don't pay as good as you did."

He took Murphy's packsaddle off the packhorse and carried it to a stall well away from Barnett's. Murphy followed him with his saddle and said he would come for his saddlebags when he decided where he was going to sleep that night.

Mathers just shook his head and asked, "Cullen, what the hell are you fixin' to do?"

"I'm goin' down to Bradshaw's Saloon to tell Clay Barnett that somebody took Bert Walker's body down, in case he hadn't heard. After that, it's gonna be pretty close to breakfast, so I might get something to eat at Irene's, if she's still in business."

"Are you sure you know what you're walkin' into?" Mathers asked, thinking that Murphy surely could not be fool enough to walk into a virtual hornet's nest.

"If you're wantin' an honest answer," Murphy said, "no, I don't. I have a pretty good idea, and I guess I'll find out for sure when I get there."

"Cullen," Mathers pleaded, "that's crazy talk."

"Paul, I can't abide a man that would order his men to murder a lawman, and I intend to see that he pays for it. I'd appreciate it if you would take care of my horses."

With that said, he pulled his Henry rifle out of his saddle scabbard, checked to see that it was fully loaded, then cranked a round into the chamber. Next, he pulled his Colt out of his holster and broke open the cylinder. He inserted a cartridge into the one empty chamber and carefully eased the hammer down. Ready then, he walked out of the stable and headed for Bradshaw's Saloon.

CHAPTER 20

Clay Barnett sat at the head of three small tables his men had moved together to create one long one. Emmett Rice sat on his right side. Always the first two to get out of bed in the morning, they were drinking coffee when Bad Eye Wilson came down the stairs and went directly to the bar.

"Gimme a bottle of that good rye," he told Pete Brice. "And bring me a cup of coffee to the table."

"That's the last bottle of that rye whiskey," Pete told him when he handed it to him. "There ain't nothin' but corn whiskey left." It was a lie, but Pete was hoping to save some of the more expensive whiskey from the gang's consumption.

"Maybe you'd best get some from one of the other saloons," Bad Eye told him. "Is that old witch cookin' breakfast yet?"

"She is," Pete replied. "It won't be long."

"It better not be," Bad Eye said. He picked up the bottle and a glass and went to the table. "And don't forget my coffee," he yelled back over his shoulder. He sat down at the table to Barnett's left and poured some whiskey in the glass.

"You startin' the day with that kinda early, ain'tcha?" Emmett asked.

"I need a little hair of the dog that bit me last night," Bad Eye said with a grin. "We oughta be gittin' some breakfast pretty soon. Pete said they was cookin' it."

Tyson Bradshaw came down the steps from his private quarters then and was almost knocked down by two prostitutes, who were in a hurry to escape Lefty Birchfield and Luther Boyd after a hard night's work. The two soiled doves were anxious to get back to their own rooms over Pratt's Saloon. Bradshaw didn't say anything to the three seated at the table. He exchanged a look of frustration with Pete as he walked by on his way to the kitchen. He had been told to stop complaining about the money owed him. Barnett had told him to simply keep a running tab, and he would be paid in full when they left.

Concerned about Irene Floyd and the two girls, he tried to bolster their courage as best he could. Barnett had given them a simple choice: do the cooking for his gang or provide the female companionship he and his men desired. Bradshaw knew he would not likely receive a dime from them when they decided they were ready to leave Newtown. He was also very much afraid that Ginger and Bonnie would be subject to outright assault when the girls were no longer needed to cook meals. Both of them were openly ogled whenever they entered the room. If it progressed beyond that, he was not confident in his ability to protect them. He thought of Eliot Baxter's sacrifice, the loss of his son to this band of mongrels.

When Luther and Lefty came down the stairs, Barnett yelled at Pete. "Go tell those women we're hungry, and bring that coffeepot back out here." Pete didn't respond verbally but did as he was told.

In a minute, Pete was back, followed by Ginger with the big coffeepot. She went around the table, filling their cups. Lefty stood, waiting to sit down after she passed by his chair. While she filled his cup, he placed his hand on her behind. She did not flinch but casually poured hot coffee on his hand.

"Yow!" he yelped and jerked his hand away. "You evil snake! Before I leave here, you're gonna pay for that!"

The incident caused a tableful of guffaws from his companions. And since it was his left hand that took a scalding, Bad Eye remarked, "I reckon we'll be callin' you Righty from now on." That called for another round of chortles from the others.

"Hurry up with that damn breakfast," Barnett yelled at her as she went out the door.

He insisted on being served in the saloon, instead of going into the dining room to eat. He preferred to sit in the back of the saloon, facing forward, so he could see everyone who came in the front door as soon as they came in. Even so, the distraction created by the hot coffee caused him to be surprised by the sudden appearance of the rugged individual holding the Henry rifle, who was already halfway back to the table. "What the hell do you want?" he demanded.

"Are you Clay Barnett?" Murphy asked, but Barnett didn't answer him. "I came to tell you that somebody cut the town marshal down you left hangin' in front of the saloon."

Unnoticed by anyone, Pete Brice silently mouthed the word *Murphy*!

"What?" Barnett exclaimed. "Who cut him down? Did you see him?"

"Yeah, you could say that."

"Well, he's a dead man. Who was it?"

"Me," Murphy said. "And the marshal sends his regards." He raised the rifle and placed a shot in the center of Barnett's forehead. In the few seconds that Emmett and Bad Eye were too startled to react, Murphy cranked the Henry twice and placed a shot in the chest of each of them. The fastest gun in Barnett's gang, Lefty Birchfield, managed to get off one shot. But since he was hampered by a still painful left hand, it was wide of his target, catching Murphy in the left shoulder. Murphy ignored the wound and pulled his Colt to return fire but was surprised when Lefty was knocked over his chair by a shotgun blast from Irene Floyd, who was standing in the kitchen doorway. He turned then, in time to see Luther lifted off his chair by a buckshot blast from Pete's shotgun.

After the sudden eruption of gunfire, there was what seemed a long moment of total silence before anyone dared to speak. Then Bradshaw and the two girls ran in from the kitchen, and Pete came out from behind the bar.

"Murphy!" Bradshaw exclaimed, unable to put his thanks into words.

"I knew I could count on Irene and Pete to help me form the firing squad," Murphy said. "Thank you both. I needed help."

Assured that their mother was all right, Ginger and Bonnie both turned their attention to Murphy. They rushed to him to thank him for caring enough to come to the town's aid, not realizing until then that there was blood on his sleeve.

"You're shot!" Bonnie cried out in distress.

"Yeah, I caught one in the shoulder from that left-handed one. I was gonna return the favor, but your mother blew him away with that shotgun."

"Mama," Ginger exclaimed. "You better look at his shoulder. He's bleeding pretty badly."

"It ain't that bad," Murphy said. "I'll go get Doc Ennis to see if he can get the bullet out of there. Mr. Bradshaw, we need to clean this mess up." He was referring to the five bodies lying on the floor. "I expect you're out a lot of money this gang owes you. So if I was you, I'd search these bodies to see if they can pay you for what you're out. 'Course, I imagine Doc Ennis will wanna be paid if he has to take care of five bodies. That's unless you and the council decide you'll just load 'em in a wagon and haul 'em out somewhere away from town and dig a big hole or dump 'em on the ground and let the buzzards take care of 'em."

"What do we owe you for coming back to take care of our problem?" Bradshaw asked.

Murphy looked surprised. "You don't owe me anything. My

only expense was the cost of three .44 cartridges, and I'll gladly donate that to the town council."

"Well, we'll certainly pay Ennis for whatever the cost is to take care of that bullet wound," Bradshaw said. "You tell him that. Come to think of it, if he's got any appreciation for what you did for the town, there ought not be any charge. You tell him that, too."

"Here, honey," Irene told him. "Let's stick this dish towel up under your shirt to catch some of that bleeding till you can go to see Doc Ennis." He was touched by her affectionate tone. "Is there anything else I can do for you?"

"I was plannin' on trying to get some breakfast after my visit with Clay Barnett," he said. "Any chance of that?"

"Oh, my stars in heaven!" Irene shrieked. "I've got biscuits in the oven!"

Ginger calmed her down by saying, "It's all right, Mama. Bonnie took 'em out of the oven. She said they're fine, maybe baked a little longer than usual, but not enough so you'd notice."

"Does that mean I can get something to eat?" Murphy asked.

Irene gave him a playful punch on his shoulder. "Of course you can. You know I'll always fix you something to eat if you're hungry," she said, not realizing she had just punched his wounded shoulder. He tried to show no pain and looked away to catch Ginger watching him. She smiled and shook her head to keep from laughing.

"I guess I could give you and Pete some help gettin' those bodies out of here, so you can open up again," Murphy said to Bradshaw.

"No," Bradshaw insisted, "Pete and I can carry them out of here. You'll start that wound to bleeding again. There's not but one of 'em that looks like a real load, anyway." He nodded toward Luther Boyd's body. "You go get some breakfast. Then go get that wound taken care of."

The three women were waiting for him in the dining room. They sat him down and fussed over him like a lost child returning home. He enjoyed the attention but had to chuckle when he asked himself how long it would last if he stuck around for a while. And he had decided that he would stick around until the town had fully recovered.

By the time he left the dining room, Pete and Bradshaw had laid all five bodies in a row outside the saloon, and they had already become an attraction as many people came out of their holes again. He knocked on the door to Elmo's on his way to the drugstore and gave him the news.

"I heard all the gunfire," Elmo said, "and I didn't know what to do. I thought all five of them might have shot you."

Murphy laughed and said, "They missed every time but once. I'm on my way to see if Doc Ennis can get that bullet out of my shoulder." He told Elmo what had happened and how they had killed all five of the outlaws in about a thirty-second gun battle.

"And Irene Floyd killed the man who shot you," Elmo repeated, amazed by the thought.

"That's a fact," Murphy said. "She killed him, but it wasn't because he shot me. It was because he put his hand on Ginger's bottom."

"I'll swear," Elmo said, and they both chuckled. "You can't blame him for that, I reckon. I've thought about it myself on occasion."

"I wish you hadn't told me that," Murphy said. "I used to have a lotta respect for you. I gotta go get some doctorin' on my shoulder." He continued down the street, and Elmo went the other way to look at the bodies.

When he reached the drugstore, he found Doc Ennis trying to decide whether to push his handcart to Bradshaw's Saloon or go up there first to see who got shot. "Well, I'm mighty glad to see it ain't you I'll need my cart for," he announced.

"You'll need more than your cart, if the town council decides to pay you to take care of the bodies," Murphy told him.

"How many?" Ennis asked.

"Five," Murphy answered and paused while Ennis nodded his approval of the good news. "But I don't know if the council is gonna decide to have you bury them or just take 'em away from town somewhere and let the buzzards have 'em."

"Did you get shot?" Ennis asked and pointed to his bloody shirt.

"Yeah, I got one in my shoulder. That's why I came to see you, to see if you can dig it out of me."

"Let's have a look at it," Ennis said. "Come on back to my examining room." Murphy followed him back to the room behind the drugstore.

"You wanna take your shirt off? Or I can just cut that sleeve away."

"I'll take it off," Murphy responded. "Ain't no use in ruining a good shirt just because it's got a little hole in the shoulder." He pulled his shirttail out of his trousers and started unbuttoning his shirt while Ennis went over to a cabinet against the wall where he kept his instruments. "You want me to lay down on that table?"

"No, you can just sit down on it while I take a look. You don't seem to be hurtin' too much right now."

Murphy sat down on the table, and Doc said, "There ain't no hole in the back of your shoulder, so it's still in there." He probed a little way into the wound before deciding he was going to have to go into it pretty deeply to find the bullet. He gave Murphy his prognosis. "I'm gonna have to put you to sleep and do some digging to get to that bullet. That's gonna take a little time, which you might not want to spend right now, so we could schedule it later on sometime. Judging by how you're moving it, you don't seem to be in much pain, so I can pour some disinfectant in there and put a bandage on it and do it when you're ready."

He paused to see Murphy's reaction to that suggestion before giving him another option. "That slug looks like it might be in the muscle and ain't in the way of any working parts of your shoulder, so you might decide to just leave it in there. Oh, you'll still have some pain until it heals up around it, but then you'd forget it was even in there. Anyway, I'll fix you up temporarily, and you can decide which way you want to go. I'll charge you two dollars for this visit and seven if I go in and get the slug out. That includes the price for the chloroform and the operation."

Murphy said he was all right with the temporary treatment. He figured Doc was anxious to get up the street to Bradshaw's Saloon to see if there was a chance to take possession of the five bodies, maybe even to fix them up to display them for a while on Front Street. So he told Doc to pour some disinfectant in the wound and bandage it, and he'd decide which way to go later. Having waited in anticipation of the decision, Doc immediately poured the iodine in the bullet hole without warning.

"Hot damn!" Murphy exclaimed and almost sprang up to his feet.

"Hold on for a minute, till I put a bandage on that shoulder." He tied a bandage around the shoulder and asked, "You need a sling?"

Murphy said no and went into his pocket for the two dollars and handed them over. Doc put the two dollars in his pocket and walked out the front door of the drugstore with Murphy. He paused to lock the door; then they walked up the street to Bradshaw's Saloon, where a crowd had gathered to gape at the five dead men who had brought the town to a standstill.

Many in the crowd gaped at Murphy as he and Doc made

their way through the spectators and went inside the saloon, where Pete and Bradshaw were putting the tables back in their proper places. There was evidence that Pete had mopped up some patches of blood from the floor. Eliot Baxter was standing there, talking to Tyson Bradshaw. They stopped talking and turned to speak with the new arrivals.

"I see you got your shoulder fixed up," Bradshaw said. "Did you tell Doc I'd take care of the bill?"

"As a matter of fact, I forgot," Murphy answered. "It wasn't unreasonable, anyway."

Bradshaw looked at once to Ennis for an explanation. "I swear, Doc, the man came back here and saved the damn town!"

Doc shrugged and replied, "Like he said, it wasn't unreasonable. If I'd known you were going to pay the bill, I would have charged him more than two dollars."

"Pete," Bradshaw said, "get two dollars out of the register and give it to Murphy."

"You don't have to do that," Murphy protested. "It was reasonable. If I decide to have him take the bullet outta my shoulder, then maybe he'll give me a break on that fee."

"I already gave you a break on that fee," Doc declared. "My normal price woulda been twice that."

"I swear, if you ain't something, Ennis," Bradshaw charged. "Pete, give Murphy his two dollars."

"Just put me down for two bucks' credit on your books, Pete," Murphy said. "That way, it'll go further."

"Now, if we're through trying to get me to work for free, tell me what you're going to do with those five bodies you've got lying out in front of your saloon," Doc said.

"We considered loading them on a wagon and hauling them out in the hills to feed the buzzards, which would save the town a little money. But we're willing to honor the agreement the town council has with you to take care of the bodies."

"Come on, Tyson," Doc declared. "I was hoping the council would see fit to up my fee in this unusual case when there are five bodies to handle."

"There has never been any discussion about a limit to how many bodies you dispose of, just a set fee to dispose of each body," Bradshaw insisted.

"You know, there's something else you might want to consider," Doc suggested. "We might want to make a display as a warning to any other outlaws. For a little extra for each one, I could fix 'em all up like they were ready for a funeral, and we could leave them out front of your saloon."

Murphy couldn't help noticing that through all the bantering between Bradshaw and Ennis, Mayor Eliot Baxter stood silent, his face held a look of faraway thoughts. With all the talk about disposing of dead bodies like they were so many road apples left after the passing of a herd of horses, he wondered if Baxter was on the brink of insanity. Ennis had just prepared Baxter's son for his funeral, his only son, and to hear Ennis and Bradshaw argue about bodies as if they were worthless clutter had to be hard for Baxter to bear. He decided to try the only thing he could think of at the moment.

"Mr. Mayor, could I borrow a couple of minutes of your time?"

"What?" Baxter responded, looking confused, as if he had been far away in his mind. Looking at Murphy then, he seemed to realize where he was. "What is it, Murphy?"

"I'd like to talk to you about something just for a minute, but there's too much noise in here. How 'bout we go in the kitchen and get a cup of coffee, and I won't take but a minute of your time? Unless you wanna stay here and listen to these two argue."

"No," Baxter said. "I guess a cup of coffee would be good right now."

So he followed Murphy into the kitchen, where Irene and the girls were cleaning up after breakfast.

"Cullen!" Irene exclaimed. "You're back already. And Mr. Baxter. What can I do for you?"

"Have you got any coffee left?" Murphy asked, and to himself, he said, *Don't let me down now.*

"As a matter of fact, I do," she answered.

"The mayor and I need a cup of coffee. I'll pay for it, and we'll get out of the way of all this work goin' on." He began to worry as Irene got two clean cups and poured coffee, because Baxter was beginning to look uncomfortable. When Irene put the two cups on a table just inside the dining room, Murphy thanked her and sat down at the table.

Baxter looked as if he had agreed to some time with a crazy man, but he sat down and dumped two heaping teaspoons of sugar into his cup. "What is it you want to talk about, Murphy? I'll freely admit that we made a stupid decision when we let you go, but we thought we had to."

Murphy held up his hands in surrender. "I can fully understand why you folks made that decision. That's not what I wanted to talk to you about. I just wanted to tell you how sorry I was to hear about the death of your son. I know what a loss it must be for you and your wife. And I wanted to tell you what a fine young man Jeff was. I didn't spend a lot of time with him, but the time I did spend really impressed me with the potential he showed. You see, I spent four years in the army, and I trained a lot of young men in that war. And I could tell in the short time I talked to Jeff that he had the makings of a fine officer. And if he had been in my unit in the army, I would have recommended him for a commission.

"When I heard how he lost his life, going unarmed against an armed outlaw to fight for the honor of a young girl, I knew I was right about him. I just thought you should know that and know that you had a son you can be proud of. He certainly impressed me. Now, I won't take up any more of your time." He started to get up from the table, but Baxter stopped him with a hand on his forearm.

"Murphy, I can't tell you how much I appreciate what you've just told me. You just verified my opinion about Jeff. I guess he just came across as just average to most people, but I knew he was special. I'll tell his mother what you have just told me, and I know she will appreciate it as much as I do."

They got up from the table and walked back through the kitchen to the saloon. Irene waved off Murphy's attempt to pay for the coffee as they passed through. Bradshaw and Ennis were still arguing about the five bodies out front.

So Baxter interrupted. "Take the damn bodies out in the hills and dump them on the ground for the buzzards. They don't deserve to be treated like decent men. Tyson, we've got some important decisions to make if we're going to save this town. Send somebody to tell Paul Mathers we need a wagon and a mule. I'll be back here in a few minutes. There's something I have to do at the store right now."

Murphy walked out of the saloon behind him and paused to watch Baxter's determined stride back toward his store, most likely to tell his wife what Murphy thought of their son. "I hope I ain't gonna be punished too severely for this," he murmured to himself. He had met Jeff Baxter when he was in the store, but he had never spoken more than a word or two with him. Jeff hadn't impressed him one way or the other. He was satisfied that the grieving father seemed to have benefited from their brief talk, however.

He had one more thing he wanted to check on this morning, so he headed toward Bert Walker's blacksmith shop. It struck him when he walked past the cold forge that Jeff Baxter was not the only young man that had been senselessly wasted by

Clay Barnett and his cutthroats. He still blamed himself for Bert's death.

You shoulda left him the hell alone, he scolded himself. *You ain't in the army anymore. It's not your job to train men to fight.*

"What's done is done!" he declared aloud in his own defense. "There's still things to do. Now, I wonder if there's any chance Bert might have put the other key to that lock on the office door around here somewhere." He hadn't asked Baxter or Bradshaw if they had it, because there was no reason for either one of them to have a key. According to Elmo, nothing had been discussed about trying to fill Bert's post, or anything else, while the town was under the siege of Clay Barnett and his gunmen.

He began a search of the blacksmith shop, looking for any keys hanging anywhere on a nail or sitting in a tool drawer, ignoring the growing discomfort in his left shoulder. But there was no key of any kind to be found. It was beginning to look like he was going to have to break into the jail, and he preferred not to do that. After all, it was the town's property. He supposed he was going to have to search Bert's little house, and he didn't like the idea of that, either. Then one thought occurred to him that he should have had before he left the saloon. He left the blacksmith shop immediately and hurried back to Bradshaw's Saloon, where they were still waiting for a wagon.

Seeing Pete standing in the front door, he went directly to him. "Say, Pete, when you and Bradshaw went through those outlaws' pockets, what did you do with what you found?"

"We didn't find much that was worth keepin'," Pete said. "Of course Bradshaw took all the money. I took a pocket watch and a pocketknife. There wasn't much else but junk, some tobacco and some rollin' papers, things like that. You can take a look at it if you want to. It's all in a bucket behind the bar."

"I would like to take a look at it," Murphy said and walked on inside the saloon. He went directly behind the bar and found the bucket right where Pete said it would be. He picked it up and took it to a table, where he dumped the entire contents out. There were several keys; one of them looked very much like the key to the jailhouse. He put it in his pocket and raked the rest of the stuff into the bucket, which he replaced behind the bar.

When he walked back outside, Robert Jessop was pulling up before the saloon in a wagon with a team of two horses. "I was coming into town when I saw Jim Anderson's boy goin' to the stable to get a wagon, so I thought I'd save Paul the trouble. I'm goin' back to the sawmill after I pick up a couple things at the store. I'll take your five guests back in the hills on the other side of the sawmill."

"I'll ride up to the store with you," Baxter said and climbed up on the seat beside him.

They're all willing to work together now, Murphy thought as he stepped away from the saloon and went down the street toward the jail.

CHAPTER 21

When he got to the jail, nothing looked any different than when he had left it when he moved out. He walked around the building to see all sides of it, just to make sure. Then he walked up the front steps and inserted the key he had found in the bucket. He gave it a turn, and the lock sprang open. *That makes things easier*, he thought. He could go to the stable and get his things and move back into the jail. Since he was officially trespassing, he probably should have cleared the move with Baxter or Bradshaw. But he didn't want to give them a chance to deny him access, because he didn't want the inconvenience of camping down by the river when there was a perfectly comfortable bed that no one was using.

Before going to get his saddlebags and a few things from his packs, he went inside the jail to look around. Everything looked pretty much the same as when he left it. Bert hadn't been the resident long enough to decide he preferred some changes here and there. He found the second office key still in the desk drawer. He took a quick check of the cell room before going back into the personal quarters. They were the same as the rest of the building, unchanged.

Paul Mathers saw him coming, so he walked out of the barn to meet him. "Cullen," he greeted him. "You want your horses?"

"No, I'm gonna leave them with you for a couple of days. I just wanna get my saddlebags and a couple other things."

"You've had yourself a pretty busy mornin'," Mathers commented. "From the looks of that shirt, I'd say you didn't get by scot-free. You gonna move back into the jailhouse?"

"Yeah, for a couple of days, anyway. I wanna see how this shoulder comes along. The bullet's still in there, and Doc just bandaged it up. If it doesn't heal up proper, I'll let him dig it outta there."

"You ain't gonna stay no longer than a couple days?" Mathers asked.

"I reckon not." Murphy shrugged. "I've got no reason to. And, anyway, Elmo came to get me when I wasn't even halfway through gettin' my new cabin up."

"You buildin' a new cabin? What happened to your old one?"

"Indians," Murphy answered. "Three of 'em burnt it to the ground while I was stayin' here in town."

"For . . . ever . . . more . . ." Mathers said, dragging out the words. "Indians! What kind? I hope they ain't comin' this way."

"Commanche, I think," Murphy replied. "And they ain't comin' this way. At least these three ain't."

"That mighta been a sign to tell you that the best place for you is in town," Mathers remarked.

"Maybe," Murphy allowed. "Or one tellin' me I need to stay home to protect my cabin."

"Depends on how you look at it, I reckon," Mathers replied.

Murphy went into the stable and got his saddlebags and some coffee out of his packs, since he hadn't seen any at the jail. Bert's coffeepot was there, however. He didn't worry about anything to cook, since he planned to take all three meals at Irene's. He was still well fixed for money from his earlier encounters with the outlaws he had dueled with.

On his way back from the stable, he decided it might be the right thing to do if he stopped in the saloon again to catch

Bradshaw and, he hoped, Baxter, if he had left his store and gone back to the saloon. His purpose was to show them the courtesy of asking if it was all right for him to stay in the jail. It was town property, he had to keep reminding himself, although he had given it to them. So he stopped in again to find that the five bodies were gone, that the crowd watching their removal had dispersed, and that the saloon was open and doing business as usual. He was glad to see that Baxter was there, having a drink with Bradshaw at the far end of the bar. They spotted him when he came in, and Baxter signaled for him to join them with a wave of his hand.

"Mr. Murphy," Bradshaw expounded, "I would very much like to buy you a drink. What's your pleasure?"

"Well, sir," Murphy replied, "I don't, as a rule, usually take a drink of likker before the noon meal. But on an occasion when I drink with the top two men in the Newtown council, I'll take corn."

"Pete, pour a drink of corn whiskey for Mr. Murphy," Bradshaw ordered. "The town of Newtown owes him a helluva lot more than that."

"I'll second that," Baxter said. "They aren't making many men that will voluntarily come in here this morning and face five desperate gunmen all by himself."

"Remember, I had help," Murphy quickly replied. "Pete here stepped up when I needed him the most, and Irene Floyd proved she's just as handy with a shotgun as she is with a skillet."

"That's true," Bradshaw said, "but it was you who walked right in and cut the head off that snake."

"It's true, all right," Baxter said, "you had help, and we're grateful to Pete and Irene for stepping up when the time called for them to. But you stepped up and lit the fuse that caused that stick of dynamite to explode."

Murphy hadn't expected this, especially from these two, so he figured there couldn't be a better time to ask the question he had stopped by to ask. "To the city of Newtown," he proposed and raised his glass. They echoed the toast, and they tossed their whiskey back. "After what you've both said about me, maybe this ain't a good time, but I stopped by to ask a favor."

Bradshaw and Baxter exchanged a quick expression of uncertainty.

"Why, sure," Bradshaw muttered. "What do you need?"

"I've got to stay here in town for a couple of days, so Doc Ennis can watch this wound in my shoulder to see if he's gonna have to operate to get that bullet outta there. I was wondering if it would be all right if I stayed in the jailhouse till he fixes my wound."

The looks of concern on both faces faded away, and Bradshaw replied at once. "Sure, you're welcome to stay there. Ain't that right, Eliot?"

"Yes, indeed," Baxter replied.

"Doc says he oughta know for sure in a day or two, so it'll only be for a couple of days," Murphy said. "I appreciate it. I'm gonna go over right now and clean up my arm and change my shirt." He thanked them again for the drink and left to take his things to the jail.

Baxter and Bradshaw watched him all the way out the door.

"All he wanted was to sleep in the jailhouse for a couple of nights," Bradshaw said. "I ain't got no objections."

"Me either," Baxter said. They looked at each other then, both thinking the same thing. "It wouldn't be a bad thing if he just stayed there permanently."

"That's what I was thinking," Bradshaw said. "We better not let him get away again."

"You know, we might be forgetting our initial concern about Murphy," Baxter reminded him. "About gunmen coming in here because they've heard of him."

"I don't know, Eliot. I've sorta changed my mind about that. Maybe when gunslingers hear about Murphy's Law, it might keep them out of Newtown." He shrugged then and said, "If they do come to our town, hell, Murphy will take care of 'em."

"I think you're right, Tyson. What do you think we should call him? Sheriff instead of marshal?"

"Whatever the hell he wants," Bradshaw answered.

The days that followed were days of recovery for the people of Newtown, Texas, much akin to the days after the defeat of an occupying enemy army. Even if it was on a much smaller scale, it was a far more personal occupation, directly affecting many individual citizens who had had the misfortune to come in contact with one or more of the evil breed. It would be some time yet before news reached the outlying farms and ranches that it was safe to come into the town again for supplies or a drink in a saloon.

After a search of the five bodies and their personal possessions, enough money was found to repay Bradshaw for some portion of the alcohol the outlaws had consumed and to repair damage done to his rental rooms. There was also some reimbursement for Irene's food costs, as well as Doc Ennis's charge for Bert Walker's funeral. Other than those few, everyone else had to settle for the end of the siege as recompense. Even Daisy Moffett and Hazel Goodings, who had been snatched from their rooms over Pratt's Saloon, had to accept the fact that failure to receive payment for services rendered was a hazard in their line of work.

One general reaction after the lawless invasion of their town from merchants and citizens alike was the desire for the return of Murphy's Law. Some business owners, like Mack Pratt, declared that they were ready to pay for the permanent hiring of Murphy. "What are we gonna do when the next gang of outlaws finds out we have no law enforcement here, no way to protect ourselves from whatever they want to do?" Pratt asked, pressing his case at the next town council meeting.

Since there was no pressure from the town council for him

to vacate the jail, Murphy stayed longer than the two days he had originally asked for while he waited for his bullet wound to heal. The wound itself was tender and caused some minor pain, but it never hampered his movement of the shoulder or left arm. After a week he found that he hardly noticed it at all. And when he went back to the drugstore to talk to Doc about it, the two of them decided to leave it alone. As Doc said, "That little chunk of metal has found a place it feels comfortable in, so I doubt you'll hear anything more from it."

In spite of concern from council members like Mack Pratt and Elmo Dillon, Eliot Baxter and Tyson Bradshaw continued to stall on passing a tax on the merchants to pay a marshal's salary. Given the fact that there were no crimes committed during the entire week after the demise of Clay Barnett and his gang, the ruling members of the council felt no pressure to act. This in spite of the fact that an employment package for a town marshal had been voted on and passed by a vast majority of the members. It came to pass that Ike Purdy was given credit for forcing the council to officially hire someone to fill the job.

Ike Purdy was a cowhand riding for the Three Crosses Ranch, a medium-sized spread with its headquarters about twelve miles north of Newtown. Too far for the naïve Purdy to ride to town every week, he restricted his visits to monthly trips. So on the last Saturday of every month, he took the twelve-mile ride to Newtown to spend his monthly wages, usually at Pratt's Saloon. It was during one of these trips to Pratt's that he had the misfortune of falling in love with a young prostitute named Daisy Moffett. Unlike some of her sisters of service, who approached their paying customers with an attitude similar to that of an unbroken bronco toward a broncobuster, Daisy was capable of compassion. She sensed a desire for true affection from the simpleminded cowhand, so she let him take his time and encouraged his childlike efforts to please her.

After that first visit with Daisy, Ike would look for her each month, refusing offers from the other women if Daisy wasn't available. Once, she wasn't available all night. Albert Smith, the bartender, told him Daisy was out of town. So he took the long ride back to the Three Crosses with most of his wages still in his pocket. Albert didn't have the heart to tell him that Daisy was still in town, but she and Hazel Goodings were being held hostage at Bradshaw's Saloon. Albert was afraid the innocent young man might attempt to rescue Daisy and get himself killed. His mind focused only on seeing Daisy. He had evidently not noticed the body hanging on a rope in front of Bradshaw's or the fact that the whole town was dead.

Unfortunately, Ike decided he couldn't wait another month to attempt to see Daisy again. So he told the owner of the Three Crosses that he had some personal business he had to take care of and he needed to take a day, maybe two days, off after only a week had passed since he was in Newtown. He rode into town after only two hours enroute, having alternated between a walk and a lope for the entire twelve miles. After tying his horse at the watering trough located near Pratt's Saloon, he left the tired gelding there while he went into the saloon.

"Howdy, Ike," Albert greeted him. "You're back kinda early, ain'tcha?"

Ignoring the question, Ike asked one of his own. "Where's Daisy? Is she back yet?"

"No, she ain't," Albert said reluctantly. "Daisy's had a little hard luck. She had some rough treatment, and she's gone to stay with a friend of hers till she gets healed up a little better. I know she'll miss seein' you again, though."

"Where's her friend live?" Ike asked. "I'll go see her."

"You know, she never told me where her friend is," Albert said, realizing then that it would have been better not to mention the rough treatment. "She didn't even tell me her name. Just said a friend." He knew where Daisy was, but he was certain she had no desire to entertain Ike Purdy right now.

Ike thought about that for a minute. He decided Albert was lying. "Pour me a drink of likker . . . No, give me a bottle. I'm gonna sit down and wait for Daisy. Something ain't right."

"There ain't no tellin' when she's liable to come back to town," Albert said. "Ain't no use in you waitin' for her to come back."

"Ain't no reason I can't sit down and drink some likker, is there? My money's good as anybody else's, ain't it?"

"'Course it is," Albert said. "I just hate to see you waste your time, that's all. Here's your bottle. That'll be two dollars." He gave him a bottle of whiskey and a glass. "You sure you don't wanna visit with one of the other girls?"

"I ain't interested in seein' anybody else," Ike declared. "I came to see Daisy." He picked up his bottle and the glass and took them over to a table where he could watch both the front door and the steps to the second floor. He started working on the bottle of whiskey in an effort to keep his courage up, and he suspected somebody, for some reason, didn't want Daisy to know he was here for her. For all he knew, they might be purposely keeping her away from him. *Maybe they're afraid I might take her away from here*, he thought.

As the day went on, Ike sat there watching the people come in and go out again. He finished the bottle of whiskey before noon. Not accustomed to drinking that much at a time, he was already drunker than he had ever been before. And since he was drunk, he yelled for Albert to bring him another bottle. Albert picked up another bottle and brought it to the table, but before he put it down, he asked, "Don't you think you've had enough?"

Ike drew his handgun from his holster. "I'll let you know when I've had enough," he slurred. "I don't know what you people are tryin' to get away with, but you're messin' with the wrong man. I don't believe Daisy ain't here. You're just tryin' to keep me from goin' to help her. So here's your two dollars! Now, go tell Daisy I'm here, before I start shootin' up this place!"

"All right, all right!" Albert said. "No need to get all riled up." He looked around him nervously as most of the other customers started for the door. He put the bottle on the table and cautiously backed away. Ike laid the pistol on the table while he pulled the cork on the new bottle.

It suddenly occurred to Mack Pratt that everything was too quiet, so he got up from his desk and left the office. He was amazed when he opened the back door to the saloon and the place was empty except for one man seated at a table and Albert behind the bar.

"Albert," he called to his bartender, "what the hell's goin' on?"

Startled, Ike grabbed his pistol and fired a shot into the wall several feet away from Pratt, who immediately slammed the back door shut again. Albert ducked down behind the bar, but when there were no more shots, he slowly raised his head again.

"Ike, take it easy. You almost shot Mr. Pratt!"

"I'm gonna shoot all you lyin' coyotes if you don't tell Daisy I'm here," Ike threatened.

Murphy was talking to Bradshaw and Pete when someone walked in the door at Bradshaw's Saloon and said, "I just heard a shot down the street." It was obvious he directed his comment toward Murphy. Before anyone had a chance to reply, however, Mack Pratt ran in the door behind him.

"I need help!" Pratt blurted. "There's a drunk cowhand with a gun, and he's run everybody out of my place!"

Murphy looked at Tyson Bradshaw and said, "I reckon you want me out of your jail. Sounds like you might have a use for it."

"Hell, no!" Bradshaw responded. "I'm officially offering you the job of town marshal. We've already passed the vote on your employment package. Do you accept?"

"I don't know," Murphy said. "I ain't seen the offer. I'll take care of this problem while I'm considerin' the job."

He walked out the door and headed down the street to Pratt's, with Pratt walking right behind him. "Has he threatened anybody?" he asked Pratt.

"I don't know," Pratt said. "I was in my office, and I didn't know anything was going on in the saloon. Then I realized there wasn't any noise comin' from the saloon, like there usually is. So I went to the barroom to see, and when I opened the door, he took a shot at me."

"Well, that don't sound too good, does it?" Murphy responded, wondering if he was going to find himself facing a killer or a drunk. When they reached the saloon, Murphy said, "You might wanna wait outside until I see what we're dealin' with."

"I expect that is best," Pratt replied.

Murphy stepped up beside the front door and slowly inched close enough to the side to peek inside. Pratt had said he didn't know if Albert was all right or not, so Murphy was relieved to see the bartender standing behind the bar but apparently not crouching behind it for protection. Then he shifted his gaze toward the center of the room and watched the man seated there for a few seconds. While he watched, the man poured some whiskey from a three-quarters full bottle. There was an empty bottle on the table as well as a pistol, and when he filled the glass, he set the bottle down on the table between the glass and the gun.

That helps, Murphy thought, since the bottle was still between the man's hand and his gun. He figured he had time to make his bluff, especially if the man had emptied that one bottle by himself. To give himself even more time, he waited until the man picked up the glass and tossed the whiskey back. Then he just walked boldly through the door and called out,

"Howdy, Albert. How ya doin'?" He walked toward the bar, his hand ready to reach for his Colt if the man made any motion toward the gun on the table. Albert looked shocked as he kept looking back and forth at Ike and Murphy, expecting to see gunfire at any second.

Confident now that he was dealing with a drunk and not a killer, Murphy turned his attention toward Ike. He walked right up to the table and said, "My name's Murphy. What's yours?"

Confused, Ike became suspicious, but it came too late. He reached for his pistol, but Murphy caught his hand with his left, then planted a hard right flush on Ike's nose. Watching from the bar, Albert flinched and grimaced as Ike's chair went over backward, with Ike still in it. Murphy reached down and picked him up from the chair, but Ike was out cold.

"You got any rope?"

Albert said he had a coil of clothesline rope.

"That'll do to carry him to the jailhouse."

Albert went into the storeroom and came back with the clothesline. Murphy cut off a couple lengths and tied Ike's feet together and his hands behind his back.

"What's his name?"

"Ike Purdy," Albert answered as he stared down at him and wondered if he was dead.

Murphy guessed what he was thinking. "He ain't dead. He's just out. He was probably about ready to pass out, anyway, after he drank all that whiskey."

Albert looked at Murphy and shook his head. "I'd rather be kicked by a mule," he said.

Murphy went to the door and signaled to Pratt that it was all right for him to come in.

"Tell me something about him," Murphy said to Albert. "What was he doin' in here today?"

Albert went on to tell him about Ike's obsession with Daisy Moffett and how Daisy felt such compassion for the simple young man.

"She was one of the women who were kidnapped from here and taken to Bradshaw's, right?"

"That's right," Albert answered. "But she was the one that got hurt pretty bad from that gang of wolves. She don't want Ike to see her in the shape she's in. She's right upstairs in her room, but she's afraid he'd go crazy if he sees her now."

"What about the other woman?" Murphy asked. "Is she in the same condition Daisy's in?"

"Hazel Goodings?" Pratt answered. "Not at all. But Hazel's older, bigger, and tougher than poor little Daisy. Hazel could hold her own in a herd of horses."

"So you're tellin' me this fellow didn't come to shoot up the town?" Murphy said to Albert. "He's just some sap who thinks he's in love with one of your sportin' ladies, and he thinks you, or somebody here, won't let her come to him. Is that right?"

"Pretty much so," Albert said. "He weren't out to hurt nobody, but he musta got the idea somebody might try to get rid of him. So that's why he took a shot at Mr. Pratt."

"Well, he did take a shot at you," Murphy said to Pratt while he thought it over. "And just shootin' a firearm in the city limits will earn you some jail time. I think it's best if we let him sober up in jail. Then I think we ought to tell him the truth about Daisy Moffett. I'm guessin' that's his horse tied up by the waterin' trough."

"I expect so," Albert said.

"I'll use it to tote him to jail," Murphy said.

He reached down and pulled the unconscious man up on his feet, then hefted him up on his shoulder and walked out the door. He walked quickly over to the horse at the water trough. Thinking of all the whiskey Ike had just consumed, Murphy thought it best not to linger. And when he got to the trough, he transferred his load from his shoulder to the saddle of the horse and rolled him over to lie on his belly. Then he untied the horse and led it up the street toward the jail. They were halfway there when he heard the sounds of Ike coming to. They were followed shortly after with the sound of the contents of Ike's stomach evacuating to the street. The horse, a chestnut gelding, sidestepped in an effort to avoid the stream running down its side, forcing Murphy to grab Ike's feet to keep him on the horse.

"Easy, boy," he said, as he calmed the horse. "I'll clean you up a little when I unload your partner."

When they reached the jail, Murphy looped the reins over the hitching rail and pulled Ike off the horse. "Can you stand up?"

"I think so," Ike answered, completely subdued.

Murphy stood him up on his feet. "I'm the town marshal, and I'm gonna let you sleep a little more of that whiskey off in the jail. I'm gonna untie you now, so you can stand a little better. If you try to run, I'll shoot you down."

"I won't run," Ike said. "I hurt my nose, but I can't remember how. Musta hit it on the table somehow."

"Probably so," Murphy said. "I'll take a look at it when I get you inside. Looks like you didn't get anything on your clothes when you threw up. You got a little on your stirrup and your horse's side, but I'll rinse that off for you."

"Much obliged," Ike said. "What am I gittin' arrested for?"

"We'll call it drunk and disorderly conduct and dischargin' a firearm inside the city limits," Murphy said as he unlocked the office door.

"Oh, okay," Ike said and walked inside when Murphy held the door open for him.

Murphy put Ike's gun and holster on the desk and asked if he had any other weapons on him. When Ike produced a pocketknife, Murphy took that, too. "I'm gonna put these in this bottom drawer of my desk, and you can have 'em back when you leave."

He took him into the cell room and unlocked the first cell. "Take any bunk you want," Murphy said. "Sit down and I'll go get you some fresh drinkin' water. There's a chamber pot for you, and I'll bring some clean rags to clean up some of that dried blood around your nose." He closed the cell door when he went out but didn't bother to lock it. He didn't think there was much possibility that Ike would try to escape.

When he came back, he was carrying rags and two buckets, one for drinking water, the other to clean Ike's face, but Ike had lain out flat on the bunk and was fast asleep.

"Just as well," Murphy muttered and took one of the buckets and the rags outside and cleaned the vomit off the one stirrup and the chestnut's side. After he put the bucket inside the door, he locked it and rode the horse to the stable.

Chapter 22

"Marshal Murphy!" Paul Mathers sang out cheerfully when he saw Murphy approaching on the chestnut horse. "Where'd you get the chestnut?"

"Belongs to a young cowhand who's come for a short visit at the jailhouse. I promised him that you'd take excellent care of him, all at the town folks' expense."

"That I will!" Mathers declared. "The word around town is that we've hired a new town marshal."

"Is that a fact?" Murphy responded. "I don't know how official it is, though. It was a pretty casual job offer, and it was made in haste by just one member of the council. The owner of this horse is the one who caused it, and he's sleepin' peacefully in the jailhouse right now. I'm sure he never had any intention of stirrin' up all the trouble he caused in the first place."

"Well, let me give you my vote on the proposal, if that'll give you any more confidence." He walked over and took the chestnut's reins while Murphy dismounted. Getting serious for a moment, he continued talking. "Listen, Cullen, the town council voted to offer you the job as marshal or sheriff, whichever you prefer, the day after you walked into Bradshaw's and showed those five killers who runs this town. Every council member was there, and we voted on the whole package to offer you, and the vote was one hundred percent in favor of it. Baxter and Bradshaw coulda told you that the first of the week, but everything's been peaceful till today. And you know how they like to hang on to the money."

"Tell me this, Paul. Did the council make any provision for another person in the marshal's office? I'm not talking about a deputy, although we need one. I'm talking about somebody to take care of the jail, do the odd jobs and the cleanin', stuff like that." He was thinking about Ike Purdy lying back there in the bunk and the possibility he might empty his insides again. "I'll take the marshal job, but not if I have to be a chambermaid along with it."

"That's just what Elmo Dillon told 'em at the meetin'," Mathers said. "And pretty much everybody else agreed. So there's provision in there for somebody to do that for you, but it ain't gonna be a high-payin' job. I'll tell you that."

"I expect not," Murphy remarked. "I reckon I'll get back to the marshal's office now and really get that place organized. Tyson Bradshaw told me this afternoon that he was officially offering me the job, so I reckon I can count on his word. I don't expect to hold this fellow in jail much longer than overnight, so you won't have this horse long."

Feeling reassured that the job was definitely his, he went back to the jail to decide what his daily schedule should be as far as keeping his eye on the town. Before writing anything down, he went into the cell room to look in on Ike. *He's either dead or sleeping*, he thought. Either way would be fine, but then he started thinking about what Albert Smith had told him about Ike's obsession with Daisy Moffett. He felt sorry for the poor man. It was a shame that his brain could be so simple that it could be turned in any direction like a wind vane in a slight breeze. He was thinking about the fact that Ike had fired a shot that might have killed Mack Pratt. But Ike had been so drunk, he'd been out of his mind.

"What the hell am I frettin' over him for?" he finally asked aloud. It was getting along toward suppertime. "I'll have Irene fix him a plate of supper and let him go in the mornin'."

He went back to his personal quarters and started rearranging some pieces of furniture he had collected during the week. When it was time for the dining room to open for supper, he looked in on Ike and found him still in the same position as before. *Maybe he* is *dead*, he thought. *I'll have Irene fix a plate with something a dead man would like.* He locked the office door and headed for Bradshaw's Saloon.

Tyson Bradshaw was standing at the end of the bar and came to meet him, his hand extended. Murphy took it, and they shook hands. "Now it's official," Bradshaw said. "Mack Pratt was in here a few minutes ago. He said you handled the gunman in his saloon just as swiftly as you put a stop to Clay Barnett and his gang. I brought something for you." He reached inside his coat pocket and came out with a badge; then he handed it to Murphy. "This thing has been burning a hole in my pocket. I'm damn glad to get rid of it. Baxter was supposed to be here to help me present it to you, but what the hell? It's official."

He became humble for a moment then. "Cullen, I know we made a bad mistake when we went with Bert instead of you, and I'm as much to blame as anybody on the council. I'm hoping you won't hold that against me as we go forward from here. Now, whenever you're ready, we'll go over your complete offer and how your compensation is broken down."

When Murphy appeared to be confused by the statement, Bradshaw continued. "You know, like how many things you won't have to pay for—three meals in the café, no charge for your personal living space in the jail, no stable fees, things like that. They all add up."

"So my actual salary won't look so small, right? We can do it at yours and Mr. Baxter's convenience," Murphy said. When he agreed to the offer, he wanted them both there, so there would be no misunderstanding. "Right now, all I need to have you confirm is that my three square meals a day are paid for, as well as the one I'm going to take back to the jail for my prisoner."

Bradshaw chuckled in response. "I'll guarantee you we'll pay for yours and your prisoner's supper tonight. Irene already knows about it. How about if Eliot and I meet you for breakfast in the morning and we'll sign the papers then?"

"Yes, sir," Murphy said when he saw Bonnie open the door to the café to turn the sign over to the OPEN side. "That'll be fine by me. I think I wanna concentrate on eating today, anyway. So I'll meet you there tomorrow." He left the bar and made it to the café door before Bonnie's leisurely effort closed it again.

Surprised, the girl stepped quickly aside. "Cullen!" she exclaimed. "You must be hungry."

"I just found out that I don't have to pay for my supper," he japed, "and I wanna get something to eat before the town council changes its mind."

Remembering then, Bonnie gave him a big smile. "That's right! Come in, Marshal Murphy." Then she turned and called out to Ginger, who was over near the kitchen door. "Hey, everybody, Marshal Murphy is here!"

Everybody was actually her sister, Ginger, and Everett Sims, who worked in the post office and must have come in the outside entrance.

"Howdy, Cullen," Everett said as Murphy walked past him on his way to his usual table. "Are you really taking that job as marshal?"

Murphy paused to answer. "I reckon so. I'm meetin' with the mayor and vice mayor in the mornin' to wrap the deal up."

"Well, I'm damn glad of that," Everett said. "That's what everybody was hoping for. Good luck."

"Thank you, Everett. I 'preciate your support. You'll be the first name I call when I'm needin' a posse."

Everett responded with a weak smile, and Murphy walked on back to his table, where Ginger was waiting with a stronger smile.

"Well, good evening, Marshal Murphy," she greeted him. "Tyson Bradshaw told us that the town would be paying for your meals now. He told us how quickly you shut that gunman down at Pratt's Saloon."

"I think Bradshaw made a little too much outta that arrest," Murphy replied. "He ain't really a gunman. He's just a lovesick cowpuncher who's smitten with a young saloon girl. When he couldn't find her at Pratt's, he tried to drink up all of Pratt's whiskey, and he found out he couldn't handle it. I left him sleepin' in one of the cells, and I'm gonna need to take him a plate of supper back with me."

"Why couldn't he see the girl?" Ginger asked. "Was she entertaining someone else?"

"No, she was one of those two that Clay Barnett's gang kidnapped from Pratt's. She was the young one. Daisy, I think her name is. Anyway, she got beat up pretty bad, and she didn't want anybody to see her lookin' like she is. Especially him, I reckon, since he's so taken with her. So she's just hidin' somewhere, I expect. I guess she don't realize it wouldn't make no difference to that poor soul what she looks like. He might even like her better now, since his face got a little rearranged, too."

"Oh, Cullen." She frowned, already feeling the young man's grief. "Did you hit him?"

He shrugged with guilt. "Well, hell, I didn't know what he was capable of when I went in there, and I had to get his attention."

"Shame on you," she said.

"He ran everybody out of the saloon and shot at Mack Pratt,"

Murphy protested. "I couldn't take a chance on him shootin' at anybody else."

"You oughta find that girl, that Daisy, and make her go visit that poor man in your fancy jailhouse," Ginger said.

"I don't know where that girl is hiding, even if I did wanna find her," he lied. "Do you really think my jailhouse is fancy?"

"Don't try to change the subject," Ginger admonished. "Surely that girl is upstairs in one of those rooms over the saloon. You're the town marshal, for goodness' sake. You can demand to search that whole building."

"I don't believe Newtown is hirin' me to act like Cupid for folks who are dumb enough to fall in love with a prostitute," Murphy stated. Then he looked at Bonnie, who had been standing there listening to the discussion, and asked, "Could I ask you to get me a cup of coffee, Bonnie? And while you're at it, tell your mama that I'd like to eat supper."

"Never mind, Bonnie," Ginger stopped her. "I'll take care of him." She went at once to the kitchen.

"I think you made her mad," Bonnie said. "She's got a soft spot for things like that."

"She's got a short fuse, too," Murphy said. "Don't take much to set her off, does it?" He rubbed his chin thoughtfully. "I never noticed that about her before. I'd best watch my step around her. I reckon I just got myself in her doghouse."

"I wouldn't worry about it," Bonnie said, lowering her voice when she saw Ginger coming out of the kitchen with his coffee. "She switches it off just as fast as she turns it on."

"Mama cooked that ham you like so much," Ginger announced indifferently. "She's cutting you a thick slice right now to go with the beans and potatoes." She placed the coffee on the table. "I'll be right back with your plate." And she headed for the kitchen again.

Murphy looked at Bonnie, who was watching him. Then she smiled, gave a little shrug with her shoulders, and winked.

He enjoyed a pleasant supper. The ham was good as usual, and the girls kept his coffee cup filled. The subject of Ike and Daisy never came up again. When he was finished, Ginger had a plate ready for him to take back to his prisoner. The only reference she made in regard to the prisoner was, "Don't lollygag on your way back, or that food is gonna be too cold to eat."

"I won't lallygag," he said, "and I'll see you in the mornin'."

When Murphy got back to the jail, he went into the cell room and found Ike sitting on the side of his bunk, leaning forward, with his head in his hands. When he heard the sound of the key in the cell door, he looked up to see Murphy entering his cell. An instant look of alarm appeared upon his face, for the only memory he had of the big man was the image of him approaching him in Pratt's Saloon. He wasn't sure what had happened after that. He only remembered waking up in the jail cell, sick in the stomach and his nose and jaw throbbing with pain. He had never been in jail before, so he expected more of the same treatment he had received on their first meeting.

"Well, I see you woke up," Murphy said. "You feel like you could eat something? I brought you some food from the dinin' room, and I'll make a pot of coffee just as soon as I bring that fire back to life in the stove." When Ike just sat there looking confused, Murphy asked, "How do you feel?"

"I felt sick to my stomach when I woke up," Ike finally said. "I threw up in that bucket. Is that all right?"

"Yep," Murphy responded, "that's what it's there for. You feel like you could put some food in your stomach now? Might make you feel better."

"Yes, sir," Ike answered meekly. "I ain't sure I can hold it down, but I'd like to try."

Murphy pulled the small bench over next to the bunk and set the plate and eating utensils down on it. "I'll go get you some coffee started. I expect you need some of that. After you eat, I'll get you some clean water and a rag to clean some of that blood off your face." He didn't mention it, but he hoped Ike's jaw wasn't broken, because the ham would take some chewing. He locked the cell door and went back to the kitchen to stir up the dying fire in the stove.

Murphy managed to get some coffee made, and Ike was able to hold down the major portion of the supper Irene had fixed for him. And with Murphy's help, Ike was able to clean up the more obvious results of his bloody nose, and there was nothing they could do to treat the obvious bruising caused by the punch. When he had done all he could to make Ike more comfortable, Murphy told him he was going to leave him alone again while he took a walk around town before darkness descended upon the streets. As he locked the office door, he vowed that he would have an assistant to take care of the prisoners, if he had to pay his salary himself.

His first stop after leaving the jail was Pratt's Saloon.

"Evenin', Marshal," Albert Smith greeted him when he walked in, his boss having informed him that Murphy was to be the new marshal. "Pour you a drink?"

"No, thanks, Albert. Is Daisy Moffett back workin' again?"

"No," Albert replied. "She still don't want nobody seein' her face all bruised up. She's still just sittin' around waiting to heal up."

"Where's she sittin' around?" Murphy asked. "I need to see her. She's upstairs, ain't she?"

"She's in Hazel's room, last room on the right side of the hall. You want me to go get her?"

"No, I can go up there myself," Murphy said and headed toward the steps.

Upstairs, he walked down the narrow hallway, almost bumping into a startled Elmo Dillon, who was coming out of a room. Upon seeing him, Elmo jumped back inside the room and closed the door. The close call caused a thin smile to form on Murphy's face but there was no reaction beyond that. When he reached the last door on the right, he knocked and waited until Hazel opened the door.

"Well, well," she clucked, "the new marshal hisself. Now, ain't this special?"

Seeing another woman sitting in a chair by the window, Murphy pushed the door open and walked inside. She turned to look at him when he came into the room, her face still bruised and her healing cuts scabbed over. "Daisy Moffett?"

She nodded, too terrified to speak.

"I need you to come with me. You wanna put on a coat or a shawl? We'll be goin' outside."

Confused, she shook her head. "I can't go anywhere till I heal up," she said.

"You don't understand," he countered. "You're under arrest. I ain't askin' you."

"Under arrest?" she exclaimed. "Under arrest for what?"

"Conspiracy to force a suicide," Murphy said, trying to think of something that sounded official. Aware of Hazel moving to a corner of the room and of an axe handle propped there, he warned her. "You pick that axe handle up and I'll shoot you down." It was enough to stop her. Back to Daisy then, he said, "Let's go! I haven't got all night. Get your shoes on and a wrap, whatever you need. Take a scarf or something if you don't want people to recognize you, 'cause you're gonna walk up the street to the jail."

"I didn't do anything," Daisy pleaded. "I don't even know what you're talking about."

Hazel spoke up. "She's right. She ain't done one solitary thing to hurt nobody."

"I reckon we'll find that out, if it's the truth, and if it is, she's got nothing to worry about. But right now, you're wastin' my time. Just as a favor, I'm willing to let you come along without handcuffs, so folks that see you won't know you're under arrest."

Making no protest to her arrest, Daisy got up from her

chair, gathered her shawl around her shoulders, and walked obediently ahead of Murphy into the narrow hallway.

Hazel followed them down the hallway to the steps, proclaiming Daisy innocent of doing anything wrong. "And folks in this town thought they was doin' a good thing when they made you the marshal. Ain't you got nothin' better to do than pick on poor workin' girls?" She stopped at the top of the steps because she was wearing only a petticoat. And Albert waved her back for fear Mack Pratt might see her.

The usual patrons of Pratt's all paused to gawk at the soiled dove being escorted out of the saloon by the town marshal.

She walked the short distance to the jail with Murphy beside her as if they were walking together, instead of her being herded to jail. When they got there, he unlocked the door, ushered her inside, and told her to sit down in his desk chair. Then he stood over her and told her why he had arrested her.

"I've got a man in a cell in there because he took a shot at Mack Pratt, even though he was too drunk to know who he was shootin' at. The reason he was that drunk was because he cares so much about you that it drove him crazy when he couldn't find you. Nobody would tell him why you weren't there, and he just wanted to find you to make sure you were all right."

Her eyes opened wide, and she gasped, "Is Ike Purdy still in there?"

He didn't answer, just continued to watch her reactions.

"I don't want him to see me like this," she pleaded. "Did you bring me over here to see Ike?"

He nodded.

"I'm not really under arrest?"

"That's right," he said. "But before you walk out that door, you ought to know he risked his life trying to get to you and save you from whoever had you captured. Because that's what he thought had happened to you. All he wanted was to make sure you were all right. All you'd have to do is let him see you, so he can see for himself that you're safe. He imagined all kinds of things that could have happened to you, and he was determined to save you." He paused then because he could see she was considering giving in.

"I think the two of you need to see each other, because both of you have got your faces beat up. I'm sorry to say that I'm responsible for the damage to Ike's face. When I went to the saloon to arrest him, he reached for his gun, so I had to react the fastest way I could. He was out of his mind at that point, he was so worried about you."

"I'll visit him," she said.

"I think you'll be glad you did," Murphy told her. "You two make a good pair with your beat-up faces. If you'll just sit there for a couple of minutes, I'll go into the cell room and make sure he's not asleep again, because this will be as big a surprise to him as it was to you. But in his case, it'll be a dream come true."

He was tempted to tie her to his desk in case she changed her mind, but he trusted her word was good. So he went into the cell room and found Ike still sitting on his bunk, having finished most of the supper Irene had prepared for him. "You feelin' any better?" Murphy asked.

"Yes, sir, I reckon I'll live," Ike replied. "I expect I owe you and Albert and Mr. Pratt a whole bunch of apologies."

"I think everybody knows it was the whiskey doin' the talkin'," Murphy assured him. "I've got somebody in the office who would like to have a word with you. All right?"

"I reckon," Ike answered, "but if it's a preacher, I ain't ready to start goin' to church. I just ain't the churchgoin' kind of feller."

"It ain't the preacher. I didn't know where to go for one." He unlocked the cell door and left it open when he walked out. Then he opened the door between the cell room and the office and called to Daisy, "You can come in now." He held the door for her.

She entered the cell room timidly, as if entering a dark part of a forest, to find Ike sitting on the bunk. His head was hanging down, and he was gazing at the floor, wondering what anybody could tell him that would do him any good.

"Ike, are you all right?"

His head snapped up at the sound of the tiny voice, a voice he knew so well, but he knew it could not be true. His eyes opened wide, and he blinked to make sure the image was real. "Daisy?" he uttered.

He sprang up from the bunk and started to rush toward her, but he stopped right away to look at Murphy for permission. Murphy smiled and nodded his consent. Ike hurried to her then, and they embraced. After a long moment, they parted long enough to start examining each other's faces and the obvious injuries.

Murphy went back into the office and closed the cell room door behind him so they could have their privacy. He grunted his amusement when he wondered how his meeting with Baxter and Bradshaw in the morning would go if they knew what was going on in the jailhouse that night.

He let the visit go on until it was time for him to take a walk around the town to make sure everything was all right. When he opened the cell room door, they were sitting on one of the bunks, holding hands and talking. "I'm gonna have to call the visit over. I've got to take a walk around town, so I'll walk Daisy back to Pratt's to make sure she's all right. And I'll lock you back in your cell for the night."

"I can't tell you how much I 'preciate what you done, Marshal Murphy," Ike declared. "I was sick with worry about Daisy. But I think I'll make it now." He looked at her and said, "Maybe Marshal Murphy will let you come visit me again sometime."

"I wouldn't worry about that, Ike," Murphy said. "I'm cuttin' you loose tomorrow mornin' after breakfast. You ready to go, Daisy?"

"Yes, sir, I'm ready," she replied. "I can't wait to tell Hazel how wrong she was about you."

"Don't spread it around very far," Murphy said. "I don't want to get a reputation for bein' softhearted."

Ike, still not sure he had heard Murphy correctly, had to ask to be sure. "You mean I'll be free to go after breakfast?"

"That's right," Murphy replied. "Have you got any money? I didn't search you when I arrested you."

"Yes, sir," Ike answered. "I've still got most of my last month's wages. Have I got to pay a fine?"

"No, but you'll have to pay Paul Mathers twenty-five cents to get your horse outta the stable."

Ike nodded, then looked back at Daisy again. "Can I come see you tomorrow, after I get outta here?"

She told him she expected him to, which caused him to grin wide enough to break the scab on his lip.

So they hugged goodbye, and Murphy locked him in his cell again. Then he escorted Daisy back to Pratt's and stood at the door to watch her hurry through the busy saloon to get to the stairs before he went on his walk around the town. He had decided it best not to go inside with her, thinking it might call more attention to her, the one thing she was trying to prevent.

Chapter 23

Leaving Pratt's, he continued his walk toward the south end of town, planning to make a circle, walking both sides of Front Street, checking the doors that should be locked, and saying good evening to those still open. When he came to the Newtown General Store, it was long past closing time, but he walked all the way around the store, checking to make sure Eliot Baxter had not left one of the back doors unlocked. Then he crossed the street and walked back up the other side of Front Street, all the way to the stable, before crossing over again and heading south again. He made casual stops at the two smaller saloons between the stable and Bradshaw's Saloon. At Bradshaw's, he always went inside to chat with Pete for a few minutes. Bradshaw's was the busiest saloon in town. As a rule, if there was any trouble brewing in town, it was most likely in Bradshaw's or Pratt's. So he liked to check those two carefully to nip trouble in the bud if he could.

"Marshal Murphy," Pete Brice greeted him when he walked up to the bar. "Are you drinkin' tonight?"

"Evenin', Pete," Murphy returned the greeting. "You know, I think I will have one shot of rye whiskey tonight."

"Right," Pete said. "What's the occasion?"

"No occasion," Murphy replied. "I just thought I'd have

one tonight. I feel the need." He also wanted to propose a silent toast to poor, pathetic Ike Purdy and hoped that Ginger Floyd never found out what went on at the jail that night.

Pete poured the shot and Murphy tossed it back. He was returning the empty glass to the bar when he heard the offer behind him.

"I'll buy the next one, Pete."

Murphy turned to find Elmo Dillon behind him. "Well, good evenin', Elmo," he said. "I wasn't gonna have but one shot. But I don't wanna pass up an opportunity to go down in history as the only man Elmo Dillon ever bought a drink for."

Elmo threw some change on the bar. "Here, I'll pay for both his drinks," he said to Pete. "So now he can claim two titles."

"I declare, Elmo, what's come over you?" Murphy couldn't resist making him squirm. "What happened? Has there been a big boom in the tailorin' business?" He knew Elmo was anxious to know for sure if he had seen him upstairs at Pratt's, when he had almost bumped into him coming out of that bedroom.

"I just figured somebody ought to at least buy the new marshal a drink of whiskey," Elmo claimed, as Pete poured a second shot for Murphy and set it in front of him.

Look at him, Elmo thought. *He had to see me. I almost ran into him!* He was certain that Murphy had seen him, and that he was pretending not to have, just to make him sweat. Still, maybe he really hadn't seen him. It had been fairly dark in Francine's room. *He saw me, that dog.* He wanted to ask him why he had arrested Daisy Moffett, but he couldn't without confessing that he had been upstairs at Pratt's when Murphy arrested her.

"So what's going on in our town tonight?" he asked, giving Murphy a perfect invitation to report anything newsworthy.

"Nothing much," Murphy answered, declining the invitation. "Seems pretty peaceful. How 'bout you, Pete? You have any troublemakers tonight, so far?" Murphy asked as he tossed back the second shot.

Pete shrugged. "Nope. Like you said, seems pretty peaceful."

"In that case, I reckon I'll finish my walk around," Murphy announced. "Thank you for the whiskey, Elmo. I've got a good memory, so I won't ever forget you bought me two drinks to welcome me back to the marshal's job." He nodded to the bartender and said, "Pete." Then he turned and walked out the door.

He continued down the street, checking the locks and doors, until he came to Pratt's Saloon, where he had dropped Daisy off and started his walk around. This time he went inside the saloon and walked over to the bar. Albert met him with a big grin.

"Evenin', Marshal Murphy," he said. "Hazel Goodings told me to pour you a drink of likker when you came in and charge it to her."

"She did?" Murphy responded, surprised. "Why did she say that?"

"For arrestin' Daisy," Albert said. "She said she's now a big believer in Murphy's Law. And I am, too. That was a helluva nice thing you did for that poor feller."

"Well, I'll be . . . ," Murphy started, genuinely surprised by their attitude toward Ike. He would have thought they might have other feelings for the little man, seeing as how he ran all their business off and shot at the owner. "Hold off on that drink," he said when Albert reached for a glass. "I just had two shots of whiskey with Elmo Dillon, and I don't usually take but one. So if you don't mind, I'll wait till I'm in here again, and tell Hazel I surely appreciate it. I'll catch her sometime when I'm in here and she ain't busy, and I'll thank her, too."

He left the saloon and returned to the jail, expecting to find

Ike asleep. He was wide awake, however, too excited to go to sleep. And he wanted to thank Murphy over and over, so Murphy stayed and let him talk for a little while. He finally had to cut him short and tell him it was time to go to bed.

Ike was up and out of his bunk when Murphy opened the cell room door the next morning. As soon as he saw Murphy, he asked if he was going to get his breakfast now. Murphy told him he had to wait until the café was open, that they had to give Irene time to cook it.

"Believe me, those women at Pratt's don't get up very early, so you'd be waitin' there, too, even if you skipped breakfast. I've got a meetin' at breakfast with the mayor and vice mayor, and I won't be back here till that's over." He paused when Ike gave a sigh. "But that won't be a long meetin'," he assured Ike when his face broke out with disappointment. "You'll have time to eat your breakfast and go get your horse. Besides, women appreciate it when you give 'em a little time to get ready in the mornin'."

"I reckon you're right," Ike confessed. "I know I must look like a fool to you, but I ain't never met a woman who was as kind to me as Daisy is. I know I don't look like much, and I ain't got no money or land, but she treats me just like somebody who does."

"I expect she just genuinely likes you, Ike. What are you plannin' to do after you see her this mornin'?" Murphy asked.

"I'm gonna ride back to the Three Crosses Ranch and ask my boss if he could see his way clear to raise my monthly pay to thirty dollars, like the rest of the hands make. Then maybe I could help Daisy out a little bit so she wouldn't have to entertain as many customers as she does now."

Murphy didn't know how to respond to that statement, so he just said, "Well, good luck with that. I'm goin' to breakfast now. I'll be back here as soon as I can." He wondered if Daisy realized Ike had the mind of a child. He felt compassion for him, but there wasn't anything he could do to help him.

"Good morning, Marshal Murphy," Bonnie Floyd greeted him cheerfully when he walked into the dining room.

"Good mornin', Miss Floyd," he responded, returning the formal greeting. "I'm gonna sit at that table over by the window." He pointed to the table.

"Oh?" Bonnie replied. "You don't want to sit at your usual table? What's the matter? Is your usual table too close to our noisy kitchen?"

He smiled. "No, I like bein' close to the kitchen, but I'm supposed to have a breakfast meeting with Eliot Baxter and Tyson Bradshaw this mornin', and I thought they might prefer it. Just bring my coffee, if you don't mind, and I'll wait on the food till they get here."

He went over to the table and sat down, and Bonnie called back through the kitchen door, "The marshal's here and wants his coffee!"

In a few seconds, Ginger came out of the kitchen with his cup of coffee. She stopped at his usual table and asked Bonnie, "What's he doing over there?"

"He's got a meeting with Mr. Baxter and Mr. Bradshaw, so he thought it might be better to sit over there," Bonnie said.

"Well, here's his coffee. You take it to him," Ginger said and handed the cup to her. Bonnie took the coffee to him.

"What's the matter?" Murphy asked. "Is she still mad at me about that thing with Ike Purdy and Daisy Moffett?"

"I didn't think so," Bonnie replied. "At least she hasn't been talking about it this morning. But she saw you come in, and that musta reminded her, so she mighta turned on her little show of wrath again."

"Sometimes a lawman just has to do his job," Murphy joked. "I'll just try hard not to cause her any more pain, and maybe someday she'll forgive me." He shook his head and tried to make a sorrowful face.

She gave him a playful punch on the shoulder, and he flinched slightly. "Oops," she blurted. "Wrong shoulder!"

"Between you and your mother, I don't know if there's a real chance that thing will ever heal. Don't tell your sister you banged on that wound. I don't want her to enjoy any satisfaction out of it."

Bonnie promised she wouldn't tell her and returned to the kitchen.

He sat there for about ten minutes before Bradshaw and Baxter came into the dining room together. Murphy figured they had probably met briefly before coming in to make sure they were in agreement with the package they intended to offer him. Ginger came out of the kitchen to give them a cheerful welcome, then led them to the table before hurrying back to the kitchen to send Bonnie out with their coffee. When Bonnie brought it to the table, she took Bradshaw's and Baxter's breakfast orders and knew that Murphy would have his usual.

The meeting got underway immediately. Baxter had the council's offer all written out for Murphy to take with him. Primarily, it guaranteed a monthly salary of one hundred dollars, plus three meals a day at the café, provided living quarters in the back of the jail, paid stable fees for his horses, and included a salary for a handyman of thirty dollars a month. Murphy was satisfied with the offer but wanted to add an ammunition allowance. They agreed to a reasonable figure, and the deal was done.

"I have to make one additional request, however," Murphy said. "I need to take a short ride out to the Rocking-J Ranch this morning to give Lionel Jacobson permission to graze his cattle on my land. I'll be back this afternoon. Is that all right?"

Baxter and Bradshaw looked at each other but could see no reason to object.

"The town's pretty peaceful right now," Murphy said. "If there's any trouble, it ain't likely to start until closer to suppertime, and I'll be back by then."

Ginger walked by on her way to the kitchen with some dishes, so Murphy said, "I'll need a plate for a prisoner in the jail, Ginger."

"A plate for poor Ike Purdy," she replied sarcastically. "How thoughtful."

The two council members decided to stay and have more coffee and possibly a slice of pie. So when Bonnie came to the table with a covered plate for Murphy to take to the jail, he stood up and shook hands with both of them before taking the plate. "Can't let it get cold," he joked. "He might not wanna come back to our jail."

When he got back to the jail, he gave Ike his breakfast and poured him a cup of coffee from the pot he had left sitting on the stove in the office. "While you're eatin' your breakfast, I'll get your horse for you. I've gotta take a little trip this mornin', so I'm gonna need my horses. I might as well get yours while I'm at it."

"Much obliged, Marshal," Ike said. He dug in his pocket and came up with a quarter, which he held out to Murphy.

"What's that for?" Murphy asked.

"My fine," Ike replied. "You said I'd have to pay a twenty-five-cent fine for stablin' my horse."

Murphy laughed. "I did say that, didn't I?" He took the quarter. "All right, I'll pay your fine for you."

He left him to eat his breakfast and walked up the street to the stable. When Paul Mathers came out to greet him, he handed him Ike's quarter. "That's the fee for Ike Purdy's horse. If you don't mind, saddle his horse up while I saddle

Nosy. I'm gonna take the packhorse, too. I've gotta take a little trip this mornin', and I'm in a hurry to get goin'."

"Where ya goin'?" Mathers was compelled to ask.

"Rockin'-J Ranch," Murphy answered. "And I told His Honor, the mayor, that I wouldn't be out of town any longer than a couple of hours. I told him that if there was any trouble to send for you."

"Yeah, that'll be the day," Mathers remarked. He went to get Ike's horse.

When he got back to the jail, Murphy found Ike ready to go. He had even wet his hair and made an attempt to slick it back, but his breakfast looked to have been hardly touched.

"You were supposed to be eatin' your breakfast. Is there something wrong with it?"

"No, sir," Ike replied. "I was just tryin' to wash up a little bit. It looks mighty good. I'm fixin' to get at it right now."

Murphy didn't make any comment, but the expression on his face was one of pure impatience.

"I forgot you said you was in a hurry," Ike said. "I ain't really hungry. I don't need to eat that."

"Now you're tellin' me a lie," Murphy said. "I'm gonna stay until you eat that breakfast."

"You're the most decent man I've ever met, Marshal Murphy. I can go without breakfast if it'll help you out."

"I'll tell you what I'll do," Murphy declared. "I need to get started, but I can't leave the jail unlocked. If you'll promise me you'll sit down on the back steps and take your time to eat that plate of food they fixed for you at the café, I'll lock up and get started. When you finish, just leave your plate and cup and your utensils on the top step back there, and I'll take care of 'em when I get back this afternoon. Is that a deal?"

"Yes, sir," Ike replied. "That's a deal." So Murphy returned Ike's gun and holster, and his pocketknife. Then with his coffee cup in one hand and his plate in the other, Ike followed him outside where he placed them on the steps.

Murphy extended his hand, but Ike hesitated, not certain, so Murphy took hold of Ike's arm and shook his hand. "Good luck to ya, Ike. You take care of yourself."

He left Ike speechless the entire time he took to lock the office door and get on his horse and ride away.

"Yes, sir," Ike said softly after Murphy had gone.

He followed a trail out of town, one leading northwest, that was an occasional trail for the cowhands that rode for the Rocking-J Ranch for a night in Newtown. It was a trip of about the same distance as the Three Crosses, which Ike worked for, but in a different direction. So he asked Nosy for a little extra, and the big bay gelding answered the call. By alternating between a lope and a walk, he arrived at the Rocking-J ranch house in a couple of hours. It had occurred to him when he was halfway there that Jacobson might be out on the other side of his range. So he was happy to find him at the ranch headquarters.

"Un-oh," Jim King called out when he saw Murphy approaching the barnyard. "Who's in trouble now? Here comes Marshal Murphy."

"Howdy, Jim," Murphy answered. "You're right. It is officially Marshal Murphy. I just took the job this mornin', but I ain't here on official business." He pulled up before Jim and dismounted. "Matter of fact, I never know when any of your boys are even in town. They don't ever cause trouble."

"They know I'll kick some butts if they do," Jim replied. "What brings you out this way?"

"Like I just said, I took the job as marshal in Newtown, so I wanted to let you and Mr. Jacobson know that I had, and that you're welcome to graze my land anytime you want. If you've been over that way lately, you'll see where I started buildin' my cabin again. But that's as far as I'm goin' with it for as far as I can see now. I'm gonna go back and pick up some tools I left buried there. Then I'll be stuck in town from now on."

"I expect you'd like to tell Mr. Jacobson the news," Jim said. "And you're gonna need to rest and water your horses if you're planning to turn right around and ride back to Newtown." He looked back toward the barn and yelled, "Peck!"

After a few seconds, a young boy appeared in the doorway of the barn.

"Come get these horses and take 'em to water."

The boy came immediately to take care of Murphy's horses.

"Come on, Cullen," Jim said, "let's go find Mr. Jacobson." They went to the ranch house to report to Miss Atha, who in turn went to get Lionel Jacobson from his study. A few minutes later, Jacobson appeared in the parlor and led the two men back to his study.

"Good to see you again, Murphy," Jacobson said as he sat down at his desk and motioned for Murphy and Jim to take a seat. "Have you come to sell me that hundred and sixty acres by the river?"

"Not exactly. I thought you'd like to know that I don't plan to do anything on that land anytime soon, since I've taken the marshal's job in Newtown, so you're welcome to use it as if it was yours."

"That's mighty neighborly of you, but you might as well let me make you an offer on it, and you wouldn't have to worry about it anymore."

They were interrupted then when Miss Atha came to the study door and announced that dinner would be ready in thirty minutes and that she was expecting Mr. Murphy to eat with them.

* * *

Back in Newtown, when Murphy was not even halfway to the Rocking-J Ranch, Ginger Floyd heard a timid knock on the outside entrance to the dining room. She was curious to see why whoever it was didn't just walk right in. The sign was turned to the OPEN side. So she went to the door and opened it to discover a slight young man holding a plate, a cup, and some eating utensils. The poor man's face looked as if it had been kicked by a mule.

Thinking him a down-and-out beggar, she asked, "Are you looking for something to eat?"

"Oh, no, ma'am. I just et, and it was mighty good eatin', too. I was in the jail last night, and Marshal Murphy had to go somewhere early this morning, so he let me sit on the back steps of the jail and eat my breakfast. He told me to leave the dishes right there on the porch and he'd take 'em when he got back. But I thought the least I could do is bring you your dishes."

She stared at him in disbelief, and she had to ask, "Are you Ike Purdy?"

"Why, yes, ma'am. How'd you know that?"

"I heard that Marshal Murphy arrested you yesterday," Ginger said.

"Yes, ma'am, he did, and he had every right to 'cause I drank so much likker till it drove me crazy. I even shot at somebody, and I ain't never done that before. But Marshal Murphy, he's the decent-ist man I ever met. When he found out I went crazy because nobody would let me see Daisy Moffett, he let me sleep all that likker off."

"Maybe you can find her today, if you don't drink any more whiskey," Ginger said.

"Oh, I will. I saw her last night." He chuckled when he thought about it. "Come to find out, Daisy wouldn't let nobody see her, 'cause of the way her face was beat up." He paused to chuckle again. "You know what he done? He arrested her!"

"You're fooling me. Arrested her for what?"

"I swear, I'm not foolin'. He arrested her 'cause she wouldn't come to the jail on her own. But when he took her to the jail, he told her he was just foolin' her and she could go in and visit with me or she could turn around and go back to Pratt's. She said she'd go in to visit with me. We found out it didn't make no difference what shape our faces was in. Well, anyway, here's your plate back, and it was real good eatin'. I'm goin' to see Daisy down at Pratt's."

She stood there holding the dishes while she watched him walk away. Then she turned around to discover Bonnie standing in the kitchen doorway, watching her.

"Aren't you glad you let Cullen know what a rotten dog he is for keeping those two apart?" Bonnie asked her.

It was close to two o'clock when Murphy finally made it back to his partially finished cabin at Brady Creek and the San Saba River. But he was only three miles from Newtown at that point. So he hurriedly dug up his tools and loaded them on his packhorse and started for home, which was now on Front Street, in the back of the Newtown jail. He was happy to see no billowing clouds of smoke rolling off the buildings in the distance when he caught first sight of the town. Maybe nothing catastrophic had happened while he was away from his post on his initial day as town marshal. So he rode casually up Front Street to the jail, where he stopped to leave the tools his packhorse was carrying before continuing on to the stable to leave his horses. After answering all Paul Mathers's questions concerning where he had been and what he was doing, he walked back to the jail.

It wasn't until he went past Bradshaw's Saloon that it occurred to him that he had not seen Ike's dirty dishes when he'd left his tools on the back porch of the jail. When he got back to the jail, they were not on the front steps, either, so he walked around to the back to see if Ike had stuck them someplace out of the way and he had just not seen them. "He took the dishes back to the dinin' room," he thought aloud. "I shoulda known he'd do something like that." *Maybe Bradshaw will think I hired Ike Purdy to work for me at the jail*, he thought and chuckled. "I'm sure I'll find out when I go to supper," he announced.

CHAPTER 24

"Good evening, Cullen," Ginger Floyd greeted him when he walked into the dining room. He couldn't help noticing that her tone was considerably less frosty than it had been at breakfast.

"Good evenin', Ginger," he responded politely.

"Your usual table, or would you rather sit somewhere else?" she asked, smiling sweetly.

"The usual one, if that's all right."

"Any one you want, Marshal Murphy," Bonnie said as she walked out of the kitchen with a cup of coffee for him and placed it on his usual table.

Thinking something strange was going on, he went to his usual table and paused before sitting down. He looked at Ginger's smiling face, then at Bonnie's smiling face. Looking back at Ginger then, he accused her. "You've been talking to Ike Purdy. He came in here with the dishes and shot his mouth off, didn't he?"

Both girls smiled at him sweetly.

"I want the cup back," he said. "He shoulda gave you the plate and the fork. That cup is mine."

"Old softhearted Murphy," Ginger teased. "What was it you said? Something about playing Cupid?"

"She baked you a pie," Bonnie said.

"Your mama?" Murphy asked.

"No, Ginger baked you a pie because she felt bad about acting so snotty with you this morning," Bonnie said.

"I call it humble pie," Ginger said, "because I wanna apologize for thinking you didn't care a nickel's worth for those two people."

"I don't think I've ever had any humble pie," Murphy remarked. "You didn't have to do that."

"Don't worry," Bonnie said. "She just calls it humble pie. She made it with dried peaches."

"Oh," Murphy responded, "then I'll bet it'll be good." He was glad things were back on a friendly basis with Ginger. It made his mealtimes much more pleasant to be on good terms with the people who fed him.

He enjoyed his supper, and the pie turned out to be pretty good, as well. So he left the dining room and walked out through the saloon, where he paused to talk to Pete.

"Everything all right?" he asked.

"Yeah, I think everything's all right," Pete answered. "I was a little worried about that fellow over at the card game." Murphy turned to look at a table where there were six players. "The one with the silver band around his hat. He's been making a lot of noise. Says his name is Clint Bailey and he's passin' through on his way to Austin. Everett Sims was in the game, but he wasn't doing any good, so he dropped out. He said Clint Bailey claimed he was a cowhand for the Lucky-6 Ranch, but he don't look like no cowhand. He looks more like a gunslinger."

"How's he doin' in the game?" Murphy asked.

"Seems to be doin' okay. I think he's ahead, so far. He ain't caused no fuss, but Sims thinks he's dangerous."

"I'm gonna make my evenin' walk around, and I'll drop back by to see if there's any chance of a problem," Murphy said.

"Much obliged," Pete said.

So Murphy walked outside and started his walk around town. Everything seemed to be peaceful in the little town as he did his usual checking. When he got back to Bradshaw's Saloon about thirty minutes later, he went inside and discovered that the man, Clint Bailey, was no longer there. When he asked Pete about him, Pete said there was no problem. Bailey had won a couple of big hands and had decided to call it a night playing cards. "Said he was gonna go spend his winnings on likker and women, so it was too bad we didn't have any women. So I expect he went on down the street to Pratt's."

"I reckon I'd best check on Pratt's again," Murphy said and went back out the door.

He was halfway to Pratt's Saloon when he heard the first shot, so he broke into a trot. When he heard a second shot, he ran the rest of the way, cranking a live round into the Henry rifle, ready to fire. When he ran in the door, everyone in the saloon was running around in a panic.

Seeing Murphy, Albert yelled, "Upstairs!"

Murphy went up the stairs two and three steps at a time, his rifle ready to react to whatever was waiting. At the end of the hallway, he saw the man with the silver band around the crown of his hat. His six-gun was in his hand, and his hand was hanging down by his side. In his first quick look, Murphy saw a body lying halfway out of Hazel Goodings's bedroom door and a second body in the dimly lit hallway, at Clint Bailey's feet. In the poor light, he could not identify the body at Bailey's feet, but he could see the glisten of blood running down Bailey's face.

"Let that pistol drop to the floor," Murphy ordered Bailey. "You're under arrest for murder."

"The hell I am!" Bailey responded. "They jumped me, so they got what they deserved. I was just defendin' myself."

"He's lying, Murphy," Hazel shouted.

"Shut your mouth!" Bailey threatened, "or you'll get the next one! Take my advice, lawman. If you wanna live, you'd best back outta this hallway and let me get on my horse and I'll be out of your way. Like I said, they attacked me, and all I done was protect myself."

"I'm afraid I can't do that, Bailey. Ain't that your name? Bailey? I'm puttin' you under arrest until I find out what happened here. Hazel, what happened?"

"He was my customer, but he saw Daisy and Ike in that vacant room across the hall and decided he wanted to go one time with her. She said no. He grabbed her, and Ike tried to help her, so he just pulled that pistol and shot him. Daisy jumped on him then and clawed him pretty bad, so he shot her, too."

"You gonna believe that ol' tramp's word over mine?" Bailey demanded.

"I'm satisfied it's got a better chance of being the truth than yours, so that's what we're goin' with, until we get a chance to talk to some more witnesses. So let that firearm drop to the floor."

"I ain't goin' to jail," Bailey informed him. "Maybe you ain't smart enough to notice that my six-gun is already in my hand. One quick move and you're a dead man."

"Is that your final decision?" Murphy asked.

In answer, Bailey started to raise the gun, only to take two steps backward when the .44 slug from Murphy's rifle struck him in the chest. While he struggled to keep from falling, Murphy cranked in another round, and now, with time to take aim, he dispatched him with a bullet in his forehead.

"It's all over!" Hazel yelled out, and then all the doors in the hallway opened. Soon the hallway was lit up as women and customers came out of the rooms, holding lamps.

Murphy knelt down over the body of Daisy Moffett to confirm her death. There was a bullet hole right where her heart would be. Then he checked Ike Purdy and found his fatal wound in just about the same location. He didn't move for a long moment, thinking about the pathetic turn of events for the unlikely young couple.

"It's a damn shame, ain't it?"

Murphy looked up when Hazel spoke. "Yeah, I reckon it is," Murphy answered her. "They didn't have a chance of makin' it in this world. Not much future for either one of them alone, and none at all as a couple."

"Well, they'll always be together now," Hazel said. "You know, I think they might be happier wherever they are right now."

He stood up and looked her in the eye. "You really believe that?" She said she did, so he said, "Then I'll believe it, too. Let's take a look at what Clint Bailey is carryin' in his pockets and see if he's got enough to pay for a decent burial for Daisy and Ike."

Hazel didn't take time to reply but went to Bailey's body immediately and emptied all his pockets. "That lying SOB," she said as she counted a roll of Union greenbacks. "He said he had just enough money left to pay for his last ride, and he was savin' it for Daisy. He's got close to a hundred and fifty dollars here."

"You take a hundred and put the rest back in his pockets for Doc Ennis to find and claim for his undertaker services," Murphy told her. "You can use the hundred to have Doc give Ike and Daisy a fancy funeral."

"Doc ought not charge that much to give 'em a decent burial, even a fancy one," Hazel said.

"Then you keep the rest for makin' the arrangements," Murphy said.

Hazel grinned. "You know, Murphy, you're already gettin' to be my favorite marshal."

"That's what all the women say," Murphy replied.

He looked back toward the stairs at the group of men who

had come up the steps to gawk after the shooting stopped. "Couple of you fellows wanna give me a hand carrying these bodies downstairs?"

Several men rushed over to help. The two fastest ones picked up Daisy; the next two took Ike. The fifth volunteer took a look at the obviously heavier body of Clint Bailey and promptly turned around. So Murphy pulled his body up and, with Hazel's help, got it situated on his shoulder, and took it downstairs.

"Already sent somebody to get Doc," Albert said when Murphy got downstairs, so he carried Bailey on out to the street and set him down next to the other two. Then he waited with the bodies until Doc showed up.

The little town of Newtown experienced a relatively lengthy period of peaceful existence after the unfortunate murders of the two young lovers, Daisy Moffett and Ike Purdy. To the mayor and vice mayor of the town, this appeared to justify their decision to hire Cullen Murphy as the town marshal after having vacillated on this issue for so long. Over a time span of about three weeks, the most serious offenses were crimes of public nuisance and intoxication that required a night in jail to sleep off a drunken episode.

The fear the town council had that Cullen Murphy was a name that would attract notorious gunfighters from all over the state of Texas turned out to be unfounded. It appeared now that if the name had become well known at all, it was because gunfighters were severely dealt with in Newtown. And the little town was so remote from the major towns and too far into the Texas Hill Country to attract anyone seeking a name for themselves with a handgun. Eliot Baxter and Tyson Bradshaw were satisfied that they had made the right decision for their town and were no longer irritated by the term *Murphy's Law*. Had they known of a chance meeting in a saloon in Waco, it might have caused a ripple in their peace of mind.

* * *

About a hundred miles away, Tom Thorne, owner of the River House Saloon on the Brazos River, was standing at the end of the bar, talking to his bartender, Shep Keenum. The subject of their conversation was a man whose dark, deep-set eyes and thin, curved nose gave him a hawklike appearance. He was sitting at a table, eating a bowl of red beans and ham, his back to the windowless corner of the barroom. Well known in this part of Texas, his name was Spade Atkins. Spade was not his birth name. Few people outside his family knew his given name, but many people knew him by the name Spade. They said it came from the many gun duels he had participated in and the fact that there was always a grave to be dug when he left.

"How's he doin'?" Thorne asked. "Is he lookin' for anyone?"

"He don't seem to be lookin' for anybody," Shep said. "I asked him where he was goin'. He said nowhere. He was just wanderin'—"

"Uh-oh, look who's comin' here," Thorne interrupted. "I thought he'd gone back to New Orleans."

Shep turned to look toward the front door. He chuckled, amused, when he saw the slender man dressed in black from his boots to his hat. "Nah, he's still been comin' in about every other day. But ain't he the lucky one to come in today? He talks about the same thing every time he comes in here. Today he's gonna see one close up. Good thing he ain't wearin' his Colt today." He paused. "Did I tell you about that?"

"No. Did he wear a gun?" Thorne asked.

"Yeah, he did. A nice 1860 Army model Colt single-action revolver. And he was wearing a fancy black leather fast-draw holster. Said he strapped it on once in a while just because he liked the feel of it on his hip. I told him he ought'n not be wearin' a weapon unless he was prepared to use it." Shep chuckled. "He said another feller told him that one time, and he damn sure nearly got shot. And he said his gun wasn't even loaded." He paused then while the man in black walked up to the bar.

"Howdy, Liam," Shep greeted him cheerfully.

"Howdy, Shep, Tom," he returned. "What's going on in the River House today?"

"Well, I'll tell ya," Shep replied. "Today might be your lucky day."

"Really?" Liam asked. "How's that?"

"You remember how we're always talkin' about gunslingers and fast-draw artists?" Shep asked, and Liam said he remembered. "Well, that feller sittin' at the table in the corner, eatin' a bowl of beans and ham, is known by every gunslinger from here to San Antonio."

Liam's eyes lit up, and he jerked his head around to look at him. "Really?" he repeated. "You're not japing me, are you?" He couldn't help staring at the man. "He doesn't look like a fast-gun artist."

"They look like everybody else," Shep said. "They're just faster with a handgun than everybody else. But take my word for it, you're looking at the real thing. His name's Spade Atkins, and he's gunned down four men for sure that everybody knows about."

Liam was struck in awe. "Spade Atkins," he repeated. "I've got to meet him!"

When he started to head for the table, Thorne stopped him. "Maybe you better not bother him, Mr. Black. Spade can be kinda touchy about strangers approachin' him." He didn't say it, but he was also thinking, *Especially a stranger dressed like an undertaker.*

"I'll be polite," Liam said and started for the table. He got only halfway there before he was stopped cold.

Having watched the stranger in black ever since he'd walked in the door, Spade put his fork down and put his hand on his six-gun, which was lying in his lap. "You got a problem?"

"No, no problem," Liam said at once, stopped by a voice that sounded as if it came from the bottom of a well. "They say you're fast with a gun, and I . . ."

"Who said?" Spade demanded.

"Uh, Shep, the bartender," Liam sputtered, thinking he might have made a mistake. "I don't carry a gun myself. I just wanted to meet a real gunfighter. I mean, one with a famous name like yours, Spade Atkins."

"Well, now you met me, so go away and let me eat," Spade said.

"Yes, sir, I appreciate your taking the time. Now I've met a famous gunfighter, and I've met the only marshal who's faster than the gunfighters." He turned to go back to the bar.

"Wait a minute!" Spade demanded. "What are you talkin' about? Who's faster than any gunfighter?"

Liam stopped and shrugged. "You've probably heard of him, Cullen Murphy, the town marshal in Newtown."

"I never heard of Cullen Murphy," Spade said. "Hell, I never heard of Newtown. Where the hell is that?"

Liam was genuinely surprised. "Newtown's in San Saba County, and Murphy's the reason gunfighters don't go there anymore. They even call it Murphy's Law." He started to return to the bar again.

"Hold on there a minute," Spade said. "Come on back here and tell me some more about Newtown and this fast-gun marshal. Murphy's Law, you say . . . ?"

TURN THE PAGE FOR AN EXCITING PREVIEW!

BREAK MURPHY'S LAW, FACE MURPHY'S WRATH.

From the bestselling Johnstones comes the latest adventure in the wild life of Cullen Murphy, a West Texas legend in the making with big dreams and fast guns, and whose word is the law.

Life is hard in the Old West—but so is Cullen Murphy. Orphaned as a child, he drifted from town to town across a merciless frontier, taking any job he could to survive. Ranch hand, cattle driver, Confederate soldier. Whatever it took, he was up for the task. But when the Civil War ended, Murphy was ready to settle down and start his own ranch in Newtown, Texas, a beautiful but untamed stretch of land with no marshal, no jailhouse—and no defense against trigger-happy lowlifes looking for trouble.

In this godforsaken corner of the West, Murphy *is* the law.

First, he stakes out a spread of his own. Then, he clears the countryside of outlaws. But now, a pair of dirtbag cowhands from a nearby ranch arrive with a sinister message from their boss. His name is Oakley Jackford, a big-time cattle baron who's been using Murphy's land to graze his cattle—and he doesn't intend to stop. To make sure Murphy hears the message loud and clear, the cowhands beat him up and burn down his house. Big mistake. Because a man like Murphy doesn't get scared off. He gets mad, gets his guns—and gets revenge . . .

NATIONAL BESTSELLING AUTHORS
WILLIAM W. JOHNSTONE
and J.A. JOHNSTONE

A WEEK FROM NEVER

THE SECOND THRILLING INSTALLMENT IN THE MURPHY'S LAW SERIES FROM THE GREATEST WESTERN WRITERS OF THE 21ST CENTURY!

Live Free. Read Hard.
williamjohnstone.net
Visit us at kensingtonbooks.com

Coming soon, wherever Pinnacle Trade books are sold

CHAPTER 1

"You sure your cousin knows what he's talkin' about?" Cleve Carter asked Beaver Branson as he sat on his horse at the top of a low rise beside the stage road between Waco and Austin. "He mighta got his days mixed up, or they mighta changed their schedule, 'cause that stage ought to be gittin' here by now. It ain't but forty miles back to Waco."

"He knows," Timothy Branson answered. Everybody called him Beaver because of an overbite that made his teeth look like those in a beaver's mouth,. "He works in the Waco station and he'da told me if they changed the date they're sendin' that money to Austin. They'll show up here any time now."

"They better or I'm liable to have a little talk with your cousin," Carter threatened. The five outlaws were waiting on the south bank of a little river about four miles past a stage station. Cleve Carter, the leader of the gang, planned to strike the stagecoach after it crossed the river and was pulling up on the other bank.

"You want me and Calvin to go on back on the other side of the river and get ready?" Hank Welch asked Carter.

"Yeah go on back over there and get set up in a good spot. Make sure they ain't gonna spot you before they go into the river," Carter said. "Signal me as soon as you get the first sight of 'em."

"Right," Hank replied, and he and Calvin Darcy crossed back over the little river to conceal themselves in the trees that lined the banks. After another quarter of an hour, however, Hank pulled out of the trees and rode out to the edge of the road to take a look back toward Waco. He jerked his horse to a stop when he spotted the stagecoach in the distance. "Son of a . . ." he started. "They're comin', but it ain't just the stage! There's a couple of guards ridin' ahead of it! I'll tell Cleve. We might wanna back off." He rode back down to the water's edge and called out, "Cleve! The stage is comin', but there's two guards leadin' it! Whaddaya wanna do?"

Damn! Cleve thought. *I didn't count on that!* "Just two?" he called back.

"That's all I see," Hank answered, "but I expect they might be US Deputy Marshals."

"Well, what did you expect? That's just good news. Means there's a big payday ridin' in that coach for us. Hell, there's five of us. We need to hit 'em hard before they know they're in trouble. We'll knock those two marshals down, and I don't think that feller ridin' shotgun will give us any trouble at all after that. He'd have to be crazy to. If there's any passengers inside who wanna give us any trouble, they'll get what they deserve, too. Go on back and get ready. Tell Calvin we'll knock those two deputies down for good first thing. If they try to get behind the stage for cover, you and Calvin can cut 'em down."

"I'll tell him," Hank replied. He wheeled his horse around and loped back to where Calvin was waiting anxiously to hear whether or not the holdup was still on. "We're going ahead with it," he told Calvin. "There's too much money not to."

"What if there's more marshals ridin' inside that stage?" Calvin responded, not sure it was such a good idea if that was a possibility.

"Then I reckon we'll just shoot it to pieces," Hank answered. "Cleve said we had to hit 'em hard and make sure we knock those two marshals outta the saddle. Then him and Beaver and Ed are gonna stop the stage and take care of the driver and his guard. Me and you'll come up behind 'em and take care of anybody tryin' to jump out the doors."

"I swear, I don't know if we oughta go ahead with this job or not," Calvin hesitated. "We'll be wanted all over the country if we kill those marshals."

"That wouldn't be near as bad as if you ran out on this job and had Cleve Carter on your trail. We've got a stagecoach comin' at us carryin' enough money to make us rich. Cleve's right—take the money and kill the witnesses. We'll just make sure those two marshals on horses are took care of and the rest will go all right." He hesitated before saying his last thoughts on the matter. "Let me make one thing clear. If you decide you wanna cut and run when the shootin' starts, that shot you feel in your back will be from my rifle."

"Hell, Hank, whaddaya wanna say a thing like that for?" Calvin responded. "You know I ain't the kind to run out on the gang, right?" Hank didn't answer, his eyes glued on the road and the approaching stagecoach. "You ain't never had no call to say something like that about me."

Ignoring the opportunity to apologize for the remark, Hank said, "Get ready. They're just about here." They both got off their horses and tied them in the trees, then gave their rifles a quick check before moving closer to the road to hide behind a clump of bushes. "Wait here till they ride past us. Then I'll run across the road, so I can get a better shot at the one on that side of the coach. If they ain't dead after Cleve and them hit 'em, we'll cut 'em down when they try to get behind the stagecoach." He gave Calvin a hard look. "You ready for it?"

"Hell, I told you I'm ready,' Calvin insisted. "Don't worry 'bout me."

"Here they come!" Hank warned. "Get ready!" They hunkered down behind the bushes, gripping their rifles while the two deputy marshals rode past them. A few yards behind them, the horses pulling the stage followed the deputies down into the river and started across. "Don't miss!" Hank whispered, and ran across the road as soon as the coach was in the water.

On the other side of the narrow river, the other three outlaws waited, each man waiting for the right moment when the horses were pulling the stage out of the water. Cleve Carter's shot was the signal to fire. The sound of his Winchester when the bullet struck the guard sitting beside the driver had not faded before Ed Moore and Beaver Branson fired. Both riders were struck and both came off their horses. As Carter had figured, the wounded deputies struggled to take cover behind the stagecoach where they were met with the rapid fire from Hank and Calvin. The massacre of the guard detail was completed as the deputies were hit time after time until both bodies were floating in the shallow water. Waiting terrified, the stage driver sat paralyzed by the sudden attack.

"Pull that stage up here out of the river," Carter ordered, then stood there until the coach rolled up on the road and stopped beside him. "Halt!" he ordered. Eager to see the treasure he knew was inside, he pulled the door open, only to be met with the point-blank blast of a Colt .45, knocking him to land on his back. Wells Fargo detective James Silverton's last act to serve his employer was to die in a hail of gunfire from Beaver Branson and Ed Moore. The money he was protecting was hidden in a canvas sack behind the backrest of Silverton's seat in the coach.

"Damn!" Beaver exclaimed. "That was a dumb-fool thing to do." He grabbed Silverton's coat and pulled him out of the stagecoach to land on the ground beside Carter.

"I wouldn't say that," Hank said. "Hell, he knew he was a dead man, so he decided he weren't gonna go peaceful. He sure surprised ol' Cleve though, didn't he?"

"There ain't no money in here," Ed declared after looking around on the floor and under the seats.

"The hell there ain't," Hank responded. "Get outta the way!" He grabbed Ed by the arm and pulled him out of the coach. Like Ed, he didn't find anything. "They didn't send a stagecoach down to Austin, guarded by four men with nothin' in it," he said. Then he took hold of the backrest where Silverton had been sitting and gave it a hard yank. When the seatback gave a good four inches, he was motivated to give it a stronger one. This time, the whole back of the seat gave way to reveal a canvas sack holding five fat packs of twenty-dollar bills. The discovery caused an eruption of cheers and inspired Hank to destroy the remaining seat backs, but there was no more hidden treasure to be found. He looked over at the stagecoach driver, who was shivering under the watchful eye of Calvin Darcy. "Where'd they hide the rest of the money on the stage?"

"There ain't no more money anywhere on the stage," the driver stuttered. "I swear to you, they was just takin' whatever's in that sack to a bank in Austin. I ain't got nothin' to do with that money. I'm just a stagecoach driver. How 'bout you just let me drive the coach on back to the station? I can't identify nobody."

"I reckon you're right," Hank said as he drew his pistol again and shot him twice in the chest. He holstered his pistol and said to Beaver, "Like Cleve said, don't leave no witnesses."

"What are we gonna do with the stagecoach and them four horses?" Beaver asked.

"Ain't gonna do nothin' about 'em," Hank replied. "Maybe they'll run off and start their own stage line somewhere." He laughed at the thought of it.

"You reckon they'll pull that stage back to that station back yonder?" Beaver asked, still concerned about the matter.

"I don't give a nickel's worth what them horses do," Hank told him. "Somebody'll come along and find 'em." He went over to check on Cleve then, who was lying on the ground mortally wounded, with Ed and Calvin kneeling beside him. "Is he gonna make it?"

"Don't look like it," Ed answered him. "He got two right in the chest. He's tryin' to hang on, but I don't think he's gonna make it."

Hank knelt down beside him and took a look at the blood pumping out of the bullet holes. Then he leaned close over him. "How 'bout it, partner, you gonna make it?"

Cleve's eyes flickered open when he recognized the voice. "Hank"—he struggled to speak clearly—"always my right-hand man. Don't let 'em leave me. I'm hurt bad, but I'm gonna make it."

"Don't you worry about it," Hank said. "You know I got your back. You just lay right there for a minute or two while we make sure we've got everything we wanna take with us. Then I'll get you ready to ride. He looked at Ed and Calvin then and shook his head as he got up on his feet again. "Let's see what those bodies have on 'em that we might want and catch up those two horses they was ridin'." Then he walked around behind Cleve, drew his six-gun, and put a bullet hole in Cleve's forehead. When the other three jumped in reaction to the sudden execution, Hank said. "He weren't gonna make it. Might as well put him out of his misery, right?" When nobody answered, he said, "I reckon that makes me boss now, so let's get the hell outta here. One of ya check that stage to see what kinda food they packed with 'em. Probably a lot better'n what we brought with us." He looked at Beaver and asked, "You still sure you know how to get to that hideout you told us about?"

"Yeah, I'm sure," Beaver answered. "It's almost straight west of where we are right now, over in the hills, about a two-and-a-half-day ride from here." He hesitated a few moments before asking, "What about Cleve? We gonna dig him a grave?" It seemed the least they could do would be to bury him.

"Nah," Hank responded, "maybe whoever finds him will think he was riding with the stage or got shot by one of 'em. And they can bury him."

It was the middle of a Saturday morning when the stranger riding the unusual-looking horse turned off the river road onto the main street of the remote settlement called Newtown. Located in the Texas Hill Country, Newtown was not on a popular trail to any major cow town or railhead. In spite of that, it was a town that had continued to grow in size because of the availability of cheap land and dependable water for the small farms and ranches. Like every town in Texas, Newtown had suffered financially since the ending of the war that divided north and south. But it was finally in the healthy stages of recovery that showed a promise of continuing growth.

The stranger entering the town on this particular chilly morning was accustomed to the stares of the people on the street as he rode the length of Front Street. His horse always caught the casual eye. It was a white Appaloosa with black dots and solid black shoulders and hindquarters: there weren't many like it. While the unusual horse caught the eye at first, the rider was also an interesting study. A tall man of slender build, he had a sharp face with a nose similar to a hawk's beak and a thin mustache that drooped to his chin. Dressed in black from his flat crowned hat to his soft leather boots, he had the look of a well-oiled killing machine under his buffalo overcoat.

He walked the Appaloosa slowly up the main street, leading a black packhorse behind him, slowing even more when he came to the jail. He pulled his horse to a stop, looking for a sign that would identify the marshal's office, but there was none. So he figured the marshal's office must be in the jail and guided his horse to the hitching rail, where he dismounted. Finding the door unlocked, he walked in to discover Marshal

Cullen Murphy seated at his desk, cleaning an 1860 Henry rifle.

Murphy looked up when he heard the door open. *Either an undertaker or a gunslinger*, he thought. "Can I help you?"

"Are you the marshal?" the stranger asked.

"That's right, I'm Marshal Murphy. What can I do for you?"

"My name is Spade Atkins." He took a moment's pause to judge if there was a spark of recognition of his name. When there was none obvious, he continued. "I've just rode into town. Never been here before and I always like to check in with the marshal or sheriff whenever I hit a town for the first time."

"Why is that?" Murphy asked.

"Because I'm a professional gambler and I like to let the local law enforcement know I play a straight game. I depend on the luck of the cards and that's all. Sometimes I win, sometimes I lose. I've been winning more times than losing, and as long as that continues I'll keep doin' what I like to do and that's gamble." He stepped in front of the iron stove heating the small office and opened his heavy buffalo coat to permit some of the heat to get inside it.

"There's no law in Newtown against gamblin'," Murphy said when Spade held his coat open. "There is a law against firin' a firearm inside the town limits, though. I notice you're wearin' a fast-draw holster, most likely totin' a revolver with a five-inch barrel."

Spade smiled. "That's strictly for self-protection. Unfortunately, sometimes the people I'm playin' cards with ain't as honest as I am. There ain't no law against protectin' myself, is there?"

"No, I reckon every man oughta have that right no matter where he is," Murphy answered. "The place where it makes a difference is when one man pokes at another man to make him mad enough to draw his weapon, knowing all the time he's faster. You look like you're pretty handy with that sidearm you're wearin'. You pretty fast with that gun?"

"I get by, I reckon," Spade replied. "I wear it mostly for show just to make it look like it might be risky to try me."

"How's that been workin' out?" Murphy asked.

Spade smiled again and answered, "Well, I'm still dealin' the cards."

"Well, Mr. Atkins, like I said, it's against the law to shoot a firearm inside the town limits, except in a situation where somebody attacks you and you have to defend yourself. But if somebody calls you out and you accept the challenge, then the law insists that you take it outta town to settle it. That don't happen very often here, but when it does, they usually take it down by the river."

Spade chuckled. "That's good to know. Since I plan to spend a couple of days in your town, maybe you could tell me where I can find a room to rent. I haven't gone up the whole street yet, but I didn't see a hotel so far."

"We don't have a hotel in town yet, but there are a couple of places to rent a room, depending on which you prefer. A lady named Pearl Johnson runs a rooming house back toward the south end of the street. You passed it if you came up from the river road. You can rent a room there for the night, if you're looking for a nice quiet place. If you wanna stay close to the gamblin', there's a couple of saloons in town that rent rooms upstairs. They're the two biggest. Bradshaw's Saloon is also the best place to eat. They've got a dinin' room built on the back of the saloon called Irene's Café. It's run by a respectable lady named Irene Floyd. You can also rent a room upstairs. The other saloon where you can get a room is Pratt's Saloon. You can pay for the companionship of one of Pratt's saloon girls, if you're of a mind to. Bradshaw's Saloon doesn't offer that."

"That café you said was in the back of the saloon, do they serve three meals a day?"

"That's right," Murphy replied. "It's a regular café. They'll be openin' up for dinner at noon."

"Good, 'cause I didn't have anything left for breakfast this mornin' but a piece of beef jerky. This town is farther from Waco than I thought it was," Spade remarked. "I think you've told me all I need to know, Marshal, and I appreciate it. I can't think of but one more place I need to stop at."

"The stables?" Murphy guessed. When Spade smiled and nodded, Murphy said, "North end of the street." He got up from the desk then. "I'll walk out with you." He walked to the door and held it open for Spade.

Damn! Spade thought when Murphy stood up, surprised by the size of the man. *I won't have to worry about taking dead aim. It'd be hard to miss him.* He walked out the door and Murphy followed him, unaware that he was already being sized up by the stranger.

"That's a mighty fine-lookin' horse you're riding, Mr. Atkins." Murphy couldn't help but admire the black and white Appaloosa. "That's one of those Palouse horses bred by the Nez Percé Indians, ain't it?"

"That's a fact," Spade answered. "I got him from a man who bought the horse directly from a Nez Percé breeder. I inherited him when that man passed away after a spell of heart trouble." He elected not to go into further detail, but he could have told Murphy the man's heart trouble was brought on by the bullet in his chest. It was a shame. The man had never really been seriously ill a day in his life. That was before the little dispute at the card table that resulted in a face-off between the two former friends.

"Well, you can depend on Paul Mathers to take good care of the horse," Murphy told him. "Paul's the owner of the stable. And you can't see it from here, but it's right at the end of Front Street. If you had come into town from the north, the stable would have been the first thing you saw."

"Much obliged, Marshal, 'preciate the help," Spade said as he stood by his horse, preparing to step up into the saddle. He paused for a short moment to make a quick evaluation of Murphy's potential as a possible opponent in a quick-draw competition. Unlike most of the professional fast-guns, himself included, the marshal was not the typical willowy gunslinger whose hand hung naturally to fall on his gun handle. Murphy was tall and brawny, with wide shoulders over a muscular chest. He looked to be more suited to steer wrestling. Spade liked his chances in a face-off against the marshal. He stepped up into the saddle and turned the Appaloosa away from the rail to continue his slow walk up the street to let the people he passed admire his horse. The remote little town may not have heard of Spade Atkins before, but they would be familiar with the name when he left. That much he was sure of.

Cullen Murphy stood outside a few minutes to watch the stranger as he rode up Front Street. He wondered if Spade Atkins was going to cause as much trouble as he looked capable of. This in spite of his visit to the jail to announce his peaceful intentions. Newtown was not a town big enough to cause a professional gambler to ride all the way from Waco. And it was not on the way to one that was big enough, either.

Murphy had to wonder about the real reason Spade Atkins showed up in Newtown. He turned around and went back into the office to finish cleaning his rifle.

www.ingramcontent.com/pod-product-compliance
Lightning Source LLC
LaVergne TN
LVHW030908080826
845145LV00010B/2814

9780786051373